FOREIGN
DEVILS

Also by Irvin Faust

Willy Remembers

The File on Stanley Patton Buchta

The Steagle

Roar Lion Roar

FOREIGN DEVILS

A NOVEL BY

IRVIN FAUST

ARBOR HOUSE

NEW YORK

For Jean

"Let us have peace."
—U. S. GRANT

FOREIGN
DEVILS

I

Well you cannot hold back any longer. Close your eyes, hold your nose, grab air and jump. Even as you did 32 years ago into Lake Powhattan at scout camp and they had to fish you out. Christ where did *that* come from? An omen? Stop that! How many times have I told you, *ordered* you not to be superstitious? You are a *great* swimmer now. All right, don't yell. All right. So jump. Must I? Don't ask stupid questions. Very well; must I? YES. OK, OK. Three days ago the President's advance party left for Peking. There, that wasn't so bad. No, but I'm out of breath. Psychogenic, get on with it. Don't push so. I have to with you. All right. They left for the Forbidden City. Ah. It is the first time since '49 Americans will have pierced the holy gates. The Chien Men. The first time they will stroll up Legation Street. Don't stop. Yes, Chinese Gordon and the Opium War and Marshall and Wedemeyer and Pat Hurley and Chiang and the Long March and *The General Died at Dawn* and the *Panay* and Sun and the Missimo (did the boys make out with her at Wellesley? Stop!) and the Right Harmonious Fists and 1900. There you've done it! You've made

13

the connection, that wasn't so godawful, was it? Then why am I sweating? Stop asking so damn many questions and get on with it, Yenta Telabenda. Leave the old lady out of it. All right. We are talking history, imperial history. Granted, well? Well what? For 49 months you have been screwing off, you write one goddam book and you rest on your goddam laurels. I have not been resting. I know, I was only kidding, trying to loosen you up. Don't be so damn good to me. So get down to the friggin nitty gritty. Don't use that, please don't, next you'll say it's a whole new ball game. *Assez!* Well? Well, you've been constipated for over five years, rationalize *that,* promising first novelist. I can't. So move it. All right, two nights ago Channel 4 and Nixon's flyboy, a professional: "I think of *all* passengers up there, not just the President." Well said, did Jimmy Doolittle say that in '42? When he laid those first blessed eggs? Where the hell in China *did* he land? Never mind, you're screwing off again. Oh don't get so goddam sore, I was just streaming a little, don't you recognize my highly lauded style yet? Touché, you're not as dumb as I look. Bet your ass. Stalling. Oh shit.

I, Sidney Benson, am settling down tonight after 49 blocked months. Blockaded. Yes, that. It is important to admit. Admitted. I have the feeling, the peculiar, pulsing feeling that it just might work. (It better work, boychik, you're driving everybody including yourself nuts.) Nixon, the Foreign Devil, reenters the Forbidden City. After 72 years. The Boxers, the Right Harmonious Fists, the *I Ho Chuan,* weaving, squirming, jabbing in the sacred air even as he settles down. It just might. Twelve years ago it did not. Hell I was just a neophyte then. Don't use that word. Beginner? All right, don't get smart. Well it did not work. How well I remember. Yes, it was a story about a Long Island kid obsessed, *possessed* by the Boxers, dancing, kowtowing all over the place, driving his father up the wall, mixing it all up with Fu Manchu. Your second story. God, second? Yes, you had the ideas then, but not the knowhow. You mean I've got the knowhow now? Smartass, move it. Well it was pretty bad, but I sent it off to Rogers at *Novel.* Who turned it down but was very nice about it. Yop, a hand-

14

written note; I'll never forget that. So? He was right, it didn't work, but it had a seed. Will it grow now? Howinhell do *I* know? God how I hate to return to old themes, I'm so goddam superstitious about failure. Benson! OK. Hell, it's no crime to flunk the first time around. That's the ticket, go on try it, you'll like it. . . .

Well first, who, what, where is he? You know, we've worked it out. A correspondent? Yes. Sure? Positive. Why? For beautiful, logical extension of self. Of Sid Benson. Of *Sidney Birnbaum. Benson,* I have the papers to prove it. All right, you but not you. How he, you, I kvelled, thrilled, kvelled to the exploits of Quent Reynolds and Floyd Gibbons, even down to [mentally] wearing the eye patch. Catharsis and a marvelous method exercise. Very well then. Let's see, he needs a good waspy name. Why? Oh you know. Why? Logical extension of self and a method exercise. Toushay. Also they didn't have yiddle reporters back then. Agreed. Something between Harding Davis and Stephen Crane. Not bad. God how Ben Stillmore pushed the hell out of those two. Don't worry about Stillmore, he's not worrying about you. I beg your pardon, we are all in this together. Bullshit. Well it only came up because I'd been thinking about the Philippine campaign, I mean at the turn of the century, you know, Dewey and Aguinaldo and the atrocities—the water cure, the neck cure, the dumdum bullets, tying them in with My Lai. Well? No, Stillmore milked the Spanish American War dry, at least for now; in ten years, who knows? That's my boy; so the name? Well, get a B in there, yes let the Ph.D.'s play with that. B. Bakely. Blakely. Blake. Yes. Christian name? How about Morris for the cuntman uncle? *Christian.* Norris. Beautiful. Norris Blake. I like it, I like it and I *will* get used to it. You always have. Yes, that's true, isn't it? Go. No reason, however, why he cannot be *in* the Philippines on assignment. For whom? A problem. Dana of the *Sun* was dead. Bennett of the *Herald* was living abroad, reporting polo and yachting. And they didn't believe in by-lines. But Stillmore pushed hell out of Hearst and Pulitzer. Screw Stillmore! All right, Pulitzer and the *World.* Norris Blake on assignment in the Philippines, covering the war against the Insurrectos. *Beaucoup* by-lines. Let's see, my first by-

15

line was in '39 when my boys at Washington "snapped the cords" for 42 points to beat Seward Park for the city title. You loved a cliché even then. I beg your palm. Oh go on. Well there it is, dispatches, by-lines, big-shot reporter. Not quite, there has to be continuity. He's writing a book? Hellyes, see you can do it if you try. A book. Go. Interweaves dispatches in this book. Go. *And* then his own novel. Well maybe. Whythehell not? A novel in a novel in a novel. We'll *see*. Shoot, why can't I ever follow my first impulse? Are you kidding? You get away with murder, now don't sulk. Shoot, what about a title? No rush, you always have to be so goddam tidy. Well it makes me feel better. So call it BOXERS for now. All right. Shoot. Stop saying that. Shit. That's better, much better, you know I hate it when you get prissy.

Well, back to the notes on the Harmonious Fists. It's a good thing I never throw anything out. Damn good thing, *this* time, trouble is you keep every piece of shit you ever wrote. You're starting, don't start. I apologize. OK. I had a long talk yesterday with Lou Feng at Bronx Science, I've been rereading Purcell's *The Boxer Uprising* and Chester Tan and Christopher Martin, and there are all those missionary and legation diaries. True, also your marvelous gifts of invention. Thank you, how about that failed story? Forget it. Very well, as Stanislavsky said, I am now sitting on all that (historic) emotion, now to push down the pipeline, *qui s'appelle* Norris Blake. Working star of Newspaper Row. Born 1866, Troy, New York. College, two years, Union. To the big city in '89. Bewitched, bothered, but never bewildered. Worked for the *Times* and *Post*. "Stolen" from latter by Pulitzer in talent war with Hearst. One of the breed of daredevil reporters public loved in 90's. Unmarried, though surely not unloved. Julian Ralph, Jim Creelman, Bonsal, Crane, Davis. Blake . . . well? Oh God, here I go.

BOXERS (working tit.)

CHAPTER ONE

In April of 1900, the supposed dawn of a bright new century, I was on assignment for the *World* in the village of San Miguel, outside of Manila in the Philippines. I had been sent out to the islands a year before by Mr. Pulitzer to cover the American war against Emilio Aguinaldo and his so-called Insurrectos and I had endeavored to the best of my ability to portray the amok running on both sides in that gory and inglorious campaign. (My God, it's moving. *Flowing.*) Looking back from the vantage point of three years in time (Good, '03), this most brutal of wars, and make no mistake, war it surely was, began I would say in December, 1898, when, on the cessation of formal hostilities, Spain had given up the Philippines for some twenty million dollars. We had, of course, already begun to heed Mr. Kipling's advice to take up the White Man's Burden and nobly uplift our little brown brothers, but in the islands we now took up the effort with a vengeance. (Nice touch.) Aguinaldo, however, a most unusual native leader, one who, had he the advantage of western birth, would surely have been a senator, an M.P. or perhaps even a newspaper reporter, soon came to the conclusion that American troopers were no better than Spanish, that domination from without was still domination—worse, oppression—no matter the name of the country or how noble its stated aims. In a remarkable conversation I held with this diminutive, swarthy, stalwart leader in his headquarters near Manila in March of '99 entitled "Aguinaldo Speaks," I quoted him as follows: "We welcomed the Americans as partners in arms in defeating the common enemy, but at no time did *I tell them* that they could come into our country as our masters." He said this in Tagalog, which I speak after a fashion, but the italics are mine, yet if ever a man spoke in italics it was this one. Aguinaldo further said that he had been deceived

17

—and I asked him twice to repeat this, which he did—by Admiral Dewey, General Merritt and above all by the President, serious charges all, but as far as I can see in taking his viewpoint, something the conscientious reporter must ofttimes do, disturbingly true. Indeed at the time I wrote those words I was tempted to *add* that if one objectively examined the events in the world over the past two decades relative to major powers and undeveloped countries—that is, if one could divorce oneself from one's western heritage—one would have to question Kipling's premise, or at the very least the powerful implication that we of the civilized world know what is best for our yellow, black and brown brethren. That they vacuously welcome our arrival, or if perchance they do not, they are insufferable and brutal ingrates. (Too fatuous? Prescient? Maybe, but Benson-Birbaum-*Blake*.) Since the Mahdi overwhelmed General Gordon in '85, resistance to our civilizing efforts seems to have multiplied as seen by the Abyssinians' fierce struggle gainst the Italians, the fight of Madagascar gainst France, the rebellions in South America, Kitchener's troubles in the Soudan and our own problems in Cuba and the Philippines. Little did I know as I thought those sentiments that I was in a very real sense looking into a globe of the future and that that future would soon explode in the great Chinese uprising which—as if to justify my presentiment—would pit the yellow man of this carved-up behemoth gainst most of the imperial countries of the world, the "great hairy ones," including the newest, Japan. That last, I must add, seems a puzzling contradiction, for is not the Japanese of the yellow race? Indeed I confess I cannot tell him from the Chinese, though my learned medical friends tell me that one has an added flap over the eyes, however I always forget which one that is. Yet I have concluded, to my own satisfaction at least, that Japanese behavior is not too strange since it has adopted western ways and in entering China as a "most favoured nation" was merely aping this most western of methods.

I have said little did I know I was gazing into the future. I must question that sentence. For did I indeed *not* know? I must wonder. The dedicated, intelligent newspaper reporter surely possesses a sixth sense as to what is to come; I confess that I am no less the recipient of this gift than any of my renowned colleagues. (Essence of Blake. Shut the hell up already. OK, OK.) It came as no great surprise to me then when in early April of the century's first year I heard certain disquieting reports from a fellow reporter named Emil Heingold, a writer employed by a Berlin newspaper who had been dispatched to Luzon in the vain hope that he would shortly be painting in words the picture of an American defeat and withdrawal and the Kaiser's triumphant entry into the islands. Withal, Herr Heingold and I shared the common experience and dangers of our craft which lifted us above national rivalries and we soon became fast friends. It was from him, prompted by some fresh native rum, that I learned of the unrest on the mainland of China, more particularly in Shantung Province where the Germans were strongly entrenched. Something deep within my being instantly stirred. That sixth sense, that gift of which I spoke. It whispered softly but insistently that this trouble was part of the pattern which I was only then just beginning to recognize, a piece of the overall picture I had seen at first hand in the Philippines and which the world would do well to heed, which the *World* would do well to report. Though suffering from the aftereffects of an attack of fever, I hastened to Manila in thrall to my intuition. I had to investigate. Naturally I had access to the highest official sources, including Arthur MacArthur himself, newly appointed as military governor, having covered his wide-ranging campaigns through the islands and we held each other in the highest professional mutual esteem. But in cases such as this I knew that official sources are not necessarily the most fruitful. I made straight to the mission quarter of the city and as luck, or rather my sixth sense, would have it, discovered what I was seeking, or should I say was by now convinced I was seeking. I found it in the persons of Father Bernardo O'Shea and the Reverend Andrew Townsend, both of whom confirmed the most dire of my suspicions. For as any reporter worth his salt can verify, when native passion erupts gainst the white man its first battering wave is invariably

19

hurled at the religious messengers of our society, those men whose oerarching belief in their God is so powerful that it compels them to go forth and convince the heathen to believe as they. Truth to tell I have sometimes wondered if we are not too presumptuous in this practice as I have seen splendid degrees of morality and ethic in some of the most naked tribes. (Pushing too hard? So gamble.) Still the fact remains that we are forever consigned, it seems, to the mission of conversion, with all of its attendant perils, and peril there is in abundant measure. As Dr. Livingstone might testify if he could speak from his jungle grave.

Father O'Shea, a Spaniard with Kilkenny in his paternal blood, had been in the Philippines for ten years and had maintained strong contacts with the mainland, where he had laboured for nine previous years. From his fellow clerics he had received letters wherein I first encountered that ominous word—BOXERS— or as the Father called them in Mandarin the *I Ho Chuan*. Quite literally the Right, or Righteous Harmonious Fists, really an appropriate title if you were a Boxer, calling to mind for this reporter the exquisite skills of James J. Corbett. The good Father, a friendly open soul, save when he spoke of the sect in question or Protestants, had worked in Chihli Province adjoining Shantung and as a student of matters Sino knew a good deal of this strange and mysterious society which even now has the power to send shudders through the consular spines of our world, to say nothing of little children in their beds. Reverend Townsend, a Methodist minister from Baltimore, on the other hand, had come ashore shortly after our troops, yet had equally valuable information. He received this from his brother, a missionary in Tientsin. Naturally Father O'Shea placed a good deal of the blame for the unrest on the Protestant missions and Reverend Townsend blamed the Catholics, but twixt them both, in a series of remarkable conversations—some in Mandarin, which I speak crudely but serviceably, having spent eight months in China in '94 presumably to report the Sino-Japanese War, in reality to investigate the white slave trade, which to the disappointment of Mr. Pulitzer proved negligible—I was able to glean an incomplete but provocative picture of that esoteric movement.

One must really begin by delving into Chinese history, which for centuries had been one of a series of rebellions. As each successive dynasty was toppled, largely due to economic and social discontent, but also, it seemed, because of a recalcitrant trait in the oriental character, a new and temporarily popular ruler would emerge. In my mind's eye, as the clerics spoke, I could see the terrible tong wars of New York and San Francisco and I instantly identified these as minor rebellions gainst local dynastic rule, thus I thoroughly understood the situation. Now the rebels who threw over each regime invariably were members of a secret society, many of which thrived since time immemorial, as the Chinese dearly loved mystery and conspiracy, the two going hand in hand. (Fu Manchu? Forget that nonsense.) These sects were generally formed around the Peach Garden Legend, a beloved myth whereby sworn brotherhood among several gods became the Chinese ideal, a concept that indeed is not unattractive to this western mind. One of these sects, according to Father O'Shea, was called the White Lotus and it told its followers that man lifted himself out of his miseries the same way that the lotus rises out of the mud. (Too much exposition? Yes, but necessary, recall how they panned you for not communicating. Fuck them. Attaboy, but explain anyway.) I, at this point, mildly praised this picture, only to be sharply informed by the priest that the White Lotus also practised devil worship and demonology. I lapsed into silence, but filed that information away for further study, as any good reporter would.

To continue then, as the centuries rose and fell, in China a mere breath in the winds of time, the ideas of the White Lotus took root and became a part of history, some of it actual, some of it legend, but none the less believed in. This history created certain gods—or god-devils—to use the Father's phrase—who were popularized in plays, operas and novels of the people and who in these works blamed the country's troubles on foreigners and especially on Christianity. The Boxers, he explained somewhat contemptuously, merely borrowed these evil gods and their so-called magical rites in performing their acts of vengeance gainst the missions and all things foreign.

Yet who indeed were the Boxers? (Yes, get off the pot.)

21

Merely, according to my clerical friends, peasants, illiterates, rascals and ex-soldiers, many of whom scavenged the countryside after the end of the Japanese War. Ah, I thought, an oriental Ku Klux Klan; I said nothing. All of these groups, agreed both holy men, certainly had their grievances, as indeed we all do, but rather than struggling manfully to rectify them as *we* do, or resorting to healthful prayer, these people joined the Boxer movement, one of the several rebellious sects, but this one in the right place at the right time. At least for the cause of mischief. And on the instant the people were seduced away from salvation by promises of *present,* or corporeal immortality, gainst which attraction the church could not compete. I could readily understand that. (Hellyes.) To ensure loyalty the Boxers added several other gifts, such as flight and the ability to walk on water. My friends added glumly that the uninformed mind, alas, has always been attracted to witchcraft. I did not point out, for I did not yet know, that many Boxers in good standing were of the gentry, even lords and poets, that knowledge would come later. For now it was sufficient to learn that so powerful were their seductions that a ladies auxiliary known as the Red Lantern was formed, much, I might add, as ladies groups often form in this country to partake of the largesse.

Of course, said Father O'Shea, these Boxer-peasants were not entirely to blame in their violent hatred of Christians, since the converts to Protestantism were invariably favoured in the courts and in matters of trade and taxes by local officials. A fact supported by Reverend Townsend, save that his converted rascals were of the Catholic stripe. In any case, both were agreed, after nearly coming to blows, that of all the western enclaves, the Germans in Kiaochow were the most outrageously oppressive to the people and this I could verify from Emil Heingold's treatment of our Philippino houseboys. Naturally the flame of revolt was only fanned by oppression: missions were attacked, churches and shrines defiled. Both clerics showed me clippings from the *North China Daily News* telling of these desecrations; in these clippings I first encountered the dread slogan: *"Fu Ching Mieh Yang."* Words as ominous in English as in Chinese: nothing less than,

"Support the (Ching) Dynasty, Destroy the Foreigners." A chill of forboding permeated my being on seeing this; that sense to which I am both master and slave, and it bade me file those words in the back pages of my heart wherein reside the portentous headlines of our time.

"But what of the government?" I enquired. "Surely it is in its interest to support western rights."

Both men spat in unison. There ensued a babble of vituperation which slowly I sorted out. They were calling the curses of hell down on the famous—or infamous—Empress Dowager, now world renowned, the wily old concubine, who in the Reverend's words, had a disgusting passion for eunuchs. This was the person, this she-devil, who actually ruled China. And she had thrown in with the Boxers, of this they were sure. Further talk of the Empress Dowager then produced a most astonishing change in Father O'Shea's behavior. He seemed to fall into a fit or a frenzy in which he proceeded to hop and skip and dance and weave about in the most astonishing and unchurchly manner, betimes crossing himself and groaning Hail Marys. During this entire performance, Reverend Townsend looked on with me and nodded his head in grim approval.

"What in the world . . . ?" I ejaculated.

"You are witnessing authentic Boxer ritual," replied the minister. "Authentic, most authentic. He is summoning their devils in order to catch and hurl back our bullets."

"In other words," I vouchsafed, "invoking immortality."

He glanced at me, then away.

"You might say that," he muttered.

The capering priest at this juncture resembled no one more than John L. Sullivan in his cups, but of course I made no mention of this. At this point, as if prearranged, the Reverend Mr. Townsend began to weave from side to side, slowly at first, then with gathering speed until he too was both opponent and partner in the dance of the Harmonious Fists. Not knowing whether to applaud or join in, I did neither; I looked on sagely until both clerics began expectorating. Only then did I withdraw, thanking them both profusely. As I left the compound, the men of God were jabbing and hooking the air with spectacular fury and at the same time spitting out the devil. I confess to a feeling of strange exhilaration mixed with downright fear as I wrote my impressions in my bamboo hut, fortified by a beaker of rum.

So. Here then were the Boxers. The terrible villains of our chronicle. Or were they? I shall let the reader be both judge and jury. Suffice to say that from that day onward reports of murder, rapine, loot and arson began to arrive daily. As for this reporter, I knew only, as if commanded by the gods of the fourth estate, that I must be there on the mainland to see at first hand the unfolding story and to tell it to the *World*. In late April I presented myself at MacArthur's headquarters and informed him of my wish, my *compulsion*.

"You wish to observe this storm," he said.

"I do."

"Is there not," he smiled, "danger enough in the Philippines?"

"I have seen both bolos and water cures."

"You are nothing if not frank," he said, a smile still playing about his lips.

"In my profession," I said, "a dishonest man is a lost man."

"Well and truly said, Blake. In mine also." He rose. "You are in luck," he said crisply. "We have been ordered to send a warship to the Gulf of Chihli. You may go along if you wish. You will receive no favour or special privilege."

"I expect none, General," I replied.

"Good. You sail in three days."

He held out his hand and I clasped it. He wished me Godspeed and I wished him well in his difficult mission. I turned on my heels and left. It occurred to me, though only briefly, that we might never meet again.

That very afternoon I packed up my several belongings including pith helmet, two canteens and my writing materials. I purchased a pair of leather boots from Heingold and sent the following telegram to Pulitzer: "Grave trouble erupting in China. U.S. involved. The *World* needs me there for firsthand report." I

24

did not check the telegraph office for a response, but spent the next two days brushing up on my Mandarin.

On April 30, 1900, I was gazing at the receding shoreline of Luzon. I was on board the *Eagle,* an American armoured cruiser. My quarters were not the most comfortable, but no matter. I was the first reporter from this country to set sail for the troubled giant, to see and report that awful catastrophe the world has come to know as The Boxer Rebellion.

It is a start. What a start! A start. *Beautiful* start. A start, don't hex yourself. Yes. Superstitious *asshole.*

||
_____

The countdown has begun. He leaves this week. Reston writes about Peking. WINS talks about Chou, as do all the magazines. Channel 5 has a special. So does 13 with James Mason narrating. On 4 he's searching for the Nile, on 13 discovering Mao. You pays your money and takes your choice. Mason reminds me that the Manchus ruled in 1900. They had conquered and finally wound up with the Empress Dowager, and as outsiders they wanted to lock out all other outsiders. Good simple T.V. point. Too simple. The Manchus depended on the foreign powers to keep theirs, but when the Boxers sparked popular resentment and she saw she couldn't beat them, the wily old conk played footsie. OK? You're so damn smart. Sure. Here is simplistic T.V. history: Opium, Manchus, Boxers, treaties, Open Door, Sun, Kuomintang, Chiang, warlords, Japs, kidnap, pact, Mao, Long March, Yenan, Manchuria, Manchukuo, Manchu puppet, Pearl, the Hump, Flying Tigers, Burma Road, surrender, Civil War, Hurley, Marshall, China hands, sell out, Joe Mc, Nanking, Formosa, Gates of Heavenly Peace. Hell I won third prize in a '38 citywide World Geography contest for "The Concomitant Ramifications of the

Sino-Japanese War." Won a silver star. Old lady Schluder passed it around the room and W.J. Boody Jr. swiped it. I know he did. Little Texas bastard. The *Times* thumbnails a Nixon interpreter, a Yale man, who learned Mandarin in two years. Shoot—*shit*—Norris Blake learned it in eight months.

PEKING LIFTS BAN ON A DOZEN BOOKS

Including *The Three Kingdoms*. One of the books the Boxers ate up. Starring Kuang Yu, God of War. How tall was he, Scotty Reston? How long was his beard? What color was his face? What about his eyebrows? His eyes? Come on, big shot reporter, do your homework, like you know who. Give? OK, he was *nine* feet tall. Beard *two* feet long. Face a dark jujube. That means the color of a plum. Eyebrows like sleeping silkworms, eyes bloodshot as a phoenix's. That's filling in the gaps, Scotty baby. Name two other popular novels. Shit, *Water Margin* and *Pilgrimage to the West*. How about that? Who is featured in *Pilgrimage*? "Monkey," that's who. Shee-it, everybody wants to get into the act. Let them. I've got Blake. And my Boxers. Does Chou know they predicted the Red Guards of '67? Hear this, Joe, a saying of Chairman Sid: THE RIGHT HARMONIOUS FISTS KICKED IT OFF FOR YOU.

Oh baby it's working. I just know it. How? I'm getting the old jism back. You haven't had it in five years. Yes, since I finished *Interplay*. That's right, what else? I'm not afraid to get up in the morning. Check, what else? I go a whole day without thinking about breathing, eyes, ears, jaw, heart, blood pressure, piles, liver, baldspot, fungus on big toe, imminent failure of gravity. Christ it *must* be working. Well something is. God, do I *really* have a second book in me? Could I be so lucky? My name is Benson. Birnbaum. Worse, could Birnbaum be so lucky? Why not? Screwed, I'm always screwed. Always? Always. Now? I don't know, maybe . . . could I be so lucky? Why not? Yes, why not, I'm *Benson*. OK, Kid, hang on to it. I will, I will, but. What? Will it keep going,

God will it keep going? Don't worry, it always tells you, doesn't it? Yes it always does, but . . . But now what? Do I really *want* it to work? Whathehell kind of question is that? Why've you been going nuts for five years if not for this? Yes but. But what, for Christ sake? I'll be a total slave to it, I know I will. So? Do I want to be a goddam slave again? Remember how it was that time; can I take it? Take what? Slavery. You have no choice, have you? So when rape is inevitable, relax and enjoy it. You are so right, goddammit, and I do enjoy!

He's off today. They got a thousand kids out of school to wave him off, the sonofabitch. Some memory. What's that? Some memory, they got you and all the other scouts to line the route and cheer for FDR in '37. That was different. Balls, they got you out to La Guardia when Jim Farley opened it. Hmmm, formerly it was just a garbage dump. Yop. Used to be called North Beach. Yop. So, don't bring it up, it's ancient history. Damn well told, none the less valid. Don't use that big shit word on me, buddy. You're right, you *do* have the old jism back. Damn well told. Ah. But you know, much ancient history of late. Yes, much. I am thinking suddenly of the old Nixon, the man in the white suit, Checkers, good cloth coat, the country can't stand Pat. You're my boy. Ike. Yes. Oh gee that was the summer. What summer? You know. Well spit it out if it's that important. Shoot, shit, you know, dammit get off my back, Bligh, you're supposed to shrink to a pinhead when I've got my confidence. Say it and I'll shrink. The summer of her and Versailles and the Tower. Aha kid, name the city. The City of Light. I'll accept that for now. Where else? Genève. OK, too, don't stop. The other her. Why? That's enough. OK, where else. New Mex. Why? Enough. Why? Shit, I don't have *that* much jism. *Bon, j'accepte, pour maintenant.*

Hell I felt so good last night I decided to step out. Socially. It was the first time in over four years I even had the urge. I did not call Sue. What for? Screw her. I did something I haven't done in what? 18 years. B.S. Before Sue. I bought a *Post* and looked up the Friday night dances. Not plays, not movies, basketball, hockey, but the dances. They were still there, two full pages. Nothing changes in the Big Apple, nothing basic; everybody palpitating to connect; in 2001, the *Post* and dances. And there, between "Educational Get-together-Film-Lecture For a Something Different Evening" and "The Sociables" at La Martinique I saw it, just like the bad old days: "Kew Gardens Young Israel Presents. Miguelito and his full sized orch. For Matures of All Persuasions." Why the hell not? Didn't Sue come out of a rat race? More history. '55. Jesus. Manhattan Center. Trim, slim, but not in the hips, what would they feel like? Standing at the bar, nonchalanting with Eloise Greenfinkel, the ball breaker. Leech. Shall we? Why not? We did. I touched the hips accidentally on purpose, they bounced, what would they *look* like under the silk, the rayon? Sid Benson. Sue Hayden. Silence. Then, "I think about eyes a lot." I was hooked. Soulmate. Stupid, don't think about her, you can bet your ass she's not thinking about you. That is correct, *vous avez raison,* but why Young Israel? I don't know, I wanted to get back to my roots. My ruts. Don't ask why, OK ask me. Why? I don't know.

So I shaped up and shipped out. Crosstown bus, then another down to 53rd and Lex and the Independent. Out to Union Turnpike. Click. I was here once, to the Renaissance in '52, with Ardele Valyana of the chorus, *Brigadoon,* subway circuit, my showbiz segment. Ancient, ancient, don't think on it, don't think period, it only gets you into trouble.

I cabbed it over to Young Israel. It looked familiar. It should. Oh Jesus, or oh Moses, I was here in—'47? Yes, '47. With the boys. Readjusting. OhmyGod, 22 friggin years old, el Conquistador. So much hydrogen hydroxide under the bridge, so much. Chick Winokur and Soc Zlotsky and Arch Goldberg and the rest of the boys. All a little crazy, all making up for the lost years. Did Arch meet his wife here? Why I believe he did, the three-time loser, poor bastard. I wonder where he is now? Still wheeling and dealing? Hell forget him, he forgot you.

I stood across the street and clocked in the arrivals, as the

boyiss and I used to. Not much. No, not much. Careful, Gloria
Steinem is listening. So why aren't you here, Glo? I'd even forget
your nonsense. "It is *not* nonsense." Yes, Susie, I hear you, Susie.
Knock it off. Christ you got Captain Bligh off your back for to-
night, don't let *her* push you around. Check and double check.
Those two aren't bad. Not bad at all, whadayou think, Chick? I
like the puppy all by herself to the left of the door, that's action.
Male chauvinist pig! OK I started across, slowly. It was strange,
very strange how my pedal extremities were dragging. I mean I
was actually holding back. *Shy?* The craziest of the crazies in
Neosho, Liverpool, Verdun, Mainz, Bad Nauheim, Marseilles, shy?
Yes, him. He. You. I. Me. Hell the last time I was shy I was
Birnbaum at Ellie Illowhite's 11th birthday party and at first did
not want to play wink. Got over it fast and by her next party
maneuvered all the post office numbers around to me, especially
Nita Nassi's, the Talyaina. What did I say about ancient history?
Very well, I was shy. But years of dedicated and purposeful pussy
chasing had reeducated me. There. I pushed myself across that
street and paid my dues and entered the temple. I got the invisible
number stamped on my wrist in case I wanted to leave and get
back in. Leon Blum couldn't leave. Buchenwald. '45. Liberators.
Third Army. Bones, bones, piled up bodies. Ilsa Koch. Lamp-
shades. Patton gets sick. The mayor of Weimar hangs himself.
Back to *important* matters. You are 46, your wife has left you,
you are a day to day sub, you are looking for a little contact with
a member of the opposite sex. What? Where did you come from,
Bligh? I just want to keep it honest, Mr. Christian. Ssh, not here.
Well? OK, a little action. That's more like it, I'll see you later.
Not if I see you first.

I walked around the outer perimeter of the large room. City
Center. Manhattan Center. Reece's, Liverpool. Same deal. All
the blank, straining faces, the eyes. No wonder she thought about
eyes. Look at them. What happens when they disappear into the
cheeks. They become large, aqueous, imperfectly shaped balls.
Balls, you and your education. It's not my fault I'm educated,
I'm the world's greatest artist, only nobody knows it. Look at
those two over there. Aloof and alert. No.

31

Then I saw her.

A singleton, sitting at a table, sipping a drink. Too comely to be action, too ugly not to be. Totally intriguing. A man with hair combed forward, was leaning over her, working his ancient points. She shook her head and smiled faintly. He wouldn't take no for an answer, she looked away and crossed her legs. He looked at his boy, also with the Caesar hair-do, shrugged, rolled his aqueous masses to save face and walked off. I kicked the chains off my ankles and moved in. OhmyGod, what do you say?

"How do you do?"

Her head turned slowly. The two liquid balls searched mine.

"How do you do?" she said.

"You wouldn't care to dance, would you?"

Was that a smile? Christ I was at Ellie's first party.

"No," she said.

"Oh."

But the head did not spin away. It kept looking, searching. Where had I seen that look? Ohyes, '43, '44, '45 for starters. The U.S.O. Service Club, Red Cross, overseas, rat race special. What did I do when they looked like that? Sure. I gazed for an instant, then flicked away. Then back. Then away. Her responding look puzzled, interested. The old game plan surged back.

"Why did you put it in such negative terms?" she said.

"I guess . . . self defense . . ."

"Oh?" This time an out-and-out smile.

"Well I . . . the truth is I don't go to these things very often."

She liked that; I know she liked that.

"Neither do I. In fact I was just thinking I don't know why I came."

"Why did you?" I said.

"Oh lack of something better to do. Why did *you*?"

Don't say to meet you.

"I'm writing a novel," I said. "And I'm collecting material." Shit, 20 years ago I would have let it go at that, but you have to swing with the times. "And if you believe that," I said, "You're dumber than I look."

32

"I don't believe it," she smiled. "But it *is* possible, isn't it?"

"Yes." I took a chance. "As a matter of fact I am writing a novel. But not about this."

She examined my bona fides, oh how she examined. I passed.

"What is it about?"

I shook my head.

"I never talk about it. Neither did Hemingway. We both believe that you let it out of your head if you do. It's sort of like the Indian's fear of having his picture taken. They say you're plucking out their soul and keeping it."

She nodded and said, "Yes, I can understand that. Do you still want to dance?"

"I'm not sure," I said.

"I deserved that. But if you do, I do."

It was all there. Like ice skating, once you learn, you never forget.

"All right," I said, after pondering with my aqueous balls.

She rose and we walked to the floor side by side. Miguelito was playing what I used to call a rhumba. She raised her right arm and I took her hand and stepped into my remembered side, to-gether, step. Whatever it was, we were going to rhumba. She was a little tight, but game, and allowed me to do the pushing. We moved silently, nothing fancy, not yet.

"I'm Ellen," she said.

"Where's your magic violin?"

"That's *Evelyn*," she said. "Evelyn and her magic violin."

Jesus she was right. Was I getting senile? If I didn't watch it, I'd soon be saying swing and sway with Danny Kaye.

"You're right," I said. "Just testing. Who did she play for?"

"Phil something or other."

"Spitalny." I felt better, much better. "I'm Sid Benson," I said.

"Hello."

"Hello."

So there it was, nice and easy. We had another rhumba, then a drink, another dance and soon we were ice skating around the floor like Roseland partners and I was doing a few little breaks

33

and dips, my trademarked specials from the old days, and after another drink even a mambo, yes mama loves papa, papa loves mambo. All as simple as yesterday. I had almost forgotten that soft moveable crease they have in the middle, that molds under your hand like latex, only no latex here, or spandex or playtex. This was a hunnert proof protoplasm, the old living material.

Ellen Mayer. Between 35 and 38. Assistant buyer, Saks luggage. Three years college, Hunter. "The stupidest day of my life when I quit." Next to the day she got married. She didn't say it, she didn't have to. Maybe I'm crazy, but I'm not stupid. After another drink, a blackberry sour of all things, even though quite paternally I warned her about the sweet stuff, she spilled. They always love to spill to writers; one thing about us, we may not be great talkers or great writers, but we are great listeners. I learned that from a Louella Parsons interview with a pseudo Steinbeck. She said he wasn't particularly handsome, clever, bright or charming, but oh how he *listened*; he hung on every word Louella said, made her feel she was the only person in the world. Since then, when impression-making, oh how I hung. Ellen loved it, more, she *needed* it—to be the only person in the world. She ventilated, calmly at first, then as I caressed her every word, not so calmly. She had known after six months with Sy somehow it wasn't going to work. But she had tried, yes, she hadn't given up. She was infatuated with him. Her word, not mine. Uh huh, yes, uh uh and I see. Once I touched her hand in quiet understanding and she touched back. Divorced two years; thank God she had gone back to work when the kids were young.

"Yes," I said at last. "You had that feeling of failure from the start and were subconsciously hedging your bets."

"Are you sure you're not a psychiatrist?"

"Nope, a writer. It's not that hard to figure out."

"Oh but it was. For me."

She seemed to sigh it all out. She was still very much in control, they always are—the careful ones—but the dancing, the sours, the ventilating, the listening were perceptibly shining up her aqueous orbs. The talk, the music spun away from us and we were two people who had connected in New York and how often does *that* happen? There have been two things that will move time for me in my history, writing when it goes and a score at a rat race. Suddenly out of the dragging mists of my recent life, I had the best of my two worlds. Before I knew it, it was phone number time. Naturally I'd forgotten my black book and a pencil, something that to her delight verified my amateur status. She wrote it carefully down and gave it to me. I tucked it into my wallet.

"May I take you home?" I said.

"If you want to."

"Now don't make me say I wouldn't have asked if I didn't want to. Just say yes or no."

That caught her a little off balance as it always did. Big shot. Down, boy, you can't even touch me now. R-r-r-ats!

"Yes," she said apologetically, squeezing my hand.

We took a taxi. She lived in Flushing off Kissena Boulevard, near Queens College.

"That used to be a reform school, before it was a college," I said in the quiet, turning dark.

"How in the world do you know that?"

"I just know it. I once did a story about it. A reform school kid and a jump into time with a college kid and a jump back to the reform school. It never got off the ground."

"I'm sorry."

"Don't be. Most of my stuff never gets off the ground."

"Oh Sid," she said.

I didn't want to, I wanted to be very proper in the cab. But she seemed to open when she said that. The old jism took over and I put my arms around her. Protectively I think. She came in quickly and we kissed. I kept my mouth closed even though hers opened experimentally and we kept kissing until we were breathing; then firmly I pulled away. She sighed and settled back. Ah, I had protected her against herself; it worked with Mai Lewkowitz at Marble Beach Day Camp in '47, with Jody Cohen in Camp Redlock in '48 and yes in '52 in Paris, down by the Seine, it *always* worked. I may have been too stupid to follow it up, but don't blame the noble impulse.

We sat quietly until we got out. I paid the man and we walked to her building. It was a 50's apartment house; I know them well, Horatio, places of infinite loss. I could close my eyes and walk through the courtyard, hear her take out her keys, open the outer door, walk us through the long hall to the elevator. In fact I did close my eyes. I only opened them in the elevator. She was very serious as we rode up. We got out at seven and walked down the thin hall to her door. Oh so many hallways, so many doors. Now came the tricky part. Her kids were at her mother's, I could have asked to come in; I didn't.

"Well," she said, turning and lifting her face, "I really had a lovely evening, Sid. And when I least expected it."

"Those are always the best," I said.

I bent and kissed her. Oh I forgot to mention. I could bend because I was wearing my elevators. Not that I'm short, I'm five eleven and a quarter. I learned to wear elevators from Sonny Tufts who was six three or four but couldn't stand the thought of anyone on the set being taller. In my case, I had to top six feet. Come now, Mr. Christian, if you hadn't mentioned it, I would have. Kiss off, mac.

"I had a good time, too," I said. True.

"Will I see you again?"

"Do you want to?" I thought I would say that, for now I had a nice little edge.

"Yes."

"Then yes, you will," I said.

I had it all played out in my mind. I would lean over again and kiss her. She would kiss back. I would reach for her breast and she would let me, even cover my hand like Miriam Lichman in '42 and press it in. Then very gently I would remove her hand, remove mine and step back. She would be breathing hard and fast, even as Miriam, and looking bewildered. Then she would burst into tears. Like Miriam and Jane Finestone after City Center in '49; God how Jane had bawled. I would let her cry it out, put her head on my shoulder. "It's OK," I'd say. "Thank you, Sid," she'd reply. "It's OK, kid, it's OK." She would cry some more, then, "Oh there are so many rats in the world, you don't

36

know . . ." "I do know, I know." Then quiet and gentle breathing. "Do you want to come in, Sid?" "No, sweetie, not tonight." The look of gratitude. "Thank you, Sid." I would kiss her—dry—spin and walk away, blue-balled but uplifted. What about the action? Stupid, there will soon be enough to give *you* seconds.

She looked up at me. I leaned over and kissed her and she sagged into me. I reached upstairs and she let me. Then by heaven, she covered my hand with hers and pressed it in. Before I could stop myself my other hand snaked to her coat and I expertly undid the buttons and she pressed harder into me. I reached down and yanked up on her dress as if I were Sid Birnbaum with Nita Nassi in Van Cortlandt Park. I drove my knee between her legs; Nita loved knees. She opened for an instant, then snapping together, she brought her knee up and into my groin. I gasped and bent double. I felt her pocketbook slapping me on the head. Then I saw the bag on the ground and she was leaning against the door, sobbing.

"You goddam bastard," she said hoarsely between sobs. "You lousy rotten bastard. You're all alike."

I tried to talk, to say no, I wasn't, but I couldn't. I felt her reach down and saw her hand sweep up the bag. I heard a key scraping, the door open and slam. I was still bent over, looking blankly at the strings of my spittle. I thought I could hear her moving around in her apartment, but I wasn't sure. Slowly I straightened up. I took a few careful steps and discovered I could walk if I kept my legs apart. Jesus, I thought, I hope she didn't give me a hydrocele. Well buster, what did you expect, chopped liver? Oh shit, here we go. You could have been Leslie Howard, but no, you needed instant gratification, you goddam SDS. Don't rub it in. Hungry, too hungry; remember '51 and Shirley Bender in Grossinger's? Hungry then too. Oh shit, leave off already, will you? So of course we fought all the way back, Captain Bligh and Fletcher Christian.

It was two A.M. when I got home. I threw off my coat, ran into the kitchen, kicked Bligh in the ass, pulled out the Boxers, and began to write. It took a little while, but finally I got some goddam relief.

37

III

CHAPTER TWO (BOX.)

We put in at Hong Kong for coal and to be joined by several other ships and from whence I filed my first dispatch, then we headed north through the Formosa Strait. It took us 13 days to steam through the China and Yellow Seas, past the brown, muddied waters that identified the discharging presence of the Yellow River, around the pointing finger of the Shantung Peninsula and into the Gulf of Chihli. It was an uneventful voyage, smooth and powerful, the ironclad throbbing beneath our feet and thrusting aside the eastern seas as if warning of its might and an answer to the gauntlet that had been thrown. Captain James MacGregor of Charleston, South Carolina, was the ideal host and he made every effort to see to my wants and needs, but these of course could only be satisfied by our arrival in Taku Harbour and the sight and sound and clash of China.

The first of my desires came to pass—at least in part—on the 13th night.

We arrived by the light of the moon and stars on May 18. We dropped anchor. And there spread all about me in the soft spring glow was as strange and conflicting a sight as I had ever seen. An eerie armada, some 30 warships, the arrayed might of the western world, and interspersed amongst them dozens of Chinese junks, their ancient and graceful forms topped by sails of matted cloth. My first reaction—after an appraising review of the colorful sight—was quite an ominous one. Could these primitive vessels, I thought, possibly be manned by the very members of the secret sect I had come to investigate? I peered westward; I could make out the darkling hulk of the mainland. I thought of the devious oriental character and my mind's eye clearly saw crouching, weaving, grinning shapes preparing for who knew what? I managed to banish these pictures only by a supreme effort of will. I was a writer of fact, not of fiction. Surely, I reminded myself, the admirals of this mighty fleet had looked to its security. For added reassurance I studied the great ships. Their sturdy iron bulk. Their firmly pointed cannon. Ah there were the insignia I knew so well: British, French, German, Russian. Above all, the familiar and comforting shapes of the ships of the United States. I was suddenly ashamed of my childish premonitions. A man of my experience, I chided myself, should know better. I smiled at my mechanical friends, wondered how I could be so foolish. In retrospect I can only ascribe those peculiar sensations to the spell of China; little did I know they were not to be the last. But for now, as if to prove my reportorial objectivity, to myself if not to my employer, my trained mind flashed to an opposing thought: could not this awesome power poised against a horde of peasants, as represented by those primitive craft, be thought of as unsporting odds by all lovers of fair play, especially in America and Britain where we go at the game hard but square? I wondered. Ah but no. The openness and honesty of the nation whose ship of war had borne me hither rose up to refute the notion. And as if to give weight to the point were we not under the command of Admiral Kempff himself? Need I say more? Already his firm and fair approach to this mission had won the respect of his countrymen. Soon his gallant refusal to strike the first blow would gladden our hearts and his steadfastness under fire when it did come, as come it must, would be well known to every schoolboy and requires no further word from me, except to note that it will ever be an inspiration and model to generations of officers and gentlemen still unborn. Indeed in a remarkable conversation I held with this gallant sailor on the following afternoon on board the *Newark* he revealed that he was ever conscious of carrying his nation's reputation on his shoulders, a weighty load, but did not Hercules carry the weight of the world? Pointing oerhead, he vowed he would never do anything to besmirch that fair banner. Perry could not have said more. As I gazed aloft with him I must admit to a glow of pride at the sight of the tried and true pennant, but again, as I shook the Admiral's hand and wished him Godspeed, I quickly suppressed the emotion; the able reporter must bend ever backward to attain impartiality, even though the facts warrant otherwise.

What were the facts?

They were sad and filled with danger. For one, a full report on the terrible murder of the Reverend S. Brooks of the British Society for the Propagation of the Gospel. I had heard of this in Manila, but now learned the story in detail of how the deed was done some 50 miles south of Chinan, near the Yellow River in Shantung Province. Suffice to say that after merciless treatment, the martyred hero was decapitated and both his head and body dealt with in the most barbaric manner. I was also told of the destruction of three villages and the murder of 61 Roman Catholic converts, mainly of French persuasion, at Paotingfu, only 90 miles from Peking. I could not help but think of the grieving Father O'Shea. I learned of the shameful and pusillanimous behavior of Yuan Shih Kai, the governor of Shantung and of Yu Lu, viceroy of Chihli. They, together with Tzu Hsi, the Empress Dowager, sometimes known as Nala, sometimes known as the Western Empress, ever suspected of the poisoning of her coequal, the Eastern Empress, were doing nothing to help us, in fact in true oriental style were hindering our efforts. There was the discovery of more Boxer placards with their dire warnings to foreigners. Finally, for now,

41

there were the alarming reports of Mr. MacDonald and Mr. Conger, the British and American ministers in Peking; I personally read these dispatches and felt I could gainsay the popular belief that our diplomats behaved as "ostriches," their heads in the ancient sands of Peking. After all, were we not here?

Yes, events were moving at an ever-increasing rate and we were a very real part of them. But for the moment, alas, we were to be inert actors in the play, since all personnel had strict orders to remain on shipboard. Not wishing to add to the captain's burdens, I contented myself that first night with poring over the maps he had kindly loaned me and prodding my memory for details of the region. On my first sojourn, in '94, I had spent several days hereabouts, both in Chihli and around Kiaochow Bay and in cruising the Yellow River. I had seen at first hand the many mission stations and now I remembered thinking: Will the cross and Buddha ever merge? Oddly enough, the Catholics seem wiser in this, adapting some of the eastern ways to their program, whilst the Protestants adhere to unswerving principle, which made the murders in Paotingfu seem all the more puzzling. The oriental character again, I thought, shaking my head. Then I recalled to mind the city of Taku, more a town, identifying it on the map as the harbour for Tientsin, one of the two great cities of the region. I traced the Pei Ho River north and west, up past Peking, noted how it drained the areas of Chihli Province wherein the drama would surely be played out. (That prescience again, Blake or Benson? Blake AS Benson.) I thought I had the picture firmly and truly fixed in my mind's eye as I lay down to sleep in fits and starts. But reality and expectation rarely conform in Cathay, as I was soon to discover.

Dawn. The harbour and my first glimpse of the country in six years. We are in deep water outside Taku Bar. The junks are gliding past, their owners nodding and waving. How foolish seem my fears in bright daylight. Bugles are blowing aboard the ships of war, which are a multicolored fleet. Some vessels are yellow, others white, still others black and white and still others gray so that they will melt into the fog of battle. Some are belching their acrid coal smoke, ominous black columns which connect the clear blue sky above to the troubled yellow waters below. Little steam tugs bustle to and fro. Sailors are scrubbing the decks, some on horizontal ladders are painting the sides. Soldiers and marines call to each other in a babble of tongues. Some loll about, some pace nervously. I can make out Zouaves in their red caps, Russians in their flat ones. British midshipmen, no more than boys. The spiked helmets of the Germans. Around me our boys in their felt campaign hats, made famous in Cuba and the Philippines. Across the busy water the now well known guns of the forts stab out at us. They seem to say: "This far and no farther." The land stretches away on either side in silent acquiescence. I feel I am an American Marco Polo as I gaze out on the enormous table-flat plain that disappears into the horizon line. Quite literally it seems to walk softly off down the centuries. I know that some hundred miles to the north the Great Wall curves down to the sea, then bends north to Manchuria, that land so coveted by the Russians. I take my notes and make several sketches, although the dazzling scene cries out for a Graves or a Gaul. I talk to several fresh-faced lads who hail, with equal patriotism, from city and farm. They run the emotional gamut from extreme tension to let the devil take the hindmost. In the afternoon the captain lifts the regulations for me and has me rowed to the Admiral's ship where the remarkable talk I have mentioned takes place. I am rowed back and telegraph two dispatches to the *World*. That night I mess with the Captain. As the sun sets through the porthole and the stars ascend, I gaze longingly out at China.

"Well," says the Captain. "I see you are chafing."

I nod without speaking. This southerner whose father perhaps fought mine has caught and understands my mood, for he shares it. But he understands, too, his military responsibilities. After some quiet talk, we bid each other good night. I smoke a final cigarette and retire for the evening. But I cannot sleep. Out there, above the endless land mass, can I hear cries in the night? Railway cars screeching to a halt? I rise and stare out of my porthole. China stares dumbly back. Ships' lights are dimmed. All is silent.

The following day no longer brings the novelty of the new, colorful as the new may be. The new in and of itself is soon old to the experienced writer; save as preface to the play, it wears out its welcome. I find myself pacing the deck with some of the marines. That afternoon the Captain summons me to his quarters.

"You will wear out the deck."

"I cannot help myself."

"Yes, I know." He is silent for a moment. Then he rises and assumes my China stare, as I have come to label it. He turns. "My orders are to cooperate with you in every way. My superiors," he smiles, "surely know the power of the press." Then he is all business. "Can you be ready at ten o'clock tonight?"

The ineffable weariness falls away. My sixth sense stirs. "You mean. . . ?"

"Yes."

"I can and will be ready."

"Good. Be patient a while longer. Remain in your cabin."

That is all. That is more than enough. I return and assemble my meager kit. Somehow I live through the evening. Precisely at the hour of ten there is a knock at the door. Controlling my heartbeat, a trick I learned on my first trip to China, I open the door and stand aside. Ensign Joseph Kubersky of Brockton, Massachusetts, enters.

"Are you ready, sir?"

"I am."

"This is for you."

He hands over a small silk bag tied with a drawstring. It clinks in my hand.

"One hundred taels of silver. I would keep it inside my shirt, sir."

I follow his excellent suggestion. One hundred ounces of silver could be quite a lodestone on the mainland.

"Follow me, sir."

I walk in his footsteps up to the deck and back to the fantail. I notice that no one has crossed our path. He points to one side, then holds out his hand. I grasp it.

"Very best of luck, sir. Don't let them land any uppercuts."

"Not if I can help it."

The sturdy lad, a fine son of Poland, but American to the core, steps back, salutes and spins away. I look over the side. A rope ladder dangles into the darkness. Is that a junk far below? I slip my musette bag over my shoulder, clamber over the side and feel for the ladder with my foot. I find it and step carefully but quickly down, paying quick thanks to my activity at the New York Athletic Club. It is *indeed* a junk. A short, square figure eases my foot to its deck. In the light of the moon I examine my companion. He is gowned, fully queued. He bows.

"I am Chang Shen," he says.

Not to be outdone, I, too, bow.

"I—," I begin, but he holds up his hand.

"I know who you are," he says in barely accented English. "Into the cabin, please." His manner is quite respectful yet strangely firm for a Chinese. I do as I am bid and crawl into the cramped quarters. I peer up through the matted cloth and I see the stars; they are moving. No, it is *we* who are moving. I remain thus for approximately three quarters of an hour as timed by my pulse rate. Then the stars stop. I hear a gentle knock and the whispered words, "You may come out."

I crawl out, but still remain in a crouched position, since this is my exotic friend's posture. We are at a wooden pier some several hundred yards above the lights that indicate Taku.

"It is all right," says Chan Shen, rising. "You may stand."

It feels good to stand up and stretch. I note that my sciatic nerve twinges slightly but pay it no heed.

"Who are you?" I enquire.

"A Christian," he says simply. "And a friend to your navy."

"Yes. So I see."

I reach inside my shirt and withdraw the money bag. He holds up his hand and shakes his head.

"Please," he says.

I know instantly that I have erred. It will not be the last time in this strange land. I replace the bag.

"However," he says, "I will give *you* something." He smiles at what he knows to be his presumption. "I wish," he says, "that it were a cross, assuming of course that you do not have one. However, I do not wish to increase your jeopardy and if you carry one, I advise you to throw it overboard now."

"I . . . do not carry one."

He sighs.

"I give you a word."

"A word?"

"Yes. The word is 'assumption.' "

"Assumption?"

"Yes."

"As in the assumption of the saviour?"

"Precisely."

"Hmmm. Curious."

"Merely keep the word in the darkest corner of your mind. Do not use it hastily. But perhaps when you need to use it, you will know the time and do so."

"I see. I fully accept your explanation."

He bows. I return the bow and step lightly up onto the wood planking. I survey the lights of the city. When I turn back the junk has already glided off. I think I see a hand raised in farewell. I raise mine. I look out at the ships, at their great chimneys and heavy masts fiercely spiking the silent sky. Suddenly I shiver. I turn back. I am alone.

AH.

46

IV

During the famous week I sub just one day, at Washington Irving, in American History and the Problems of Democracy. "The Treaty of Versailles." Seniors, some juniors. They are bored stiff. The future of America. The other days I spend at Columbia, mainly at Kent Hall and the East Asian Library. Surrounded by oriental scholars, some of whom for all I know are related to the event, I handle the books of '01, '02 and '03 very tenderly, but even as I do, the pages that tell of murder and riot and torture flake and tear away in my hand. Excitedly I read the day to day trivia in the stiff upper lip diary of the beautifully named Lancelot Gibbs. I trace the adventures of one, Pierre Loti, who sends his dispatches to *Figaro,* but *after* the rebellion, not like a certain American correspondent who simply had to be where the action was. I read of *China in Convulsion.* Its author, Arthur H. Smith, a missionary of course, has dedicated his book to his wife, who labored hand in glove with him for 30 years to save the heathen soul. I study the names of the dead—the martyred—missionaries. I do not find the names of the Chinese dead, unless they are Christian converts.

At night, with my heavenly, raging, magnificent, liberating tyranny firmly fixed in my frontal lobe, I sit and watch the tube. The great banquet. Our man in Peking grinning. Chou, his face an Aztec mask, thinking. Back to the Open Door? And the diplomatic John Hay. So America can also get its piece of the action? "Most favored nation" clauses. Anson Burlingame, American, the first foreign envoy to reside in Peking. In '68 appointed by the *Chinese* foreign ministry as High Minister Extraordinary and Plenipotentiary to the U.S. and Europe. The allied ambassadors presented to the emperor in '73. They do not kowtow, merely bow five times. Senator Albert Beveridge, Jan. 9, 1900: "The Philippines will forever belong to the United States and beyond them is the huge China market. The United States will keep both." My first lesson on Asia and old lady Schluder: "Now here in the Yangtze Valley was the British sphere of influence. This was the German, in Shantung. The Russians had Port Arthur, Manchuria and Mongolia, the French Yunnan Province, the Japanese Taiwan, Korea and Fukien Province. Today the Japanese have Manchukuo which is the new name for Manchuria so you see some changes have been made. We of course insisted on the Open Door Policy which is only right and proper to keep China free." Uncle Chou blinks. *The Bitter Tea of General Yen* and *The General Died at Dawn.* Nils Asther blinks. Coop makes a great speech on freedom. Akim Tamiroff, American-Russian, playing the Chinese warlord, smirks. He knows from spheres of influence. Ah but Madeleine Carroll. What did W.J. Boody Jr. say about her? I'd walk 39 steps to get to her ass. Crude Texas bastard. Even studied his mother's ass. Besides Madeleine doesn't screw. How could she, her legs are always crossed?

Chou, jaw flexing, thinking of the eight invading armies, the Allies? The American marines? Admiral Kempff? He looks at the man asking for the Open Door. Perhaps. Is that the flick of a smile?

My God, he is almost pathetically appealing. In a sad way. Yes, that. The pained and painful smile. The bulging jowels, they're not. fat, but bunched muscle from years of clenching. The effort of will

48

to carry it off, to keep from falling over his own feet. Our Emperor Dowager, if you can't beat them, join them. Neck bobbing in awkward toast. No shoulders, how is that possible. Seymour Sigelman in 6A had no ankles, but no *shoulders*? At a given signal Eisenhower up in the sky yanks and raises and lowers the arms which grow out of his neck.

Smartass bastard.

Holy cow, as they say in India, look at that ballet! It is pure Boxer ritual. Of course. Resist the invader, death to the foreigner. Bob and weave and stretch and shrink and rise up. Perhaps the choreographer's grandfather was a Right Harmonious Fist. Maybe the ballerina's grandmother was a Red Lantern?

Hell, they are everywhere. The gymnastics are nothing more than the climax of physical and mental exaltation. *They* told us. It is the only immortality we know. Uh oh, he is grinning again and clapping. Chou is almost smiling. Joe Mc is lurching around in his grave. The senators from Formosa are plotzing.

So The Forbidden City at last. The Imperial City. The Yellow City. The Violet City. The Tartar City. The Chinese City. At the palace lived in by the last emperor, the final thin-blooded Manchu. And who was that, oh student of history, oh expert in foreign affairs, homework doer, symbolist of Great Walls? Henry Pu Yi, that's who. And what was his real name? Hsuan Tung. And who deposed him? Sun, Sun Yat-Sen. Well technically speaking, he abdicated. What happened to him? He became the Japanese puppet emperor in Manchukuo né Manchuria. Who opposed Sun after the abdication and pushed him into exile, was short, thickset and looked like Clemenceau? Hell, Yuan Shih Kai, the pusillanimous viceroy-warlord of Shantung. The potsy player with Boxers. Aha the thlot pickens. Yuan Shih Kai. Akim

Tamiroff. General Yang-Yen-Yuan. Enough! He only went to Whittier, *you* went to C.C.N.Y.

That night I treated myself to a Broadway play, my first one in six years. I picked *Lenny* because I once saw Bruce downtown when he was already on the skids and I knew he couldn't be that bad. I'd heard the records. So I went. I treated myself to a good seat downstairs and I saw *Lenny*. I cried all the way through. I walked out as they scraped him off the bathroom floor, sat him on the toilet and took his picture. I couldn't stand to see a smiling actor take a curtain call and twinkle off, although Cliff Gorman was marvelous with his Cagney stance and Julie Garfield delivery. I went to the Edison and sat at the bar and drank V.O. and water and suffered. God how I suffered. For didn't he say it all, in one overpowering speech? Yes, all. No *rachmunes*. Oh Jesus, no *rachmunes*. No pity. That is it. No pity, as with you know who. Who? Fuck you, Bligh, ask General Yang-Yen, he had no *rachmunes* either. He didn't deserve any, Mr. Christian, and aren't you being quite ambivalent? All right, all right. After all, he *could* have kept his mouth shut now and then, he didn't *have* to be so compulsively seeking punishment, he *could* have compromised. Bullshit, Bligh, that had nothing to do with the price of eggs. Oh? Free speech, obscenity, balls, Lenny Bruce was persecuted because he was a New York Jew. Oh lord, not the paranoia again. True is true, the whole world hates a *New York* Jew, including you; double zero, double double zero. It even rubs off, they hate a New York gentile worse than a Colorado Jew. Well well. The smartass New York Jew, see; everyone out there is green with envy, looking on, watching him make out, crack wise, tickle the ivories, noodle the licorice stick. Actor, painter, writer, the talent exploding out of every pore. Go on. Shit, it's got nothing to do with noses or Christ. No? No. The New York Jew, isn't he always out front? So? Just look at Sergeant Ambrose Detweiler of Baton Rouge asking Benson to fix him up in Joplin. With Carol Winthrop, who finds the N.Y.J. the cutest thing in her Missouri life. See PFC Jimmy Jackson of

Biloxi howl till he cries at Benson's routines with Abe Glassman of Bensonhurst. Look, Sleepy Starbuck of Winston-Salem, eyes bulging open at the Benson lindy hop in Red Bank, the Benson combo in Liverpool. So of course they hated Benson-Bruce, the corkscrew, the nigga luvva, but not for the latter reasons, schmuck, for the former!

I went to bed after the eleven o'clock news, but I couldn't sleep. *Lenny* bothered me. I was the only person in the theater who truly understood it. In fact it reminded me of a few minor setbacks in my own life. And before you curl that goddam lip and say, Minor? I'll say it for you, minor. My, aren't we touchy tonight. I *told* you, don't start. *I* am the captain, sir, and the question still holds, minor? Well, setbacks. That's better, Christian, you know I like it when you're honest. How's this for honesty? I had not been able to think about those setbacks for years. Splendid, and why was that, sir? Must you always know? Not always, but most of the time. Because I am the Jew Pope, OK? Infallible. And these—things—indicate fallibility. No one is perfect, my boy. I'm not your boy and *I* was. Perfect. Ask Schluder. Ask Nita Nassi. Ask the old man. Do tell. Never mind, use any objective rating scale of perfection you want and see how high I come out. Well, there is the voice of confidence again. Damn right. But. Yes. That's what hurt so. When? '38. What? It. What it? Don't be so fucking Odetsian, it, the thing, the business in scout camp at Ten Mile River. Your Yellow River. I was going to say that, you're stealing my stuff. Obvious, too obvious, go on if you can. Oh I can, you don't think I can, but I can. As a reborn, functioning, fully integrated human being, I can. The Boxers, God bless them, have given me the strength. . . .

I, Birnbaum, was 13. King of the Schoolyard. Speediest wheels on the block. Chinning record, no gypping. First choose, always first. And I was a *non-swimmer*. I fully admit it, after 33 years. Thank you, Fists. Very clearly, as in the Peking sunshine I can see the hero now. Bunched in against the bus window, alongside Robert

51

Dopp (né Dopplinsky), all everything load, but a swimmer and surface diver. I see him shivering all the way up the Jersey side of the Hudson, past the Bear Mountain Bridge and the Red Apple Rest, I see him staring at himself—this person—beneath the icy waters of Lake Powhattan, breathing those waters, once, twice, thrice and out. This hero. A non-swimmer. No reason. No early trauma. A fact. Complete loser of ego identity. As soon as he hit the water. The hostile environment. Nazi Germany. This Birnbaum was the complete, total hydrophobe. I admit. Trustworthyloyalhelp-fulfriendlycourteouskindobedientcheerfulthriftybravecleanandrever-entandscaredshitless. I writhe in bed, but I see him. I confess to him. There, gazing at Sid Birnbaum in the globe of the Brothers Bus Company. Projecting to that 50-yard swim test. His lips are moving. What is the hero, this shitheel saying? On my honor I will do my best to do my duty to God and my country and to obey the scout law. To help other people at all times, to keep myself physically strong, mentally awake and morally straight.

He sat and talked like that all the way up, this star of 181st Street, this swivel-hipped clean-up hitter. He sat thus on the bank as Norman Hooplock, jello tits and all, plunged in fearlessly and huffed and puffed for 50 glorious yards, while the (perfidious) troop cheered. As Jerry Bimstein swan-dived and cut the water like a knife, as Bobby (Load) Dopp turned into U-238. It hurts, oh it hurts, but I am taking my medicine on that bed, even as Henry Pu Yi. The puppet, the deposed emperor of 181st Street.

That afternoon dipped and darkened and still the ex-king sat, towel about fuzzy pubes, until they had all qualified and disappeared down the road to Seneca Compound. And only he and Mr. Dernberg remained.

"You can do it, Sid," said Dernberg.

The staring head shook.

"I know you can, fella."

"No I can't."

"Try."

"No."

"Just jump in a little. Get in over your head. Or you'll never conquer it. If anything happens, I'll be right beside you."

"... I can't."

"Oh forcrissake then, get back to the compound. Report to the crib tomorrow morning."

Mouth twisting (sneering?), jock bulging, Dernberg walked off down the road. The nothing-king sighed. Stared at the water. Sighed again. Then he rose and pulling the towel tightly about private things, trudged off down the road. I writhe on my rack of pain. But wait. The lay-up champ has stopped. He's turned. Turned away and begun to cry. I reach up and brush my eyes; this is rougher than I had bargained for. I think of Norris Blake, breathe deeply and return to Birnbaum, who has turned once again. He is walking out onto the dock, dropping the towel, closing his eyes and stepping off into space. I am falling, Norris, Captain MacGregor, I am falling. The water. It slaps hard and jams into my nose and yes, just as the bus window had said, I am sinking. All right, life, start to flash. So long, Nita, and your hand jobs. Goodbye, W.J., I forgive you for staring at your mother's ass, I did it too. Adios Hohner Chromonica, beautiful licorice stick and the Benny Goodman plans. I hereby bequeathe the captaincy of all teams to Jerry Bimstein. You shouldn't have left me, Sue, I was coming to myself. I-he-we touched bottom. Oh Jesus Christ it was dark down here. But shit, it's just two parts hydrogen, one part oxygen. Miraculously, as Archimedes himself said, we began to rise. Of course, we were displacing an equal volume of water. We broke into the air, into coolness, gulped, coughed, choked. And went down again. This was a goddam Otis elevator. And this time not one lousy life picture. Oops, up again, above the transparent membrane of my bedroom, then, shit, kicking, pushing, swinging, fingers apart in how-not-to-swim, grabbing for oozing handles and then somehow believe it or not, suddenly at the blessed ladder, wrapping it around, arms, legs, chest, neck. Hugging, coughing, spitting, oh shitting against the wall. Finally, after two thousand years, there he-we were up on the dock, on all fours, weak, dizzy, funny, but back in the sneering world. And after all the carrying on, after flopping over and blinking up at the trees, who was sneering most of all?

Who?

You, for one.

I am not sneering. Who?

Lord Baden-Powell. The hero of Mafeking, the founder of physically fit and morally straight. The sonofabitch was laughing at me.

He was a very honorable man.

Don't I know? Christ, don't I know? But I got it out on the table. I gutsed it out. You heard, you saw. I beat it, finally and at long last. Fuck Baden-Powell, the British Empire was shit for the birds anyway.

I see. Then what happened?

You bastard. The next morning I reported to the non-swimmers' crib.

V

Shanghai.

"No dogs or Chinese allowed." Foreigners crossed the bridge free, natives had to pay. The *Shanghai Mercury* covered the Boxers, step by bloody step. He walks through the halls of the industrial exhibit. On the wall Lenin. 1900: The missionaries, he said, camouflage the policy of robbery. Our man rises after the banquet, strides to the platform, pauses, then leans into the bank of microphones, the gathering of notables:

"At this time I just want to say that this has been a magnificent trip and who beside me would ever have thought I would be here after being shafted in 1960 and '62, yet I came back which is the quality that counts the most in this world and here I am standing before you today."

The little Chinese lady with the short hair translates. Polite applause.

"Now I just want to say this. During the years of my growth and development, many of the persons of my generation were preoccupied with frivolous activities. I never had that kind of good *mazel.* It is of no little note that while I studied and debated and worked like a canine to help support my mother and dad and other members of my family, these people were making out like minks."

Translation. Much applause.

"In this respect, therefore, they clearly resembled members of the Ching Dynasty."

Chou nods sagely. Translation. Enthusiastic applause.

"Being only human, there were occasions, however, when I would say oh feces, climb over the great wall behind our house and hurry out to seek a variety of socio-economic experiences."

Pause, rapid-fire translation, loud burst of applause.

"These then were my first crises in dealing at initial hand with the peoples of another culture. I determined from those first enlightening days onward to pursue these critical relationships with intensity."

The Chinese girl nods briefly, translates, waits for applause and nods to herself again.

"I then read avidly, especially in Sino-American literature. Such works as *The Yellow Stream,* by I. P. Daily, *The Women of Hong Kong,* by Ah Fon Goo and *The Spot on the Wall,* by Hoo Flung Shit."

The little girl. Good applause.

"During that period of growth, development and crisis I built a simple code of belief and action which I share with you and discreetly urge you to adopt. To friend and foe alike I would say: If your heart is not in China, get your ass out."

The little lady sprays her translation. Murmurs. Applause.

"I just want to tell you that we have made a very long march in my country since the days of One Long Pan and his lee-woll-ower."

Translation. Oriental hear hears.

"On the other hand there are five fingers. And at this momentous occasion in history, as the world follows with bated breath what we say here"—Chou smiles—"even though areas of disagreement remain, I just want to say that many of your war lords were also make-out artists."

The words. Intense applause.

"The categorical fact is, as we look at the history of these two great peoples, the well known fact is that many persons on both sides of the yellow curtain were born with a silver spoon in their mouth and don't you forget it. However, as we all know, except those who have been cruelly brainwashed by the carping critics, God must have loved all the people who never made out, he created so many of them."

Chou applauds wildly. The lady translates, all applaud wildly.

"So at this high tide of history, at the climax of the week that will change the world from the year of the rat to the generation of the swan, that will create for us millions of temples of heavenly peace, I want to and will propose a toast. To all those people who made me eat the material with which you fertilize your land: Up yours with gauze for the cause!"

The little girl launches into her singsong. When she finishes, Chou stands and claps in rhythm. All stand and clap with him. Chou raises his glass. All raise glasses. He stands before the microphones of the world, smiling down, the sweat collecting above his lip.

I am definitely coming to myself. I feel it in a hundred little ways. Plus a few big ones. Hungrier, healthier, hornier. In fact I have begun to feel strong enough to face the competition. *That* strong? Yes. Three nights ago, I got myself together and went out to a lit'ry party. For three first novelists. At the Gotham. They didn't give me a party for my book five years ago, so they can go screw themselves when *Boxers* comes out. The three novelists were all shitting green. Already wondering if they have a second book in them. After all, how many of us *have*? Also the reviews, ah the reviews. Well I can tell them, eager little beavers, that they're promising, that there's a book somewhere but this is not it and Joyce did it better. In two months it will be what have you done for me lately? I will read no reviews for *Boxers,* others can do it, I can do it. None? None, it will be totally misunderstood anyway, which is their problem, not mine.

The night, however, was not a total loss; I met an emphatic editor named Bertha Green, who really understands me, that is, she is able to read between the lines. I thought you would never accept a woman editor. Bertha is different, she is not jealous of my talent, she came to terms with her lack of it a long time ago, she does not wish to compete and she will pour her creative energy into constructing, in her words, an autobahn for my art. German? Yes, probably a Nazi and attracted to my New York Jewishness, however she is objective enough to separate my talent from the attraction. You'd sign with a Nazi? Shit, I just *told* you, I am just the vehicle for my art, it's my talent which must do the driving down the autobahn. That is curious, most curious. For you maybe, not for Bertha and me. Only I do not touch her till I see proofs.

Well, last night I also went to Jim Tomkin's on East 35th Street. Jim is the last gentleman even if he is loaded, but withal a very decent guy. And smart. He published my second story. In fact, he and Rogers are the only ones who publish good fiction. You mean fiction or good fiction? Both, it is just not being published. Perhaps the reading public is trying to tell you something. It's trying to tell the world that we need more novels like *Interplay*, but no shitheel editors who only get behind it to the tune of 653 copies. *You* don't read fiction. Why should I? You think any novelists are included in that 653? I never thought of it that way. That's the trouble, you never think, you just shoot from the hip, never giving me the right. Oh my God, don't kvetch so. I have to, or no one will know I exist, there, you see that individual over there? The one with the beard? Yes, that one, he writes a book, gets a review and grows a beard, the phony boloney; that's Stillmore. The one who also writes historical fiction? Pardon me, *I* write fictionally-oriented history. Sorry. Jesus Christ, Bligh, get on the stick. I said I was sorry; Stillmore seems a quiet enough sort, rather self-contained. Balls, that's his professional pose, he's a social worker. Well he looks quite competent. Bullshit. What's a social worker doing writing novels anyway? Do I do social work?

No, but you do substitute teaching. That's different, I do it to stay *alive,* he probably has a spastic colon and lives on Gelusil, I happen to know he is lusting after the N.B.A. even though he says prizes are meaningless and would be embarrassed if he won. How about you? How about me? You already have an acceptance speech written, you wrote it five years ago. I did not, do not, I plan to refuse it. Oh come now. Well I'm *contemplating* refusal. Look, he's t.l.'ing the *Times* man, Norris Blake wouldn't be caught *dead* with a *Times* man, look, he's talking to Jim, why Jim? I bet Jim knows somebody on the N.B.A. Look, he's going into the bedroom, what for, a quick bang? Look, he's got his coat on, what's he got his coat on for, it's only eleven o'clock? He probably has to get up early to go to work. Balls, he's going home to write. Look, look at those two over there, they got their coats on, and there, that one, and over there, shit it's a mass exodus and they're all going home to write, everybody in this fuckin party is going home to write, all over this fuckin city they're sitting down at desks, at kitchen tables, at warping planks, on rotting floors and writing like crazy and setting me up to get loaded here and seduced by poetasting broads who must get laid by writers.

I said goodnight and thanks to Jim, grabbed my coat and rushed home.

VI

CHAPTER THREE (B.)

Slowly but surely I walked into China. I felt quite calm now that I was committed to a course of action, but together with the calmness there throbbed very near to my skin an alert intensity that has ever accompanied me into danger. For Taku and danger would be, I knew, one and the same. In the darkness my knees flexed and extended, my boots rose and fell and that danger drew nigh. (Up yours, Stillmore.)

At last I was within its outer edge. Taku at this time boasted some 10,000 inhabitants, most of whom huddled in its tight nucleus; out here were the flimsy huts and shanties that mark the suburbs of the orient. I walked steadily past this ramshackle quarter and into the heart of the town, which I identified by the packed-in dwellings, the brightest of poor lights, the widest of narrow streets and the stench of open sewers. Now several inhabitants scuttled by, their eyes downcast, taking no apparent notice of me, although I surely knew better. Finally I came to a small cross street, on either side of which were arrayed a number of disreputable-looking taverns. I considered briefly and made my decision; if you are out to probe the heart of the local matter, you can do no better than to explore the scenery within the neighborhood public houses. I chose one that sported as its trademark what I took to be a faded and lopsided cat, but which on closer inspection, aided by some worn lettering, I identified as the Blue Dragon. I entered.

Within was a scene with which I was most familiar, having viewed it in its many guises in Manila, San Miguel, Hong Kong and Honolulu, to mention some of my more recent ports of call. Along one side of the room ran a long, mottled bar that held up the elbows of some half-dozen men, all of whom required this support. Scattered about were several old tables and chairs around which were seated as motley a crew as one was likely to find outside the Tenderloin. Drinking and spitting, some into, some outside spittoons, seemed to be the chief activities.

I paused only briefly, then walked forward into this den of certain iniquity. Long experience in these places led me, however, not to the bar, as one might suppose, but to a vacant table. There I seated myself, the composed and occidental cynosure; this time eyes and faces made no pretense of looking away, although askance was another matter. Quite satisfied, I ostentatiously reached inside my shirt, not, as some of my tavern-mates were doing, to scratch my armpits, but to untie the drawstring of my money bag. I slipped my hand inside the bag and drew out several taels which I dropped on the table with a clang. Holding the bag from without, I reached in and deliberately drew the string taut. A moment of silence, of interrupted activity, descended, followed by a perceptible increase of talk, drink and expectoration. I hadn't long to wait. Momentarily, it seemed, I found myself looking up and into the uncomely features of a fellow, whom for want of a better term I shall call the bartender.

"Sawrt fiss?" he said.

I studied the bartender for an instant, then shook my head. I could easily have said, no wantee fiss fiss, but I despise pidgin

English; it is my firm conviction that the Chinese mentality, properly trained and nurtured, can surely grasp at least the rudiments of a foreign language.

"I do not care for salt fish," I said in Mandarin. The owl eyes blinked, though the face, more Mongolian actually than Chinese, remained unchanged. Again an intake of silence invaded the premises.

"I will have some absinthe," I said, still in Mandarin. "You have absinthe?"

The surprised fellow nodded and retired behind his station. He returned in a minute with a cracked cup that contained a dark green, oily liquid that I tasted and generously identified as absinthe, albeit mixed with a high percentage of local dirt. I downed it in one breath-holding gulp, then pushed a tael toward him.

"Another."

He picked up the cup and the silver and walked to the bar and returned with my libation. This time I smacked my lips at the swallowing. Every pair of red-rimmed eyes was now fastened to my corpus like sets of bleeding cups. I belched politely and stood up.

"My change, please," I called out loudly in the native tongue. The bartender did not alter his expression; indeed he was a model of oriental impassivity, although I must say in all fairness that I had seen some of them laugh and even on occasion cry. He fetched me several Mexican coins, foreign currency being quite acceptable in this unhappy land. I extracted one and left it, pocketed the rest and humming a Philippino folk tune, I sauntered out.

I walked outside, onto Taku's Broadway, 10th Avenue and 14th Street rolled into one. It was quite deserted, but I was not deluded by the lack of discernible physique. I walked with head high and squarely forward, to the end of this main artery, in the opposing direction from whence I had come. Out here the air was cool and dry with the slightest taste of dust in it. Lights and civilization, such as they were, dropped away behind me and I was fully exposed to the natural—or should I say unnatural—elements. I halted and lit up a cigarette—Turkish—that being my one particular weakness, and I remained at that spot, smoking and inwardly smiling.

I had not long to wait.

With great snorting exhalations and a clicking of syllables, two bodies descended heavily onto me. The ground rose up and fetched me such a clout in the forehead that flashes of Ursa Major and Minor danced before my eyes. I felt a hand snaking into my shirt. Then, with alacrity, I retaliated. (And how, Stillmore!)

Firstly I grasped the offending arm with both of mine, applying a lock of such pressure that a squeal of sour anguish rent the atmosphere. That accomplished, I rolled quickly into a neck stand, thrust my hands into the ground and landed lightly on my feet in a crouched position, arms upraised, fully prepared for any offensive or defensive action. (Try *that,* Stillmore.) However, the invading duo were now staring in surprise and no little disbelief, one flat on his back, the other squatting and nursing a limp arm. I recognized them as two of my spittoon companions, from the other side of the room. Recognition did not breed contempt; on the contrary, it filled me with a newfound energy. I danced about alertly on the balls of my feet, flicked my nose with my thumb and motioned the pair toward me. They were, I must say, possessed of a single track mind, if not an overly intelligent one. After a period of recuperation, despite my well-balanced stance, they launched themselves at me amidst some oriental blasphemy, most of which eluded my translation. Murmuring a paean of thanks to Ruby Robert Fitzsimmons and his generous teaching at the athletic club, I side stepped, causing one of the oafs to trip over his own feet and at the same time I clipped the other with a smart rabbit punch that sent him sprawling. (Fat bastard. That's enough now . . . I said that's *enough.*) This time, when they assumed the vertical, they did so with much less steam and with looks of puzzlement. Poor fellows, I quickly added to their discomfort by dancing between them, left hooking the target to one side, right crossing to the other, combining both blows with the famed Fitzsimmons corkscrew. There are not many so fortunate as to be privy to Bonny Bob's secret and I hereby publicly acknowledge my debt of thanks to the great gladiator. I somehow think I brought no dishonour on my teacher; soon both ruffians were lying face down, completely in a daze and not too eager for combat. I sat down on the back of one and grasped the inert arm of the other, twisting till vocal awareness returned.

"Now," I said in their tongue. "Now you lie there and listen to me." I bounced once and twisted. "Are you listening?"

"A-i-i-i-i," they squealed. "Yes."

"You will," I said, "take me to the Righteous Harmonious Fists on the morrow."

"A-i-i-i, we cannot do that," moaned the one beneath me.

I clouted him alongside the ear.

"You will do this," I said sternly.

"Yes, master," they said in unison.

"You know where they reside?"

"Oh yes, master."

"Good. Then it is arranged. Now you will lead me to a place where I can sleep tonight."

They looked at each other. I let them. Then I rose and yanked them erect, holding each by the scruff of the neck. I knew very well that at the first opportunity they would take to their heels, for nothing is so cowardly as a bully shamed, but it was not for naught that I worked for Joseph Pulitzer. I reached into my money bag and drew out two taels. I slapped each one into a greasy, albeit receptive, palm. Then I dropped their arms. Behold. They looked down at the silver, at each other, then at this strange adversary who smote them with such fury one minute and rewarded them the next. Ah the occidental mind.

"There is another tael for you when you have done what I wish. Now lead on. I will follow."

One of the villains suddenly bent far over and touched the ground with his forehead. I let him and glanced at the other. He, too, kowtowed. Now I despise the subservient acts of royalty as much as the next republican, but in a pinch one uses what one can. I bade them both rise, which they did, then waved an airy hand. With a very good pace, considering their recent exertions, they struck out down a side street in a direction diagonal to the Blue Dragon, with the western emperor close behind.

We continued on, a fast-striding threesome, until we reached a foul-smelling edifice that, in distinction to its neighbors, contained an upper story, rather an upper level. They stopped at the door, stepped aside and motioned for me to enter. I shook my head and pointed for them to precede me, which, with no nonsense, they did. I followed. I perceived, within the dim interior, that they were talking to an old woman. I drew nearer. Her face was more parchment than skin, her eyes were high and huge, made so by her tightly drawn white hair. Quite patronizingly then, I thought, she detached herself from the sibilant pair, glanced at me, then turned away. She picked up a lighted candle from a sideboard and tottered away on tiny, bound feet. She said nothing, but the incline of her head was unmistakable; I followed as she padded away and up a flight of stairs. On the upper floor she bustled down a narrow hallway and entered a room. I was close behind, for her every move bespoke impatience. The room was small, but had an air about it. On one side squatted a lacquered lowboy, in the center was a plain bed made fancy by a silk spread, although it was quite worn; yet I could discern dragons and chimeras prancing on its faded blue face. Torn, dusty rice paper hung from the ceiling. It seemed that before the trouble this was a house of some distinction, perhaps the residence of Taku's grand concubine; at least my fancy mused along these lines. The grand party, if indeed she was, placed her candle on the lowboy, nodded curtly without looking at me and tottered out. I stepped to the door. I could hear whispering below, in particular the word "devil" over and over. I smiled. Without a doubt I was the most primary and hairy of the species. But I was suddenly too weary to speculate on their opinion of me; it had been rather a full day. Reaching down, I yanked off my dust-caked boots and carefully brushed them off. I placed them close to but not directly beneath the window so that they would properly air out; as any infantryman can vouch, from Caesar's legionnaires to MacArthur's troopers, if you take care of your footwear, it will take care of your feet. Without removing anything more, I threw aside the coverlet and lay carefully upon the surprisingly firm bed. I did not speculate on its history, that would have kept me awake the entire night, but fixing my mind on the hour of six, a mental gymnastic I had been taught by Phineas Barnum and to which he attributed a good deal of his success, I drew the silken beasts of the orient over my weary form and quickly fell into a light but thoroughly sound sleep.

I was aware that night, as at a great telescopic distance, that the two scalawags occasionally skulked in my vicinity, doubtless with delusions of plunder, but my trained mind caused me to moan a stern warning, so that my slumber remained undisturbed, save by visions of boxing, prancing monsters. These, however, I found quite amusing. Precisely at the stroke of six, I awoke, totally refreshed, ready for whatever challenge the eastern day would bring. My room, in the spring dawn, was exposed in all its shabby gentility, a scene I found suddenly sad. But one cannot afford softer sentiments when a mission is in train. I shrugged off the emotion and quickly drew on my freshened boots, ran a casual hand through my hair and clattered down the rickety stairs. I found my companions in revolution seated at a table and being haughtily served by the taciturn old woman. The inclined plane of her neck guided me to a chair and she deigned also to serve the foreigner. Soon a steaming gruel that I have since learned was sorghum, a type of millet, was placed before me. I found it surprisingly tasty, though to be sure it was hardly breakfast at Rector's, and I spooned it down in short order. The hot tea was also quite good, not up to my favorite chocolate perhaps, but after all this was Chihli and not 14th Street. I gulped it down and then drew out two taels which I placed on the table. I rose. The old party neither picked up the money and bit it nor flung it in my face, which I must confess disappointed me a little. No matter. As I left, she was standing proud and erect, gazing out the window, having preserved every shred of the dignity that marked our first encounter. I do not know her name, nor will I ever see her again, conditions peculiar to my vocation and true of countless others in this world, yet I will never forget this particular ancient of China, fragile, worn, ageless as the mountains of Mongolia; I can only hope that somehow she has returned to her former eminence, or that her ancestors have made a proper place for her.

Outside once again we struck out through the suburbs, away

from the ascending sun and on a path that took us through much of the town. Taku was beginning to come awake and the hurrying, averted eye was everywhere, including the two pair beside me. But ever curious, by nature and profession, I looked at everything and studied each example of exotica. And by heaven, right there, very near to the Blue Dragon, I saw it! The blessed, accursed sign. My first Boxer placard! There was absolutely no question but this was that famed bit of literature, the oriental vox populi. It was nailed to a post that thrust squarely up in the intersection of the Broad Way and a fairly large muddy cross street. I stopped my guides, though sorely against their will. They cast furtive looks all about and urged me on. I would have none of that nonsense. I walked straight up to the post and with beating heart I read:

> So as soon as the practice of the I Ho Chuan has been brought to perfection—wait for three times three or nine times nine, nine times nine or three times three—then shall the devils meet their doom. This will of heaven is that the telegraph wires be first cut, then the railways torn up, and then shall the foreign devils be decapitated. In this day shall the hour of their calamities come. The time for rain to fall is yet afar off, and all on account of the devils.

Yes, it is true—the hair on the back of your neck can stand erect, your spine can turn to ice and force the cold stuff into the thousand byways of your being. I can vouch for the reality of those clichés of fear—nay terror—and despite my well-practised discipline, they played no little havoc with me as I absorbed those words. When finally I and they had their fill, I turned away; I noted with some surprise that I was the only person before the placard; whether it was just me or still early in the game I could not tell, most likely some of each. In any case I proceeded to shake off my chilly symptoms and rejoined my two companions, who behaved for all the world as if they had never seen me.

"Very well," I said crisply, "we go."

They lit out with no further urging on my part. I right beside them. This time, to their immense relief I am sure, I made no detours. Nor, surely, did they. Taku was soon far behind us. After a half-hour or so we turned sharply to the north and continued on across the plain. As we walked, the gray earth turned to fields of reed and herbage. We stepped high through the spring grass and though the going was hard, we did not slacken our pace. For two more hours we ploughed on, until finally we reached a change of scenery. At this I stopped and raised my hand. Before us was a series of odd-looking cones, all the same shape, though of varying size. Each one was surmounted by decorative earthenware. I looked to my guides.

"Tombs," said one. "Burial places."

"One and the same," I said dryly. I looked around. "All the same family I should guess."

They looked at me with what I gathered was respect. They nodded.

"Well," I mused aloud, "not so very different from us, after all."

They glanced at each other.

"Come on," I said.

We started out once again, veering around the tombs and their intricate toppings. Farther on we saw several more family groupings, but we did not pause to investigate. Nor did we make any further stops until we broke through a clearing in the tall grain and beheld the river.

"Ah," I said, "the Pei Ho."

Again they did their glancing thing which I considered was good for them, considering our tenuous relationship. They then pointed. Tied up to a steep and muddy bank was a small, newly painted junk. It was shining black with the much loved Chinese monsters cavorting on the bow. Close by, on the shore, attached to the boat by a rope was a broadly smiling Chinese, one of those orientals I have noted who broke the mold with (gleeful) vengeance. He bowed as we approached and he and my companions exchanged a Maxim gun greeting.

"This is Yang," said one.

Yang smiled even wider and bowed six times, though not quite kowtowing. I nodded curtly and withdrew a tael.

"Very well, let us proceed," I said, tossing him the coin. He snatched it up like a starving dog and bowed six more times. "Yes yes," I said. "Come on."

I stepped down onto the craft. One of my men stepped in also, at the stern, and took the rudder. The other, together with the cheerful Yang, harnessed himself to a tow rope attached to the mast, and at a loud grunting signal from the helmsman, they bent forward, one behind the other, and stepped into the boat's inertia. With a creak and a groan we started upriver. In no time at all we were moving at a very nice clip; they were both small, but quite strong, especially Yang, who had sharply sloping shoulders and Ruby Robert can show you what *that* means. I stood with one foot on a gunwhale and surveyed the picturesque scene sliding past. The straining towers walked on a narrow path that soon dipped down to the river's edge, rather the river rose to their level. Beyond them the plain stretched far off, now thickly clotted by the tombs we had seen earlier, causing me to wonder if China gave more of its land to the dead than the living. The villages that we occasionally saw answered me, so shabby and tightly packed were they. Alas, in addition they were soon to know arson, rape and pillage. For now, it would seem, they resembled poor, overcrowded villages the world over. The mystery of the orient was nowhere to be seen; there is nothing mysterious about poverty.

And so we glided on into China. From time to time a junk with silently staring passengers passed us on the journey downriver to Taku. Now the herbage gave way to the tall sorghum which had made my breakfast so long ago; it blotted out the countryside and formed a curtained backdrop gainst which our towers laboured on their path. Creaking, grunting, breathing, we continued, tucked into the slit between the curtains of grain, until the sun was high in the sky and the two men were soaking wet and acrid from their work. Still they did not slacken their pace; slow and steady, like slant-eyed tortoises, they pulled us inland. Not until it was two or three o'clock did I decide to assert my authority.

"You may stop now and eat," I called out.

In a thrice they were out of their harnesses and had us tied up to the bank. Yang rummaged around inside the cabin and emerged with some chunks of old black bread and rice, and of course, tea. He cooked the rice and brewed the tea, using a lantern as a stove. The rice was bland, the bread hard and tasteless; both were manna. The tea scalded my tongue, but was oddly cooling. With much lip-smacking, we downed our feast. Then without a word from me, the man at the rudder exchanged places with his companion on the path, and with the indefatigable Yang, edged us forward. Twas as if we had never stopped, so neatly and smoothly was it accomplished and soon we were gliding along as before.

I began now to indulge in a bit more reportorial introspection than heretofore. I thought deeply about the wiry, bent figure in the lead harness and I saw him as a person in his own right, not merely a yellow integer in a sea of millions. Could it be, I thought, that he has the feelings that we possess? Sadness, happiness, envy, avarice, etc.—the so-called higher emotions? I pondered that and reached my conclusion. Yes. From that essential starting point, I began to build a mental picture of him. From his stance and musculature I deduced that he had been either a coolie of feces, that is, the fellow who carried the two steaming pots on a stick across his shoulder, or else a jinricksha coolie. Something in his manner, a certain dignity, persuaded me that he had chosen— quite consciously—the latter career path. I pictured him trotting skillfully through the foreign concessions with his fat European cargo perched behind, lost in stock or grain market reports unaware that before him ran a man, not a beast of burden. Year after year the poor fellow had accepted his lot. Yet under the bland exterior lurked the humanity I have described, a sensitivity to himself and his surroundings. Somehow there formed in that brain the image of a different existence, the rural life—no the marine life. And so with the savings of all those years, all those miles, he had retired, perhaps with his family, perhaps not, and opted out for life on the river. Why, Tom Cruikshank, a reporter for the *Herald*, had done much the same thing and now lives quite happily, *sans famille*, as captain of his own fishing boat in Sheepshead Bay. Hmmm, I pondered, were we not all jinricksha pullers for the Bennetts and Pulitzers of this world? Well well, I did not in the

71

least care for *that* concluding thought to my sketch. To banish it I leaped lightly onto the towpath, I walked to the subject of my mental article, grasped his line and began to pull along and in unison with him. Ah this was more like it. This was pitting muscle and energy gainst a visible and physically resistant force. For several yards we were a finely matched, yoked team. Then, to my astonishment, the most startling change took place in Yang's behavior. He stopped, shook his head violently and began to jabber so excitedly that I could barely grasp a word save the constant negative. I turned. I looked the question.

"He says," the other tower called out, "that you should not pull."

"But I want to pull," I exclaimed. "I wish to pull. It is good exercise. And it will help us go faster."

At this, upon my word, Yang burst into tears.

"You are shaming him," sang out the man. "And before his friends. You are saying he does not tow properly."

"He is an *excellent* tower. It is only—" Suddenly I stopped talking. Of course. How foolish of me. Particularly after having granted him human feeling. Whereupon I let go the rope. And promptly committed another faux pas: I took out a coin and offered it to him. He shook his head stubbornly and wiped his eyes with the back of his sleeve. I realized again what I had done and pocketed the coin. I patted the back of this poor fellow who had his own standards of pride and workmanship. Then, finally using my head for something else besides a helmet rack, I dropped to one side and let the other fellow pass; I had no doubt that *he* would snap up the coin, but I had made enough western errors for one day. Quite happily now, the two pullers got us going again, if anything with a bit more energy. I in my turn served my exercise compulsion by merely walking, also a fine anodyne for the vapors, especially if one varies the routine by walking backwards and sidewards. Soon, although I was, as ever, mentally busy, twas not with morbid philosophy, but with a deeply perceived appreciation of this countryside and my place in it. We fell into a rhythmic pattern that I found most calming. Mile after mile after mile.

Only to be fully jolted from my reveries by the war.

To be more precise, a precursor of the war. It is close to four o'clock. Yang, ever nimble, steps neatly around it. So does the other tower. Lost as I am in my thoughts, I stumble on it. A dead body, Chinese, gazing forever at the sky, already black and leathery. I cry out in surprise. My three companions, for whom I suppose death is a next door neighbour, laugh aloud. I silence them with my best imperial look. We continue on, but now I am alert to any obstacle. What kind of land have I come to? Who are these people, one of whom a few moments before shared some sort of bond with me? Why was I driven to the ends of the earth simply to see and tell what I see? I could not answer myself then, nor can I now. I have asked Mr. Henry Stanley the same questions and if ever a man was never at a loss for words, it is he; he looked at the ceiling, the floor, the four walls, at me and asked if I wouldn't care to have a drink. So I—we plod on. I find myself envying the certain blankness of the three minds around me, until I also control that emotion. Newspaper writers on assignment can ill afford envy.

Another five miles, or 15 *li,* slip beneath our feet and suddenly the man at the rudder stands and points to the west. The two men before me stop. Yang is pointing. I follow his arm, but can see nothing except the giant millet. But the other fellow is slipping out of his harness.

"What is it?" I enquire.

"We leave the junk here," he says.

I am about to say, but why? but something new in his voice and manner, restrains me.

"Very well."

I take three taels out of my bag and hand them to Yang. He bobs merrily. All three bow at each other. Then with a quick motion, the two men plunge into the sorghum. I am right behind, no longer thinking. Yang, the boat, the river journey are but one more memory. This, at last, is action. The huge stalks whip into my face, I thrust them aside and hurry forward. My pathfinders bend the grain back and slide through in the same motion and soon I have adopted their method. We are moving rapidly now. We work our way forward for a good three quarters of an hour. Then we burst out into a small clearing. The clearing is populated by a large collection of tombs. The men walk stealthily to one on the outer perimeter and peer around it. I join them. Carefully I peep out. Dropping away, almost at the tomb's wall is an inclined plane that terminates in a dusty, scooped-out valley. Down there in the valley are a body of men, at least 75. They are drawn up in a huge V. Within the V is a very strange sight indeed. Two men are drawing circles in the dust with their fingers. They are wearing red scarves around their heads. I circle my thumb and forefinger and peer out through my natural microscope. Clear and sharp, if in miniature, I can read on the scarves the word, *"Fu."* Happiness. Curious, most curious. About the wrists and ankles are red bands. I rub my eyes and clear away the strain. Ah, now the two men of happiness are erect and folding their hands upon their foreheads. They gaze at the sun. Their mouths move. I can hear, in a thin stream, a Chinese singsong. I do not understand the words. And now, by jingo, they are falling heavily backwards, as in a sudden fit or fainting spell. No one in the silent throng makes an effort to impede their fall. They lie there in the dust, still; but yet their mouths are moving, although no sound reaches my ears. Suddenly four men dart forward, grasp the stricken ones by the shoulders and raise them to their feet. The helpers bark some words at them. They respond, but even at this distance, their speech is slow and thick. Now they are nodding, slowly, heavily. There is a commotion in the ranks. See there! Two swords are passed from man to man until they reach the first men in the V. These hand them to the red scarves. They raise the swords to the sky, then slowly begin to parry and thrust, then to weave and take exaggerated dancing steps. They are most graceful. Gradually they accelerate their tempo until they are swooping and leaping with tremendous speed and skill. It is a shadow dance of two expert swordsmen, scathing, whipping the air with their weapons. Suddenly they stop. They point. At the joint of the V, a man steps forward and removes something from each sleeve. Pistols! He raises both arms.

74

He points the pistols. The shots fan out in waves through the valley and over the plain. The two swordsmen drop to the ground, clutching their breasts. A great moaning rises out of the throng. It beats against the tombs and about our ears. The moaning men pound their chests and tear at their hair. I stare in fascination at the brutal murder, the disconsolate mourners. Then, as the wailing rises to a crescendo and the men begin to rip their clothing to pieces, right then, a miracle! The two dead men sit up! All is silent, still. The two men slowly rise and face each other. They reach into their gowns and hold up their hands. I can make out something between the thumb and forefinger. I construct my instant microscope again. By heaven those are bullets! They are holding the missiles that felled them! The transfixed spectators emit a truly horrible scream; they jump high in the air; they come down on all fours; they rise, they dance. It is a dance of convulsions. Some are actually frothing at the mouth. Can this be? Yes. Oh yes. I have found them. I have found the Boxers! I have seen their magic, their immortality! I am so transported, so hypnotized that I barely notice my two guides. Suddenly, before I can raise a hand to stop them, they have leaped up. They are running forward, into the valley. AND I HAVE NOT EVEN PAID THEM. I shout after them, return at once! They stumble and go down. They rise and scramble forward and fall again. And as they scramble and trip and get up, all this time, they are shouting and pointing. And where are they pointing? Why to a tomb, behind which is crouched a devil. A *foreign* devil. A *primary* devil. Finally they reach their true masters. They grovel at their feet. The immortals look down, then look up the hill; their eyes follow the curve of the tomb and find what they are seeking. They raise their swords and slash the air. Silence. The dancing ceases. They slash again, and yell. The dance begins anew, even more terrible, if that is possible. This time my erstwhile companions join in.

I look down on the amazing scene. I draw out my writing pad and make a few pertinent notes. The two leaders brandish their weapons gainst the purple sky. I note that. Then they lower the swords and begin to stride up the hill toward the tombs. The yelling, jerking mob dances along behind. I replace my pad. I straighten the kerchief about my neck and square my pith helmet. Then I step out to face the *I Ho Chuan*.

God he is cool. Ice. He is ice. So am I. I am. I am cooler and stronger than I have even been in my life. So why are you pissing in your pants?

VII

What the hell, if Blake can take on the Fists, I can face Hannah Birnbaum. Oh? Yes, oh. The duty visit. Call it whatever the hell you want, I can and will, it's been nine weeks. Ten. All right, ten; the only reason I stay away is not to upset her. Her? Us. Us? Me. All right already. Anyhoo, keeping a good grip on Blake's cool and Yang's toughness—somehow that was also reassuring—your security coolie—OK, I admit it, I admit it, so hanging tightly onto these two, I took the subway up to 181st Street.

I got out and walked the two blocks up the hill, averting my eyes from Pleasant Arms and although I hoped it wouldn't be there, see how honest I am? there it was. It is always such a shock, isn't it? Yes it is and you are not going to bug me on this, I've had it up to here with guilt and horseshit and I have too goddam much Blake-Yang jism to fall for your reaction-formation traps. We'll see. Yes, we'll see.

All right then, there it was. "Isidore's." That's all. For 33 years. "Isidore's." It should have said "Hannah's." Right is right. From the very first day; but no, the man is king. Perhaps king shit, but

77

king. So, loyal to her man. We had here Fanny Brice. Ah yes. I took the deep breath and entered. Oh lord, there she was, small, square, packed down into herself like a take-out Breyer's. Sitting in her chair in the back, reading the *Enquirer*. Her *World*. Manny was polishing the fountain.

"Hello, Ma."

She looked up from Dean Martin's latest.

"Well, what was your hurry to see me?"

Eight weeks ago, no nine, no ten, that sent me storming out into the night. I smiled.

"How are you, Ma?"

"How should I be?"

OK, I was used to that.

"You shouldn't answer a question with a question, Ma."

"That's not a question."

"OK, Ma. How you doin, Manny?"

"I'll make it, Sidney."

"How's the *shiksa*?" said my mother.

I gave Manny a look; he still polished.

"What?"

"How's the *shiksa*? Hello, Plotkin," she smiled. A woman around her age walked in, picked up a *Post,* dropped a quarter on the counter. Manny rang it up and gave her a dime.

"Hello there," she said to my mother. "How's your awthritis?"

"Rotten," said my mother. "It settled in my right shoulder."

"Mine settled in my left shoulder blade. Did you hear about McGillicuddy?"

"No, what?"

"She got mugged. In her own vestibule. In broad daylight."

"Was she hurt?"

"Just a black-and-blue mark on her arm. You know her arm, just touch it and it gets black-and-blue."

"What was he?"

"Who knows? He had a knife."

"That louse."

"What do you expect, they'll all cokies."

78

"They'd mug their own grandmothers, what do they care? This is my son, Sidney."

"How do you do?" I said.

"The writer?"

"Well. Sometimes."

"You write about what's happening to this city. That's real life. Just like *The Godfather* was real life. Did you know that, Birnbaum?"

"Sure I knew. It was Lucky Luciano," said my mother.

"No, it was Anastasia, the one that got killed in the barber chair."

"Gloria Vanderbilt married an Eyetalian?"

"Yop. That was Di Cicco."

"That's right. He didn't have a nickel. Then she married Stokowski."

"I always wondered why such a beautiful girl would marry him. I don't care what they say, that's December and May."

"Didn't I tell you it wouldn't last?"

"Yes you did."

"Sure I did. Tell your son he should come around more. Goodnight, Birnbaum."

"Goodnight, Plotkin."

She walked out. It was quiet, very quiet, except for the polishing.

"So?" said my mother.

"So?"

"So?"

"If you mean Sue, she's all right, I suppose. I haven't heard from her lately," I said.

"Naturally. She deserted you."

"Manny," I said, "why don't you go for supper. I'll take care of the customers."

He looked at my mother and she gave him her go if you want shrug.

"OK," he said. "Either of yez want anything?"

"You going to Fischler's?" asked my mother.

"Yes."

"Bring me back a pastrami on rye very lean with a sour tomato and a Dr. Brown's Cel-Ray. You want something, Sidney, I'll blow?"

"No, it's all right, Ma. Thanks."

Manny put on his hat and coat and walked out. We were alone, God, we were alone.

"You shouldn't say anything in front of him," I said. "He knows your whole goddam business." Christ, *I* was worrying about the neighbors.

"So what? True is true."

"The way I was carrying on, *I* would would have left me."

"For better or worse. Through thick and thin."

I tried to stop myself, oh how I tried, now Bligh, you know I tried. I know.

"Is that what Papa said?" I asked.

What a rotten, lousy sigh. The eyes misted over; they went no further.

"Your father was a man. She's a woman."

"So?"

"Shut up. A customer."

I looked around. A young black man walked in. He saw us.

"Hello, Mom," he said, walking over to her.

"Hello, Jackson. This is my son, Sidney, my youngest of two. He's a writer."

He held out his hand and I shook it.

"You got a wonderful mother there," he said.

"I agree," I smiled.

He nodded at her.

"My usual, Mom."

"I'll get it," I said.

He looked at my mother.

"It's OK," she said. "He made them all his life. He's an expert."

"An egg cream," he said.

I walked behind the fountain and mixed up his egg cream, using the spoon to receive the seltzer; that's the trick. I handed the glass to him. He shredded a straw, put it in the soda and carefully tasted.

"Mmm, almost as good as hers," he said. Slowly, studiously, he worked his way to the bottom, even doing a little Shep Fields rippling rhythm along the way. Then he swiveled around and off the stool, walked to the other side, picked up a *Post* and an *Ebony* and gave me a dollar-fifty. I looked at her.

"Twelve cents the egg cream."

I rang it up, punching the numbers with exquisitely remembered skill, even using my own button. I slipped the dollar into its drawer and slipped out the change and gave it to him. He held out his hand and I shook it again.

"Nice meetin you, Sidney," he said. "You got a real mother there. Good night, Mom."

"Goodnight, Jackson," she said. "Now be on time with the job in the morning."

He grinned. "Sure Mom. If you say so." And he walked out.

She shrugged with her head.

"The *shvartz* call me Mom. They all call me Mom."

"You got a great touch with them," I said.

She nodded.

"Me and Mrs. Roosevelt. He loves egg creams. A *shvartz* who loves egg creams." She sighed.

I looked at my watch.

"You just got here," she said.

"I know. I have to do some research."

"You're writing another book?"

"Sort of."

"You going to finish this one?"

"I hope so."

"She took the *kinde*?"

"Who?"

"The *shiksa*."

"Yes. I . . . we thought it was best for now."

"I always said someday she'd call you a dirty Jew bastid. Did she called you a dirty Jew bastid?"

"Ma, please. Don't start, OK?"

"Who's starting?"

"I don't want to discuss it."

"Sure, it'll go away. To Africa. I wouldn't be one bit surprised if she got a *shvartz* from Africa. That's all you see today. White women with *shvartz*. It's digusting."

"OK, ma."

Manny walked in, thank God. For it was surely getting to be a *shonda* for the neighbors. He gave her the sandwich and the Cel-Ray. She examined the pastrami carefully and picked away the fat. "His meat is gettin lousy," she muttered. She held out half the sandwich to me.

"No thanks, Ma."

"You better since you got nobody to cook for you."

"No it's all right. Really."

She took a huge bite and began to chew. I could hear her loose plate sucking against the gums. I looked at my watch.

"Well, Manny," I said, "time to shove. Nice seeing you again. Take care of things, will you." As she watched the sandwich, I took out a five-dollar bill and held out my hand. He took it and I transferred the taels to the greasy palm.

"Don't worry, Sidney," he said. "I'll take care." He winked.

"You just got here," she said.

"I have to get to the library before it closes."

I walked to her, bent and kissed her cheek. It tasted like parchment. She sighed. Quickly I walked out. As the door closed behind me, I could hear her voice:

"Take a paper, a magazine."

There I did it. You saw me. Yes, you did, but don't stop now, not with all that bloody jism. OK, OK. I walked up the hill past the house. The house? Yes, the house, Pleasant goddam Arms. And? And this time I did not look away. Bully. Up yours, Bligh. I walked into that hall, yes I did, that cat-piss hall. Where? Where W.J. and I used to look over all the sure lays in the building, including his mother. Ah. And I read on the walls, the clean yellow walls: "Tru lov fo eva." and "Mary is a hua." Nita is a hua? No, Mary, *Mary*. I walked on. I walked to the third floor. To 3E. W.J. Boody Sr. S. Gonzalez. All right, to the fifth. I took the lousy fifth. I. Birnbaum. Leandre Peters. I stared at the door. I have dreamed about that door. Dreamed? Yes and you know it, you ball-breaker; I'm in no mood to take shit from you. Says who? Says me. So? So, he walked in and Hannah said, "Did you find something today?"

"No," said Isidore.

"Did you sit in Bryant Park all day?" said Hannah.

"No," said Isidore.

"What did you do all day?" said Hannah.

"I watched the board at Goldman, Sachs," said Isidore.

"After what they done to you," said Hannah.

"Yes," said Isidore.

"After the knife they put in your back?" said Hannah.

"Yes," said Isidore.

"Why don't you call Sam Cushman?" said Hannah.

"Why should I call Sam Cushman?" said Isidore. "I gave him his first job off the boat."

"You should call him because the *kinde* need what the hell to eat," said Hannah.

"That sonofabitch of a Hoover," said Isidore.

"We might as well break up home and move into a furnished room," said Hannah.

Then what? Is that all you can say, then what? As you well know, Mr. Christian, this is far from all I can say; however, the appropriate and pertinent question is then what? You know then what. But I love to hear you tell it. Still trying to keep me honest? That, sir, is a full-time job, as they say. Why don't you throw it up to me for bribing Manny? Bribing who? Bribing Manny. Bribing who? All right, Benson-Birnbaum, you happy? My dear boy, it is not a question of happiness, but of justice; at the risk of sounding the bore, or should I say, knowing your concern with Baden-Powell, the Boer, then what?

Well, Abe was upstairs studying geography with Hy Pincus. Yes? Isidore said they should all only have a black year like his black year. In his native tongue, of course, which was not Mandarin. Of course not. Yes? He then said, come on, Sidney, we're going out for a walk. Yes? Well Hannah said don't keep him out all night, we still got a piece of ground chuck for *essen,* thank God. I see. And so we went out. Ah hah. Yes, we went out; and I walked out of the Pleasant Arms. Where? You pertinacious s.o.b., down to Fort Washington Avenue, stride for stride with Sid and Isidore, to 170th, to 165th. Yes? Over to the Drive and down and still down, scrambling, panting, cursing. So. Yes so. To the grass and out to the point. Their point. Our point. At the water's edge I stopped. And stared out at Jersey, golden glow, Palisades Park, the U.S. of A. Then what? Christ, Isidore pointed and said, OK, sonny. Yes? So Sidney, the little hero, with no looks, no smart shit, took out his Hohner Chromonica, the one he always kept on him just in case, slicked it with his tongue and began to play. Play what? "My Country Tis of Thee." "God Save the King?" I told you what he played; oh did he play, with heart and soul, his Manhattan serenade, letting freedom ring from every high tor. Until? Until Isidore spit in the river. I see. No wonder Franchot Tone hated your guts. Oh get on with it, Mr. Christian.

"Why can't you ever play that note right?" said Isidore.

"I don't know," said Sidney Birnbaum.

"Try it again," said Isidore.

So Sidney Birnbaum lifted up the Chromonica, inserted, saw the mercury note, pounced.

"Forcryinoutears, what is so *difficult?* What the hell is wrong with you? Your grandfather had a perfect pitch."

Sidney did not tell him to remove the paternal load, to stick or shove it. Or Grandpa. Nor did he suggest defecation in his hat. Very patiently he lifted the instrument, licked it and blew.

"Shit."

David wiped his eyes. Saul patted his neck.

"It's OK, sonny," he said. "Just sit here. You don't have to play."

So they sat. Very quietly. Listening to the river and to Hendrik Hudson and his loyal son. And all the rotten mutineers. Yes, they listened and looked. At the lights of Jersey. And America. And then little by little Hendrik Hudson's son began to talk. Softly, but oh so surely. He did. He did. He talked about how one day he would grow up and write *the* book. The book that would expose the whole lousy candy business. Sarah Sweetmeat would have nothing but black years when *he* got through. And then the good, the loyal men, would come back to the fold, walk through those gates and take over and make nothing but fine, pure candy that had no flies or rat shit in it, so they would *never* have to close down and they would knock the kishkas out of Loft and Fanny Farmer. This Sidney Birnbaum would do.

And Isidore, he leaned forward, into Jersey, and dropped his head between his shoulders and said, your words and God's ears.

VIII

You trying to give me a complex, Bligh? Whatever do you mean?
Come off it, you know damn well what I mean: non-swimmer,
clinker artist, big-shot dreamer. Facts, my boy, facts; you wanted
honesty. I want *balance,* fairness, objective reporting. Can't we
leave that to Mr. Blake? Don't get smart or funny or come the
acid with me, fella, and don't mix up fact and fiction, you know
damn well, for example, that I am a *fantastic* swimmer today, the
king of Jones Beach, not to mention the Caribees. Do tell. Yes I
do tell; only ycu left me shitting green in the goddam crib and I
cry *foul.* Exactly what are you asking for? The other side of the
goddam coin, the obverse, the complete picture. Complete? Yes,
I have, with few exceptions, been a king, a hero, and those exceptions have oftentimes been upgraded to hero status. Such as? Such
as Ten Mile River. Go on. Granted I spent two summers in the
crib, granted I almost drowned the winter of '38 at the St. George
pool where Dernberg took us for our 2nd class test, granted I did
not make class president my first year at G.W., that my clarinet
loaded up on clinkers, that Nita Nassi stopped playing with my fly

in Van Cortlandt Park, that she started walking home with W.J. Boody Jr., granted all this. Granted. What about the following summer? What about it?

I rode up on that bus. Oh I did. I rode up on that bus. I did not say a word, did not sing *Trail the Eagle* or *Stand up and Cheer*. I stared into the window at the yellow-bellied sapsucker. At Birnbaum, the nothing. When we got out and walked down to the lake to qualify I went up to Hank Lingstrom, king of the waterfront, and said, "I'm not jumping in, I'm a non-swimmer and I will report to the crib in the morning." With that I turned around and walked away to Seneca compound.

The next morning I reported to the crib. I crept into the cold water and scrunched down, tried a few strokes, got the lousy stuff up my nose, coughed, spit, choked and floundered to the edge, where I hung on till my fingers hurt. In three feet of water. Hank Lingstrom, the 6 foot 4 sonofabitch, laughed his Swede head off.

"Come on, Birney, get your head in that water, hell it's only water."

Well I tried. I certainly tried. No one can say I didn't try. I saw Baden-Powell watching from Mafeking to Macao, but every time I tried the dead man's float and felt my feet leave the wood floor, I got crazy and began to inhale and that was that. Causing Hank to say, first thing every day, "Hey, Birney, give us your dead man's float." Lousy greenhorn. Meanwhile Bobby Dopp was surface diving like a porpoise out in the lake, Jerry Bimstein was making seascouts and nobody was passing off to me in the full court basketball games. I caught pink eye and poison sumac that summer and Robert Baden-Powell followed me everywhere. On the nature trail, on sick call, in the latrine, at bird study and star gazing. On the night they all took turns sucking Norman Hooplock's tits, Powell said to me, "Is this what you come up here for?" To which I replied, no sir, not me, I got the real thing, a *Talyaina*. Oh? he said, lifting his monocle, are you getting veddy much lately? And of course he had me there.

That year Isidore made a little bit selling buttons in Harlem and they sent me to camp for six weeks. At the end of the third week they came up to visit. Sure enough the first thing he said was let's see you swim. Oh, it's Sunday, I said. So it's Sunday, let's see what I'm paying for. I sighed and changed and we walked down the long, long trail to the crib.

"What's this?" he said.

"They don't let us in the lake without a buddy."

"Oh."

So I crawled in. I hunkered down to my neck and then stroking with my forearms, leaning forward, I walked along the wood floor. I peeked up. Hannah was beaming. Isidore frowning.

"Get your tail up and show them a dead man's float."

Hank.

I lay down in the water, took in a mouthful and started to choke. Oh this time the sonofabitch didn't laugh; he was kissing ass for tips.

"Hi," he said, shaking hands with them. "I'm working to get him to relax and float. Once he does that, he can swim. But he keeps fighting me."

"He can't swim?" said Isidore.

"Oh he *could*. Swimming is like walking. Anybody can do it."

"Can *he* do it?"

"Give him time, Mr. Birnbaum, Rome wasn't built in a day."

I climbed out of the crib and ran up the hill and kept running until I hit the ashes of the Saturday night campfire. I sat in them until it got dark. I didn't cry. When I walked back to the bunk, they had gone.

"Your parents couldn't wait, they had to catch a bus, where the hell you been?" said Bobby.

"Shitting bricks."

"Well they left this."

He gave me an envelope. I opened it. Inside were two dollar bills. Nothing else.

Well that night I went to supper with the rest of the bunk. In the middle of the creamed chicken I said excuse me, got up and walked outside and kept on walking down to the lake. I took off my clothes, walked out on the dock, spread my arms, closed my eyes and stepped in. The water slapped me. I slapped back. It jammed into

89

my nose, I spit it out. I went down, I came up. The ladder said here I am, come and get me, I said fuck you. I thought about the cramp that was sure to paralyze me so soon after eating, I said, up yours, cramp. I knicked around in a circle and I pounded the water with my arms and outstretched and separated fingers and kicked toward the bottomless well. *I didn't go down.* My head, straining far back, *didn't go under.* I flung a glance at the shore. It was *moving.* Shit *I* was moving. I thrashed in a bigger circle and came back to the ladder when *I,* not it, wanted me to. Then I pushed off and thrashed around in a great circle. A hundred miles out. In the middle of no-man's water I suddenly stopped, gasped, held my nose and pushed my head and chest under. *I didn't go down.* I bobbed right up. I tried it again, this time, kicking, thrashing away. I stayed on top of the water and felt it slip away under me. Now I tried calming down. Slow, nice and slow and easy; I dropped a bit lower in the water, but still did not, *could* not go under. Then I tried it. I took a breath, stuck my head in the water and stretched out. I lay there, you lousy rotten Swede, I lay there. I kicked. Harder. I could feel my heels breaking air. I began to stroke, to cup and reach and stroke. I was sliding downhill, going like goddam 6o! Finally my lungs gave out. I lifted my head, got a snoutful, but instead of going nuts, coughed and spit and sneezed it out. Only then did I puff my way back to the ladder. I crouched, backside to it, grasping loosely and I looked up at the sunset. Lord Robert Baden-Powell was nodding.

The next morning I walked down to the lake and told Hank I was not entering the crib.

"Come on, Birney, be a man."

I walked to the lake, spread out in the fireman's dive and dropped in. I came up, took a breath and struck out, away from shore. When I came back he was clapping and pointing.

"I knew you could do it," he yelled, "I knew it if you only listened to me."

Cheese and crackers there was no stopping me. I mastered breathing and the six-beat crawl in a week. The side stroke, with powerful, gliding scissors kick, the breast and inverted breast in another week. By the end of the fifth week I was disrobing in the water and swimming 100 yards. The passes began to come my way on the basketball court and when Hank came down with the runs and acted like a fuckin baby, I took over the crib and even taught Georgie Weintraub how to do the dead man's float. Three days before we returned to the city I passed my swimming merit badge.

When I got home in August, I rushed Isidore over to the Palisades Park pool and swam four laps, each lap a different stroke; he took us on the whip and the loop-de-loop. In September, the first day of school, I walked home with Nita and W.J. although he didn't like it one bit, which as they said in Russia was toughsky shitsky for him. Very casually I asked Nita if she wanted to rehearse that evening. Of course, she would. And W.J. slunk away to study his mother, front, back and sideways.

I picked her up at seven and we walked to our old place near Van Cortlandt Manor. I ran a few scales, then pointed the licorice stick downtown to the Madhattan Room of the Hotel Pennsylvania and then over to Jersey and the Meadowbrook and then I gave her the B.G. nod. My vocalist ran through choruses of "Stardust," "Our Love," "Tangerine" and "They Say." When I was satisfied with her phrasing and intonation, and only then, I let her play with my fly and I munched some *genuine* tit.

Now that, *that* is the full story.

I was reviewed in *Metronome* on September 21, 1943, after a gig at the Crowder Service Club, I was called a young comer in the Jerry Wald mold, which I resented even as Jerry resented the Artie Shaw shtick. You really are funny, Fletcher. Mr. Christian. All right, but you really are. Why am I really funny? Because you never seem to learn, didn't we just go through this? Did you not just massage the past, flip through it like a pack of bubble gum cards? I read that review, too, that guy didn't know his ass from a hole in the ground, and as for never learning, well I have accepted that, it's part of my goddam charm. You don't mean that, you'd have to stop fighting me. Who's fighting? I accept everything you say. You're incurable. Accepted. A bore. Accepted. A boor. Accepted. You're a mediocrity. You sonofabitchofasmartassbastard; who was the world's greatest clarinetist? Benjamin Goodman? *I* was: who was the world's greatest actor? Brando? *I* was, although he was the only one who could compare. Who said I'm still big, the movies have gotten smaller? You? G. Desmond-Swanson. Go on. What was Brando's greatest picture? *Waterfront*? *The Men*; his first. As what character did he stink the most? Fletcher Christian? That was the second most, no, as Marchbanks, opposite Kit Cornell, I tell you, far above Cornell's quarters twas an awful pew. I'm delighted that, as you might say, you are back in the ballgame. I wouldn't say that; and I'm back in the ballgame because I have considered and rejected Brando for Norris Blake. I see, whom do you prefer? Something between Leslie Howard and Julie Garfinkel. You mean John Garfield. You go to your church, I'll go to mine, OK I want a kind of British-Jewish Bill Holden, the Bill of *Sunset,* not *Wild Bunch*. That's rather ambitious, how do you propose getting him? Don't be naïve, I'll conduct a nationwide talent search; I'm also considering making the film into 12 separate chapters, à la *Elizabeth R,* which is an update of the *Perils of Pauline,* but I want Saturday night, not afternoon. Twill be the *Pickwick Papers* of our time. *That's* the idea, each week, all over America the talk will be Blake and how on earth will he get out of his latest scrape, to be continued, what do you think, Bligh?

I think you should jolly well get off the pot, onto the stick and bite the bullet.

X

_____

CHAPTER FOUR(B.)

The two sword-bearing leaders, with their babbling ragamuffin followers in train, came to a halt. I raised my hand, palm outward, in the traditional gesture of peaceful greeting, understood and respected the world over even amongst the most savage of tribes. Stanley, Livingstone, Speke, Burton had strode through Africa with palm aloft, as had Nellie Bly on her oddessey, not to mention Norris Blake in the dark interior of Luzon. Never had it failed them or me. To ensure its success I said, in my most careful Mandarin, "Good afternoon, gentlemen, peace and happiness be with you."

The angry buzzing ceased; an expectant silence reigned in its place. The taller of the two, obviously the leader of the leaders, smiled, albeit imperiously, which all in all I took to be a good sign.*

_____

* Because of Mr. Pulitzer's blindness, he was a stickler for physical detail. In my dispatch, therefore, I described the fellow thus: "The head Boxer was two inches shorter than this reporter, putting him at five feet ten

97

He lowered his sword, which had been pointing in the region of my left ventricle.

"You speak our language, foreigner," he said in precise Mandarin.

I enfolded my arms and rested on my left leg, both for reasons of presence and the shooting of the sciatic pain into my right thigh.

"I do," I rejoined. "I have studied it and find it most appropriate to the good sense and honest passion of the Chinese people."

His eyes narrowed in that smile. Then in perfect, if somewhat Anglicised English, he said, "A pretty speech, devil, now why should we not kill you?"

I was, to say the least, taken aback. However, having learned from Aguinaldo that honesty is the best policy in dealing with these native leaders, I gave full vent to my surprise.

"You speak English!" I exclaimed.

The fellow turned to his band and translated my sentence into Chinese. A burst of laughter greeted his words. He turned back to me.

"I always keep my followers fully informed of all that transpires," he said. "It is a facet of leadership I find most productive and one that I commend to the superior military minds of the west."

I detected a note of sarcasm veiled with irony in those words, but I did not dwell on it. Indeed, my busy mind was already into other things, principally casting this interview onto the front page of the *World*. Not immodestly, I had already placed it on a par with Crawford's interview of General Grant, or the conversation with Sir Henry William Gordon, the martyred hero's brother, just before the fall of Khartoum. I was positive that Mr. Pulitzer would recognize its importance, doubtless employing Walt McDougall to produce a six-column cut, or a cartoon as memorable as the one that had destroyed Blaine. For headline I tried out:

---

inches, a good size for a Chinese. His weight was on the light side of 170 pounds. His features were blunt, a thumb of a nose set in a square face, chin blocky. The eyes were dark green and narrow; they narrowed further when he smiled, which he did more often than the humour of the situation warranted."

98

Reporter Runs Remarkable Risk
and
World Writer Wages War of Words

But I rejected them as too sensational and settled on:

Blake Be-Devils Boxers!

In all frankness I thought it had a fair chance of ringing down through the ages, even as "Rum, Romanism and Rebellion." Satisfied for the nonce, I returned to the business at hand; one might have thought that a good quarter-hour had been consumed by my professional introspection; in actuality it was but a few seconds. And the halo of importance that now ringed our words convinced me I must surely keep one step ahead of this surprisingly cagey fellow.

"You were educated at a missionary school?" I suggested.

The shadow of a frown touched his countenance, to be replaced by the omnipresent smile.

"Very well educated. In Shantung, at the Witung Mission. And converted to a true Episcopal believer. I was properly baptized and named. Thomas." He seemed to expectorate that last.

I bowed slightly.

"That is no longer your name, I take it?"

Again the frown, which I now saw was surprise, again the quick control of it.

"I am Kuang Yu."

"I am Norris Blake."

He inclined his head. Then he tossed my name over his shoulder to his men. I could hear "Bake" and "Brake" buzzing through the ranks.

"You have not as yet answered my question, Mr. Blake," said Kuang.

"Will you answer one of mine first?" I said. "You see I am a newspaper writer. I am employed by the greatest newspaper in the

99

world, aptly named the *World,* and 200,000 people could read the answer to my question."*

That was indeed a calculated risk. For there are two classes of what I call interview subjects: Those who bridle at our very approach, as typified by Queen Victoria, and those who clearly expand six inches in circumference under questioning; James Blaine is a prime example of this group. I waited on my quarry with baited breath. Kuang Yu drew himself up and pushed out his chest. Ah.

"Very well," he said, with subtly feigned indifference. "What is the question?"

I hoped that Dave Sutton, our City Editor, had the good sense to use bold face, took a deep breath and said, "Why did you leave Christianity and join the Boxer Society? for obviously that is what you have done."

He clasped his hands behind his back, including the sword, and closed his eyes. I drew out my writing pad and pencil. He opened his eyes. Looking straight at me, he explained the question to his men. I saw heads nodding and ominous laughter. He nodded and all was still.

"Obviously, I am a member of the Boxer Society," he said, "although I prefer the Right Harmonious Fists. However, at the mission I was a model Christian. I always said my prayers and made up several of my own. I was a choir boy. Then one day I grew very ill—as you know, our country is filled with disease—and I was sent to hospital. A Chinese hospital. I was able to walk there in the company of two priests. When we arrived I saw a dozen of my countrymen stretched out on the floor in terrible agony. But as soon as I walked in, the doctors—the Chinese doctors—hastened forward and took me to a fine chamber and gave me the finest of care. . . ."

I wrote my notes in my specially devised short hand method, then looked up. His visage was filled with deep emotion, part anger, part anguish. At such times the good reporter interjects the bridging phrase.

* 300,000, if Pulitzer ran it in the Sunday edition.

"I have seen that in my own country in hospitals in the south," I said. "A white man will always be served before a colored man, no matter when he is brought in."

He flashed me a look of appraisal.

"Yes," he said. "But your doctors were no doubt white. These were Chinese doctors, *Chinese*."

I did not bother to say that the two colored doctors I knew were guilty of the same practice. What I did say was, "And the favouritism shown the Christian convert disgusted you . . ."

"Yes. Disgust. Yes."

He spat. Every man jack of them spat.

"Then," he continued, "after treatment I fell into a deep delirium, not unpleasant, mind you, but one that caused great concern to the mission staff. They offered up a constant stream of prayers for me."

"Yes?"

"Now, in that illness I had a vision. As plain to me as your standing there. I dreamed—" he paused and studied me; the eyes were slits, but he was not smiling—"I was the son of Christ."

"I see," I said. "Very like Hung Hsui Chuan. The Heavenly King." I referred of course to the leader of the Taiping Rebellion, who was finally put down by Gordon and his Ever Victorious Army. Gordon, as we well know, was the greatest Christer of all.

His eyes, now cunning, showed respect mingled with amusement.

"Very like," he agreed, "save that Hung thought himself the younger brother of Christ."

"I am aware of that," I said dryly.

An abbreviated bow and he continued:

"I recovered. In fact, I believed that I owed my recovery to my father's intercession, not to mention my grandfather's. Upon leaving hospital, I was hurried back to the mission in great pomp and ceremony. The very first night back I left my bed and ran to the Yellow River with the express purpose of walking across it, for was I not the son of our Lord?"

I said nothing.

"I entered the river and I walked. I continued to walk as the waters arose above my chin, my mouth, my nose. I drowned."

"Drowned?"

"Yes. Or believed I did. The next thing I knew I was lying on the shore with men and women gathered about me, not from the mission, but poor, ill-clad people, who were offering up prayers for me to *their* gods."

"Their gods."

"They saved me," he said simply.

"The gods of your countrymen . . ."

"Precisely. These *heathens*. They saved me."

"Hmmm."

I decided to gamble and let the devil take the hindmost.

"I venture to observe," I said, "that the most critical part of your experience was that you were not able to walk on water."

"Not only not able," he said, stamping his foot, "but drowning in the very act. Do you hear? Where was your God? My *presumed* God?"

"He had obviously failed you," I observed mildly.

"He was a fraud. He *is* a fraud."

"One could very well think that," I vouchsafed.

His agitation was now quite evident. He walked to the end of the first rank, spun on his heel and returned to me.

"I recovered," he said with a new harshness in his voice. "That is, I recovered physically. But my heart was empty. For if I was not the son of Christ, then I was nothing."

"To say the least."

"I returned to that hospital and began to help my suffering countrymen. Still behaving like a good Christian, you see. Oh I was praised to the skies for my good works."

"But you did not believe?"

He thrust his sword into the earth.

"Of course not. Haven't I told you?"

"Yes, you did."

"Very well then. I cared for my fellow countrymen. But in caring for them, I discovered something that tore at my empty heart. I discovered that they possessed the faith I lacked."

"They believed."

"Ah yes, scrivener, they believed. In the Middle Kingdom. In China. In the Eight Diagrams. In the White Lotus—"

"Which lifts itself out of the mud as man lifts himself out of his misery."

The smile returned.

"You are clever. Yes, that is so." He pointed at his weapon. "And they believed in the Great Sword Society."

"Aha."

He wrenched the sword out of the ground and held it aloft; the afternoon sunlight glittered on its burnished blade.

"*This*," he said softly, "is China. The China of history, of invulnerability." He lowered the sword. "One night a band of my countrymen came to the mission. Not for conversion, or to pray. They came to destroy it. And they did. They sacked it, left it in ruins. In the process I was struck by a bullet."

My mind raced back, then ahead.

"But you did not die?"

"I was not *hurt*. This they saw. This they passed on, one to the other. These men, these *I Ho Chuan,* for that is who they were, carried me off, back to their camp. They told my story and all bowed before me. Yet did I still think I was unworthy."

"In other words you were not convinced of your worth."

"Have I not said so? That very night I had a vision, a *true* vision. I awoke sweating and trembling, but filled with a strange new power. For I knew at last who and what I was." He drew himself up, adding at least a half inch to his height. Why not a seven-column cut? I thought. "Thomas of the Witung Mission was the son of the God of War," he said.

Something pieced together in my mind, something I now realized I had been groping for.

"Kuang Yu, by jove!"

"So," he smiled, "you recognize the name."

"But of course. And you are the son of the God of War?"

He bowed.

"At your service," he said. "And now, Mr. Blake, that I have answered your question and satisfied 200,000 of your countrymen, don't you think it is time we killed you?"

So, I thought, he has a one-track mind. And that track led inexorably to my demise. Well, his western antagonist also had some ideas about his ending and they did not include this denouement. Dispassionately, I considered my precarious situation and came to my decision.

"I confess," I said, "that since we had conversed like civilized men, if not friends, I assumed that you had changed your mind. At least, that was my *assumption*."

With amazing dexterity he flipped his sword skyward, spinning it in the sun, then caught it by the handle in its flashing descent. He threw his head back; the air resounded with corporeal laughter. When that subsided, he translated my words to his men. They were equally, if more brutally, amused.

"So you think that idiot, Chang Shen, can save you?" he said. "You think his—*your*—God can intercede for you? Fool. You will be the tenth man to die with that word on your lips." His laughter was now quite mirthless; all the cruel history of the orient, from the great Khan to the Empress Dowager, infused the metallic sound. Yet, withal, my mind somehow was untouched by my mortal danger; Leonard Wood has told me he experienced the same sense of detachment under fire in Cuba; it is as if the mind leads a life of its own. Well here was one mind that still thought of a day's work for a day's wages and it grasped this particular bull by the horns.

"Kill me if you must," I said under cerebral leadership, "that is, if you think it will profit you. Remember, however, that my employer, Joseph Pulitzer, almost single-handedly delivered the oppressed Cubans and Philippinos from tyranical masters and in so doing proved forever that the pen is mightier than the sword."

Slashing the air with the device I had just mentioned, he created vibrating silence. The cold green eyes, barely visible in their oriental sockets, measured me.

"I have heard of that," he said. "Tell me, Mr. Norris Blake, exactly what are you proposing? If indeed, I *do* spare your life."

It occurred to me that McDougall's illustration could well occupy the full width of the front page.

"Just this," I said. "Take me with you. Let me observe your fight to free yourself from Christian oppression. Let me report this to the world *through* the *World*."

He did not reply. In fact, suddenly, as though an internal curtain had descended, he seemed no longer part of the scene. His head fell slackly to his chest, his eyes rolled about blindly. His co-leader, then his men, stepped back; he fell to his knees, then began to jerk and to moan in the most awful yet piteous manner imaginable. I stared in wonder, for without doubt I was one of the few white men to be privy, nay a party, to a Boxer trance. As we watched in awe, in curiosity, he seized his sword, plunged it into the ground, then beat his way about it as though Excalibur were magnetic. It seemed impossible that the man could sustain this level of exertion, yet he not only did so, he increased his tempo until he resembled nothing so much as a giant, disabled humming-bird. Froth gathered at the corners of his mouth, like salt on a jagged wound. I considered, then rejected the taking of notes, for this tableau would surely sear itself into my journalistic soul.

Then, as suddenly as the fit descended, it lifted. He climbed quite steadily to his feet. He pulled the sword out of the ground and slid it into its scabbard. He turned his smile on me and extended his hand. I extended mine and east met west in the western manner. His men gave out with their version of three rousing pips.

"Welcome, oh mighty pen," said the son of the God of War.

Instantly, and with no questions asked, I was accepted as part of the Boxer band. For my part, regardless of the evidence of subsequent breakdowns in command and discipline, particularly in and around Peking, I had ample proof of their adherence to positive leadership. And positive leadership there surely was, despite Kuang Yu's manifestations of conceit and ego, of which there were many. Yet they never, it seemed, interfered with the task at hand. In this he was ably abetted by the other swordsman, Liu Sim, who served as a combination aide-de-camp and executive officer. As for me, mounted on one of the half-dozen horses they possessed,

I became the chronicler of the company, with official sanction, and in this capacity, received even a certain amount of deference, for the writer in China, unlike our country, still commands respect bordering on awe. I suppose it is the magical element that resides in the markings on paper produced by the human hand, an age-old wonder of man, here raised to the highest and most satisfactory degree.

I had my horse, but all the men rode on a beast of some sort—mule or donkey—and one fellow, a strangely silent Mongol, even had his own camel, which was responsive to no one but him. With amazing speed and fluidity then, we moved out and into the countryside. I was naturally not informed of our destination, but was otherwise free to talk to the true believers. In the main, I soon discovered, they were peasants from the Province of Chihli, but members of the gentry were present, some from Shantung and most bitter over the German presence there. I met and talked with several veterans of the Japanese War, who were particularly venemous in their attacks on the *Wojen,* quite literally, the dwarfs, who had invaded their country. Two of these, oddly enough, were my erstwhile guides and it was astonishing, considering their former shiftiness, to see them behave so straightforwardly, as well as to hear their well articulated hatred of the midget enemy. It is indeed odd, I mused then, and do now, how a cause of passion, deeply believed, can turn riff raff into men of purpose. (American Revolution, use the American Revolution. Much too obvious. *I* want it.) The men of Lexington and Valley Forge, et al, I would say, proved that.

Each morning, even as Ruby Bob in his gymnasium, the men drilled. Only their drill was like no other in the world, or its armies, had ever seen. With Kuang and Liu at their head, facing always southeast, each one bends over and bangs his head on the ground three times. As if this were not enough to scramble their brains, they rise, somewhat unsteadily, and proceed to pull at the ears, yanking so hard away from the head as to cause what we call the cauliflower effect. They then attack the mouth, stretching the orifice so broadly that in some cases it reaches the poor ear. By now they resemble the clay heads our children pummel beyond recognition. But this is not all. They flash the hands, feet, shoulders and knees about in a variety of shapes and contortions, each movement of which is supposed to convey a special sign; when this has been accomplished to each one's satisfaction, they fall straightaway to the ground in a kind of epileptic orgy, everyone attempting to outdo the other in the writhing and spitting departments as well as in terrible and incomprehensible sounds.

After some three days of this, Kuang asked me if I would not like to partake of the exercises, the better, as he said, to understand them. Nothing loath, I said, why, certainly. Whereupon I struck the old noodle on the ground stood up and yanked at my unsuspecting ears and mouth, then flung every jointed member to the four winds. I had been forewarned by Kuang that when I grew exhausted and longed to sink down, this was the very moment to renew my exertions, to push myself beyond pain and torment, and by jingo, he was right! On so doing I felt a marvelous lightness throughout my body, as if gravity were an undiscovered law, a kind of peace mingling with violent power, yet finding the two opposing forces perfectly compatible. Just when the ectsasy, and I use that word advisedly, was nearly more than I could bear, I saw myself, as from a great distance, plunging in a great arc to the ground. At which place, except for a deep rushing noise in my ears, I felt myself to be a huge, empty shell. How long I remained like that I do not know, but I do know that when I came to I was totally renewed and refreshed, although soaked to the skin. I looked at myself; my hands, feet and knees were bleeding, yet I did not feel pain or even discomfort.

"By heaven," I said to Kuang, "but that was a most interesting experiment!"

"Thank you for your approval,' he said. "Do you see that rock?"

"Yes."

"Try and lift it."

I bent over and tugged, but it was a huge thing, and gravity having returned to the scene, my effort was of course useless.

"Well," he said, "at my command you picked up this rock and carried it lightly from that tree to this place."

I looked at him, at the rock, at my bleeding hands.

107

"How extraordinary," I murmured. "It must have been some form of hypnosis."

He folded his arms.

"Call it what you will," he said rather darkly. "However, I do not indulge in trickery. That is a western habit." His mien, his manner then suddenly changed. "Come writer," he snapped, "we ride." And the mercurial fellow flung about, strode off and cracked out his orders.

And so we mounted up and rode. For another day, and still another, steadily north by northwest. Across the plains of China we rode. Whenever we entered a new district we would go straightaway to the local magistrate, where the two leaders would parley, and Eureka! many bread-cakes instantly appeared, to be followed by numerous strings of cash. The eager official would invariably say, "Now you will go away, won't you?" and after some more receipt of the above ingredients, why we went away. To the next district, where they were even more generous. In this fashion we comfortably ate up the mileage as well as the bread-cakes. I have developed a keen sense of pace from galloping around the one-and-five-eighths miles of the Central Park reservoir, so I judged that we covered a good 180 *li,* or some 60 miles. And once we found the rhythm of our journey, it was not at all unpleasant. Each night I clambered off my mount, tethered him, ate, then slept sound as a top, fully clothed, with my saddle for a pillow. The cool, bracing air I found excellent for the adenoids and the smooth, hard ground was just the ticket for calming my sciatica. As dedicated to my religion as the Boxers were to theirs, each night before slumber, I carefully wrote up my notes and mental observations; if these latter remained in my mind this long I knew they were worthy of permanence. I must confess that I found life with a secret, rebellious sect quite pleasant and soothing to the nerves. Even though I knew that, as inexorably as the setting of the huge, golden ball toward which we rode, all good things must end.

Our finale began to unravel on the morning of May 27. On that day at around eleven o'clock I heard a thin, almost delicate whistle.

Someone up front pointed. Far off to the east a curl of blue smoke rose straight up then trailed off parallel to the ground. The men began to jabber excitedly and I turned to Kuang Yu for an explanation. Oddly enough, he was nowhere to be seen, although only a moment before he had been at my side. I twisted about to Liu, but his eyes now had that eastern blankness that told you communication was out of the question. At times like this one waited; I waited. Presently, a murmur ran through the ranks, rippling from back to front. The band seemed to split in two and down the center aisle strode the leader. Ah but quite a different leader. His face, hands and arms were now the color of a ripe plum. His eyes, which moments before had been clear as a child's, were blood-red. Slowly he turned. The men, even their mounts, stood transfixed before the son of the God of War!

But only for a moment.

Without a signal, or none that I could discern, they dived into their convulsions. Oh but this time they outdid themselves. No demon of mortality could survive such fits. They were urged on by both Kuang and Liu, who at the climactic moment held their swords at arm's length and somehow contrived to leap over them, a feat that Barnum's prize acrobats would have envied. Twas the pinnacle of all exorcisms. And at the moment of unendurable pain, they swung into action.

The two leaders leaped onto their horses without so much as laying a hand on a flank. The men followed suit, although a few cheated by leapfrogging, including this reporter. Pointing their swords toward the line of train smoke, Kuang and Liu uttered a scream that outstripped anything I had heard from the bolo-wielders of northern Luzon. They dug deeply into their horses' sides and the poor animals sprang forward with cries of pain. We all followed. I found myself in the midst of a sea of rising and falling bodies, yet when I could peer overhead or at the ground beyond I could see we were racing with incredible, if even, speed. A wild, screaming gibberish mingled with the pounding as we charged on. Suddenly we were atop a rise and now plunging down, without slackening our pace. There, stretching away, meeting itself on the horizon, was our goal, the railway line. And beside it was the station and its small town.

"What place is that?" I shouted at Liu through the screaming thunder.

His face flashed at me and his mouth formed the word, "Paotingfu." Then he was galloping on.

So, it was not to be the main line, the one that ran from Peking to Tientsin and thence to Taku, but the trunk that tied into it. What in the world were we up to, I saw no trains down there? I was not long in finding out.

In a cloud of gray dust, the men jammed to a halt. They leaped off their animals and made post haste for the station. As if by magic, quite appropriately, clubs, knives, ancient rifles appeared even as they ran forward. Now Kuang was pointing with his sword. Now two men sprang for the telegraph poles alongside the tracks, scurried to the top in a thrice and with three mighty swipes slashed the wires. An oriental hurrah, silenced by a wave of Kuang's sword. He pointed again. A knot of men rushed into the station. Wild shouting, a half dozen shots, the smashing of glass, followed by the exit of chairs, tables, desks. Terrified humanity finally made its appearance in the person of a young woman and a middle-aged man, both of whom followed the furniture out of the window, both cutting themselves, but paying no heed to their wounds in their fearful flight. A shot and the man dropped. Kuang held his sword aloft and in the moment's respite the woman disappeared into a house across the street. Luck was on her side, for now other duties occupied the men. Liu was running forward, followed by another detachment, angry, wild, yet strangely disciplined. With their weapons they dug beneath the tracks, buried a small bundle, then hurried back. Silence. Then a small, hard explosion and the line rose into the air, buckled and descended like two limp snakes, lying finally and uselessly across each other. The men had no sooner cheered this event when Kuang, who seemed to be everywhere at once, was again pointing. To a man they remounted, the scrivener included, and raced out alongside the leader, past the break and down the line. It was quite incredible how, despite the noise and confusion, not a soul appeared. Clearly they had been utterly terrified. Or well warned.

Then began the wild, (in)famous ride north and east to Fengtai, where the railway met the Peking line. I must say now twas one of the great tragedies of my life that the *Shanghai Mercury* got the story out first, but that was only because of a cut wire; the fact remains that I was the *one* and *only* correspondent, eastern or western, directly on the spot; and herewith is the fleshed-out report of the rather sketchy account I managed to get out later in that frantic week:

With a terrible efficiency Sherman himself would have admired, the Boxer band cut its swath of destruction to the junction town. Two wooden bridges were set on fire. Even as flames leaped and roared, they were off down the line, ransacking a textile factory, then away, chopping down telegraph poles, slashing wires, and still away. All night we rode, into and through six stations, destroying each one faster than the one before. Yet I must add that before looting could commence, commands were shouted and we were galloping to the next town on our terrible mission. The sun was licking at the sky behind us when finally we dashed into Fengtai, but 15 *li* from the Imperial City.

What went before was now prelude. With Kuang Yu at every turn a dark wraith of vengeance, the men of the *I Ho Chuan* raged through the town like a storm of screaming locusts, leaving in their wake a trail of destruction: a burning station, a burning round-house, smashed locomotives, ruined repair shops and store houses, a charred handful of native houses that someone yelled belonged to converts. And most awful of all, the ripped-open homes of the foreigners. Yet, as before, whether through good fortune or some warning system, no one was to be seen. That is, until we reached the last house.

As Kuang and a dozen of his men burst into this one, a man, a woman and a child emerged as out of a terrible dream. They looked about, dazed, almost beyond fear. Three foreigners, perhaps Americans; I never did find out. The man held the child in one arm. In the other dangled a pistol, but it seemed useless in the

111

grip of the senseless owner. At that instant a Boxer swung off his mount and rushed at the woman. I would gladly have traded my pen for a sword right then, but alas, I had neither that nor a fire-arm. What I had, though, was a pair of bellows for lungs.

"WAKE UP, MAN!" I roared.

He jerked up out of his nightmare. The arm raised and stiffened, the pistol cracked. The immortal Boxer fell. He struggled upward, then toppled back, forever still. I was suddenly aware of a presence beside me. I looked up from the dead man into the eyes of Liu Sim. He read my question: of course a bullet will kill, yet was not this man protected by your spells, your gods?

"His faith was not strong enough," he said with a shrug.

I did not have time to mull that over, for danger was again surging toward my countrymen; blood was thicker than curiosity. I galloped forward. I dismounted and with bridle in hand ran toward the man who was staring at me really quite stupidly. Well I must have been a regular sight, with my smoke-blackened face and garments and eyes by now as red as Kuang's.

"Quickly," I shouted. "Mount and ride for Peking. You have no time to lose!"

He roused himself from his trance and yelled to the woman, "The horse, Jane, run for the horse!"

I held the animal steady as the plucky woman ran over, mounted and reached down for the child. The man handed him up, then swung on behind them. He looked down at me.

"I do not know you, sir," he said, "but God bless you, who-ever you are."

I gave the steed a sharp whack on the rump and he sprang away. The huddled family clattered down the main street, past the home they might never see again. As they drew abreast of the front door, they swerved as if in farewell, and just then one of the Boxers ran out. Now they were past him. He raised his rifle and took aim; even with that ancient, rusty piece he could not have missed.

To my total, utter astonishment, Liu whipped out a pistol and shot the Boxer dead!

All my poor head could do was swing from one to the other, from the prone figure in the dust to the mounted executioner. Then to add to my amazement, he slid off his horse and in perfect English said to me, "Assumption forever. Now up and off to Peking."

Well I had seen quick turnabouts in my time, after all I had been through the Philippino campaign, but this capped them all. I can honestly say that thought and speech failed me, although for the briefest of instants. When they finally returned, I stepped back and held up my hand.

"What sort of game is this?" I enquired.

"This is no game, Mr. Blake," he retorted. He made a skilled sign of the cross. "God is everywhere, is he not? However, if Kuang Yu comes out *you* will be fair game, for he learns all that happens."

"But . . . what of you?"

He smiled. "Am I not immortal?" Then he turned all business and thrust the reins into my hands. "Quickly," he snapped.

My professional mind entered the scene; grasping its essentials in a flash, it bid me tarry no longer. I flung myself into the saddle. I gazed down at this strange new ally.

"Before I ride, I must know something," I shouted.

"Yes?"

"The men who shot you and Kuang back at the tombs. I saw you fall. Yet you were unharmed. It was a trick, was it not?"

A quizzical expression touched the oriental face. He shrugged. Then I heard a sharp explosion. The house of the rescued family burst into flames; yelling Boxers ran out; at their head was Kuang. I dug into my horse's flanks, he sprang forward. Wisely, I veered him to the left and we brushed Liu, who turned out to be a consummate actor. He fell over in a heap and as we dashed off I could hear a stream of Chinese oaths floating oerhead. I clattered past Kuang Yu, who had halted and was gazing up at me, his jujube face a study in contrasts.

"Farewell, Son of War!" I shouted. "Perhaps we will meet again."

I was now clear. I turned in the saddle and looked back. Two men had raised their rifles. Kuang slashed curtly with his sword and they lowered them. I still looked back even as I spurred my horse onward. Kuang Yu stood against the flaming tableau of Fengtai, smiling, his sword pointing at the sky.

Well? Well? Let's go out and get drunk.

XI

I woke up filled with power and glory. Also under a tent. Quiet you, you had your grog. As I was saying, I awoke with strength, determination, resolve and no hangover. It was my day to sub, I even had a call from Washington Irving. But with Blake four-square behind the decision, I said the hell with it; let the children of American suffer, they were lousy critics anyway. With Blake by my side then, with Bligh locked in his cabin, I shaved, showered, sipped and sallied forth. I walked down Broadway to 106th Street and sat on my all time favorite bench, the stone one with the carved-in letters that said, "IN MEMORY OF ISIDOR AND IDA STRAUS WHO WERE LOST AT SEA IN THE TITANIC DISASTER, APRIL 15, 1912. LOVELY AND PLEASANT WERE THEY IN THEIR LIVES AND IN THEIR DEATH THEY WERE NOT DIVIDED."

Lovely and pleasant in their lives. In death not divided. Long before he became impossible, before she misunderstood him, before they broke each other's bananas. And as I sat in the glow of that glorious union, I decided to do it. Call Sue. Yes I would. I would call and charm her and rush over. We would plunge down together in our own *Titanic,* clean off the choking barnacles and pull our way to the surface, renewed, replenished, reconsidering. From far far away, muffled, hollow, yet terribly clear, I heard, *You cannot do it.* I plugged up my ears. You are *gutless.* I stood up, walked around the bench and sat down again. All was quiet on the west side front. Well, said another voice, a Leslie Howard-Julie Garfinkel-Bill Holden voice, you must do it, you know. I know, I know, maybe in a little while. Gutless. No, now. Soon, gutless, *now.* All right, yes, now!

I got up and walked across Broadway to a phone booth, took out a dime, inserted it. No dial tone. I punched the phone. No dial tone. I took out another dime, considered calling the operator, but if there was no dial tone . . . I shrugged and stepped out. *Gutless.* I stepped in, inserted the dime, no dial tone. I punched the phone again, kicked the booth and flung myself out. With Blake matching me stride for stride, I walked two blocks to a drugstore, entered, bought a pack of stainless steel blades so I could get change, stepped into the phone booth and shoved in a dime. It pinged; perfect dial tone. I dialed. No ring. I hung up. No dime. I leaned my head against the door. Carry on, said Blake. You *can't.* I took out another dime, inserted and dialed the operator. It rang, by Jesus. She came on. I have lost a dime. I'm sorry. Is that all you've got to say? May I have your name and address? I gave her my name and address, no stamps please, I prefer cash. That is not our policy, sir. Well change your policy, I never write letters, I'm illiterate. I'm sorry, sir, you'll have to talk to my supervisor . . . Can I help you? I have just lost three dimes, one in this booth and two in another booth. What is the number of this booth? TR 3-4593. What is the number of the other booth? I don't know, I left in a pet. I see, what is your name and address, sir. Sidney R. Benson, 502 West 115th Street, 10025, apartment 4D, but I already gave that to the other operator. I see, sir, then you won't have to give them to me. I already did. I'm sorry, sir, we'll mail you a refund. That's what the other one said. I want cash, silver taels. I beg your pardon, sir. Three dimes. That is not our policy, sir. It is not my policy to accept stamps. I'm sorry, sir. It used to be your policy. We have changed our policy, sir. Stamps never stick for me. I'm sorry, sir. The glue is harmful to my tongue papillae. I'm sorry, sir. You give cash to the Republican National Convention, why can't you give me cash. I'm sorry, sir, that is not our policy. If you send me stamps, I'll send them back to you. You may do anything you want with them. May I shove them up your ass? I'm sorry, sir . . .

I stood outside the booth and leaned against it. I said to the druggist, "Conglomerates should not be permitted under the Sherman Anti-trust Act," and I walked out. I went straight home and with Bligh rattling around in his cabin, with Blake right beside me, I called Sue. Since the call went by way of London, it went through. She was home.

"It's me, Sue."

"Sid?"

"Yes. How are you?"

"All right, Sid, how are you?"

"Better, much better. How are the kids?"

"Fine. Carlie did very well on her boards."

"What was her verbal?"

"610."

"That's not so great, considering who her father is."

"It's fine, Sid, whatever she got is fine."

"OK, I agree, she does what she does, right?"

"Well, I'm glad to hear you say *that,* at least."

"I told you I was better. How is Garth?"

"All right. Still struggling in French. I probably shouldn't even mention it."

"No, you go right ahead and mention it. French is not easy even if I got a 98 on the regents. Some people simply don't have an ear for language. Are they handling the social adjustment all right?"

"Fine. You know them."

"A chip off their old lady's block. Can I come over tonight?"

". . . Oh Sid, let's not start that again."

"But I'm working everything out, I am. I feel great. Sue, I'm working on a book. It's going beautifully."

"I'm glad."

"You don't sound so glad."

"I'm very glad. For now."

"I know just what you mean. But this is more than now. I know it. I feel it. This book is transforming me, it really is."

"Are you getting help?"

"Sue, please, you know how I feel about that."

"Yes, I know."

"I don't want anyone tampering with my talent."

"Yes, I know."

"Look what it did to Ben Stillmore."

"All right, Sid."

"Can I come over?"

"No, Sid."

"Please."

"No."

"Don't you want to see the book?"

"No."

"I'm asking in a nice way, goddammit."

"No, Sid."

"All right, all right, I don't want to upset you. I never want to upset you again."

"Sid, please don't threaten me."

"Who's threatening? It's merely a calmly considered statement of the state of things. Which is pretty shitty. You don't wish to see me, is that correct?"

"That's correct, Sid."

"Very well. Good bye, Sue, from the song of the same name."

"Good bye, Sid."

She called back in ten minutes. I let her ring eight times, then picked up.

"Are you all right?" she said.

"I'm great. Terrific."

"You shouldn't talk like that, Sid."

"How else can I talk? Can I come over?"

"No."

"OK."

"And I'm not going to call you back. That was stupid."

"So bend a little, be stupid. Don't be such a piece of iron."

"That's funny, coming from you."

"Sue, I didn't *ask* you to call."

"I know."

"Hell, I'm glad you did. See? When did you ever hear a piece of insight like that from me? I told you I was a hundred times better."

"Well it beats saying oh shit."

"There. You recognize it, too. How about it?"

"I told you, no."

"Forever no, or now no?"

"For the indefinite future."

"How about giving me a little light at the end of the tunnel? Tonight?"

"No. N.O."

She hung up. I waited two hours by the phone; she didn't call back.

Late in the afternoon I got on the subway. I always get on the subway when I'm upset. Or when I have to think. Or when I'm in a blue funk. Or when I'm all three. I decided to join the army between 242nd Street and Flatbush Avenue. I went with Jack Teagarden after the A train. I signed the contract for *Interplay* after the Coney Island BMT. When City College dumped in 1950 I rode the Lexington Avenue local for five hours. The gloom, the screeching, the crowds, the blank eyes, chest to tit, the defeat of Manhattan's rock bed, the generations of immigrant sand hogs, they all settle my head and my stomach and my back. So this time, in a fog, what Birnbaum used to call his sadsong, but which Benson recognizes as a hard, if temporary, minor depression, I wandered down to the 103rd Street IRT station and got on the train.

I stared at the car cards, at the magic markered *Luis 137, Hitler*

II, Crazy Cross and the penetrated L&M girl, but none of it really registered, artistically, sociologically, pain-in-the-assedly. I just stared. I do not think I came to until we reached Franklin Street. Yes, that was the first station I noticed. Perhaps it was Benjamin, perhaps Roosevelt, but even as I searched the connection, we were past it and I was standing. At Chambers Street I stepped out. I walked upstairs and east, past Church and Broadway. I paused at City Hall, then continued across the street to the bronze Horace Greeley gazing toward his beloved red-brick *Tribune*. I perked up a bit there. I sat down and contemplated Horace. I had always admired this tough, pure, disturbed man. So had Blake.

He had?

Oh God, who let you out? I let myself out, you know you can't keep a good man down. Wisecrax it gives. I'm just trying to cheer you up, you need it during a sadsong. This is *not* a sadsong. No? No, it is a minor setback along the upward road to recovery. Very well, answer the question, did Blake admire Greeley? He did, but he and I both detest Whitelaw Reid, his successor. Why? Because we are for the underdog, that's why, and Whitelaw, who by the by ran for vice president with Benjamin Harrison on the Republican ticket in '92 and was soundly clobbered by Cleveland and Adlai Stevenson, because this Reid was for the overdog and it serves him right that grandson Ogden has turned Democrat, and as you may or may not know, Blake went to the *World* after an offer from Reid and the *Tribune* precisely because, even as Ogden, Pulitzer cared for the poor souls below 14th Street, to say nothing of Cubanos, Insurrectos and Boxers. Well, well. Yes, well well, so stuff that in your breadfruit and eat it!

I got up and walked to Park Row. Newspaper Row. There they were, or should have been. The old *Times* building. Now Pace College. Beside it the *Trib*. Dana's *Sun*? It shone for all no more. At the other end of the Row, at Ann Street, Bennett's *Herald,* the great competitor, no longer there, but always there. Above all, across from the *Times,* where the new buildings of Pace stood, across Printing House Square and Benjamin Franklin, there facing City Hall so he could grab scoop after scoop, there Pulitzer had built his *World* in 1890, ten years before the Boxers, 16 stories high, golden-domed, the most modern of the modern. High up in the turret, bespectacled, bearded, old-countried editor and with him the star reporter, 100% Amahrican. Standing together and gazing east to the Brooklyn Bridge, the first great story, illustrated, then slowly revolving and shaking their heads over the push carts and blood-sucking tenements, the subject of oh so many crusading editorials. Then spinning their globe and stopping at Luzon and making their plans and there Joseph sitting alone and tracing a desperate journey up the Pei Ho and into Fengtai. Hold on, he was blind. Sure, the better to *feel* China, from Taku to Pekin. Peking. Pekin, just now I prefer the old spelling.

I sat down across the street and I looked at where the *World* should be. Was. I spent the afternoon there. Looking. And Listening. To what? To the flea in my ear. To Iago. What saying? Who needs her? Not me. If she hasn't got a *shvartz*, she's got somebody else. And how. Somebody else is taking your place. And how. Who? I don't know, I don't know, I don't want to think about it. Who? I don't know, maybe Rabin, her new boss. Name must have been Rubin. Yes Rubin. Or Rabinowitz. That too. Probably putting out during dictation. Yeah. Between the salutation and truly yours. Between the date and the salutation. And the body. And truly yours. And the P.S. Yeah, she always came fast. How about what she always said just before? What, what did she always say? Don't be coy. Yes, what she always said, the profanity. All right, Mr. Christian, the profanity. Yes, she liked to say that. To Rabin? To me. To Rabin? No, yes, maybe, I don't know . . . LEAVE ME ALONE ALREADY!

I got up. I ran across Printing House Square and stood in front of Pace College. How many times had Norris Blake stood here, right here, before going up to see the boss? Before checking out the new assignment?

Many times, Sidney.

Come on, Christian, move it.

Wait. Many times, sir?

Yes, many. Standing right there. I could see him from my 16th-floor window. I mean Dave Sutton could see him for me.

Come on, Christian.

And then what, sir?

I said why is he waiting, send the boy up.

Christian!

And he came up?

He did. In our brand new Otis elevators. Right to the top door under the golden dome.

Now that's an order, Mr. Christian.

And you looked out over New York?

Off course. This boy was my eyes. We looked out over the *World*.

Jesus.

Now I will not stand for this nonsense.

You planned the Luzon assignment together?

Off course.

I'll see you hanging from the highest yardarm in his majesty's fleet, Mr. Christian!

You got his telegram on China?

What a missive! (chuckle) That reckless boy.

I *command* you.

Sir . . . did you ever give him . . . personal advice?

Off course. I was like his priest. Or his rabbi.

I'm warning you.

Did you ever give him advice . . . on affairs of the heart?

Many many times.

I'm disgusted with you, Mr. Christian.

What . . . what did you tell him, sir? I mean what was the gist of it?

Christian!

Never, and I do mean never, take no for an answer.

Where are you going, Mr. Christian?

Up yours, to never take no for an answer!

I took the train back uptown. I dug into the trunk and found the case, right on top of the Chromonica. I ran back down and took a cab. All the way out to Bayside. Then I walked the two blocks to the Palm Garden Apartments. I opened the case and took out each quiet, well-behaved part and I screwed them together and there it was black and slim and shiny and perfect. Sidney's rod. I screwed on the mouthpiece. I ran a few scales and noodled a bit. It had been a good two years, and I was drunk at a Scarsdale bar mitzvah, but it was all there. I walked across the street and stood under 2G. Then I closed my eyes and pointed up and began to blow. I blew "Body and Soul" for starters. Nice and easy. With a few Hawk breaks, transposed of course. Then just as nice, just as easy, "Someday Sweetheart." Then "Who?" And "After You've Gone."

A few heads popped out of windows. I heard the pitter patter of little coins. I bowed and swung into "Goody Goody" and then "It's Been So Long." Not a clinker, not a single goddam clinker. Then into "Dinah" and "Moonglow." And "My Old Flame" and "I Got It Bad and That Ain't Good," "How Long Has This Been Going On?" and finally "Why Don't You Do Right?" *sans* Peggy, but *avec beaucoup* feeling. I opened my eyes. I heard applause and some more coins. I took a bow. I looked up. No head in 2G. I was killing Artie Shaw in our battle of music, to say nothing of Rabin-Rabinowitz, but no head. Hell, I lifted the licorice stick to my grooving chops and I let go; and with the greatest phrasing of a distinguished career I implored, "Don't Be That Way."

When I opened my eyes, she was standing beside me, wiping her face.

"All right," she said, "you win. But just for a little while."

I sat down on a straight-backed chair and she smiled before she could stop herself. So did I.

"I always liked a straight chair," I said.

"How well I know."

I tried not to sigh too deeply, but didn't quite succeed. On the other hand, I did not push it too hard; this one knew me, oh how she knew me.

123

"How's your mother?" she said.

"Like always, complaining."

"Well that's a good sign."

"Yes it is," I said, "in her case."

"Is she complaining about me?"

"Why not?"

"Yes, why not."

She could have offered me some coffee, a scotch, a Pepsi, a lousy glass of water. I got self control. She sat in the easy chair, the one we got at Sloane's in 1961, her legs tightly crossed, calves bulging, dress up to here. Disgusting, Hannah would have said, all exposed, if there had been anything to expose. I checked. I looked carefully, though cagily, for what the ladies' magazines call the unsightly gap between garter belt and stocking, the no-man's land that drove Birnbaum crazy, only to remember with a sudden jolt that my wife had been wearing panty hose for three years. Miserable goddam things. German invention, naturally. How could I forget? W.J., wherever he was, would never forget; he knew every inch of his mother's underwear. Yes, how could you forget? Down, you. He went down. I went down. Not all the way, however, which was a bit embarrassing. I almost expected W.J. to yell, hey look at Birney with the semi! I too crossed my legs.

"Nu?" I said.

"Nu?"

"I meant what I said on the phone. I'm back on the beam."

She toodled an airy clarinet with all ten fingers.

"It seems to me I've heard that song before," she sang.

"It's from an old familiar score."

"I know it well, that mel-o-dee."

I got up, semi or no semi, walked across the room and kissed her on the cheek.

"See," I said, "we're a team. Goddammit, we're a winning team. Like Adam and Eve."

"Like Mutt and Jeff."

"Like Horowitz and Margareten."

"Like Maggie and her drawers."

I bent over and turned her face up and kissed her on the mouth. She let me. I squatted down beside her, her hand in mine. She was looking at me solemnly, shaking her head.

"*Mishugena* nut," she said.

"That is redundantly superfluous."

"DADDY!"

I looked up, frowning. Carlie was at the door, blue sweater, ape haircut, tie-dyed jeans. I changed to a smile and got up; she ran across the room and flung herself into me. I bent back slightly at the crotch, put my arms around her and kissed her clean, smooth cheek. God, she looked, felt and tasted exactly like Jody Cohen, '48, queen of the campus. We encircled each other and looked down at mother.

"He's coming back, isn't he?" Carlie said.

"We'll see, honey," I said.

Sue looked up at us.

"Yes, we'll see."

"That's out of the parents' handbook. I don't know what there is to see. You don't have to protect your woman's vanity, you know."

"Hey wait a minute, girlie," I said. "That is mah ol lady you're insultin."

She squeezed me and put her head on my shoulder; I smelled Chanel number five: Millicent Charnak, CCNY '51, Lewisohn Stadium, top row.

"You can stay in my room," she said. Then she spotted it, the licorice stick, on the table. She ran over and picked it up as Sue and I exchanged looks. "You brought your clarinet," she squealed. "Oh, daddy, play something. Wait." She thrust the clarinet at me, tumbled into her room and returned with her record player and one record, before I even had time to mug. She plugged in the player and set the record on it. It was a 78. "All right," she said, "you know, play." She dropped the arm. I heard the slow, wailing beat. I raised the clarinet and as Benny came on, I slurred with him into "Goodbye," his closing theme. We played it out together, every note, every break. When we finished, she sighed

125

down to her little rump and turned to the flip side. B.G. and I swung into "Let's Dance," his opener. As we kicked and drove, she got up and with eyes closed, herky-jerked into a frug-watusi-monkey that would have had the killer-dillers plotzing in the aisles. When we finished, she applauded and kissed me, then threw herself down beside the player.

"All right," she said, pointing, "take it, Mr. B."

I shook my head, rolled my eyes, put the clarinet in my mouth and played a dozen notes. She shot a hand up.

" 'Cherokee,' Charlie Barnet," she screamed.

"Twenty lucky bucks."

I thought, raised the stick and played; this time she didn't even raise her hand.

" 'I Can't Get Started,' Bunny Berrigan."

"A case of O-Henry bars. OK, dig this."

I played, she closed her eyes, wrinkled her face, rocked back and forth and blurted out. "The 'Dipsy Doodle,' uh . . . uh . . . Larry Clinton!"

I grinned with ecstasy at Sue who was grinning right back. I motioned to her and launched into:

" 'I Got a Right to Sing the Blues,' Jack Teagarden!" they both screamed. We all broke up. "Daddy, daddy," Carlie shouted, "tell us about the famous battle of music. You know."

"Which one? I'm a battle-scarred veteran."

"You know, the one you played against Tommy Dorsey."

"Who was known as?"

"T.D."

"What else?"

"The Sentimental Gentleman of Swing."

"What did Shep Fields play?"

"Rippling Rhythm."

"How come?"

"One night he and his wife were sipping sodas through a straw and she blew the wrong way. Rippling Rhythm."

"What was Charlie Spivak?"

"The Sweetest Trumpet This Side of Heaven."

"Brazil."

"Where hearts were entertaining June."

"Big noise blew in from—"

"Winnetka!"

"Racing with the—"

"Moon!"

"Those cool and limpid—"

"Greeneyes!"

"Who was the greatest?"

"You."

"No, no, the *real* greatest?"

"Jack Teagarden."

"What did he play?"

"Slip horn!"

Sue and I applauded.

"OK," I said, "just because you're good." She took a deep breath, a contented breath, who used to take that breath? Sue Hayden. "Well," I said, "this was in Lancaster, P.A. At F&M College." I paused.

"Franklin and Marshall," she said. "For Benjamin Franklin and John Marshall, the first chief justice."

I waited.

". . . The *greatest* chief justice. John Jay was the first chief justice."

I picked up the stick and squeaked out, "That's right." She pounded the floor.

"OK," I said. "We were down there on this gig and the college kids had their dates, oh from girls' schools like Beaver and Cedarcrest. F&M was all boys then, that was before all this goddam sexual integration"—she pounded again—"well I had been with Teagarden two weeks and had learned his book by living on coffee for six days and nights. No reefers, mind you, though, hell, I knew guys on reefers full time. In '46. So what else is new? Anyway we got this date because Jimmy Dorsey, who'd had it originally, and Tommy, were having one of their celebrated arguments—"

"*The Fabulous Dorseys* was on T.V. last week."

"Poo poo for the birds. Someday I'll tell you the whole, complete inside story." Her eyes grew big. "As I was saying, Teagarden was the greatest, he was the closest thing to a colored singer and musician the white race has ever produced, and the band was playing real good, mostly young guys just out of the army and dying to prove ourselves. Of course we didn't have the rep Tommy had, but with people in the know like *Metronome* and *Downbeat* we were right there with the big boys. I think Tommy may have suspected what he was getting into, but he was such a gutsy guy—nobody in the world had more chutzpah than Tommy Dorsey—well he had talked himself into thinking he could beat any band that ever blew. He went on first and I must admit he played real good. He did all his old standbys: "Song of India," with that great intro, "Marie," Jack Leonard's big hit, Sy Oliver's "Opus Number One" and of course "I'll Never Smile Again," by Frankie and the—"

"Pied Pipers!"

"Kee-rect. Well the kids whooped it up, even the neckers came out of their cars to hear the action. Then us po' lil country boys came on. We warmed up with a few easy things, then sailed into our book and did "Sheik of Araby," "Aunt Hagar's Blues," "Peg O' My Heart." Well the kids stopped dancing altogether and you know what *that* meant. They were pressing in around the bandstand to hear this live, hundred percent, pure, un-electronic music. Jack gave us the downbeat and away we went into "Red Wing." Right smack in the middle he nodded and I stood up and—"

I stood up, pointed the clarinet at the kids around the bandstand and swung into my head arrangement. When I finished they broke it up. All of them. Then ever so slowly, with Jack on the vocal, I eased into "I've Got a Right to Sing the Blues," our theme. I finished in hushed silence. Slowly I lowered the clarinet.

"Afterward," I said softly, "Tommy came over to Jack and I saw them talking and I saw Jack nod. Then Tommy came over to me and said, 'How would you like to work for me, kid?' I was bowled over. Here I was out of the army six months and playing with Teagarden and the great Tommy Dorsey was offering me a job. It's the big scene in the *Sid Benson Story*. I looked over at Jack and he sort of had his head down the way he did when he was sad and right then and there I said, 'I'm very flattered, Mr. Dorsey, but I want to stay with Mr. Teagarden. He's been great to me.' And you know what Tommy said?"

"YOU GOT A LOTTA CLASS KID!" They yelled.

"Gize whys," I said. "Goddam gize whys. I shoulda known it was a con job." Carlie rolled back and waved her legs in the air, then she sat up and said, "More, more." I shook my head. "Show's over. Our next broadcast will be from the Aragon Ballroom in Chicago. Hey, haven't you got some work to do?"

"I did it all in study hall."

"You mean you've got nothing to read or review or prepare for?"

"Ugh."

"OK, ugh, let's go. By the way, where's your lil brudda?"

"Over at Gary's" she said. "They're working on a spectroscope."

"OK, you go work on one also. You'll be the first lady Ph.D. in physics to come out of that school."

She wrinkled her nose. Anna Yamanaka, Osaka, '45.

"I don't know if I like the idea of being a lady," she shrugged. She got up and hugged me and I hugged back, this time careful not to be careful. "Night Mom," she said and breezed out.

We were silent. Then I got up and sat on the arm of Sue's chair. I stroked her face and she rubbed it gently against my hand. I slid down in the seat and said, "We got the two skinniest asses in captivity."

"Mine isn't so skinny."

I nodded and kissed her and we played with tongues. Then I drew back and said, "She's OK, she's gonna be great."

"You really think so?"

"I do. You're doing a great job."

"Except when you're the competition."

"Come on. I ship bulls to France, to Argentina, I'm just a big bull shipper. You're the solid citizen."

She looked at me, the kind of look I got before she ever saw a sadsong. I kissed her and she slid into me and without any guiding, so help me Hannah, her hand was on my semi. It lay there very quietly; I did not make a move, I even stayed at half mast, for I knew she was thinking and when this one was thinking . . . And *I* thought, with everything considered, floor show and all, I had a chance, at least for the night. Wham, bam, thank you, Sam. She drew her hand away, brushed back her hair and sighed.

"No," she said, "that wasn't right."

"Am I complaining?"

"No. But you have a right to."

"I got a right to sing the blues."

"And I got a right to feel low down."

"So?"

"So I think you'd better go, Sid. Before we start something we'll both be sorry for."

I was tempted to say, who's writing your stuff, but I was afraid Bligh would answer, I am, she's a Wac in Africa. Instead I got up very quickly. Hell, let every kid in the class see me sticking out.

"All right," I said quietly. "I agree with your basic position." I unscrewed the clarinet and tucked the poor little parts into their places. I held out my hand. She took it, then kissed me on the cheek.

"Goodnight sweatheart," I said, "till we meet tomorrow."

"Goodnight sweetheart, sleep will banish sorrow."

I spun dramatically on my heel and walked out.

As soon as I got home I began to write.

XII

CHAPTER FIVE (B.)

With a hearty vengeance I applied boot and spur to my gallant little steed and to my finely tuned sense of pace he seemed to answer my punishment with—if that were possible—even more speed. At first I galloped with the afternoon sun over my left shoulder so as to maintain a northerly attitude, but as soon as I cleared the last of the clash and ruin of Fengtai and entered the quiet steppe, I veered into a sweeping semicircle and raced around to the east, calculating that I should strike the main line about equidistant to Peking, hoping upon hope that it was still intact. My sense of direction, rather my feel for it, proved accurate, which in my excited state of mind and body was a great comfort, as after a run of some nine or ten *li* I espied the tracks. Another and more general comfort was the fact that my powers of emergency, my emotional counter-offensive as it were, seemed to be functioning as well as ever, in fact—if questioned on the subject—I would have to rate them at their apogee. Also, and this was no small thing, my luck was holding up remarkably well, although I have always felt that luck was a direct product of skill times opportunity. As if to verify my arithmetic, there, stretching as far as my tired but satisfied eyes could see, was a shining secure railway.

As soon as I came alongside the iron arrows, I eased up on my faithful mount and settled into an easy, though far from relaxed, canter. Then guided by the genius of western industry, I rode toward the Imperial City. And now that my corporeal self was fixed on a solid course, the journalistic portion of my being was free to roam into and over the professional aspects of the case. It did not, as one might think, tarry on the prospect of the city of a thousand tales and dreams that lay before me, no, that would come when it would come and to wallow in romantic speculation of the fabled place would be uneconomical effort. What I was concerned with now was the self-interrogation that contained the six omnipresent questions which are the staples of our trade: who, what, why, when, where and how. And added to these the query that I modestly consider my particular contribution to the reportorial art: OH?

And so as I bounded along I probed the basic entreaties.

Who was countering the Boxers all through the province? What was happening up and down the line? At Taku? At Tientsin? even more important, in the capitals of the world? Why was this terrible conflict taking place? And why was it sweeping inexorably from one awful climax to another? When would the next blows descend? Where would they descend? How would they descend? How would they be dealt with?

I responded to each question with the facts in hand, such as I knew them, and also with a projection of my trained imagination. All of this information, this mass of data, added up to one inescapable conclusion: I was in a remarkable place in a remarkable time in history and I would not trade this place or time for all the rice and tea in China, as tantalizing as I found that thought to be.

OH?

Ah there it was, my petite contribution. To that question I had to own up that I had no answer, nor I might add do any of my most skilled colleagues, and that is why it is so perfect for the 20th-century journalist. It is not an eyebrow-lifting syllable, nor a weary one, nor is it supercilious; on the contrary, it is circumferential and pregnant with the yearning and striving of those of us who ride to the four corners of this earth to catch and report the reaping whirlwind.

I heard a train whistle.

Instantly my physical, psychological and philosophical selves merged into one and I was on the unified *qui vive*. Hinging my knees to act as cushions, I stood up in my stirrups and peered up the tracks. My straining eyes were soon rewarded by the telltale plume of smoke. I sat back, patted my faithful partner on his sweat-laden mane. It suddenly occurred to me, even as I urged him on, that he deserved a name, as did any good friend, in particular a nick-of-time-friend. I rifled quickly through the lists; I discarded them all and then quite by inspiration, which is often my wont, I came upon it: Herald! Of course. Not only symbollically accurate, but a wry pleasantry that Mr. Pulitzer would surely enjoy even if Mr. Bennett would not. I leaned forward and whispered, "Just a little faster, Herald, old friend, we're getting there, but not quite quick enough." Upon my word, the faithful little fellow snorted and bounded ahead and maintained that accelerated pace until our quarry came into view. And quite a surprising quarry it was, for this was no two or three or four-car linkage; even from this distance I could see that. Another half-mile and I was abreast of the rear car. There were seven others, plus the huge, straining locomotive. I smiled to myself. Skill times opportunity had produced luck; my *World* nose smelled news.

I cut over to that rear car and seemed to pull each one to me as Herald stretched out for the front one. By now heads were poking out of windows and arms were waving. *Uniformed* arms. But not any *one* uniform. Well! I tapped the slick flanks; the first car came back to us, the car where the leader or leaders were sure to be ensconced. As if to say yes we are, an important-looking head poked out of a front window, a head that held maturity, yet youthful dash in its pepper-and-salt moustache, sideburns and sombre expression. I cupped my hands.

"Who is on this train?" I shouted.

The neutral countenance considered the question.

"Guards," it snapped.

"Guards for what?"

"Who wants to know?"

"I do."

"Who are you?"

"Reporter."

"Reporter for whom?"

"The *World*."

"The New York *World*?"

"The *World*. The *World*. We dropped the New York sixteen years ago so as to represent our international rather than provincial character."

Gray eyes digested this information.

"We are guards for the legations," said their owner.

A surge of excitement coursed up my usually objective spine; they had called up the guards, they had called up the legation guards!

"May I come aboard?" I hollered, employing the naval metaphor despite the blue army uniforms behind those windows; twas a calculated gamble. But one I had to take. The official face pondered. Then the blue arm beckoned. I saluted and reined in Herald until the car had almost passed us by. Then as soon as the rear platform hove into view, I swung the responsive little fellow toward it. He seemed to understand perfectly; with no further word from me, he increased his tempo to match that of the train. For about an eighth of a mile we ran together as though joined by an invisible chain. Then I leaned forward and whispered, "Now Herald, old boy, you continue to run with us until I return, do you hear?" For good measure I said the same thing in Mandarin. He snorted. I disengaged my feet from the stirrups then, pulled up my legs and in one motion hoisted up and squatted on the saddle, still bending far over. In this position I resembled nothing so much as a coiled watchspring. Holding my kinetically precarious balance, I timed Herald's upward sway and at the felt instant I leaped for the railing which was some two feet from my head. The trick, as it had been

134

taught to me by Mr. Jesse James, in '81 in Missouri, where I had been sent by my parents for reasons of health, the trick was to maintain absolute calm and confidence in your ability to pull it off.* Jesse was a good teacher and I apparently an apt pupil, even after all these years. My hands grasped the rail and my feet reached for and found the bottom step. I hauled up, vaulted and voila! there I was, firm on the platform. Before me stood the moustache and the grave visage; they belonged to an officer of the Army of the United States, a good two inches shorter than I, though far from diminutive. He stood at attention.

"Captain Jedediah Whitmore," he said. "At your service, sir."

"Norris Blake. At yours, sir."

"What can I do for you, Mr. Blake?"

"The situation," I began, speaking loudly over the train noise, "it is precarious?"

"Most precarious."

"What's that?"

"MOST PRECARIOUS."

"I see. Calling up the guards is a serious matter."

"A serious what?"

"A serious MATTER."

"Most serious."

"Pardon?"

"MOST SERIOUS."

"MAY I ASK HOW MANY YOU HAVE?"

"IN TOTO OR FROM EACH COUNTRY?"

Aha, that is what I was after.

"FROM EACH COUNTRY, IF YOU PLEASE." I whipped out pad and pencil.

"THE OFFICIAL OR UNOFFICIAL COUNT?" he asked.

"OH?"

* Mr. Howard, his alias at the time, turned out to be my first professional interview, the remarkable conversation taking place in his hideout and subsequently appearing in the Troy High School *Sentinel* the next fall; this was most fortunate since the dirty little coward who shot Mr. Howard did so the following year.

My seventh journalistic commandment; it wound around and poked at this business.

"WELL, SIR, AS EVERYONE KNOWS," he shouted, the hound to my hare, "THE MINISTERS PETITIONED THE TSUNGLI YAMEN TO BRING US UP—"

"YES," I broke in, "THE TSUNGLI YAMEN. THAT IS THE . . ."

"FOREIGN MINISTRY," he shouted dryly. "IF I MAY ATTACH SUCH AN APPELLATION TO THOSE WEASELS."

"HARDLY AN INDEPENDENT AGENCY?" I suggested.

"WELL PUT, THOUGH MILD. TOTALLY UNDER THE THUMB OF PRINCE TUAN AND HIS SHE-DEVIL."

Odd, I thought briefly, how satan was so loosely assigned to both sides of this conflict; no doubt, though, that he relished his current popularity.

"AND HOW DID THE WEASELS RESPOND TO THE MINISTERS' REQUEST?" I asked.

"AS WE MIGHT HAVE EXPECTED. THEY GENEROUSLY ALLOTTED US 30 GUARDS FROM EACH COUNTRY."

I looked up.

"EGAD! 30!"

"PRECISELY OUR SENTIMENTS. AND I AM SURE, THE SENTIMENTS OF YOUR READERS."

"I AM POSITIVE. OR I DON'T KNOW AMERICANS."

"NATURALLY," he rejoined, with obvious satisfaction, "WE COULD NOT BE BOUND BY SUCH A FIGURE."

"NATURALLY."

"THEREFORE, THAT OFFICIAL 30 ROLL CALLS OUT AT—" He waited until my pencil dropped; he cupped his mouth— "52 AMERICANS, 75 BRITISH, 75 FRENCH, 75 RUSSIAN, AND JUST TO KEEP THEM HAPPY, 30 ITALIAN AND 30 JAPANESE."

"HMMM, SIX COUNTRIES, 337 MEN."

"THAT IS CORRECT."

"HARDLY AN OVERWHELMING NUMBER."

He permitted himself the semblance of a smile.

"OH WE CAN HANDLE THE CHINK. EVEN WITH HIS MUMBO JUMBO."

"YES. I'M SURE YOU CAN."

"MUMBO JUMBO NEVER STOPPED COLD STEEL."

"THAT IS TRUE." I reflected on Kuang and Liu and *their* cold steel. "WELL CAPTAIN, YOU HAVE BEEN MOST COOPERATIVE. PERHAPS NOW I HAVE SOME NEWS FOR YOU."

His eyes lifted.

"PERHAPS YOU WOULD CARE TO CONVERSE IN A BIT MORE COMFORT," he suggested. "PERHAPS SHARE A CANTEEN OF TEA?"

"WHY THANK YOU, THAT WOULD BE A BIT MORE LIKE IT AFTER THE DAY I'VE SPENT."

"FOLLOW ME, SIR."

He entered the car, I right behind. We walked down the aisle, passing the stalwart rescuers of the countries he had mentioned, all of whom glanced at me then away with diplomatic awareness. I sensed quickly that they ranged from old China-hands to spanking new arrivals from Manila, Hong Kong, Port Arthur, Shantung, Formosa and perhaps even Genoa and Marseilles. Whitmore paused at the front seats where four officers were standing.

"Gentlemen," he intoned, 'this is Mr. Norris Blake, a journalist from the New York *World*." I sighed but did not interrupt and he said, "Mr. Blake will report on our labours out here and also has some information which may prove of interest. Mr. Blake, may I present Captain Searington."

The British officer stepped forward and shook my hand.

"Lieutenant Borodofsky," said Whitmore.

The Russian stomped forward in his great boots. Cossack, I told myself, assaying the steppe of a face. We shook hands.

"Lieutenant Boncoeur."

Clicking his heels, the Frenchman bowed. I, too.

"Lieutenant Tujama."

The tiny Japanese saluted at an odd horizontal angle. He was really quite natty in his western-style uniform, although it was several sizes too large. *Wojen*—midget enemy—I found myself thinking, with some surprise.

"Shall we sit down, gentlemen?" suggested the American.

We did so. The captain picked up a canteen and a mess cup and poured from one to the other, then handed it to me. The tea was cool and strong. I swigged again; yes, the tang of rum.

Quickly I reflected on the potages our troops around the world stored in their army issue and came up with pineapple juice, cocoanut milk, sugar cane distillate, and of course rye and corn whiskey. "Thank you," I said, handing him the cup. "That was most refreshing." He passed the cup to an orderly and waved him away.

"And now," he said, "what news?"

As they all assumed the controlled alert, I leaned back and replied, "The Boxers have torn up the Paotingfu line."

A lightning glance of concern flashed around the group, which I must say I enjoyed.

"The telegraph line alongside the railway," I added, "has been cut."

Another flash. I continued:

"Bridges, stations, factories, stores, all the way up to Fengtai have been burned or smashed."

A moment of silence, then, "A pwetty kettew of fish," murmured the Briton in the upper class British manner. It rather resembled what the Chinese did with l's and r's, a fact I found oddly congruent, though at the moment I had no appropriate use for it; therefore I filed it away for the future, since a reporter, like the economical housewife uses everything, wastes nothing.

"Yes," I said, "Fengtai was, or by now, will be destroyed."

"Sacré bleu!" ejaculated *le français.* Even the phlegmatic Whitmore evinced some unhappiness. Each, in his national way, reflected on my report. I perceived reminiscence, speculation, comparison, sadness, joy, determination, outrage. Finally the Briton:

"Wewr gentewmen," he exclaimed, "I expect we can handew the fiwthy beggahs."

A moment of inner translation and he was followed up by grunts of assent. At which point I stood.

"I have not the slightest doubt that you can," I agreed. "And so now I must take my leave."

"You are not accompanying us into the city?" asked Whitmore.

"Thank you, no. I prefer to nose about on my own hook. It is a peculiarity of the trade. And my horse is still running alongside, I must see to him."

"Yes of course."

All rose.

"I am pleased and honoured to know you gentlemen," I said. "As will be all America. Although I know you do not need it, I wish you luck in your Christian endeavors."

They bowed, clicked, saluted, murmured and tightened the upper lip.

"I'll see you out," offered Whitmore.

"Thank you."

I turned and with the captain behind me, strode down the aisle. When I came to the platform I turned back and held out my hand. He grasped it.

"Give them hell," I smiled, "you and the other hairy devils."

"Never fear," he answered solemnly. "By the way, you may have need of this." He took out his order book, tore off a sheet of paper and dashed something across it. "This will assure you safe passage," he said, "right up to Mr. Conger." He handed it to me. I folded it and slipped it into the pocket of my tunic.

"That is very kind of you," I said, "Although frankly I like to worm my own way into the sanctum sanctorums."

"As you wish." He nodded. "Well, I see your horse awaits you."

"Once again, captain, *au revoir* and good luck."

"Good luck to *you*, Mr. Blake."

Resting on a rear leg, his left hand on his sword, he threw me a careless salute. I returned it, then vaulted over the rail and landed lightly on the platform step. Judging Herald's pace and tempo, I hoisted my weary but obedient form into space. The cooperative fellow settled under me. I leaned over and untied the reins, pulled sharply at them and clucked at him. The train pulled ahead.

"Oh by the way," I shouted, "where are you from?"

He did not answer for the briefest of moments. Then:

"Manasquan, New Jersey. With a *Q*."

I waved. The train with its still, blue figure, shot away to do the devil's own business.

The vast plain. Gradually sloping upward. Disappearing into the mountains of Mongolia. I am alone. No, not alone. I and my trusty partner, shiny, foam-flecked. We walk. Past tombs, some most noble. Through thickets of green cedar where we pause to cool down. We continue on, past another tomb, huge, grand, an empress's? It is enclosed in marble gates and stands beside a white stele. All are reflected in a fine, limpid pool. But is it a pool, or our imagination, or a Boxer trick? Herald ignores frowning ancestors, strides in and fetlock deep, proves it is no trick. I get down beside him and douse myself with the liquid that will forever surpass tea or for that matter scotch whiskey. Side by side then, we walk on.

Still no sign of Peking. But I am not surprised. Yang, our man of the river, had explained: "Peking does not shout out its presence. It stays quiet and suddenly reaches out for you. You know you are there when you feel it reaching out." This suits me quite well. Patiently we walk toward the out-reach, neither anticipating nor denigrating, trained as I am by years of coming upon the magnificent and awful places of the world, though admittedly none so rare as those of the Middle Kingdom. Again the empty plain. Again the tombs. Then again the plain. All the afternoon. Trudging steadily onward.

We round a bend. And there it is.

A great crenelated mass, floating on clouds of dust.

"Peking, old boy," I confide to my companion.

He is impassive.

Very well. We walk just a bit faster. Toward a city that is quite without visible foundation. Why this is indeed magical! Despite my professional sang froid, I am rather impressed. It is still six or nine *li* off, but the oriental air, or is it the magic dust? imparts a telescopic aspect to my vision and I can make out in perfect detail carvings and claws and horns. They all belong to fantastical beasts which grow in size as we draw nearer. Chimeras, dragons, unknown monsters. They glisten in the clarifying air. While above all tower the triumphal arches, carved against the sky with delicate grace, containing masses of the aforementioned beasts. Now I can see houses up there, whose upper stories are covered with a fine golden lace. Fancy open woodwork and at the top the ever-present rows of gargoyles and gilded dragons. A black stele with gold letters towers yet above the houses. Now at last, through the dust-fog, I see a wall and a huge gate. Topping the gate, to its right, the golden rotunda of, yes, the Temple of Heaven! The map of Peking which is printed in my head now settles over this floating city. My mind's eye gazes down from a hovering balloon. I see two walled, antagonistic cities, a pair of huge quadrilaterals lying angrily cheek by jowl. The ruling Tartar City is atop the native Chinese City, as befits its status. I squeeze the gas from my balloon, descend and alight. I walk toward the Chinese City.

"Well Herald," I say, "here is the eye of the storm."

This time he snorts. I pat him. He is dry and cool now. Somehow, I think, it is inappropriate to enter Peking on foot. I halt my friend, I swing into the saddle. Sitting very straight, I walk him toward the gate. The Yung Ting Men. I can see now the roof of the Heavenly Temple, blue enamel beneath the golden rotunda. Now I can also see that I am not alone. Huge dust clouds roll off to the east and emerging out of this scrim is a caravan of Mongolian camels, their legs hidden in the dust so that they seem to be swimming in the air, also donkey carts, whose wheels, too, are hidden so that they glide magically to the city.

I break Herald into a canter and head for the leading dust clouds. Each step helps me pierce the mist, until I can discern faces and forms. First in line is one of the ludicrous animals, topped by a man, his roll of baggage and a hump, all swaying awkwardly but steadily forward. Behind him is an open cart. I can make out chairs and the upturned legs of a table. Sitting on one of the chairs is an old woman with the reins in her hands. Beside her a young girl and beside her a younger boy. The other carts are also filled with sticks of furniture and bundles and blankly forlorn faces. I have seen enough of the world's wars to recognize the fleeing victims.

I gallop to the first cart. The poor old woman starts in fear at the sight of this apparition materializing from the dust. The girl places a protective arm about her.

"Do not be afraid, granny," I say in Mandarin. "I will not harm you."

She appears even more frightened at the sound of my words in her native tongue. The girl strokes her hair. It is a gesture I have seen among the immigrant groups in New York, though rarely, alas, in my circle. I smile approvingly. She is perhaps 18 or 19, very bedraggled, quite nondescript, yet if cleaned up and properly dressed not, I judge, without character, or indeed attractiveness, if that idea could be applied to the oriental female and I see no reason why it could not.

"Where are you from?" I enquire.

"Near Tung Chou."

"What are you doing here?"

"*I Ho Chuan.*"

So, I conjecture, they are on *that* side of the fence, only some 35 *li* east of Peking. Perhaps my friend Kuang Yu. Well well.

"You are Christian?" I ask.

"Converts."

I really did not believe, I think dryly, that you were born to the faith, but of course say no such thing. Rather, I ask:

"Do you have friends in Peking?"

"An uncle and an aunt."

"That is good."

"Yes, that is good."

She has spunk. I like that. I reach into the pocket of my tunic and draw out Whitmore's safe passage.

"If you have difficulty with the guards, or anyone else among the foreigners, present this and ask for Mr. Conger." I hand her the note, wondering suddenly if this is another western gaffe, but she takes it without a word and slides it into her sleeve. She does not thank me, but then I did not expect it. Well. I tip my hat.

"I hope . . ." I clear my throat. "I hope . . . you are not too saddened by the war."

I swing Herald about and gallop for the city. Another quarter of a mile and I am standing before the main gate.

The sentries looked down and challenged me. I identified myself in both English and Mandarin, but they still seemed hesitant, so I tossed them each a tael. The gate swung open and I entered. Ahead of me stretched a road which apparently bisected the native city. On each side of the road were red walls. Beyond them woods of cedar. To my left was the Temple of Agriculture. To my right, enclosed in double walls, the Temple of Heaven. I started down the road toward the Tartar City.

It was most tempting, as I passed the famous and sacrosanct edifice, to pause and attempt entry, unapproachable though I knew it to be. Indeed, the emperors themselves only came once a year to perform their solemn rites of purification. Perhaps if this had been royalty's time I should have attempted it for an interview. But I had other and more worldly business in hand, so I resisted the impulse and continued on, past the golden dome, the blue enamel roof, the white marble esplanade and the Imperial Path that led to these upper reaches of grace, an inclined path of marble that was embossed by clawed dragons so that the holy, silk-encased feet would not backslide.

I passed other enclosures containing secondary temples and their surrounding woods of cedar, arbor vitae and willow; here and there wisps of smoke wafted skyward, dispensing sweet-smelling incense to the gods. Then the familiar gray plain returned. We picked our way across it. Far ahead were other travelers. I shifted in the saddle; the head of my war-ravaged caravan was now visible. I sighed for it and turned back. For some two miles we walked, passing through no suburbs, only the great plain that led to the living city. This loomed up ahead, now at last beginning to take shape in its lower regions. One could imagine that a roll of gauze bandage had been drawn across it up to the halfway point; above was the splendid crystal portion, behind the gauze the murky foundations, as if the Chinese City, suddenly shy about its earthier parts, had daintily veiled them. Now, too, the uninhibited sounds of an oriental native quarter floated out to my ears. The quarreling voices, the fishmongery, the cry of the peddler, the buzz and hum of the quiet people all mingled in the still air. This rich mixture of sound grew ever louder as I approached a white marble arched bridge. This, I knew from my mental map, was the real gate to the Chinese City. For this was the famous, or infamous, Bridge of Beggars. And as if to proclaim itself to this scout of western world, there were its namesakes, arrayed in their tattered ranks across the span, hands outstretched, their voices cawing piteously high above the city noises.

I looked neither to the right or left. Nor did Herald. He had been well trained; as though he had spent his life avoiding them, he stepped neatly through and around. They parted like bending wheat sheaves, whining after me, shuffling along behind. But I knew that just one act of generosity on my part and they would be transformed into a pack of snarling jackals. I had made that mistake my first day in Manila.

I felt a hand on my saddle.

I looked down at the perpetrator of such a presumption.

Our British officer of the guard would have called him a fiwthy, cheeky beggah and he would have been correct on all counts. The individual who grinned toothlessly up at me was quite the most villainous piece of goods it had ever been my good fortune to view. For reporters crave extreme cases and this person was the end product of all extremity. Calmly I halted my uneasy horse. Calmly I met the shameless gaze. Contrary to his expectation, I did not ask him what he wanted; I knew only too well. Instead I said in Chinese:

"And who are you?"

The black excavation widened. One eye had a small white ball in its center; the other regarded me shrewdly.

"A king," he responded.

"The king of beggars?"

That brought him up short.

"You have heard of me?" he asked.

"Of course. Who has not heard of the king of beggars?"

The fellow then showed wit, I'll grant him that:

"Then you must know," he said, "that I am the poorest of the poor, the sickest of the sick." His rubber face flowed dramatically

144

about the cavern of his mouth. I merely held my ground and granted him one word:

"Pity."

The shrewd eye clouded over, the face contracted in sorrow.

"Ah sir," he wailed, "you are rich. I can tell from your fine bearing and imperious manner, so you will not miss the scraps you throw me from your overflowing pail."

A clever little speech, if you analyzed it, which I did post haste. As I did, the others began to crowd about me; I longed suddenly for some of the sweet incense I had recently sniffed, or even some good thick dust. The beggar king was holding firmly onto the pommel; the situation looked anything but promising. I smiled and hunched my shoulders in apparent resignation. Then I reached dramatically into my moneybag, drew out several taels and held them up. The collection of misery ahhh'd. I reached down to the poorest of the poor, the sickest of the sick and he reached up, graspingly. Suddenly I straightened and flung the coins with all my might far back over my head. There ensued a moment of absolute and silent confusion. Followed by a great thudding of feet and the band was rushing off behind me; I could hear the scramble and snarl of the jackal pack. A pack, however, sans leader. That (un)worthy stood fast at my pommel. The moment, I then decided, required a much more direct approach.

"You look-see," I began in pidgin English. "If you no go chop chop," and with that I placed a foot against the bony chest and exerted firm and unmistakable pressure. "You savee?"

If I had never seen fear and venom mixed in equal parts in a man's face, I saw them now. The baleful eye narrowed. He drew back.

"Melican?" he rasped.

"Maybe yes, maybe no," I shrugged. "Me no talkee you."

He stiffened in his kingly pride. With that I tapped Herald's flanks and away we clattered, over the bridge and into the Chinese City. I did not look back; I had not the least doubt but that a near-century's worth of hatred for the westerner sped me on my way.

All of the sights that had been small and perfect from a distance were now exactly sized and equally perfect. On either side of the street down which I rode, the houses stood in oriental splendour, displaying for my edification their golden facades, their carvings, gargoyles, chimeras and dragons. The dust screen was here drawn away as if it were a theatre curtain, to reveal these features in all their intricate detail. Twas very clearly the upper-class section of the city and the people who padded about were well and sombrely gowned, going about their business with a hushed dignity that to me oddly resembled our Fifth Avenue. Businessmen, scholars, clerks glided about in their soft boots and now and then a mandarin, with his truculent retinue, walked haughtily by; the crowd halted, parted, he passed through and they closed ranks and continued as before. On either side of the street, intermingling with the golden buildings were the shops of this Fifth Avenue; within the cool, dark interiors, their owners, tradesmen from birth in this country, were waiting patiently for customers, doubtless counting their sapeks.

I passed under the fantastically decorated triumphal arches, which recalled days of past glory, an ironic touch when I considered the ruling city toward which I rode. As was (and is) my wont I studied the citizenry that swirled about me; they did not reciprocate. Indeed I felt that the blank eyes were strenuously averted from my curious ones and had I been a tyro in this business I might easily have supposed that blankness also filled the area behind those eyes. If so, I would surely have been mistaken; every experience I had undergone since stepping onto Chinese soil shouted: *au contraire!* I nodded agreeably to my inner self and continued to look, nay to *observe.* And in so doing came upon a collection of evidence that supported this conclusion, the conclusion that said, yes indeed, there is more here than meets (or did not meet) the eye.

I had come to a large intersection. Let us call it the Sino Herald Square (for a number of reasons, least of all the one I bestrode). On impulse I turned to the left, hoping, if possible to inspect a less fashionable area. A few steps and I was rewarded almost before my senses had prepared me for the change. Adjusting quickly, I peered in fascination (and evaluation) at my new setting. Twas as if I had just pierced a beautiful but insubstantial outer layer and had now come to the core of the matter. Back here was the rough and ready city, the rough and tumble city, the south-of-14th-Street city. The sounds that had been muffled by the adorning veneer now rose up in all their pushcart cacaphony: anger, humour, argument, excitement, complaint, disgust, derision, cajolery, resistance, insistence, delight, interrogation, response. I somehow felt relieved. This was the China I knew, the China of the bustling treaty port cities, or at least the native quarter of those cities. Shanghai, Canton, Amoy, Foochow, Ningpo. (The treaty port area, of course, was a foreign island unto itself, much like the Tartar City in this instance.) Houses here were ramshackle, some barely deserving of the title. In and out of them, inhabitants engaged in the petty but endearing acts of everyday existence; for comparison, I urge the reader to stroll through our own little Italy. They were all here: the rascal, the reformer, farmer, bumpkin, soldier, common and uncommon thief, coolie, opium smoker. Ill-clad urchins scurried everywhere, drawn by this bit of excitement, that great discovery, their thin faces not yet filled with blankness, but touched with the shrewdness of the city young everywhere who had been thrust too early into this world. Yet, with all this activity, groups of men stood about in apparent idleness, seeming to wait for something, they knew not what. They looked at me with a dull hostility as I rode by. It struck me that a Boxer torch could easily ignite these ready-mades, and sure enough, as I passed an open field, there they were, some 50 of them, going through their familiar gymnastic paces. Another large group, including the urchins, stood by, watching intently, and at certain points, as in our football matches, breaking into applause and shouting words of approval and encouragement. The surprising thing to me was that it was all quite open and above board. I saw no soldiers, police or any other figure of authority that might halt the proceedings or at least challenge them. If Whitmore and his guards knew of this, I began to tell myself, but stopped right

there as the inevitable conclusion to the thought was quite un-
settling. And if I'd had any doubts about the nature of the gyra-
tions in that field, I soon received enlightenment. It came some
distance further on and it was nailed to a pole. My second Boxer
placard. Much as I believe in constant motion in touch-and-go
territories, the reporter in me bade me stop and read. I did so:

SACRED EDICT
Issued by the Lord of Wealth and Happiness
The Catholic and Protestant religions being insolent to the gods
and extinguishing sanctity, rendering no obedience to Buddhism
and enraging both Heaven and Earth, the rain-clouds now no
longer visit us; but 8,000,000 Spirited Soldiers will descend from
Heaven and sweep the Empire clean of all foreigners. Then will
the gentle showers once more water our lands: and, when the
tread of soldiers and the clash of steel are heard, heralding woes
to all our people, then the Buddhist's Patriotic League of Boxers
will be able to protect the Empire and bring peace to all its people.
Hasten, then, to spread this doctrine far and wide; for if you
gain one adherent to the faith, your own person will be absolved
from all future misfortunes. If you gain five adherents to the
faith, your whole family will be absolved from all evils; and if you
gain ten adherents to the faith, your whole village will be absolved
from all calamities. Those who gain no adherents to the cause shall
be decapitated; for until all foreigners have been exterminated,
the rain can never visit us. Those who have been so unfortunate
as to have drunk water from wells poisoned by foreigners should
at once make use of the following Divine Prescription, the ingredients of which are to be decocted and swallowed, when the
patient will recover:
Dried black plums . . . half an ounce
Solanum dulcamara . . . half an ounce

I read and reread. Then I took out pad and pencil and set it
down exactly as I have reproduced it here, including the business
of the purging diuretics. And again, despite my enforced detachment, I felt some of the same symptoms of excitement and fear
(freely confessed) that I had experienced on seeing my first placard
in Taku. Indeed I must have sunk into a reverie of sorts, wherein
the words played havoc with my imagination, for on coming
to with a start, I realized that the group of idlers and their insolent

148

pups had begun to drift my way. Taking discretion to be the only part of valor, I gently tapped Herald into a slow walk and guided him firmly through the neer-do-wells and back toward the intersection. I heard some unflattering muttering, yet resisted the impulse to fly, which in these cases can be the explosive spark. My steed and I performed well. In a few minutes we were amongst the solid citizens of Fifth Avenue. We both snorted our relief; my good friend broke into a brisk canter. From here it was but three quarters of a mile to the Chien Men, the main gate to the Tartar City. Western faces, western voices, western ways. I applied the spurs.

The Chien Men was really a hole in a wall. A massive black hole in a massive gray wall. Looming above the wall were black dungeons, five stories high, capped by curved roofs that seemed to impart a curious softness to the grim purpose of the structures. Oddly enough, considering the situation, traffic passed in and out without interference or question, but then I had long since learned that paradox was endemic to this curious land. So without asking anyone's permission, I too entered the hole. It turned out to be an amazingly thick one, really a triple tunnel and what with the press of humanity, animals and carts, it took a good several minutes to proceed through the darkness and emerge, thankfully, into the glow of twilight.

If they had set me down blindfolded out of the Gobi desert and whipped the bandage from my eyes, there would still be no mistaking my new setting. And like an eager child I drank it all in. The Tartar City. The Manchu City. The ruling city. The foreign city. It was this last which dominated here just inside the main gate. One could see many more intersections than in the native city and the streets running off them set up the familiar gridiron pattern of a New York or a Paris. I was suddenly so delighted with this homecoming that I advanced a little way down each street smiled, stopped, looked, listened, then returned, only to repeat the performance at the next corner. The thing that struck me with the greatest force was the sheer number of jinrickshas that went scurrying by, carrying their "long nose" burden. The western world was going home, or visiting, or merely taking the air. Some few hardy souls were even doing all three on *foot!* I looked for the natives; aside from the coolies, none to be found; they had melted away, into the gate, into the servants' quarters. There was no question but that this was the important quarter (for "important" one may substitute "foreign") of a great city. But this was an inland city, so, unlike the great treaty ports, one saw none of the hallmarks of Western trade commingled with the local adaptation: the aptly named godowns, or warehouses, with their bustling compradores, the Portuguese word for Chinese overseer, or the cool, brisk taipans, the foreign managers. No, this was the diplomatic metropolis, (pre)occupied with the business of most favoured nations and extraterritoriality, rather than their practice. And the heart of such business, as the world has since learned with fascination and horrified edification, was the Legation Quarter.* After satisfying myself with the comforting aspects of my new ambiance, I returned to the main street and walked Herald east at the first intersection and into this famous, indeed legendary, area.

I found myself, as luck—or more likely intuition—would have it, on Legation Street, soon to be the cynosure of cynosures. The legation guards would have long since preceded me; in fact I would not have been at all surprised if some of the stalwart figures standing along my route were among their number. I first passed the Dutch Legation, then the Russian. At the latter I asked a concave Cossack face which was the way to the American Legation, but received only puzzlement as I said, American? United States? U.S.? and Uncle Sam? Only receiving the pointing arm and the smile on enquiring for "Melican housee."

I walked across the street and several yards on and there I saw the stars and stripes floating gently in a pretty garden. I dis-

---

* One could argue that it lay in the Forbidden City specifically on the Peacock Throne. I suggest that reality has proven otherwise.

mounted and tied Herald to a little iron dragon. Two soldiers stood at their ease at the legation entrance. I walked up to them and said, "I am Norris Blake, a newspaper reporter for the *World* and I should like to see Mr. Conger."

They snapped to a semblance of attention and one said, with the syrup of Dixie in his voice, "Ahm verr sorry, suh, the ministuh is seein no one."

"Then," I rejoined, "I will see Captain Whitmore."

That produced the desired effect. They looked uneasily at each other and the confederate nodded. His comrade about-faced and disappeared around the corner of the building, which in actuality was a good-sized Chinese house decorated with the now familiar monsters. He was back on the double, Captain Whitmore beside him. The captain was buttoning his collar.

"Ah Mr. Blake," he said gravely.

"Hello, Captain, I see you beat me here."

"By some two hours."

"I took some time to reconnoiter the area. I saw a few things that perhaps you fellows should be looking into."

"Yes. Of course. What can I do for you, Mr. Blake?"

"I wonder if I might have a few words with Mr. Conger?"

He consulted a pocket watch.

"It is close to the dinner hour," he said.

"How well I know. However, Captain, I would greatly appreciate it if you would tell him I am here and that Joseph Pulitzer has been following his situation with great interest and then leave it to him as to whether or not he will see me."

The watch shut with a resounding snap. Whitmore turned on his heel and entered the house. In two shakes of a dragon's tail he was back, with a tall, smiling party alongside, whose hand was at the diplomatic ready.

"Well well, Mr. Blake," enthused the owner of the gladhand which pumped mine as if going for water, "so good of you to come. How is Joseph? I have read your dispatches from the Philippines with no little admiration."

"He is well. Thank you. And I yours."

"A bit stiff. A bit stiff. But that is our trade."

"On the contrary, fascinating, if one reads between the lines. That is why my first thought on entering the Tartar City was to see you straightaway. I knew that would have been Mr. Pulitzer's express desire."

"And mine, too. I assure you, mine, too. Come along, you must dine with me. Whitmore, show Mr. Blake where he can clean up a bit. I'm sure you can do with a bath, sir."

"Indeed I can," I retorted, smiling obliquely at the captain. "That would be most refreshing after the day I've had. Perhaps Captain Whitmore has told you of my brush with the Boxers?"

He glanced at the captain, who looked his discomfort.

"Indeed? Well well, Whitmore, looks as if the pen is seeing more action than the sword."

"We were on the train, sir," mumbled the captain.

"Yes, of course, the train. Show Mr. Blake to a guest room, please."

"Yes sir," sighed the poor fellow.

It was half-past eight by the time I had bathed and rested up a bit. When I descended, Conger, a portly young man and Whitmore were sitting at table. They all found their legs as I entered the room.

"Well, you look a new man," said Edwin H. Conger. "Not," he added diplomatically, "that there was anything the matter with the old. May I present my secretary, Prouty."

"How do you do, Mr. Prouty," I said with a bow. "And where in our great country do you hail from?"

He looked at the minister who nodded almost imperceptibly.

"Evanston, Illinois," he responded.

"A suburb of Chicago. I know it well. A lovely town."

"Why yes," he said. "Chicago." This a bit dreamily. Well, I thought, the old homesickness; twas still a useful lever.

We dined then. A delicious repast, done in high Chinese style, my first civilized food since dining with General MacArthur on Luzon and that seemed centuries ago. Conger was quite expansive and under my innocent guidance, aided and abetted by some excellent American bourbon, he painted a picture that seemed much more grim than his confident words warranted. True, there had already been a brisk fight between the Russians and the Boxers near Tientsin, true that the Fists of Chihli were mightily stirred up over the incident, true that the Dowager Empress was backing and filling and in the long run kowtowing to them, true that Prince Tuan was also on their side—by this time I was looking askance at Prouty, who was staring at the frescoed ceiling; Conger went rambling on: But of course now that our soldiers and marines were here, all was well in hand. Prouty now took in the walls. Monsieur Pichon, the French minister, said Conger, was much too alarmist, eh, Prouty?

"I would say so, sir," said Prouty in a small voice.

I added that voice and Whitmore's eyes to my growing arsenal and continued to probe, pick, lead and guide. By the time I took my leave, I was ready for the major question. Asked pointblank as the secretary handed me my pith helmet:

"What do you think, Prouty, are we in for it?"

He stirred uneasily and said, "Will I be named, sir?"

"No. I give you my word. Merely as an unimpeachable source."

He smiled, albeit weakly.

"Then yes, we *are* in for it."

With that under my hat, simmering in my brain, and declining Conger's generous offer to put me up, I left the legation. I preferred, nay was anxious, to get my nose into less official places, so off I went to the Peking Hotel close by the Japanese Legation. There a pointed use of the minister's name produced a very nice chamber on the second floor rear, facing onto the French Legation. I was really quite fortunate since the hotel was filling rapidly with mission people from the nearby districts. I saw to Herald, then directed my clothes to be washed. Then I smoked one of the American cigarettes the minister had given me, all the while sitting at the window and looking out at the softly glowing town. The parties, the dances, would now be in full swing. Beautiful gowns, splendid uniforms, high stiff collars would be whirling their way toward the oriental dawn. The last thing I saw before climbing onto the soft bed and settling into a deep but troubled sleep were the two white-marble monsters that guarded the French Legation, gleaming fiercely in the starlight.

And now events pressed in on us from every side and with breathtaking speed. Alarums, excursions, *yao-yen,* that word that so well proclaims its meaning: rumours. How they flew about us from all sides and how they multiplied in geometric progression, only to fly out again, replenish themselves and return. The only way I can re-capture the exact nature of all that occurred is to refer to my journal (if my employer will excuse the use of that term) and present for the reader's edification my thoughts, actions and impressions that mirrored so faithfully what transpired in those hectic days. I should also mention that these sentences have never before appeared in print.

June 3—Today the German and Austrian guards arrived. Very appropriate as the kaiser and the emperor are always hand in glove. The spiked helmets are rather ludicrous, but most impressive to the natives, and, of course, reassuring to our side. The Teuton does inspire confidence, I'll give him that. At 3 P.M., also known as the hour of the Monkey, I had a remarkable conversation with Baron Von Ketteler, the German minister, who assures me the Tsungli Yamen will now be totally reasonable.* With no lack of modesty, the baron delivers his monologue for a good 50 minutes. At that point comes a knock at the door, the baron bellows *Kum,* an aide enters and reports that the Peking–Tientsin railway has been cut at Huangtsun, some 60 *li* distant. Needless to say, this concludes the interview.

June 4—I held a remarkable conversation with Sir Claude Mac-Donald, the English minister. He assures me that the situation is completely in hand. He then invites me to a cricket match on the legation grounds, the guards vs. the diplomatic staff. He exhibits choler only when the guards draw ahead.

* Alas, on June 19, on his way to the Yamen, the baron was shot to death by a Chinese soldier.

June 5—I spent the morning wandering back and forth across the canal that splits the Legation Quarter. At 10 A.M. visited the Peking Club where members discuss the Grand National, the Bourse, favourite restaurants, Dreyfus, the situation in Pretoria in the South African War. Lt. Blumenstein, a Dutchman, and Capt. Fitzmaurice, Briton, are pried apart by their comrades after exchanging views on that conflict. The ministers expressly forbid a duel, so both men retire to quarters. Much muttering. At one o'clock, the hour of the Horse, I walked to the Mongol Market behind the Russian Legation; the wives were buying up great quantities of food; in times of trouble always observe the wives.

June 6—This morning I had a most remarkable conversation with M. Pichon, the French minister. This is a man who understands the journalistic function, although he thinks *Le Figaro* represents the apogee of the art. He directs his secretary to see we are not disturbed. He then talks, off the record, on the record, *ça ne fait rien*. With utmost gravity he tells me that he is concerned, most concerned. He recalls well how China fought in '84, which should forever put the lie to the belief that she is a helpless giant. We were, he says, *tout à fait* beaten on the land. Had it not been for our navy, and, he adds modestly, our diplomacy, we should never today have Indo China. He fears that repetition of that success on land is entirely possible. He shows me letters from a Bishop Favier, who each day sees the Boxers rising and enlarging their "sphere of influence." This last with a bitter laugh. The Bishop is in mortal fear that his cathedral is next on the list of destruction. Tis no surprise to me that M. Pichon was the first minister to call up his guards. He then gives me a thorough assessment of the situation, including facts and figures which show conclusively that we are outnumbered *50 to one*. Meanwhile, he says, *les Anglais*, and he places his head on his hands and snores. I laugh with him, but ruefully. As I take my leave I ask if I may change the subject and ask a rather personal question.

"But of course."

"Where do you stand on the Dreyfus matter?"

"Foursquare."

"Should Dreyfus have been pardoned?"

"The Boxers are a terrible threat to the security of western interests."

He bows me out.

June 7—This morning I mingled with the common man. Namely the guards—in their barracks, at the hotel bar, in the streets, at the post office, in the bank, in the gardens, in the park. Their conversation falls into four categories: The quality of their mess, alcoholic beverages, the desire to "get a chink," Chinese women. Most of the talk sooner or later focuses on the latter subject. There is much speculation in each language as to whether or not "it" is true. This "it," it turns out, is the slanted or unslanted direction of a particular organ of erotic reputation. . . .

At 2 P.M. I left my quarters, walked north on Great Eastern Street, past the Belgian Legation and continued on to the Tsungli Yamen. The exotic, the mysterious, the sinister inner sanctum. To my great surprise I was passed through and graciously received by none other than Li Hung Chang, the respected, aged Mandarin, who is well known for his pro-western views. I speculate that the E.D. or Prince Tuan has sent orders for the famous journalist to be flattered, cajoled and otherwise led down the eastern primrose path. *Quel naïveté!* Yet the quavering old fellow is oddly disarming; with deep emotion and in a delicate English accent, of which he is obviously very proud, he tells me of his unbounded admiration for Generals Grant and Gordon, whom he knew very well and who, he maintains with great emphasis, will always be lessons of great inspiration to all right-thinking Chinese. He is quite certain that all will be sorted out. As Pichon would say: *pauvre innocent.*

June 8—Great excitement! The residents of Tung Chou, only 30 miles to the east on the Pei Ho, have fled to this haven. Their eyes are wide with fear, their mouths pinched with the same emotion. *Yao-yen,* the rumour factory, is working overtime. And now we learn that Prince Tuan has been appointed President of the Tsungli Yamen. Which only makes it official, since he, who is ruled by the ancient concubine, has been the ministry ruler for weeks. This day, I am sure, MacDonald will not be watching his beloved cricket; Li

156

Hung Chang will be ill with remorse.* There is now a great rush by all foreign families to the legation neighborhood where they are kindly received by the various officials. The American Methodist Mission is packed to the walls.

June 9—Early this A.M. I attempted to walk again to the Tsungli Yamen, this time to interview Prince Tuan. I am stopped. I send a message in Mandarin requesting an audience. In a note back to me, in *English,* he refuses my request, stating that he is too busy, doing all in his power to stem further foreign incursions! I consider trying the E.D. However, she: maternal, kind, august, protecting, peaceable, fostering, glorious, indulgent, grave, sincere, respectable, pious, proud, wise and brilliant—Holy Mother of the Great Ts'ing Empire, is surely singlehandedly holding the *I Ho Chuan* at bay.* I walk back to the hotel bar.

June 10—At last! By telegram we learn that Admiral Sir Edward Seymour has come ashore at Taku with some 500 British sailors and marines. He has proceeded to Tientsin and his column has been reinforced to almost 2,000 by Americans, Germans, Russians, French, Japanese, Dutch, Italians and more British. Relief is on the way! Today is my birthday. 34. Troy, New York, is the moon. I drink two glasses of scotch whiskey at the hotel bar. The American soldier beside me, Tom Cruikshank, of Dover, Delaware, confides that yes, it does slant.

June 11—More dark deeds: Last night the British summer legation in the western hills outside Peking was burnt to the ground. Today Mr. Sugiyama, chancellor of the Japanese Legation, a confident, bantam rooster of a man, was murdered at the main gate of the Chinese City. All ask what in the world he was doing there, considering the state of affairs? Alas, it is after the fact.

June 12—Seymour's column has reached Langfang, halfway between Tientsin and Peking. The news is brought to us by Hang Too Fon, a 16-year-old convert educated at the Episcopal mission

---

* He is to die just a year later. Of a broken heart?
* She would also, of course, lifting her robes, issue her famous and scandalous command. This correspondent would take the lance through the heart first.

157

in Tientsin. His information is mixed and in my opinion, mainly ominous. True, Seymour has advanced, but one train has gone back to Tientsin, so either the latter is in trouble, or he is, or both. And the brave Chinese courier says he heard gunfire ere he left and saw two men in red sashes fall. So at the very least Seymour has his hands full. We also learn that Prince Tuan has asked Sir Claude, now fully awake, to return the entire column to Taku. Need I record MacDonald's response?

June 13—The E.D. and Tuan have at last put their cards on the table, face up. They have ordered Yu Lu, that scalawag, to the railway to prevent Seymour's advance. This means open, unequivocal war. And about time. And as if a skyrocket had split the sky, the Boxers cut loose at this moment. They enter Peking and on the instant run amok, even worse than the crazed natives of Luzon. They burn the American Board Mission in the Chinese City. Also the south and east Catholic cathedrals. Reports rush to Prouty's office, thus to me. The following are also in ashes: the American Presbyterian Mission, the Society for the Propagation of the Gospel compound, the International Institute and the London Mission. Christian converts have been murdered in the most barbaric fashion. The flames of hell are singeing us here. Yet all is strangely calm.

June 14—Another convert has broken through to us. From Tientsin, a boy of 13, who proudly proclaims that his name is James. James what? Just James. What does he tell us? Merely that the foreign premises of Tientsin have been invaded! He has heard that heavy fighting is going on between Seymour's column and the Boxers, but when pressed, owns up that all this is *yao-yen*. Communication with Seymour has been broken off, so we are completely in the dark as to his fate. Or ours. Now the rumour factory, which has been closed for several days, breaks open, but with great fatalism. Strange how the Chinese character has unknowingly rubbed off on ours . . . A sally by the Boxers! It is repulsed at the Chien Men, the main gate . . . Vociferous argument this night at the bar between Whitmore and a British Captain Parkhurst: "Are we, or are we not under siege?"

158

June 15—This morning I awoke at the hour of the Snake. Nine
A.M. with a feeling of great foreboding, not unmixed with excitement. I breakfasted at the hotel, then walked down Legation Street
to the Melican house. The street was quiet, orderly. Had one not
known of the palpitating humanity that jampacked the various
buildings, one might have thought this a normal morning. One,
however, would have been quickly enlightened. A cry, a yell,
a command, a crack of gunfire, a western oath—of satisfaction or
frustration—and the reality of who and where and what and when
would hit home whilst why and how ran through a busy mind. Not
to mention, oh?

Having long since gained carte blanche to the legation I nodded
at the sentry and entered at 10 A.M. Went straightaway to the reli-
able and unimpeachable Prouty. He informed me that Yuan Shi
Kai, the wily governor of Shantung, had been ordered to Peking
with his army of 7,000, quite the most modern and best equipped
in China. The question of the hour, and the one we immediately
debated, was, considering Yuan's history, which side would he be
on? We discussed it pro and con, long and hard, then under the
convoluted dilemma of the oriental mind, gave it up as a fruitless,
not to say, exhausting exercise. I then retired to an upstairs study
which the minister had kindly turned over to me and where I composed my dispatch that covered the events of the previous day.
Since the doughty James, our courier, wished to return to his
beloved Tientsin, I would ask him to carry it there; the under-
ground convert system would somehow, I felt sure, contrive to get
it to Taku; once there, with Mr. Pulitzer drawing like a lodestone, it
must reach New York. Indeed it dare not do otherwise!

I was in the midst of the Tientsin invasion when I became aware
of a slight rustling sound. I vaguely ascribed it to the wind ruffling
the rice paper on the ceiling and continued to pursue my narrative
with characteristic intensity. Then once again I heard a clear and
louder repetition of the sound. Frowning, I raised my head. My
eyes first struck the clock over the paper lantern in the corner of
the room: twas 11:37 A.M. Then as though drawn along an airy
vector, my eyes moved to the door; there in corporeal though

159

slender reality stood the author of the sound. A Chinese girl. Covered from head to foot by a shabby gray cloak. She could not have been more than 18 or 19 years of age. She stood very still, very straight and her face was quite animated for a Chinese. I adjudged it so through fear as the pupils of her black eyes were two huge dark moons. She must, I thought, be a convert, who had been granted sanctuary by Prouty or even Mr. Conger.

"Do not be afraid," I said in my most soothing Chinese. "I will not harm you."

"I know you will not," she answered calmly in a low voice. She took one small step toward me. I peered over the rolltop desk. Of course, twas the poor girl of the caravan, the one who had fled here with her brother and granny.

"Well," I said, "so it is you." I smiled my encouragement. "I am happy that you arrived safely. And I see you have used my note to good advantage."

"I did not use your note," she retorted with, I thought, a touch of asperity. Their sense of face. I did not pursue the matter.

"And how is your granny?" I asked.

"She is well."

"And your brother?"

"He is well."

She took another tiny step. I found myself wondering if her feet could be bound. Yet, she did not seem high born. On the other hand, in the rush and press of war, who could tell prince from pauper? One thing was unmistakable: she was filled to the brim of her being with total fear.

"And how are the other members of your caravan?" I asked the poor child.

"Well. They are well. All are well."

"Ah splendid. All unhurt?"

"Unhurt. All unhurt. Well. All very well. Why do you chatter so, Norris Brake?"

"Eh?"

"Why do you go on and on and on?"

I laid my pencil down. She took three more dainty steps and

stood in the center of the room. Her dilated pupils were fixed on my confused ones. With a movement then of supreme grace, her hands flew to her throat, her shoulders lifted and in that instant the shabby cloak fell to the floor. She stepped over it. She stood now revealed in spectacular raiment: a white silk tunic, embroidered with huge flowers and gold chimeras; beneath this, blue silk trousers and soft white sandals.

"What in blazes . . . !" I ejaculated in English.

"Hush, Norris Brake. Must you talk so? Hush."

"I will *not* be silenced." This in Mandarin. "Who in the world are you? More to the point, what in the world are you?"

"I am," she responded simply, "a goddess of the *I Ho Chuan.*"

"You are *what?*"

"Why must I repeat everything? I have said who I am. Your fingers are not in your ears."

"Then," I began with a rising of the hairs along the nape of my neck, "that caravan . . . that was . . . a Boxer band . . ."

"Yes."

"My God!"

As soon as I uttered those words, in English, by the way, the most extraordinary thing in an extraordinary career took place: She practically flew to me and when she reached my person flung herself at my feet. Then she touched her forehead to my shoe three times. After which she looked up at me, her long neck arched like a swan's, her eyes suddenly and magically great daubs of lustrous gentian violet. Her pale lips parted, her voice was a throbbing purr as she said:

"How I have dreamed you would say that."

"Say what?" I enquired.

"That I am your god."

"But, that is merely a . . ." I cut myself short. The face gazing into mine was all at once the most exquisite I had ever encountered. Which included the niece of John Pierpont, as well as Mlle. Bernhardt. And twas certainly different from any other oriental face I had ever seen, giving the lie to the popular belief that they are all alike. I reached down and drew the graceful creature up to me.

"What is your name?" I asked gently in Chinese.

"Ah Soon," she replied.

"How did you know my name, Ah Soon?"

"I knew."

"Yes, but how did you—"

"I *knew*. Do not ask so much." She stamped the exquisite foot.

"Very well. If you wish."

"I wish it. I wish it." She sighed. "Do you think it is easy for me, coming here?"

"I should think not. The guards, the officials—"

"*That* is not what I meant! They are nothing. Nothing. It was myself that I had to fight, to overcome."

"Ah yes, I see . . ."

"How I fought you in my dreams, Norris Brake."

"Only to be . . . overcome?"

Again she sighed. I lightly brushed the silken hair.

"Yes," she said simply. "By a foreign devil."

"Is that," I vouchsafed softly, "what I am to you?"

"Yes. And no. All is confusion since I saw you at the gate."

"Poor sweet girl. I can see you have suffered."

"Do you think it is easy to kowtow to a foreign devil?"

"I know it cannot be. Poor girl."

"I am not your girl. I am a goddess."

"Yes. You are."

I slowly lowered my head to hers and placed my lips against her soft, full petals. I felt a tremor traverse the length of the surprisingly curved body. Then the body grew limp. Just on the point of swooning, I clasped it and her to my bosom. My strength seemed to course through her; she revived and pressed herself to me, her arms encircling my neck. Her eyes, those of a wounded faun, opened. We gazed in wonder at each other, then she drew my head down and applied a warm and insistent pressure to my lips. I was deeply touched. With the back of my hand I stroked the silken cheek. Perfumes of I know not what wonders encased my being. For the first time in my life, which included balloon travel and a transatlantic crossing on a clipper ship, I felt dizziness. I drew back until my head cleared. Then I enquired gently:

"Is it possible that a goddess can love?"

The enormous lashes brushed away a tear.

"I fear it is, Norris Brake. Now hush."

It occurred to me at that point in time that this magical faun was performing hitherto unfamiliar movements with her body and that my own body, almost without my knowing it, was responding in a like, yet complementary, manner. One of the encircling arms and and its soft hand had detached themselves from my neck and was now producing in my nether regions the most delicious and never-before-experienced sensations. I felt surely that I was being lifted up to a plane high above the one on which we stood, that from this great height I was then reaching down and raising my precious, clinging, undulating burden up to me. Entwined thus in the clouds we floated to a constellation of stars that was in the shape of an oriental chaise lounge. My reportorial self saw my familiar, moonlit hands unfolding smooth and shining garments, layer upon magnificent layer until exposed beneath those hands and the astonished eyes was a form that indeed dwelled on a Chinese Mount Olympus. Then, still on the chaise lounge, but barely aware that it existed, together we were rising up even beyond the clouds and the moon and the stars and a celestial symphony was swelling and falling and swelling within our transported selves . . .

"Norris Brake."

"Yes, Ah Soon."

"I have never known such ecstasy."

"Not even from the gods?"

"Not from gods or mortals."

"You have known other mortals?"

"Hush."

"But—"

"Hush."

"Very well. For your sake."

"Norris Brake."

"Yes."

"You are in danger here."

"Of course. We are all in danger."

"I do not care about all. I am speaking of you."

"Sweet gir—goddess."

"The Chien Men will burn tomorrow."

"It will?"

"And the southern city."

"That, too? But how do you know?"

"I know by who I am."

"Yes of course. What else will happen?"

"Taku will be shelled."

"Are you *sure*?"

"Yes, yes, I am sure."

"By whom?"

"By your Allies."

"My Allies?"

"Have I not said it?"

"But . . . I mean no offense, Ah Soon, but are you absolutely positive?"

"Please do not question me, my love."

"Forgive me. Taku will be shelled. Of that I am sure."

"I wish you to come with me, Norris Brake. You will be safe with me."

"Ah if I only could. Now that I have found you, I could wish nothing more than that. Alas, I have my responsibilities."

"Your responsibility is to me."

"In a certain sense, yes. But in another, it is to the world."

"What are you saying, Norris Brake? Remove the pebbles from your mouth."

"I am saying that I am a newspaper writer and I cannot shirk that fact. Therefore I cannot go with you."

"It is not a question of cowardice, then."

"Not at all. I would gladly be called a coward if it meant I could be with you. No, it is a duty assigned and a duty accepted."

"Ah how that rings in my ears. To know you would accept degradation for me."

"Gladly."

"And tis your duty which dictates otherwise."

"It is."

"Oh how I feared you would say that. And yet I knew it. For I, too, am bound by duty."

"Perhaps, Ah Soon, when this terrible conflict is over . . ."

"Ah you men of the west. Always perhaps and when."

". . . You have known other western men?"

"Hush."

"But—"

"Hush."

She drew me to her and although I did not think it possible after so short an interim, the celestial orchestra again crashed in ethereal waves about our enraptured selves. Upon our return to this earth, she said in a tight little voice:

"You will not join me, Norris Brake?"

"My dearest goddess, I cannot. It is torture for me to say it, but I cannot."

"I knew it. I knew it."

The pathetic creature found her perfumed legs. She replaced the exquisite garments and walked to the center of the room where lay the shabby cloak, all in a heap. With a movement of great dexterity, she swirled it into the air and about the sweet shoulders. She gazed at me for a moment, then walked to where I sat. With her long, pointed fingers, she made looping, darting motions above my head.

"You will be safe now," she said, her eyes glistening.

"And you?" I asked, touched to the quick.

"Yes," she sighed, "I will be sustained. When I lead my troops I will not be harmed."

"You lead troops?"

"Of course. I am a goddess."

"In truth you are. I'll vouch for that. An oriental Joan."

"Who is this Joan?"

"No matter. Just thinking aloud."

"You have known her? Do not tell me. Yes, tell me. No . . ."

"Dear one, she is nothing to me, I assure you."

"I believe you . . . Norris Brake?"

"What, my perfumed dearest?"

"Would you . . . ? Would you . . . ?"

Naturally I did as I was requested. I could do none other. When we had drunk our fill and the waves were in gentle retreat, she stood up and looked long and tenderly at me. Then without a word, but with what I perceived was a wrenching effort of celestial will, she drew herself together, turned and was gone.

I rode out that night, south for Taku. Not one person tried to stop me.

XIII

Are you happy now, hero?
  I am.
  There was no need for that, you know.
  Disagree. Much need.
  Christian, my boy, don't you see what you've done?
  I'm not your boy. And I've created an exquisite piece of work,
if you'll pardon the expression.
  Nonsense. You have compromised your artistic integrity. You
have grafted an externally compelled branch onto the trunk of your
truth.
  Bullshit.
  It is not worthy of you, Fletcher.
  Up thine with twine. You cannot torment me, I'm beyond you.
  Is that so? Tell me, did it slant?
  Animal!
  Did it?
  Monster with claws!
  Diagonal east? Diagonal west?

Gargoyle!

There. Very well, take it out. Cut it out. Exorcise it.

Je réfuse.

This is no game, Christian, I *command* you.

You can't command me. I am on Pitcairn Island. Far beyond your jurisdiction.

The whole thing is an abomination. For example, there is no historical evidence that the Dowager Empress ever practiced what you imply she practiced.

This is fiction.

But truth, Christian, truth is everything in fiction.

Well she *could* have.

That is quite beside the point.

It is not. Besides, Wu Hu, an empress who ruled some centuries before, practiced it. She made all the visiting dignitaries do it.

But that is not the empress in question.

I merely compressed history.

Merely compressed . . . ?

As an artist I had a perfect right.

You cannot mean that, Mr. Christian. Then there are no rules.

The rules are what I make them.

You are quite incredible. All right, let us return to the point. Sue has nothing to do with this book.

That is for my subconscious to say and for me to apprehend.

Very well, let us accept that proposition, dubious as it may be. You consciously manipulated this subconscious of yours, do you deny it?

I do. My subconscious manipulated my conscious which then manipulated my subconscious. In that case, it is perfectly acceptable, artistically speaking.

You are a scoundrel, sir.

Naturally. If I don't take your bullshit, I'm a scoundrel. What are you, for handing it out all these years?

I'm trying to help you.

Hah!

By thunder, I am.

168

With friends like you, who needs Boxers?

I'm trying to save you from yourself, can't you see that?

Let me go under, please. It's more romantic.

I am through playing games. It comes out.

It stays in.

Out!

In!

Out!

In!

Boys, boys, what in the world?

Thank heaven. You tell him, Mr. P.

Yes, tell him, Joseph.

Tell him what?

Tell him, tell the *World*. She stays. It stays. They all stay.

Nonsense, Joseph. You know this will never do. Even you know it.

Know what?

Don't listen to him, Mr. P. He thinks you're a commie.

Come, Joseph. He cannot use this helpless girl as an instrument of sexual revenge. Tell him.

I can, I do, I—

Basta, basta. Both of you. I can't hear myself think. Now, does she or doesn't she? That's the question?

Yes.

Crude, but, very well, yes.

Hmmm . . .

Well?

Well?

OK, I'll tell you. With this boy, of course she does.

Thank you, oh thank you, sir.

Uncouth, over-sexed immigrants!

Just one thing, my boy.

Yes sir?

Did you get the exclusive rights?

XIV

I got up this day at the hour of the Snake. Cobra, python, boa constrictor, anaconda. Coral. Star scout Birnbaum always preferred the coral. He appreciated the deadly pith pockets, the instant poison arcing three feet at the enemy, or so he told Boody, Jr. It had been a very rugged night. Bligh was absolutely impossible. Objection. Oh shit. Objection, *you* were impossible. Come off it, if it wasn't for Movita whom I took six different ways I would never have gotten through the night. And what about me? What about you? No one ever thinks of the leader, of *his* problems; well captains and kings have problems too. My piles bleed for you. Precisely what I would have expected from a mutineer. What else? I was on a goddam raft all night. Reversing roles, eh wot? That will be the day; look, start sailing for England already and leave me loose; as I was saying before being so crudely interrupted, I got up at the hour of the Coral, had my Familia and asked Mrs. Mary Montana down the hall if I could read her *Times*. She is only too happy to accommodate a starving artist and also to exchange some verbal communication as she is married to an engineer. So: over my Postum—I never touch coffee or tea, they are imperialist products—I read about ping pong. Pong ping. Ho hum, what else is new? Izzy and Birnbaum played this unknown, exotic game in '32 on Hannah's dining room table. And before Bligh butts in, I'll say it: Hannah was out in Coney Island at the time visiting her mother, also known as the *shviga*. God how that drove Hannah wild, Izzy calling her old lady the *shviga*. That and sucking in from the nose and swallowing. And in front of the *kinde*. Funny, the first time Birnbaum tried it in '29, it tasted good. . . . What else is new? The NVN offensive. . . . Not again. . . . Yes again. . . . All right, face it: curious gut reaction. Curious? You? I'm listening in by trans-Pacific radio. All right, listen, yes, very curious gut reaction. Curious haha or curious strange? All right, you asked for it, *I'm rooting for them*. You're *what*! You heard me, for the first time in my life, Izzy and Birney should only forgive me, but I am, I hope they win. You realize what you're saying? I do. Not only a mutineer, but a traitor. OK, you lousy goddam imperialist, you Kitchener, don't *you* realize there is a greater, a higher allegiance? Do tell, I do tell. I have read that feces too, mutineer, what of my country right or wrong? Hitler said that. So did Nathan Hale. He said millions for defense, not one cent for tribute. Lawrence of the Chesapeake said that. He said we must all hang together or we will surely hang alone. Patrick Henry said that. He said we have met the enemy and they are ours. Stephen Decatur said that. He said sighted sub, sank same. Hold it right there, mutineer; now tell me, is this what *you* fought for? I'll explain it again, *that* was a good war, a moral war. Oh I'm in stitches, I'm doubling over. Fuck you, Bligh. Naturally, your Lenny Bruce response, come now, why do you *really* want them to win? I've told you. Oh yes, higher morality. Allegiance. Yes yes, morality, allegiance, what else? What do you mean, what else? Come come, Mr. Mutineer. All right fatstuff, if they win, it gets that other imperialist s.o.b. out of the saddle, happy? Ecstatic, ta, ta . . .

At the hour of the Horse I walked over to Columbia, to Kent Hall. Hey Cap'n, *regardez*. Where? There on the wall. I don't read anything out of a spray can. *Read.* "U.S. gives up." What else? "Right on take Saigon." So you see, I am not alone. *Pauvre innocent.* What's that supposed to mean? Remember the Children's Mansion on the Drive? Yes. What did *that* spray can say? That's easy: "Vietnamese have children too." What else? That's it. What else? That's it. What else? Where? Right under Vietnamese have children too. Nothing. Nothing? Nothing. You're blocking, Mr. C. I didn't see a thing. Say it. What? It. What it? Say it!

WHO CARES?

Ta, ta . . .

I could not get into Kent. Six oriental students and a bunch of hair all with red armbands blocked my way. As we milled about the door the kid on the sundial yapped through his hand mike: "Let's hear it for all the apathetic German people. Let's hear it for business as usual, let's hear it for all you scholars and students who don't want your routines interrupted by B-52s, Daddy, what did you do when they rained bombs on the poor peasants? I went to the library . . ."

I turned around and started walking home. The boy beside me said, "Have they blocked Hamilton, too?"

"Yes. And God knows what else," I said.

"Well, that gives Nixon the election."

". . . Exactly what I was thinking. These goddam kids never learn."

"Never."

"It was the same thing in '68."

"Were you here then?"

"Right to the bitter end. The Harlem kids would have that gym now if it wasn't for them."

"They're all mouth. When it comes to tough, hard, political effort, they fade away."

"Precisely. That's thankless. No headlines there."

"You're absolutely right."

173

We walked to Butler Library. No pickets here. I wished my understanding buddy good luck, then ran up to the second floor to record the conversation.

I worked for an hour while the voice from the sundial pierced the closed windows. Finally it stopped. Only then did I decide I needed my Sino materials, my oriental stuff. I packed up and at a quarter to the hour of the Monkey (2:45) I walked outside, took the subway down to 42nd Street and walked into the great library. There I got in some heavy background work by Hu Sheng, a communist historian, and his *Imperialism and Chinese Politics* and *The Opium War Through Chinese Eyes,* by Arthur Waley. Which was exactly what I needed. With every page of the opium business I kept feeling worse and worse and better and better, the jism flowing like mad—

It titillates your moral complacency, doesn't it?

I've been waiting for you.

Here I am.

So I see. Well what have you got to say about starting a war to protect the opium trade?

Money, Mr. Christian, is the root.

Of all evil.

Oh just the root.

A matter of economics?

You might say that.

You raised that stuff in India which didn't even belong to you and forced it at inflated prices onto the Chinese market, ruining millions of lives. Millions. Why you make the Mafia look like amateurs.

I dare say.

You dare?

They didn't have to buy it.

That's where you're wrong. They couldn't help themselves.

Everyone can help himself. The survival of the fittest.

Oh? Then what happened to your empire?

A touchy subject.

Let's touch it.

Point in fact, the world has never been the same since we lost it. I'm waiting.

Waiting for what?

A renascence. The greatest of all empires. The Anglo-American Empire. Our brains, their brawn. We've given the colonies their chance and they've failed miserably. They'll welcome us with open arms.

Racist. Exploiter. Pusher. Trafficker in human souls.

Fiddlesticks. There will once again be glory and romance, something to live and die for.

Do you really think anyone in the world still believes that?

What about Norris Blake?

A reporter. One who reports. A human seismograph.

I see.

He is!

I said I saw. What of Benson?

What *of* Benson?

Only this, you goddam fourflusher: Before Sue packed up the kids and moved out, you were about to send them to private school!

All right, that's enough.

That's not enough, who was going to pay, big shot?

I was.

Who?

We were.

Who, creative artist?

I told you.

No, I'll tell *you*. The exploiter, the pusher will tell *you*. Hannah. And the lousy candy store. That's who! Here, have a fix.

I walked out into the air. Into Bryant Park. I sat down on a bench directly across from a slender young thing who read her paperback with intense vacancy. I pushed Bligh off by concentrating on her legs. They were tanned all the way up. A week in Bermuda or Nassau. Dress up to her pupick. I was absolutely, totally convinced she was not wearing pants. It was disgusting, a *shonda*. Every Tom, Dick and Harry could see everything. Does Carlie wear pants? Oh God. She'd better, the little gize why, or I'll tan that firm little bottom with my own Bermuda. I don't give a shit about the bra, I mean it will deprive the boys of all the unhooking fun, that's their problem, but I draw the line at no pants. Why? Lecher; go all the way back: Nita Nassi in '39, Miriam Gottlieb in '42, Christ, even Anna Yamanaka, Osaka, '45, yes, and Sue Hayden, that's correct, Sue, what did they all have in common; what stopped this probing, insistent hand? They did. Like hell, their *pants* did. . . .

Bryant Park. Izzy. He sat on these benches, perhaps this very one. Looking at legs, although he was also a tit and ass man. Sitting, looking, after his 42nd Street matinees. No apple hawker he. Isidore Birnbaum, now *this* was a hero. The biggest and best of the brothers in Cracow. The king of Rivington Street. Ask anybody, they all said it. Then why did he duck the emperor's army in 1913? God, how that bothered the hell out of Birney, the dumb little bastard. Dumb? Of course, dumb, Izz was light years ahead of his time, a great pacifist, an anti-war hero. But Birney did not believe this? He didn't *know* it, he'd fallen for all your Sergeant York, Charge of the Light Brigade bullshit. Oh, Isidore then was *not* a coward? He was a *hero*. He tried to fix Birney up with Zelda Cushman. Don't throw that up, he only mentioned it; as soon as B told him how spit collected in her mouth when she talked and she had no tits, he backed right off. I see; he was a good friend to his son? Good? Are you for real? He *invented* the father and son relationship. He told jokes? Did he tell jokes! Listen, why did the squirrel starve to death when he climbed up Hitler's leg? I'll bite. No nuts. Very droll. What was his favorite ad? The one about out-of-town college required? No, that was his *un*-favorite, that was a code for no Jews, see? Ah yes, is that why he planned to send B to the University of Pennsylvania? Of course, that way he would beat the system through the kid, they'd *both* beat it.

Yes. But that's a want ad, I mean a commercial ad. I give. OK, get this: Colliers, 1930, "Give your girl a gorgeous Gruen for Christmas." Hmmm. Say it fast. GiveyourgirlagorgeousGruenfor Christmas." Get it? I suppose. That slayed him, Birney too. Hannah? No, she didn't think it was so hot. It was part of that close relationship then? In a way, yes. He was a good provider? The best, never allowed evaporated milk on the table, or oleomargarine. He bought B a reversible raincoat, thus saving on the purchase of one coat. Come on, that was the style. Yes, the style; of course B never did go to the University of Pennsylvania and evaporated milk and oleo *did* make their appearance at table. That was after he lost his job. He lost his job? *Everybody* lost his job, because of your goddam capitalist, imperialist depression. A depression is merely a mental let-down. That's what your men said, that's what Hoover said, the word-bender. Well you have your sadsong, the world has its depression. Sure, next you'll tell me things equal to the same things are equal to each other. You said that, I didn't, and don't get so excited. Prosperity is just around the corner. My, we're huffy. When people are out of work, a state of unemployment exists. Calm down. We had to destroy the village to save it. Now don't bring *that* up, let's stick to the depression, these things happen, they will always happen, after all, seven good years, seven lean years. You Mellon, you Morgan, you Whitney, you Hoover, it *happened* to Isidore Birnbaum, it *happened* all right. . . . In 1931. . . . He got up at 5:30 as usual . . . he ate his orange in quarters . . . drank a raw egg . . . had his black coffee from the saucer . . . left the four-room apartment . . . took a subway down to Chambers Street . . . walked to Sarah Sweetmeat, Inc. . . . He read the piece of paper on the door: "We are now out of business as of today Sept. 6, 1931. I am vary sory. Good luck to all. J. Feibleman."

He walked inside. Feibleman was behind the old desk with his green eyeshade on, staring at the four walls.

"What the hell is going on?" demanded Isidore.

Feibleman looked this way and that way. "You can read," he said.

"What kind of horseshit is this?" said Isidore.

"Maybe it's horseshit for you," said Feibleman, "but it's curtains for me." He looked straight at Izzy.

"Don't talk that way," said Isidore.

"What way should I talk?" said Feibleman.

"You could try and look on the bright side," said Isidore, "instead of being such a gloomy gus. After all, you got your family, you got your health."

"Curtains," said Feibleman.

"Come on, cut it out," said Isidore. "Who do you think you are, going out of business, Auburn?"

"Don't talk Auburn to me," said Feibleman. "They should only have the *shvartz* year I had."

"They can't," said Isidore. "They're in the hands of the receivers."

"Fuck them too," said Feibleman.

"Now you're talkin," said Isidore. "Fuck them where they live, it's only money."

"I only wish I had your disposition," said Feibleman.

"Train yourself," said Isidore. "You think Cantor was born funny? He trained himself. Just say to yourself this whole thing is horseshit."

"Let Hoover say that," said Feibleman. "I can't."

"I give him a *hundred shvartz* years, that bastid," said Isidore.

"I voted for that," said Feibleman.

"Who didn't?" said Isidore. "Did we want the pope?"

"I feel rotten, Izzy," said Feibleman.

"Sure you feel rotten," said Isidore. "Because you take things too serious."

"It's my curse," said Feibleman.

"Bullshit, you ain't King Tut," said Isidore. "You think you're the only one in hell?"

"I don't give a shit about them others,' 'said Feibleman. "They don't give a shit about me."

"Now that's where you're wrong," said Isidore. "Misery loves company."

"Thanks a lot," said Feibleman.

"Come on, Jake," said Isidore. "Get the marshmallow out of your back and fight. You were always a fighter."

"Fight with what?" said Feibleman.

"Your hands, your back, your balls," said Isidore. "You and me together, I'm with you a hundred percent."

"That's very nice," said Feibleman. "The blind leading the blind."

"Listen," said Isidore, "you wanna make me a partner? I'll be a partner. We won't take a nickel out of the business. You on the inside, me on the outside."

"You're talkin crazy," said Feibleman. "I been pourin good money after bad for thirteen months. You don't even know the facts of life in your nuthouse."

"Facts, horseshit," said Isidore. "Here's facts. Consolidate. You don't need all this space. My uncle closed his button factory down in Jersey City and moved into a loft on 28th Street."

"Herman?" said Feibleman.

"Yes Herman. A man who went to Europe every year for the last ten years," said Isidore. "First Class."

"Curtains," said Feibleman. "Herman Birnbaum can't make a go of it, this country's goin red."

"He went down three times and came up four," said Isidore. "He can do it, you can."

"Herman Birnbaum is in shit creek," said Feibleman, "we're all in shit creek."

"I'm tellin you, he *ain't*," said Isidore. "He'll keep fightin as long as there's a breath left in his body. Is Fanny Farmer through? Is Loft? Are *they* givin up the ghost?"

"I'm gonna go to work for Fanny Farmer," said Feibleman.

"I got wax in my ears today," said Isidore. "Hit me again."

"You heard me," said Feibleman.

"You're not only yellow, you're crazy," said Isidore. "How you gonna go to work for Fanny Farmer after all these years of *fighting* them?"

"I'm sick and tired of fighting," said Feibleman. "You want me to ask for a spot for you too?"

"I'll eat shit first," said Isidore.

"Eat shit," said Feibleman.

"Jake, listen," said Isidore. "This don't make sense. Maybe you're crazy, but you ain't stupid. Don't you realize you been tellin customers all these years Fanny Farmer is horse manure? Now you're gonna turn around and say eat this shit, how can they have any faith in you?"

"Leave me alone," said Feibleman, "I'm tired."

"You're a fuckin old woman," said Isidore, "that's what you are. I got more respect for a prostitute in the street."

"All right I'm an old woman, I'm a whore," said Feibleman, "stop knockin me out."

"Is this final?" said Isidore.

"Yes," said Feibleman, "final."

"A hundred percent?" said Isidore.

"Two hundred percent," said Feibleman. "Stop torturing me, Izzy. Here take a box of coconut almond home for the kids. It's on the house."

"Shove your coconut almond up your ass," said Isidore.

OK, Bligh?

If you say so, Mr. Christian.

I say so. Now get lost.

Whatever for?

I got better things to do.

Better than Isidore?

Better than *you*.

Such as?

Such as: The sweet young thing. She has stirred and is looking around as if she had just awakened. Oh not again; don't you realize that, to use your own expression, you're just an A.K.? I'm mature, understanding, experienced, complex, tempered by time, now get *lost*. But Isidore—*Izzy* is looking *with* me, he liked young stuff . . . OK . . . I look . . . I start the bats flying in my eyes; I will her to gaze deeply therein. The sweet young thing unflips her pants-less thighs and finds her tanned legs. She clicks toward me on wedgies. Linda Adelman, Mosholu Parkway, 1951. Abreast now. I flap the wings in my eyes. She swings by, just an iota of awareness. Message sent, message received. I find my two-and-a-half legs. I nonchalant behind the swing and sway. Edith O'Higgins, Arcadia Ballroom, '47. She walks to Times Square. Pardon, Allied Chemical Square, Adolph Ochs should rest in peace. She stops. I stop. She waves. A sweatshirt with hair in a ponytail stands beneath the missing Paramount marquee. Corporal Sid Benson stood beneath the marquee. Sweatshirt waves back. Corporal Sid waved back. The S.Y.T. runs across the street and leaps into sweaty arms, bending up the back leg, dangling the wedgie. Bernice Bogbard, '44, ran across the street and leaped into khaki arms; looking over her shoulder, Benson saw the bending leg, the dangling wedgie. The corporal and the co-ed (Brooklyn) turned and walked into the exotic darkness of Alan Ladd's *China*. Dirty ponytail-sweatshirt-acne and the S.Y.T. headed for a subway and a campus bust. Poor kid, she doesn't even realize (care?) how the S.D.S. exploits, *degrades* women; doesn't realize (care?) how we put them on a pedestal and gaze up adoringly, achingly—pants or no pants. All right for her; make his coffee, cut his stencils, run his mimeos, put out for the group, who cares? You. Come on. Suppose Carlie—Stop! Tomorrow she puts on pants, now leave me *alone*. . . . I suddenly have a terrific yearning for gentian violet eyes, for perfumed, silk-clad legs.

I hailed a cab and said Mulberry Street, step on it.

On Canal Street I said, OK, you can let me out here. He stopped, I paid and got out and walked the few blocks to Mulberry. I looked all around, took a deep breath, then crossed the street and entered the Chinese City. I smiled to myself; twas the full gamut, from mandarin to opium eater; here and there a "long nose" hurried by, on the way to the city gate. On each side of the street, in the cool darkness, the shopkeepers were waiting for customers, counting their sapeks.

Coming out of one of the shops I saw her.

The gown was long and modest, the slit revealing just the top of the knee. Above that would be silk, *real* silk. She was crossing the street. She stepped up for the curb, the skirt stretched, but, modestly, not enough, the (tiny) foot caught, she tottered; I moved. I held out a western arm and she took it, lightly but firmly. She stepped up onto the sidewalk. I smiled gravely. She smiled back gravely.

"Thank you," she said in almost perfect English.

"You're quite welcome," I rejoined in English.

She paused as if waiting for she knew not what and I said:

"Are you from Chihli?" She seemed puzzled by the question; I laughed quietly and said, "How foolish of me, today it is called Hopei."

"No." Her voice was soft, almost childlike in its purity.

"Shantung?" I enquired.

"No."

As I said that, I placed my hand over hers; she made no effort to draw it from my arm. Her eyes flickered searchingly over my face as she said:

"Mott Street."

I nodded and pressed her hand; she pressed more firmly on my arm.

"What I mean," I said, "is where did you dwell before that?"

"Taiwan."

"Ah. And before that?"

"I . . . don't know."

Somehow I found that terribly touching. Apparently she sensed it for her eyes widened, rather the pupils did. They were not quite gentian violet, but close enough not to quibble. I smiled reassuringly.

"My name is Norris Blake. May I escort you home?"

The eyes, for the first time, seemed to swerve away from my face.

"Do not be afraid," I counseled. "However, I really do not think you should be abroad alone at this hour."

The soft lips parted. The slender column of a throat worked.

Suddenly I felt myself being spun around. I thought for a moment that she had worked some violent magic on me. However, I soon learned otherwise; I found myself looking down at a huge blimp of a face, a Chinese face, a face that belonged to a square Chinese body, a face that was suffused with high emotion.

"Who the fuck you think you're talkin to?" asked the face.

"I beg your pardon."

"What was he sayin to you, Laurie?"

"Well, he . . ."

I wrenched free from his grasp.

"You don't have to answer that," I said.

"Did I ask you?" said the face. "I want your advice, I ask for it."

"That is a bargain," I said.

"C'mon, Hank," she said, "it don't matter."

"The fuck it don't," he returned. "He thinks he kin walk in here and insult you? The fuck it don't."

He cocked his right arm. I could see it coming from around the corner and it was almost laughable, the roundhouse right. I sidestepped and he want skidding by, completely off balance. I helped by a light shove and he ended up in the gutter. I looked at the girl called Laurie. She was gazing full at me.

"Fu," I said with a broad smile.

Someone or something hit my head from behind. Even as I thought, how cowardly! her face was covered with a shower of sparks. At the same instant I felt a terribly sharp pain in my side. The next thing I felt was the unyielding sidewalk against my forehead; it seemed to be jumping up to that part of my cranium, making violent contact and falling away; slowly it dawned on me that the reverse was true; slowly both sidewalk and forehead came to rest. I turned, looked up at three oriental faces, one of which, even without my glasses, I could tell belonged to the one called Hank.

"Murderous Boxers," I muttered.

"What?" said Hank.

"You're a lousy Boxer."

He kicked me in the ribs. I folded up into a ball, but not before I glimpsed her face. It was positively aglow. He kicked me again. I heard the soft, musical voice saying, "C'mon, les gethehell outa here." Then I felt it: a sharp, pointed (bound?) foot in my ribs. And I saw it: the slender leg flashing at me right up to the slit. I closed my eyes. When I opened them, they were running across the street and out through the portals of the city.

I lay there for some time, dimly aware of faces peering out of windows, and of feet, eastern and western, stepping by. Oh well, let's hear it for the people of the world. Finally I partially unwound and found my tissue-paper legs. I put on my glasses, which I had removed—as is my wont—prior to talking to the young lady. Walking then in the semi-fetal position, I made my way to the subway and got on the uptown local. Blessedly it was still intact. I got out at 110th, tottered the three blocks to my building, climbed the steps, opened my door and collapsed onto the couch.

A pretty sight.

Oh, God, please not now.

There is no time like the present. What is that colorful phrase you use?

Please, I'm not in shape.

You can say that again.

I'm not in shape. Also I feel rotten.

You look rotten. The phrase.

I'll take you on tomorrow.

No deal.

Be decent. I've just had a big shock.

Decency be damned. You asked for it. Oil and water, old man.

I know, don't rub salt in the wound.

That's up to you. The phrase, what is the phrase?

Please.

The *phrase*.

You can't see the forest for the trees.

No, though you can't, God knows. Try again.

Please . . .
Come, come.
God helps those who help themselves.
Don't be banal.
Time and tide wait for no man.
Laughable.
Fat fat, the water rat, fifty bullets in his hat.
Pathetic.
If at first you don't succeed—
Don't try to butter me up.
Give me some men who are stout-hearted men.
And don't be cute.
Please, can't I get away with *any*thing?
Not this.
Why not?
You know. The envelope, please.
I ACT LIKE MAN WITH A PAPER ASSHOLE.
That's the one. Very well, now you can go to sleep.

When I woke up, I washed my face and applied iodine. It hurt good. Then I turned on the television. Columbia. Kent Hall had been liberated. I dragged my way over to the typewriter.

XV

CHAPTER SIX (B.)

Herald was as fresh as a three-day-old colt as he carried me out into open country. The enforced inactivity of the past several days had clearly been anathema to his soul and spirit, not to mention his corpus, as it had been to mine and for a mile or two I let him gallop full out, to kick up his heels, to buck and prance, to release all the pent-up equine emotion. I must also confess that the steppe and the wind and the moon and stars were wonderful tonics, a release as it were, to my own enclosed self; I reveled in my new liberty, this freedom once again to be captain of my ship, master of my destiny.

So hell-bent for leather we charged, reining in and settling down only when I judged us on a line parallel with Matou on the Pei Ho. I had intentionally kept us somewhere between the railway and the river, hoping to avoid the marauders who could be anywhere, but I felt it safe at last to veer east and pick up the waterway that would guide me to Tientsin and thence Taku. The Boxer bands

187

in the area must surely be converging on the iron devil to confront Seymour and his column and I should have relatively free access southward, or as free as anything could be in this dangerously fluid situation.

So far so good. I struck Matou at about 3 A.M., that is, what was left of it. Like vengeful locusts, the Gods of Mars had rushed through the village and picked it clean, leaving in their wake the up-turned bones of war-ravaged daily life the world over: smashed beds, tables, chairs, a child's pitifully torn doll, trampled gardens, smoking timbers, the still, unseeing, all-accusing forms.

I forced us through the ruin and stench so as to remind me once again, as if indeed a reporter needed reminding, of the horrors of human strife. Herald, of course, needed no such reminder, for he had surely seen much of this in his short life, and, too, animals have no need to partake of the wasteful efforts we higher forms indulge in. But obediently, though with head cocked to one side as if quizzing my good sense, he stepped us through the carnage. Then once again, with a snort of relief, he cut loose to the towpath of the river, the very one that had guided me north centuries ago.

Beside the peaceful gleam we cantered along.

Who might loom up out of the darkness?

What had happened to Seymour's column?

Where was the Admiral?

When would the balance be struck? The trained might of the west assert itself?

Why was I not back in Peking, transported by the opiums of amour?

Oh?

I chuckled into the night. "You're a fool, Blake." I said aloud to the neutral stream. "A bloody fool." Did I perceive Herald nodding his head?

We settled into a good pace, hidden by the screen of sorghum. I reached into my knapsack and drew out some black bread and feasted on it; this was how reporters on assignment should eat. Then I watered my gallant steed, fed him some sugar and dried rice and once again we were off. Another hour on an easterly course and we were detouring through Hosiwu, also visited by the starving locusts. Here the Pei Ho bent sharply down. It would strike the railway at Yangtsun, about 75 *li* or 25 miles north of Tientsin. Perhaps I might be lucky (or skillful) enough to run into Seymour's column. At the very least I should be closing in on another locus of action and counter-action; Dr. Newton was surely everywhere in evidence in Chihli Province this spring of 1900.

Horizontal stripes of light and darkness now layered the sky over my left shoulder. Pushing up from beyond the Gulf of Chihli, the great golden master sent his whiplike strokes clear across the horizon line, then bid them be gone and in a tremulous, hushed moment, leaped onto the scene in glowing panoply. "It can't be long now," I assured my doughty comrade.

As dawn captured the eastern sky, the scars of the holocaust began now to appear along our path and lent solid substance to my weirdly prophetic words. Here a bleached and splintered junk with German lettering above the hull's grinning monster, there on the shore a stiff and staring soldier in a spiked helmet. What nameless local infection had flared up and left behind these victims? I dared not speculate; I only knew I must press on and probe into this fevered and unhappy giant. Another still form, this one no more than a child; cleared by Herald in a shuddering leap, and then still on, past the whipped and beaten sorghum, evidence of a lightning struggle followed by a wild dash to the interior. By whom? Where were they now? I began to sense, to feel, to *smell* Boxers all about, although as yet I had neither seen nor heard one, live, that is.

Ahead of me at last lay my immediate target, the village of Yangtsun. I had expected the usual ruin and smoke; instead Yangtsun was spread out quite intact in the sparkling morning sun, in fact going quite normally about its business. I rode into town; the war could have been a million miles away, so could relief columns, so could harassing armies, for all these stolid citizens seemed to care, although, to be sure, you never can quite tell with the oriental. I shook my head and Herald gave his mane a punctuating wag. Well, since there was no history to be found here, we walked to the water's edge, stopped and ate breakfast. I had to decide then whether to continue south by the rail line or the river, both of which intersected here. Something told me, perhaps the old scrivener's instinct, that Seymour had taken to the river, since the rail was too juicy a target.* After breakfast and a good watering, I mounted and we headed south. All morning we rode, until we struck the village of Hsiku. No mystery here about where the war was; twas the all too familiar scene, but now quite suddenly too close to Tientsin for my comfort. Thus alerted, I made a wide swing to the west, deciding to bypass the city which was sure to be an eye of the storm, but which I must avoid if I was to reach my pre-ordained shelling of Taku.

So off we swept in the huge arc, the base of which would carry me back to the river, but south of Tientsin, just beyond the foreign settlements. I should pause here, ere the anti-imperialists raise their cries of "shame," and note that these latter areas are properly known as concessions, quite simply those places taken— often forcibly—from the Chinese by the foreigner and subject only to foreign law. I will not attempt to justify the existence of these tiny colonies, I will leave this to that literary taipan, Mr. Kipling, nor is it the purport of this narrative to argue against such enclaves, I will leave that to my readers who may or may not wish to join in such argument. Suffice to say that the Boxer Rebellion provided the pros and cons of the argument and twas my duty to record it, so without further digression, I will continue that report and in the process doubtless respond to many an angry cry of "Go it!"

As I have said, I rode out and then cut in, thinking perhaps to glimpse the concessions, but planning to give them a wide and healthy berth. Well I glimpsed them all right. And what a terrible glimpse it was.

The foreign settlements, the concessions, the colonies of Tientsin were in flames!

I sat transfixed. Before me the golden furnace was leaping in

* Alas, we never did meet. Well I could not report *every* event.

awful splendour toward its father in the sky, as if drawn by a great, invisible magnet. My steed whinnied nervously and pawed the ground as the inbred fear of fire gripped the poor fellow, yet he held his ground, as he was no doubt trained to do. "It's all right, old boy." I soothed, reaching over and patting the tense neck even as I fooled the both of us. "However," I added, "I do wish we could help, I really do . . ." My words trailed off as the wind shifted and the flames swept sharply away from the river and toward the main city. Should I ride in and brave it? Could I do anything except salve my conscience? I did not think so, yet . . . ? I sat there, a-pondering, agonizing. Well, as it so often does, the dilemma solved itself. Actually was solved for me.

Even as I sat in auto-debate, I felt a tremendous hoisting force from behind; it lifted me out of the saddle and tumbled my feet skyward. I glimpsed fire and sky and wondered quite objectively if the heat of the furnace had lashed out and flung me off my perch; I had heard that tale from veterans of the Chicago fire. As I thought on it, I cracked the ground; that is, the ground cracked me. I seemed to be doing a good deal of bouncing, but when I came to rest, I regretted I was not still doing the same. For I was now staring up and into a circle of solemn, sinister faces. Ah, I thought, no doubt but that the hands and arms attached to those faces had done the hoisting and bouncing. That settled to my satisfaction, I nodded and smiled.

"Who are you, devil?" enquired the most sinister face. He spoke Mandarin, though with a local dialect.

"Who are *you?*" I responded in his tongue.

A murmur passed around the circle.

"*I* ask the questions, devil," spat the sinister one. "What are you doing here?"

"I thought," I said, "you wished to know who I am?"

"Yes, who are you?"

"Well, do you wish to know who I am or what I am doing here, please make up your mind?"

"Silence, long-nosed devil! I have told you *I* will ask the questions."

191

"I only wished to know which question. After all, if I—"

"SILENCE!"

"As you wish."

He struck me smartly with the back of his hand. I looked into his eyes.

"You will pay for that," I vowed.

He struck me again.

I spat blood and looked him in the eye again. He exploded into a string of Chinese expletives which I will not translate although my jaw clenches at their remembrance. This, most clearly, was a Fist who was not anywheres near Kuang Yu's gang, surely not on a par with Kuang himself. This fellow was of the ilk that has since been featured in the world's press as the personification of villainy, and I cannot gainsay the description. When the blackguard reached the end of his obscene string, he turned to a henchman and snapped, "Tie the pig up." Which act, with alacrity, was promptly attended to.

First they dragged a pole into their circle. At the top of this pole was a placard, but containing only pictures. I craned my head up and saw an upright pig who was tied to a cross and impaled with arrows. Various Chinese figures were shooting these arrows at the ugly creature and were also carving up a kneeling goat. I have since learned that the pig meant a Christian whilst the goat represented all westerners; the Boxer mind, it seems, perceived this duality. Twas, however, a crass and barbaric depiction, completely bereft of the (angry) poesy which marked the printed placards. Well the ruffians bound me tightly to this pole, then thrust it into the ground so that I might face the foreign settlement fire. The harder I squirmed, I knew, the tighter would become my thongs; I stood stock still. The leader, if I may grant him that title, waved his sword and the scruffy band ran around in front of me; I counted fifteen. He walked to the pole and spat in my face, then pinked my cheek with his sword. I did not blink an eye, even when he held aloft the bloody point.

"You are playing the brave game, devil," he sneered.

"Thank you," I said.

His mouth worked with frustration. With an effort he choked back the venom and said:

"Well, you will die watching our fire."

"If God so wills."

"*I* will, *I, I*," he bellowed.

"You must pay for this, you know," I averred.

He emitted a roar that was clearly meant as mirth but was far wide of the mark. Then the evil features settled into a form of composure, albeit a secure and clear conscience could ne'er touch this face.

"You will die by the western method," he said. I arched an eyebrow. "Oh, so you are surprised we know such grand things?" I lowered the eyebrow. "We are not as ignorant as you think." He turned to his men. "Take your positions," he grunted.

They settled into two ranks, the first one kneeling. Their arms, a motley collection of rifles, faced the sky. So, it was to be the firing squad. Ingenious, to say the least.

"I will not tie your eyes," he said.

"I would not wish it."

"I want your last sight on this earth to be the flames of the Tientsin concessions."

"I'm much obliged."

He struck me across the mouth.

"Thank you."

The face of evil split into a mirthless smile.

"You will provoke me no further," said the cruel mouth. He looked over to his men and stepped away.

"Raise your western rifles!" he shouted.

I looked over their heads and to the flames. The face and form of Ah Soon danced there and I smiled to myself; my last sight on earth would be far different from the one he had planned.

"Aim your filthy guns!"

I concentrated on the sweet face, inhaled the delicate perfume.

"FIRE!"

Airy crosscurrents flashed cross my face, I heard the angry zzzzing of the lead. So, I thought, this is how it is. I clearly saw

193

the evil one staring. I saw his men stare. I wondered vaguely how I could see so much on earth if I were already on my way above, below, or into nothingness. Then an astonishing event took place: The men leaped up, the evil one leaped up and together they ran to me and kowtowed! Then screaming like the banshees of hell, they scrambled to their feet and rushed off toward the river. I looked down at my feet. No blood. I waggled my head. It remained on my shoulders. I wriggled against the pole. I felt it dig into my legs and back. It hurt like the very blazes. I looked into the flames. Ah Soon was smiling.

Then I fainted.

Oh for God's sake.

Yes?

Hairbreadth Harry has done it again.

Yep.

You are not going to leave it at that?

I am.

You can't be serious.

Dead serious. And Roebuck.

I'll ignore that. See here, Christian, you're overdoing, you know.

Strange, coming from you, William.

Mind yer manners. And don't change the subject. Very well, you may keep it in.

Thankee, sir.

Whippersnapper. You may keep it in on one condition.

That is?

You must continue. You cannot end it on that damned precipice.

I think I can.

You're becoming quite impossible, you know.

Billy boy, I'm becoming *possible*. Ta.

XVI

Twas the night the old nostalgia burnt down. Oh? Yes, Norris, twas, i.e., I'm seeing old friends again, I've *seen* old friends again. That's almost too much confidence. You might say that. I might and will. However, is this appropriate now that Quangtri has fallen? Pity. Anloc is in supreme danger. Tough. All right, George Sanders is gone and you're seeing old friends? Yes. Jedgar Hoover, and you are. . . ? Uh huh. How about Gia Scala? That was rough, very rough, but yes, I'm carrying on; listen bubby, the London Bridge is in Arizona, the Queen Mary's in California, what price glory and I'm *still* seeing old friends, ta, Bligh.

Soc Zlotsky, one of the boyiss, called me. We go back over a quarter of a century, Soc and I. I first met him at Upton as he told me to watch the needle. At the time I was wearing a G.I. raincoat over a sunburn acquired the day before—my last as a civilian—in Rockaway. Soc, he stared at the needle as it sank in and then passed out; they lowered his head, raised his feet and pulled him out of shock at the base hospital. A week later, sadder, no wiser, he was back in our tent and the next day we shipped out to Crowder. In Missouri, or misery as Soc called it, he became a Morse-code man and I a lineman, driving my acrophobia ahead of me up the pole. Just when I learned not to look down we were assigned to colleges under A.S.T.P., he to Rice, I to Grinnell in Iowa. After love affairs at both places, we were reunited at Monmouth in the early formed 81st Signal Service Battalion. Thence to the wilds of Jersey for field maneuvers, including the Blue Moon in Pompton Lakes and wining, dancing and romancing in the Hawaiian Paradise, Patterson. Then to Shanks in New York and the dawning speculation that we were heading for the E.T.O. Confirmed at Staten Island, December 1, 1944, on board the *Island Queen,* a converted Liberty, in which Soc got seasick as we rode at anchor. Across the North Atlantic in a 30-ship convoy, puking, always puking. To Liverpool where we recovered on mild and bitters and stand-up jobs. To Kirkby, Fazakarly, Southhampton, to Le Havre's floating docks, up the Seine to Verdun, Marville, Luxembourg, across the Siegried line to Mainz on Rhine, over the pontoon bridge to Mannheim, Bad Nauheim, Birglingenfeld, Salzberg, Weimar, Buchenwald, Regensberg, Linz, VE, Marseilles, all aboard the *SS Monterey,* to Manila via the Panama Canal, Baguio, VJ, all aboard the *LST,* to Yokahoma, Osaka, Koshien, Hiroshima, Matsuyama, all aboard the navy transport, to Yokohama, to San Francisco, Welcome home well done, Camp Stoneman, troop train, Fort Dix, ruptured duck, pass the fuckin butter mom, *mishuga,* to the borscht belt, rat races, marriage.

He called me.

"Sid, it's Soc."

"Soc Zlotsky?"

"Yeah buddy, long time no see."

"Since 1954, the year the Giants took four straight."

"That's right. Who was Mandrake the Magician?"

"Don Mueller."

"Who jumped on Durocher's back after the shot heard round the world?"

"Stanky."

"You're too fuckin much. Hey, my kid is gettin married, you havta come."

"Hugh?"

"Nah Hugh, I break his arm if he gets married now. Eva."

"Little Eva?"

"Little Eva."

"Jesus."

"Ain't it the truth."

"She used to grab my finger in the crib."

"That's right. OK, so you're coming."

"I don't know . . ."

"What's to know. So you wrote a book, big shot, hey, it's me, Soc."

"I haven't been feeling so hot lately."

"Am I the happy rabbit?"

"Stan Rojek."

"Am I Miksis will fix us?"

"Eddie Miksis."

"Am I Spooner but sooner?"

"Karl Spooner. Come back, little Shuba."

"George Shuba."

"You're a piss whistler, Soc."

"And you? Who hung out the hotel window?"

"Danny Gardella."

"See? I won't take no for an answer."

"What can I say?"

"Yes. You and Sue."

"OK yes. But not Sue. We're having trouble. Where and when?"

"Saturday after next. At the Cornwall."

"The Cornwall? On Central Park West?"

"The same."

"That was the rat race where you and—"

"Yep, I met Aida."

"That is sheer poetry, Soc."

"I knew you'd appreciate. After all, you were in on the kill. See ya, buddy."

197

I rented a tux and bought the kids the Oxford Dictionary—both volumes; I always give books, though never mine. On Saturday I took a cab down to the Cornwall. I got out, hesitated, then walked past the hotel and down 83rd Street to Columbus. I stared at 200 West, second floor, fat-bellied window; I lived there for three months in '46, while I was readjusting. LuJane Whittlesby of Columbia, S.C., nurse in training at Flower Fifth Avenue, loved it from Jewish fellas. Sprayed over the door: "Jesus Mary I love you save souls." I turned and walked back to Central Park West and the Cornwall.

I walked inside. Morris chairs in the lobby. 1946–47, Arch, Chick, Sid, Soc. Soc, also known as Fearless Fosdick; "I like mine, see ya." Soc and his law of averages: work your points all night and you must score, or at least get on base. Third time up, Aida Mittenfeld and Soc thrown out sliding into third, bare tit and that was it. Six months later, married. I consulted the bulletin board. Zlotsky-Greenblatt Wedding, Ivory Room. I asked for the Ivory Room, as if I didn't know. Second floor, down the hall. I walked up the fraying carpeted steps and down the hall. The man at the door was not stamping wrists with invisible ink, he was Soc, mustached, high-collared, bald and bellied.

"Sid you sonofabitch, I thought you'd chicken out."

"I told you I'd be here, didn't I?"

"That you did."

He hugged me. "Who was the greatest first baseman of all time?"

"Tookie Gilbert."

"Poor bastard. Who was Citation?"

"Lloyd Merriman."

"Who was Cuddles Marshall?"

"Tyrone Power."

"Who played golf instead of baseball?"

"Sammy Byrd."

"Who could hit in a rocking chair?"

"Dusty Rhodes."

"Who stretched triples into singles?"

"Ernie Lombardi."

"Who got all the publicity?"

"Clint Hartung."

"Who else?"

"Johnny Rucker."

"Who else?"

"Tom Winsett."

"Why Winsett?"

"*Life* had him on the cover."

"What did Brando say?"

"Why they so mean to me."

"What did Leo Carillo say?"

"I hear bout dis money, she no good."

"You pass, you sonofabitch, how the hell are you?"

"OK, rotten."

"Like always. Recognize this place?"

"Yes."

"A lot of fuckin water under the bridge, buddy."

"The goddam Amazon."

"The goddam Nile."

"The Atlantic and the Pacific, but the Pacific wasn't terrific."

"And the Atlantic wasn't what it's cracked up to be. Aida!"

She walked over very slowly. Deep sun tan, frosted hair. Slender. She looked me up and down, to and fro. I was always a bad influence on Soc, from the first night, the four of us in his car, me and Mary Horowitz, sit-up boff in the back seat, she always resented that. I suspected they had argued over my coming to the wedding, and he'd put his foot down. "Hello, Sidney," she said. "You're looking very well."

"So are you. What's your secret?"

"Melvin takes good care of me."

Soc winced. "Jack LaLanne," he said. "It used to be Slenderella." She winced. He took both our arms and walked us inside. Tables all over the dance floor. The bandstand and bar, however, were in place. "Right over there," said Soc. I looked. The crazy bastard had painted a white X in the corner near the bar. He dug my ribs. I dug back. Aida sighed. "OK," he said, "I gotta host, you're table 23. Garrett Buxby is sitting there."

"Lucky Bux? Very little hips and no ass at all?"

199

"The same. All the way from Oklahoma. Chick also."

"Christ, old home week. How about Arch?"

"Nah, Arch, you know him. Who the hell can keep track?"

"Yes, I know Arch."

He leaned over and said in his stage whisper, "There's a live one at your table." Aida's Maybelline flickered; they walked off, she mouthing, he shrugging.

I was feeling a little shaky, like my first postwar rat race at the Arcadia, February 10, 1946, so I walked over the X to the bar where I had a Chivas Regal and water. Soc always went first class: G.I. shirts formfit, khaki underwear french laundered, Seagram's Seven Crown, never Five. I felt better after drinking the courage and I pushed off onto the floor, now filled with tables, *mishpoocha,* friends and *shnorrers,* instead of operators, stiffs, Fearless Fosdicks. I veered off to the bandstand. Piano, drums, trumpet, tenor sax, clarinet. They were playing a thin tango version of *South of the Border* and lucky to get work. I swore at James Caesar Petrillo and walked to table 23.

Something hit me high and something hit me low.

"Mr. Outside!" yelled Chick. High.

"Mr. Inside!" yelled Bux. Low.

I spun, twisted free, very easy as I do 25 sit-ups every morning plus my yoga and 30 side straddle-hops whereas they obviously got their exercise as did Bob Benchley, lying down till the urge passed away. I dodged around table 23, a bottle spiraled toward me and I caught it tight against my chest. A fifth of Canadian Club. I circled the other way and lateraled off to Chick. He bobbled it, juggled and fought it all the way to the floor where it finally cradled into his belly. Bux sat on him. I saw two horror-stricken faces staring down. Another woman with Audrey Hepburn hair but not her chest was looking at me; beside her a solemn-looking type wearing his bar mitzvah suit. I waved. Chick shovel-passed the fifth which I caught with one hand and set tenderly on the table.

"Champeens of Lucky Strike!" yelled Chick.

"Third Army!" yelled Bux.

"Twelfth Army Group!" yelled Sid.

They struggled up, rushed over and we pummeled each other while the others looked on with frozen smiles. Chick was all gray, including his face; Bux, whose hair was the amazement of B team —thick to within an inch of his eyebrows—was bald except for two black bushy sideburns.

"You a piss cutter," said Bux.

"*Ve heizen zee, fraulein,*" said Chick.

"*Volen zee shpotzeeren mitt me,*" said Bux.

"*Nein nein,*" I said, "Mamma, Papa."

They broke up. When they came to we pummeled each other some more, then Bux waved a frozen smile over. She was dressed in a gold formal. "Now ah want you ta meet the Bernie Goodman of the 81st Signal Service battal-eone," he said.

"Benny," I smiled.

"See?" she said. "I told you."

"Ah don't give a holler'n hell. This boy was the best they is. He made that lil ol stick sit up an say uncle."

"A long time ago, buddy," I said, but I appreciated. Bux was the one southern boy who didn't think we were merely exotic fuck-offs or cocksmen, he just liked to be with us. I extended the warmth to his wife. "Hello, I'm Sid Benson. You're Miriam."

"Yes," she said, pleased.

"Hey," beamed Chick, "how about Linz?"

"Phil?" I said innocently.

"Nah, Linz, Austria."

Bux's eyes rolled toward his old hairline. I winked at Chick and he nodded. Bux was already loose-lipped and redfaced, as on the night Hitler was reported dead and he shot up the German Wac barracks and killed a bottle of schnapps. He grinned to himself. "Hilda and Hulda," he said. "Strenth through joy."

"Hello," I said quickly to the other frozen smile. "I'm Sid Benson."

"I know," she said. She was thick and straight, up and down, even her face, her ankles. "We met once."

"We did?"

"Grossinger's," said Chick. " '59."

" '6o," she said.

"Of course," I said. "Shirley. *Shelley*." She had been thin and straight.

"That's right," she said, her mouth relaxing.

"I told you he'd remember," said Chick. "Writers remember everything." Like the Bourbons, I thought, learning nothing. "Where's Susie?" asked Chick.

"We're separated."

He hesitated, then punched me on the arm. "It's cheaper that way. This is Joe and Janet."

Audrey Hepburn's hair said hello very quietly. Since there were seven chairs, she was the live one. I shook Joe's embarrassed hand. Poor bastard.

"Whachou drinkin, buddy?" said Bux. "Ol Feahless got nothin but the best."

"Schnapps."

He doubled over, gasping. We all waited patiently until he straightened up. "Canadian and water," I said. He nodded, all business, and poked his finger at everyone. "Bourbon on the rocks, scotch 'n soda, rye on the rocks, rye 'n soda, scotch on the rocks." He bent over the table and very seriously mixed the drinks, twisting and dropping lemon peel into each. Very seriously he handed the glasses around. Chick said, "Here's to the 81st, B team." We raised our glasses and drank to that magnificent crap. The out-group looked at the in-group, rather jealously, I thought. Idiots. Over my shoulder the mickey mouse band was sneaking up on *Frenesi*. "May I dance with your wife?" I said to Joe.

"Sure. Go ahead."

"Why don't you ask me?" said Janet.

"Uh oh," said Chick.

"You nevuh heard that in Japan," said Bux to Miriam. She said, did nothing.

"Well may I?"

"I don't know."

"Uh oh," said Chick.

"Welll . . . all right," she smiled.

"Uh oh," said Chick.

We put our glasses down, got up and walked to the floor. In one of the great ritual movements of our time, she turned, opened, you step up, they melt in. Plus the bonus, cheek to cheek. Mary Duckett, Liverpool, '44. I moved her toward the music and saw Soc dancing with a woman I recognized as his older sister. She nodded at me and I nodded back, he swung her around and winked and I winked back. "Why did he wink?" said Janet.

"He has a psychosomatic tic."

"All right, don't tell me. Are you really a writer?" she said into my ear.

"Yes." White Shoulders. Sue, '56.

"A creative writer?"

"Well yes, I suppose so."

I could feel her reflecting. She was an awkward dancer, but knew it and so clung tightly as I maneuvered. Elspeth Hubbard, Red Bank, '43. We moved silently in a small circle in the center of the floor. The Plantation Room, Hotel Dixie, Teddy Powell orchestra (definitely not m. mouse), Nita, '42. Finally she said into my ear, "I'm a creative writer, too."

"Oh?" (Thank you, Norris.)

"Well in a way. Short stories. Well I've written two stories."

"Were they published?"

"Oh no. I couldn't bear to have anyone else read them."

"I can understand that. I felt naked when my first one came out."
She snuggled in, I held her. Protectively? We moved counter-clockwise. "Nobody would publish them anyway," she said softly.

"How do you know?"

"I know."

"Well it's something to have written even one."

She sighed. "Have you published many?"

"Five. But I haven't written any in a long time. I'm working on a novel."

"Your first?"

"I've published one."

She seemed suddenly to become even more awkward; I put my other arm around her and we danced like that, hidden from the world by all the other couples. Sid and Olga Onewing, pure Zuni, Neosho, '43, Happy's Inn, Bob Eberly singing "Marie Elena." The band swung into the "Walter Winchell Rhumba." Reluctantly we separated and I tried to move her into a simple box step, but without my body, she couldn't make it. Smiling, I slid in and she came back to me; I two-stepped confidently and even tried some of the old hesitation dips. It made her giggle, it always made them giggle; I felt my chest expand. I heard her say, "Can you talk about it?"

"What?"

"The novel you're working on."

"I'd rather not."

Silence. Birdie Bideaux, Laurel in the Pines, '51. Then: "I love to talk about my work . . ." Ah yes, only I can't talk to anyone, especially Joe, he just wouldn't understand . . . "I don't have anyone to talk to about it," she said as I smiled into her hair, "except my dentist and I pay him to listen."

I patted her head. She drew back and looked at me; we gazed into each other's eyes; with a sigh she snuggled back. Kim Abromowitz, Camp Redlock, '48. "Are you working on something now?" I said.

"No, I'm blocked."

I stroked the back of her head. I felt her relax. "I can only resolve it by leaving my husband," she said. I kept my big mouth shut. "Only I can't. Not yet. My dentist says I can't tear away from my father . . ." She looked at me again. Janine Weinstein, G.I. war bride, Concord. '50. Ready, willing, eager to leave bed and board for the clarinetist. God.

"Everybody," I said, "needs a mother and father. That's no crime."

"But it's *blocking* me."

"*You're* blocking you."

". . . Do you really think so?"

"Well I'm no dentist . . ."

"But you're a writer." But of course.
"Then yes, I think so."
Silence. Kinetic silence. Assimilating silence. All the way to the Guy Lumbago break. All the way back to the table.

The ceremony was semiorthodox and very pretty. Little Eva from where I sat suddenly had a woman's behind. Aida dabbed at her eyes, Greenblatt smashed the glass with one stomp and Soc, in top hat and tails, looking like a fat flushed Fred Astaire, gave everything his special body english. Everyone danced with everyone, even Aida and I, and we all yelled for the "Anniversary Waltz" and clapped and whistled as the Greenblatts, alone, swooped and glided around the floor. Then some more dancing, and in a quick cut, before Soc broke in, Janet was his cousin on his father's side, from Camden, early marriage, three kids, bim, bam, boom, a computer programmer was nice and decent and impossible and for seven months they'd lived like brother and sister and she was choking to death . . . I walked back to the table and the boys and their bullshit:

"How about the Liverpool docks?"

"Soc stole all the Eisenhower jackets for the team."

"Shee-it, they was coming to us."

"Friggin A."

"He made T5 for that."

"He earned it. Remember the broad he picked up on Lime Street?"

"You mean the time he worked his points all night?"

"Yeah, yeah and just when he's makin it, she says, 'Five pounds, please.' "

"Jesus yes, an he went down to the pro station."

"Oh Jesus."

"Remember Crazy Wimplog?"

"The truck driver?"

"He shot the three SS prisoners in Gotha."

"Right in the head."

"Then took their watches."

"Crazy bastard."

"How about Stu Gold?"

"The singer?"

"Da glow of sunset in da summer sky."

"Da golden flicker of da firefly."

"Da gleam of lovelight in ya lovely eye."

"Dese are da tings I love."

"Sonofabitch. He told the broads his name was Stuart Gotz."

"Stu Gotz."

"A. Stu Gotz."

"He used his condoms for garters. Bloused his pants over his combat boots with them."

"Don't kid yourself, he used them for other things."

"Friggin A."

"Remember the Jap bimbo he picked up on the Kobe subway station?"

"She picked him up. Took it right out on the platform."

"And he brought her back to the barracks."

"An kep her there for two days."

"Ah Stu Gotz."

"Sonofabitch. Remember the Polack concentration camp?"

"Outside Salzburg?"

"Yeah. Scarecrows. They couldn't even stand up."

"They chowed down our C rations and got sick as dogs."

"They showed us where all the SS was hidin."

"Remember the one they stomped to death?"

"Yeah. Why not? But they took care of that one guard, remember."

"Yes. Said he was good to them. So they weren't all animals."

"Shh-it, he seen the writin on the wall."

"Could be. Sid had that big Polack broad."

"You're dreaming."

"The hell I'm dreaming. You played that licorice stick and she laid right down."

"You're crazy."

"Yeah? How about the lieutenant's party in Linz?"

"What party?"

"The fraternization party. He had the mayor's wife."

"An you had the police commissioner's wife."

"You're both dreaming."

"She kep on sayin *shpiel, shpiel.*"

"*Shpiel* 'Shtardust.' "

"*Shpiel 'Mein* Referee.' "

"You had her in their bedroom. Under the feather deck."

"An she kep on askin you to *shpiel.*"

"So you said sure and while you were playing up north, she was playing down south."

"Boy, you guys are really dreaming."

"You tol us, buddy boy."

"He remembers, he's just shittin us easy."

"And aftuh, you tol her you was Jewish."

"You're in dreamland."

"Oh sure. You said that's a corkscrew and *ish bin Jude.*"

"An she just looked up and said *shpiel* 'Night *unt* Day.' "

" *'Nacht und Tag,'* you plow jockey."

"Yeah. Uh huh."

"Hey go on up there an play."

"Come on . . ."

"Show the sadsack what it's all about."

"I'm out of practice."

"Shee-it, you kin play that thing in your sleep."

"No, really . . ."

"Hey little lady, tell him to play that thing."

I looked at Janet. Her eyes were shining. I got up and walked to the bandstand; I heard a patter of applause behind me. I leaned up to the clarinet man and asked if he'd like to take a break, that I'd like to sit in. He looked at the piano player who nodded. He handed me his stick and made tracks for the bar. I stepped up to the platform and took his chair. "What do you want to play?" said the piano.

"I'll try and follow you."

"No, be my guest."

I looked down at table 23 and shook my head. Bux yelled through his hands, " 'What a Difference a Day Makes.' " I turned to the band; the sax said, "I'll have to fake it," but the piano said, "Yeah, I know it, Dinah Washington's tune." I nodded and tried a few scales; gee dad, it wasn't a Wurlitzer, but it was OK. Piano and drums took off and I came in at twenty-four little hours. The Benson combo, Joplin, '43. Couples walked onto the floor and easily picked up our beat, among them Bux and Janet. She was still looking at me, no matter how he turned her, so I started to get twisty and slurry. When we finished the tune, Bux whistled with circled fingers and Soc was standing below me applauding like crazy. " 'Woodchopper's Ball,' buddy," he called up. Again I looked at the band and again piano and drums nodded; sax wiggled his fingers, well he had faked pretty good so I said OK. How's this? said drums, tapping lightly. Little faster, I said. Give me the beat, he said. I tapped, he and piano picked it up, I raised the stick, saw Reece's, Liverpool, '44, and blew. We were all a little ragged at first and I was worried about the drummer, on the first number he'd had a quarter-beat rest between each tooth and I figured he could never keep up with me, much less kick out. But with the chips down he met the challenge, which (as I've always said) proves any mouse outfit can play if you give it the chance. Don't misunderstand, Davey Tough he wasn't, nor was that Mel Powell on piano, but second time around we really sounded like we knew each other. By this time I was standing up and beginning to fool around with some head things, bits and strands that curled up out of the past, that jumped from Liverpool to Joplin to Jack Teagarden to one-nights in Reading and Altoona and Berea and South Bend and New Orleans and somehow all merged into Woody's great side. Came then the magnetized response and the old pied piper smiled to himself: a half-dozen couples began to lindy hop, some others jerked into a frug and one old guy even whipped into a Charleston. Best of all was Bux. He had grabbed Janet and was out there doing the Buxby Jump, famous throughout the E.T.O., consisting of an epileptic, all-over jerk combined with a catatonic face while the girl did her best to survive in no-man's land. It was better in suntans and combat boots, but the impulse, the effect were still there: nothing less than the spirit, the *history* of all jitterbugging, and yet it was nothing, absolutely nothing; Bux had a tin ear, he had no rhythm, he was totally uncoordinated except with a carbine in his hands, but here was this Okie filtering the Savoy, the Harvest Moon Ball, every dinky Roseland in the world through that lopsided body. As always it cleared the floor. They formed a wide circle and began to clap the beat. I could see Janet, a pasted smile, ducking under his low-bridging arms, managing a few desperate spins and twirls, but let's face it, Arthur Murray had taught her dancing in a hurry. It didn't matter to Bux in any case; she could have been Cyd Charisse, she could have sat down, thrummed her heels on the floor and cried, for all he knew. I picked up the tempo; no difference. I slowed it down, hell, he jerked to his own drum. I thought for a moment I might break up, but Lucky Bux deserved his "Woodchopper's Ball" and by God he was going to get it. Yes, I know very well it's the Jew's overreaction to the accepting goy, I mean I know it now, I felt it then, but I never gave a shit for motives if the result was good. And this was great. Or it was until his post-war life caught up with him. Suddenly his feet began to shuffle rather than jerk. The body seemed to wind down to an exaggerated slow motion, the blank face grew puzzled. I remember seeing this in Barney Ross against Armstrong, Louis against Marciano, you read about it when they say the legs were gone, or I reached for it and all of a sudden it wasn't there. I think the toughest thing to see, in Ross, in Louis, in Bux, was that sense of betrayal on their face. Joe had it even as he toppled. So did Bux. He went down slow and hard. I saw Janet staring at him. I stopped playing, but drums and piano kept going, after all they had a night's work. I saw Soc and Chick and Miriam running over. Soc yelling give him air! The circle opening. Bux looking up, trying to grin. Then vomiting all over himself. Janet holding her face. Soc and Chick raising his head. He puked again, God how he puked. Soc opened his collar, loosened his tie. He flopped over on his side and began to retch.

The North Atlantic, the convoy, retching into his helmet. Miriam bent down and unbuttoned his shirt and pulled it off. I saw something gleam on his chest. OhmyGod, he was wearing his dog tags!

I laid the clarinet down very carefully and walked off the bandstand. I kept walking until I hit the street. I crossed it and stared into the park and breathed. Someone tapped me on the shoulder. I swung around, ready for a blade, a gun, a chop, a queer. It was Janet.

"Take me with you," she said.

Quietly, thoughtfully, we walked downtown. I didn't know where we were going, but then we came to 50th Street and I knew. We stopped there and I told her about the Roxy. I told her that on June 25, 1943, I saw *Crash Dive* there. On June 27 I was in the army. I told her that Roxy Rothafel was one of my father's great heroes and I showed her where the stage door was supposed to be, where W.J. Boody Jr. and I waited to see the Gae Foster Girls. The rest of the world could take the Rockettes, give us the Gae Fosters. We continued walking. I showed her where the Astor was supposed to be, the clock where Judy met Bob Walker. I showed her the dim Astor Lounge and Lenny Herman and his band. I showed her Child's Paradise where Glenn Miller played before he hit it, the featured band being Freddy Fisher and his Schnickelfritzers. I showed her the Fiesta Danceteria, the Palladium, the Arcadia and Roseland, the *real* Roseland, with hostesses and tickets and no matter who came and went, always Ovie Alston. I showed the Paramount and the Strand and something called Loew's State where I had seen Julie Garfield in *Force of Evil*, inspiring me to become the new Julie Garfield. Spencer Benson. Yes.

Then we walked to Eighth Avenue and back to 50th, to a gigantic parking lot.

"This is Madison Square Garden."

"It's a parking lot."

"It's the Garden."

"I thought that was down around Penn Station."

"Ersatz. This is the Garden. See that?"

". . . Yes."

"That's Davega's. See that across the street?"

". . . Yes."

"That's Jack Dempsey's. And Roger's Corners. Featuring the Korn Kobblers."

"You . . . loved this place, Sid?"

"Yes. I did. *We* did. The balcony was steep and a hundred miles up and one false step and you were down in the center ring. My father took us to see Clyde Beatty and I punched a kid named Norman Hooplock in his fat belly because he said Sells Floto was better than Barnum and Bailey. I think I saw Hank Luisetti and his one-hander here, but I'm not sure, but I did see Lenny Maidman and Sid Trubowitz and Art Hillhouse and Bill and Bun Cook and Frank Boucher and Neil and Mac Colville and Cunningham and Bonthron and Venzke and Fenske and Joe Mangan and the typographical mile and a stiff named Luigi Beccali and another stiff named Taisto Maki and a one-armed hurdler named Marsh Farmer and a Jewish hurdler named Allen Tolmich and Wayne and Blaine Rideout and Elmer and Delmer Smith and little Phil Reavis, the world's greatest high jumper inch for inch and Greg Rice and his hernia and the City College dumpers . . . Shit."

"Dumpers, Sid?"

"Yes, dumpers. We won the NIT *and* the NCAA in '50 and the next year dumped. Lost games on purpose."

"That's awful."

"Wait a minute, it wasn't their fault."

"How could it not be their fault?"

"You have to know the Garden. Or the way it was. Every tinhorn gambler waving a bill in front of a kid. What did they know? Hook shots. They didn't even know, half of them, where they were going to sleep the next night."

"They had so many girl friends?"

"Christ. They were *ghetto* kids."

"Oh."

"After it broke I said Kaddish for them for six months. I haven't been inside a shul since."

"Oh Sid."

"Hell, it was overreaction."

She touched me on the arm. I glanced down. She had the clarinet look. Oh it had been so long. I covered her hand. The look, the look. I got very tough with myself. "I didn't tell you to work my points. There was a time I would have, but not now."

"I know."

"The guy in the powder-blue flannel suit, double-breasted with the single button and rolled lapel, the double Windsor, the slight peg, the Wildroot and the pomp, he would have, I guarantee, he would have."

"Was he so so awful?"

"A bastard. A make-out artist. After one thing."

"I don't believe that. I wish I had known you then."

"Do you want to come home with me?"

"Yes."

I didn't touch her in the cab. I mean the way it was she leaned her head on my shoulder and relaxed all over and I just sat there. Electra, smelectra, as long as you love your father. At 112th and Amsterdam we got out. I bought a pizza at V&T and we walked to my building and took the elevator up. We held hands. We held hands. Then we walked into the apartment.

I hung up her coat, turned on PAT and slid the pizza into the oven. When I walked back in she was looking at the books. "Where's yours?" she said. I took it out and handed it to her. She held it like it was a Tiffany lily and turned to the title page. "By Sidney T. Benson. What's the T?"

"Just T. I made it up. It rolls better."

"How's therapeutic?"

I looked very closely. I have been on to the con since the age of twelve, but so help me, this was legitimate.

"Embarrassing," I said.

"Then we won't use it."

I looked and she looked back. I touched her cheek, then spun and walked into the kitchen. I took out the pizza, poured the Ruffino, returned and served. She was tucked up on the sofa, shoes off. Marilyn Remo, 83rd Street, '46. Somehow I thought her dance floor awkwardness would carry over, but she was completely at home. I told myself it was my (therapeutic?) manner and not experience and we clinked glasses and drank to literature. Then we ate. All the while, and very cooperatively, PAT poured out its theme song cycle. When it was finished, I asked if she'd like to hear some of the real thing? Of course. I dug in the closet and came back with a stack of B.G. 78's and very delicately placed them on the table and turned it on. "Goodbye" came on. "Would you care to dance?"

"I don't know," she smiled.

"Well while you're making up your mind we'll move closely together in time to the music."

"All right."

In stocking feet she was up to my shoulder. She leaned against it and I put both arms around her and we shuffled around off the edge of the rug. "Rose Room," "It Never Entered My Mind," "More Than You Know," "My Old Flame," "How Long Has This Been Going On?," "I Got It Bad and That Ain't Good." We finished near the window, looking downriver. She turned her head up, closed her eyes and very lightly I kissed her. She opened her mouth and began to breathe. I pulled back, she pulled me down, I pulled back, she pulled me down. Well I had done my best. I took the shackles off my hands and she began to shudder all over. Then she slid around to my ear and said, "Undress me."

"You sure?"

"Yes I'm sure."

Still standing, she lifted her arms and I peeled off her dress. Then I took off her slip, her shoes and that goddam panty hose. I left the bra for last, recalling my problem with hooks. ("Push together," said Nita.) It came off easily. With each item she was a bit less composed and I found that terribly touching. I kissed her

213

lightly all over, especially the well-remembered pressure points (which every boy scout knew would make a girl scout come). Then, very tenderly I led her into the bedroom and arranged her on the bed. Quickly I undressed and again ran over her body. Frankly I was amazed at myself, it had been so long between drinks and I could have pole-vaulted out the window, but I did not want to take advantage and I want that for the record. On the other hand I knew damn well this one needed an orgasm for all kinds of reasons including self-concept, so I surely wouldn't overdo gallantry. When I had worked out the delicate balance to my satisfaction and made mental notes of every caress and corresponding moan, I stroked the inside of her legs, gently opened them, rolled above her and looked down. Her eyes flicked open. I felt her knees snap together. "I can't," she said.

"You can't?"

"I'm blocked."

"What *is* this?"

"I want to but I can't."

"Cut the shit."

She began to cry. I rolled over onto my back. She cried it out and we lay there. Then, because I can't stand blanks, I very quietly sang "Someone to Watch Over Me," chorus and refrain. When I finished she touched my hand and said, "Sid?"

"Yes."

"Don't be mad."

"I'm not mad."

"I can't help it."

"I heard you."

"I'm—"

"The goddam Boulder Dam. I know."

She began to cry again. This time I sang "There's No You." When it was very quiet, she said, "No matter what you think, I'm not a tease."

I turned over and patted her head, "I know, baby."

"Do you mean it?"

"Yes. I know you're not. Come on, let's go inside."

"Maybe if we just lay here for a while."

"Lie. No, it doesn't work like that. It would only get worse."

"I'll take a drink. I'll get drunk. That worked once with Joe."

"No, I don't want to take advantage." (Hear that, out there?)
"Besides, you wouldn't enjoy it or you'd probably get sick as Bux."

"Ughh, that was disgusting."

"Hey leave Bux alone. He'd probably say any broad that wants to get laid but can't is disgusting."

"I had that coming to me."

"Well just leave Bux alone."

She reached down and put her hand on it. I pushed her away. "Don't do me any favors," I said.

"I only wanted—"

"Don't be stupid."

"All right, Sid."

She got up and walked into the living room. Suddenly I reached down and slapped the head. It went down. "Dumb bastard," I said. I got up and walked inside. She was on the couch, still naked, feet tucked up. Still stinging from the slap, I sat down beside her. She leaned against me and I put my arm around her; I considered playing with a nipple, but saw each successive action and rejected the idea. I didn't know what to do so I sang "As Time Goes By." Then I looked at all my books. And it hit me. I walked to the bookcase and pulled out *16 Famous American Plays* and *Six by Odets.* In each one I flipped to *Waiting for Lefty,* the third scene, *The Young Hack and His Girl.* I gave her the Odets book. She looked at it and at me. "I was in this in 1953," I said. "I played Sid."

"Born for the part," she smiled. Thank God.

"Well *I* thought so the first time I read it. I really thought he wrote it for me."

"Maybe he did. I believe in those things."

"I did too. It was at the Cherry Lane in the Village. I read for the part and Jim Posner said, OK, you're Sid, he's you. I was terrific in rehearsals—"

"Of course."

"I was the greatest rehearsal and classroom actor in the world. It was money in the bank. Opening night I walked on, felt the lights, said, "Hello, Florrie," and froze.

"Oh Sid."

"I wanted to. Desperately. It was all there, everything I'd worked on, I was a method actor, and yet I couldn't."

"You . . . blocked?"

"Yes. Completely. I walked off. It ruined the show. I was crazy for three months. I haven't looked at this thing since then."

"Really, Sid? You're not just saying it?"

"Really baby. No shit."

"I believe you."

"I'll tell you something else. That's the story of my life. I played great clarinet—"

"And how."

"And the recording ban finishes the big bands. All the vocalists made it big."

"You have a very nice voice."

"Not good enough. Not for me. I don't have the box. But I was a fantastic actor. I would even astonish myself with the stuff I did. In *class*. They all told me I was the next big romantic star. So I do *Lefty* and freeze."

"I'm so sorry, Sid."

"Don't be. I'm the world's greatest writer, only nobody knows it yet."

"I know it."

"No you don't. But I'll make it, don't worry."

"I know you will."

"How do you know?"

"I just do, that's all."

I kissed that nipple. "Will you read this with me?"

"I could never read lines. Not even in high school."

"Do it for me."

"I . . . I just can't, Sid."

"I'll help you. If you'll help me. Just ignore all the punctuation, that's the secret. Just talk it, don't read."

"I get so self-conscious."

"Well just listen to me and answer with the words on the page. It's really very easy. Please."

". . . All right, Sid, I'll try it . . ."

"OK, now you're talkin. Sit right there. Get comfortable. Think about this guy you're crazy about. Have you ever been crazy about someone?"

"Yes."

"All right, think about your father hating his guts—"

"He did."

"Great. So you're even crazier about him, right? OK, that's the scene. Only it's 1935 and it's your brother who hates your man. OK? Think about that. I'll go outside and come on and we'll take it from 'Hello Florrie.' OK?"

"I'll try, Sid."

"I know, sweetie, I know." I kissed both nipples and walked into the kitchen. I closed my eyes, connected with Strasberg and the Studio and Stanislavsky and they directed me to Izzy and the candy factory and Feibleman and Hoover and his fish and prosperity is just around the corner and when I was so pissed off I couldn't hold it, but somehow did, I walked slowly in. She was sitting stiffly. Good. I said Hello Florrie and she looked up from the book and in this little voice said Hello honey, you're looking tired. It caught me. I stopped and said nah, I just need a shave. God, I had gotten through those terrible lines! She gave me a brave smile, a real Franny Farmer smile and I walked up to her and we were kidding each other through the first sad passages, bouncing it off each other, re-acting the way Spence Benson and Natalie Windsor did all through rehearsal. Very easily then we moved into the Paris gown bit, the Movietone News and the kiss. It was hard and wet and I was her man. Then we were into her dumb brother and the big-shot money men (Hoover, Goldman Sachs, Feibleman), the pacifist speech, her eagerness to shack up with me, the blues—the 1935 blues, the slow dance in the center of the room, pressed tight, hanging on for dear life, screw the old man, then my old Pat Rooney soft shoe. The books were on the floor. I

217

was shuffling, grinning, she was staring, eyes moist. She sat down. I was on my knees with my face in her lap and we were both crying. And she began to moan, "Oh yes, Sid, I want it, go in, please, go in." She lay on the couch and spread wide. I reached down, she was very wet. I slid in and touched her and she shook from top to bottom. I was rounding third, Soc.

I thought of Sue.

I went down like a melting candle.

She opened her eyes. "What's the matter?" she said.

"Nothing."

"Please stay in."

"No."

"I *want* you to."

"No."

"Why not?"

"I'd be taking advantage. The big man is taking advantage."

"But you said—"

"I know what I said."

"Sid, you'll be doing me a *favor*."

"Not in the long run."

"I don't understand you, Sid."

"That's lousy dialogue."

"Don't make fun of me."

"Some fun. Writers are nuts, OK?"

"*Men* are nuts."

"Have it your way."

"Sid, don't be like that. Sid . . ."

"Yes?"

"I know I can do it. If that's what you're afraid of. I won't be stupid again."

"That's not what I'm afraid of. I told you. You're too easy and I have a conscience."

"I know that. But I resent what you said. You think I do this with every Tom, Dick and Harry?"

"OK, you don't. I'm sorry. That was mean."

"Yes, it was."

"I said I was sorry."

"All right, Sid . . . Sid . . ."

"Yes?"

"Will I . . . will I see you again?"

"Oh Christ."

"I won't, will I?"

"I don't know. I don't think so."

"All right, Sid."

She didn't cry. She just got up and put on her clothes. I put on my shorts. "I'll take you back," I said.

"No. The wedding is all over by now. I'll get a cab to the hotel."

"Where are you staying?"

"The Taft."

"Charley Drew and songs that teacher never taught."

She tried a smile. "Everything means something, doesn't it?" she said.

"Now that's good dialogue."

"See?"

I walked her to the door. She held out her hand. I took it and she shook it firmly. "Goodnight, Florrie," I said. "You look tired."

"Nah, I just need a shave. See, I can do it too." She turned and walked out. I heard the elevator.

I didn't have any pills stashed away—I had thrown them out after the first chapter of BOXERS, so I took three Anacin. I changed the sheets and crawled in and gazed up at the ceiling. Just as I was about to drop off, naturally Bligh came calling. Big hero, he said. I know, said Christian. You could have helped the poor thing out. I know. But you had to be the big hero. Yes. You liked her. Forcrissakes 20 years ago I could have *loved* her. Aha; you had enough there to choke a horse. Don't get filthy, yes I did, didn't I? What happened? You were peeping, you horny son of a bitch. Sue. Yes. Anything else? Sue. Yes, I understand, but what else? Isn't that enough? What do *you* think? Yes, that is enough. Must we always go into this song and dance? I don't, you do. Oh dear. Just whathehell are you driving at, Bligh? Please don't come the innocent with me, you know bloody well. Oh? I'm surprised you didn't have a premature come. You're disgusting. And you? What about me? The facts, sir, just the facts. Oh shit. Yes, m'boy?

If I had laid that sweet young thing and she had come, probably for the first time in her life, I would never get her off my back, is that what you wanted to hear?

Precisely.

XVII

We've given Okinawa back to the Japs.
    What else is new?
    Back. To the Japs.
    All right. But shouldn't you say Japanese?
    Yes, but we gave it back. Look at Sato, he's crying.
    It's been a long time. He's entitled.
    Did Namura cry? Did Kurusu?
    I daresay not.
    Friggin A not. You ever hear my poem about him?
    Yes.
    Saburu Kurusu didn't give a damn, so-o-o
                he took it on the lam,
                   but after he belted Pearl
His plans we sure did ferl. I've heard it.
    We gave it back.
    Well we gave India back to the Sepoys and Kenya to the Mau
Mau.
    But the Japs.

Ah yes, that's different.

Of course it is.

Why?

Well is this what Si Buckner died for?

Who?

You know who. General Simon Bolivar Buckner. Named for another great liberator. Is it?

What?

Christ, what he died for?

Pull yourself together. You ought to be concerned with Haiphong and blockades and interdiction and Wallace and Mays and the Mets and missions to Moscow.

That's a Commie movie.

Interesting point.

Christ, even Agnew was at 'the ceremony!

Can't count on anything, can you?

Not a goddam thing.

Well why don't you get down to some real, honest-to-goodness imperialism?

You smart bastard, I will, I will, I will . . .

XVIII

CHAPTER SEVEN (B.)

I saw myself as at a great inverted distance descending slowly from clouds of heavenly purity back to the sanctified earth of the Middle Kingdom, whence great songs and showers of incense welcomed me and bade me linger awhile.

The world flickered before my eyes.

I stared as an old woman whose face had been folded into a thousand creases arranged herself against a background of mountain, river and flame. As I watched, she approached and passed under my nose a kerchief that exuded the most powerful yet delicate of aromas. Upon seeing the confused eyes of the patient, she grinned, showing a wide expanse of healthy red gum, and cackled over her shoulder:

"He lives. He breathes."

He also speaks.

"Who . . . are . . . you?" he enquires.

That was funny, delightfully funny and she gave vent to her

merriment in the aforementioned rising cackle, as did her confreres gathered all about. When her mouth returned to the trembling normal she squeaked.

"A peasant. An old peasant. As are we all. Harmless and peace-loving. Now who are you, Long Nose?"

"Norris Blake. Of the *World*. At your service."

Hilarious. Joe Miller. Toto the Clown. Whoever called these people inscrutable? Why they were the very models of risibility. I decided whilst they howled that I and I alone must figure out what had transpired. Let me see: Flames. Thugs. *Boxers*. Murderous leader. Guns. Firing squad. Ah Soon. Darkness. I looked at Tientsin. Still there. The foreign concessions. Still burning. I looked for Ah Soon. I saw the mirthful crone. Oh. Then I felt them: My wrists, my ankles. They shot their own flames into my arms and legs. I looked at myself. Bound to the stake. But no question that I lived, breathed, ached.

"Would you please be so kind," I asked, "as to untie me?"

They grew serious. They palavered. Then an old male party approached with a wicked-looking broad sword. He raised same. It trembled above his head and gravity did its work. I closed my eyes. I heard a thin cheer. I opened my eyes. I was free. I rubbed the raw and offending parts of my corpus and as I did so, noted some head shaking, whispering, pointing. Another old woman, similar to the first in the folding area, came nigh, both hands cupped and filled with mud, plain mud. I began to say no thank you, but she, brooking no nonsense from the invalid, slapped the oozing concoction on my raw, chafed parts. At once the stings evaporated into thin air.

"Thank you, granny."

She cackled, shyly I thought. I looked about me. Wonders were on the increase. Herald grazed peacefully some five metres distant. I whistled. He raised his head and clattered up.

"Good old boy," I said, stroking the faithful mask. "So you out-smarted them, too, eh?"

He looked at me rather severely as if to say well what else did you expect? Then resumed his dinner. I reached into my shirt for

the bag that was still there and withdrew a handful of silver. I held
it out to the ancient nurse.

"No," she said firmly.

"Please."

"No."

"May I ask why not?"

"Yes you may ask." She turned and they whispered amongst
themselves. Then turned back. "In your sleep you muttered one
word over and over."

"Ah, and that word was . . ."

"Assumption."

"I see. I will ask no more."

I bowed. So did she, quite charmingly. I returned the taels to
my bag. I drew Herald around and stiffly mounted. I waved at my
rescuers.

"May the Saviour protect you, too," I said.

They all made the sign of the cross. All at once, above the flames
behind them, a beautiful face appeared. The beautiful face frowned.
"Forgive me," I said silently, "tis only to make them happy. I am
quite without religion, in fact I am rather taken with your teach-
ings." The frown turned into a beautiful smile, the exquisite face
nodded, then returned to the flames.

Forelegs up to the sky, hola, and away!

Steady and true, east by south, for three hours we rode alongside
the railway. The sights of strife multiplying as we neared Tangku:
the telegraph line down, also a telephone line, although wonder of
wonders, another single strand of Dr. Bell's genius still stretched
intact up and down the tracks. A bridge burned out, a train smashed
up, three dead soldiers, two Russian, one *Wojen*, a half-dozen
Chinese corpses. I applied the boots.

Saturday, 8 P.M. Tangku, 18 *li*, six miles west of my destination.
Even as we approached I could see and sense and smell the turmoil
and excitement; yes, war has its own repulsive yet attractive excre-
ments. I cantered into town and not a soul took notice of me, a cer-

225

tain sign that great events were in train, since I must say in all modesty that I am usually marked out by looks, greetings, angry silences, curses, cheers, hallos, *something*. Here twas nothing, only the hustle and bustle of preparation. They knew not for what; I knew.

I made my way through the pack to the railway station, usually a sure barometer of the military weather. Yes, even more troops, mainly sailors and marines and mainly Russian, some mounted on sleek, well-fed horses, all newly arrived, I judged, from Port Arthur. Well leave it to the Russ!

I continued on beyond the station and past the godowns, these occupied by Austrians, whom I have always classed as imitation Prussians, not bad fellows if the fight were modest, but watch your rear if it got fierce. Sentries now everywhere and at last some challenges:

"Halt (or *"Achtung!"* or *"Arrêtez!"*), who goes there?"

"Norris Blake, Journalist. The *World.*"

"What is that?"

"A newspaper, man! And I'm about to make you famous."

"Pass."

I galloped on over to the Taku Road. Here all was quiet, ominously quiet. And so on into Taku.

I had come full circle. I was back to my beginning. But this was far from that beginning. Yet also, I knew, far from the end. Somewhere, I suspected, at the apogee of the circle. Or was it the perigee? Either way, hellfire was in the offing and I blessed a certain *exquise* for putting me onto it; hellfire was the bread and meat of my ilk, God help us.

9 P.M. My single great impression is one of compressed silence, hemmed about by the barking and howling of the dogs. These Baskervilles know something. Well I do too. But like them, I know not how or when. I ride for the Town Hall as a sentry who has been promised fame tells me all the women and children have been evacuated there. I ride past that first mean tavern, my first lodging.

A lump in my throat. Cathay, your spell is heavy.

Midnight to 4 A.M., Town Hall. The women and children, all white-faced and silent but totally courageous, are packed into the narrow confines. No amahs that I can see; all the servants have run away. How can one blame them, poor creatures? Yet? Yet, would they return in future in another and dastardly guise? I wonder. I am reminded of an incident of the African war:

Zulu: "You be killed, B'wana, if you no go way."

Master: "But you are my trusty house boy, Ombego."

Zulu: "Not by me, B'wana, by boy nex door."

Yao yen fly about. The Boxers have taken Tientsin. They have not taken it. Seymour is in Peking. He has been destroyed. Yuan Shih Kai and a hundred thousand troops will save us. Will turn on us. Will remain neutral. Will, oh the devil take it! Everyone is splendid, but none more so than these western women. They are angels of light. One, Mrs. Katherine Hearinghouse, wife of a British taipan in Shanghai, here on holiday and trapped, makes the best of a sticky wicket, to say the least. Her skin is a glowing pink, quite transparent in the Chinese starlight; years in the orient have this way with our women. (Did I say "our"?) She has her charming little girl, Rebecca, with her and tells me, for publication, that her faith is in God, England, the Queen and the foreign office in that order. How can one doubt we will be victorious in the face of such conviction!

Sunday, 2 P.M. A train loads up with many of the weary refugees and leaves for Tangku. Others have the Hobson's choice of leaving for the ships in port or remaining. I turn Herald loose in the courtyard, bid him behave and I leave with a party of women and children for the *U.S.S. Monocacy,* under the command of Captain Wise, whom I know slightly from my previous sojourn in Taku harbour. Kempff has already issued his famous command that will resound in all the history texts through the ages, alongside Bunker Hill, that no act of war had been committed against us, so we would not fire the first shot." May we continue to produce officers like this . . .

The day is a confusion of ultimatums, from the forts to the

ships, 31 strong, to the forts. Mr. Johnstone, a Chinese scholar, leaps to momentary fame on the front pages of the world, as he patiently interprets for both sides.

Finally it is settled. 12 midnight is set as the witching hour. The Chinese must surrender by then or the foreign navies will open fire at 2 A.M., June 17, my mother's birthday. I could save them much time and travail, but of course keep my counsel. The channel is being mined by the enemy and he is taking every advantage of the time, our sportsmanship and patience. I find Mrs. Hearinghouse in a hatchway and tell her what I fear is in store. She rocks her baby bravely and unflinchingly and in the same motion reaches out to touch my arm. Ah sainted motherhood!

1 A.M. The scoundrels, yes, scoundrels, sir, have jumped the gun and opened fire! The very first shot flies in a whining parabola straight for the British *Algerine,* but thank God, passes harmlessly through her rigging and splashes over the stern. A great cheer. Kempff does at last what he must do. I dash up to the bridge. The noise is deafening and quite sensational. For five and a half hours we reply. Tis a re-enactment of Manila Bay, only on the international scale.

6:30 A.M. Small boats are putting off from the Japanese ships. They are pulling for the North Fort. Every breath is baited. Fire and shell pass overhead as the boats row into the blazing hell. By dawn's early light they land. The midget soldiers charge in splendid array. They disappear. All pace with great emotion, but with outward calm. At 7 o'clock the rising sun hoists itself over the parapet! Cheers, handshakes, much back-slapping.

7:30. Boats put out from the *Algerine.* I know we have been designated a refugee ship, so Uncle Sam will not see too much of the fun unless I move quickly. I say farewell to Mrs. Hearinghouse, probably forever, kiss the innocent babe. I do not ask Wise for permission; he cannot or will not grant it. I climb down a ladder and as a boat passes beneath, launch out into space and land amidst some startled British marines. "Keep quiet, men," I counsel even as they exclaim, "you will be heroes in a week, I promise you."

"Welcome aboard, lad," sings out a hearty.

8:30 A.M. We grind up onto the shore and leap out. The water is cold, the mud clings. Bullets singing. Shells scream in their deadly arc; one hits a boat; it disappears. We splash for land. I turn for a look at the *Monocacy*. Curses! A shell has struck. I hesitate. The fire flares up, then as quickly dies down. Good, brave lads. I turn back and with the marines make a dash for the Outer North Fort.

We reach the glacis. We cower down. Captain Lloyd Hugh-Benson of Brighton, 36, married, father of three, raises his arm and points. We leap up and rush for the incline. Tis a cold, wet, gray morning, just right for fighting and dying. The man beside me, Sergeant John Drooker of Southport, 45, unmarried, grunts, grasps his arm, curses, apologizes and drives forward. We break now onto a concrete inclined plane, shielded miraculously from the fire; the Chinaman thought he would be the only one to come this way, but that is the history of losing armies since the beginning of time.

We hurl ourselves over the top of the parapet. Bayonets, of which the British are past masters since French and Indian days, clean out the yellow man in two shakes of a pig's tail. He streams away toward Tientsin, there to fight another day. Down comes his flag. Up spins the Union Jack. Three rousing pips. Oh well, next to the stars and stripes, this is best . . .

At 10 A.M., when quiet once again reigned, we went round to inspect the scenes of invasion. Ruin, blood-spattered scenes everywhere. Headless, armless corpses. Blue-jackets collecting and building huge mounds. Torches. No tombs for these poor souls, only the black, acrid smoke spiraling toward the neutral sky. Kempff ticks off the casualties:

Algerine—one officer killed, one badly wounded, three men killed.

German *Iltis*—the commander badly wounded and several men killed when a boiler exploded.

Russian *Konetz*—two officers badly wounded, eight men killed, ten badly wounded, 70 hurt from an explosion in the powder room.

French *Lion*—one officer killed, one wounded.

On returning, we saw every flag in Taku Bar flying at half mast. Ah Soon had indeed given me my story.

Mrs. Hearinghouse and Rebecca were safe. The child had slept through all!

How was that? Fair. Fair? Fair. I see. Yes, rather thoughtful, controlled, perhaps too controlled, all in all, well, fair. You said that. Now don't sulk. I'll do what I damn please; as a matter of fact I thought it was excellent, right down the pipe. Oh of course you would, you have a spontaneous love affair with every word of yours that slashes paper. Don't we all? Perhaps, but we're talking about *you*. Well you don't have to be so goddam specific about it. Of course I do; look here, the business of the English woman. Yes? Sue again? Maybe. Or little Janet? I don't know, maybe, I never tamper with my talent. Pardon me! Go screw yourself. See, you are sulking. OK, so I'm sulking. Good; now the business with the complexion, a bit much don't you think? I do not; Mary Duckett, Liverpool, '44, wall job, had just such a complexion; all the limey girls had it during the war; listen I even considered saying it was due to Pear's soap. What in the world do you know of Pear's! Some memory; the encyclopedia the old lady picked up in a rummage sale on 181st Street in 1930, you remember how she loved rummage sales? Ah yes. However, I thought that would be reaching a little. It would indeed; Captain Hugh-Benson was bad enough. You caught it! Of course, you threw it; was that really necessary? Shee-it, tickle posterity's ass a little, remember *Interplay,* the cigarette Johannsen smoked? *Benson* and Hedges . . . Yep, Hitchcock can do it, *I* can do it.

ENOUGH!

XIX

Shouldn't you be paying attention to Moscow?

I could care less. Two ribbon clerks. Banker and broker. Pishee payshee.

Isn't the expression, I couldn't care less?

Either way I could care less.

Kremlins, Nicky, Alexandra, Rasputin, Anastasia, the Finland Station . . .

Yes yes. You've heard of their Irish general?

No.

Tim O'Shenko.

Not too good.

Well I told you.

How about Mays?

I wish he weren't back.

You can't be serious!

I am. Completely. Now I can't hate the Giants. I can't turn to the boxscore lusting for them to lose 13 to 11. They lose, he has a big day, see? Now . . .

You could care less.
You're getting the message, boychik.
Bombings at Columbia?
Not Kent Hall, so let em bomb.
What is it with you, Christian?
I've been thinking.
Uh oh.
I believe . . . I'm ready.
You mean?
Yes. Mona.
Are you *sure?* I know you have all that jism, but . . .
Yes, quite sure.
The ship? Paris? Geneva?
Yes, yes and yes.
Brunhilda?
Such a sadsong.
Don't I know? Don't I?
Yes you do. I have to admire this, old man.
Thanks. I think though, no, I *know* I have to do it third person.
I'll accept that.
I need the distance. And the proximity.
I said I would accept.
Also Benson. He must go.
Ah.
Alan. Yes, Alan. Katz.
Why?
I like it, that's why. And I can call him Tab.
Tab Katz.
Yep. And say he chases pussy. That's a little play on words.
Do tell.
I thought you'd appreciate. Bligh?
Yes?
Stick around, will you?
Of course I will, Fletcher.

THE BOUNDING MAIN

July 1952, and the *Vasco da Gama,* Portuguese ancestry, Pana-
manian flag, Italian crew, German music, was a wallower. He could
see that as he leaned over the rail and pointed down at the cubic
litres that flooded and clashed in on themselves, basically an interesting and scientific sight, but right now shit for the birds. For at
this moment his forehead was lifting off each time the *Gama* wal-
lowed down and he was kept busy feeding the fish, even as Garrett
Buxby eight years before, even though there was nothing left to
feed with.

After he finished his 16th feeding session, he decided he could
not really count on a helicopter and cool white hospital sheets, so
he made his way along the deck that kept snapping at him until
miraculously he reached an open door and an alcohol smell and
a big beefy nurse to whom he confided he did not feel too well.

"Zee zick?"

"Yes."

"Take zis."

She handed him a husky, bullet-shaped pill which he quickly
stuffed into his mouth and swallowed. He looked around for some
water. The nurse shook her head.

"*Nein nein.* Ziss iss zuppozitory. Put in za rectum. *Mein Gott.*"

He looked around the room sheepishly. She shrugged, gave him
six more pills, wrote his name down and said, "Remember, za
rectum. *Gott!*"

He nodded softly and walked out and went topside and this
time watered the fish. Then he walked below and stopped at the
first head he came to and sat down and took his temp rectally with
a suppository. Almost immediately he felt a calm warming sensation that sizzled up into his belly and seemed to line it with velvet.
Gingerly he let go of the hand grip and looked around. He mopped
his sweating head with a wad of toilet paper. He took a deep
breath and looked at the floor; it was cowering down and purring.
He took special note of that head, the only place he had felt like
Alan Katz in two days, and he patted the iron walls. Then he

wrapped the five remaining, precious bullets in his handkerchief, stored them where he could connect when things got rough, stood up, pulled, zipped and belted and walked out. Suddenly his knees were marvelous gripping hinges in riding, *mastering* this baby.

That night he went down to his first supper.

"Hey look what's here," said Jay Pintchik, the Staten Island teacher, who of course developed his sea legs riding a nickel ferry. Alan smiled and nodded at his table mates, whom he hadn't seen since breakfast off Sandy Hook, when everything still seemed rosy.

"Feeling better?" said Mr. Bruckel, the Munchen Grill on East 86th Street.

"Much better," he said. "Thank you."

"Plenty bread," said Mrs. Bruckel. "And *kartofel*. Pack za stomach."

"Uneeda Biscuits," said Wendell Finestone. "That's what we recommend for car sickness." Since Wendell was the owner of Fine's Motel outside of Monticello, he should know; Alan filed that away. He smiled and swallowed. He felt his eyes roll and his stomach elevator up and down, but he hung in. He hung in all the way through supper. He even hung in with the conversation, using his Julie Garfield-Nick Conte delivery because he felt so grateful to feel like a person again. Ergo so anxious to please. Also he felt clean and new. That was the real pleasure. The clean feeling and the newness. Cut new from the crap of the old (new) world, still a week from the new (old) world, suspended with all his cleanness and newness in this third world. He filed that away too, under "Emotional preparation, Stanislavsky."

After supper he went topside with Jay and Wendell and took a spin around A deck. All at once he was meshed with the deck, the water, the sky, they were him, he was them, deep within the newness. So he was very receptive when at 8 o'clock Wendell said let's see what's what. They walked down to the casino and sat around a bolted-down table and ordered drinks. They listened to a gemütlich combo play things that brought tears to the eyes of Mrs. Bruckel at the next table. He did not tell anyone he could play fine clarinet, for he saw that as a past chapter in his life and besides he didn't want to sit in, so he fingered the bullet in his pocket and sipped his white crème de menthe. Wendell sighed over his Jim Beam and looked around the room and said that, that, and that. What? Go. Come on. All right, watch. Wendell got up and walked across the room and when the band struck up "Donna Clara" he bent low and asked a "that" to dance. She shook her head, so did the second one, but he was a Fearless Fosdick and the third "that" shrugged coolly and mouthed why not? They danced right through the break and Alan studied them (as he studied everyone since taking up dramatics) and admired the way Wendell kept the ball bouncing until they were holding hands between numbers, which frankly he had never suspected with this cool "that." Jay, who in Wendell's words was more bullshit than boy, did not dance, but soundtracked with sardonic aloofness those that did. How pathetic, how stupid, how this, how that. More bullshit than boy.

When Wendell came back to the table his eyes were wide. "No question," he said, sitting down, "she is hungry."

"Didn't she have supper?" Jay asked.

"Hungry for it. *It.*"

"Oh," said Jay. "How do you know?"

Wendell ticked off points. 1. Belgian. 2. Married to a fifth consul. 3. Husband re-assigned to the States. 4. Going home to see mama.

"So?" said Jay. Alan smiled.

"So I've seen them come through the motel on singleton vacations. Hungry."

"What about the friend?" said Jay.

"Now that is a reality factor. Two singletons together. They get crazy. Each refuses to give the other the idea she goes. That confirms the fact, see. If they go in isolation they can always convince themselves it never happened."

"I don't see that," said Jay.

"Do you see it, Alan?"

"Yes," he smiled.

"There."

Wendell loungingly avoided looking toward the fifth consul's wife until the combo returned to the stand. Then he jumped up and said to Alan, "OK, you got the friend."

"How about Jay?"

"I don't dance," said Jay hastily.

"I don't know if my stomach is up to it."

"Then dance on your back. Talk. Come on."

He got up and with hinging knees walked with Wendell to the girls' table. He stood there riding the ship as Wendell said, "Ladies, this is my good friend, Alan Tab Katz. Alan, this is Martha and this is ah—"

"Billie," said the tight-haired, eye-lined friend.

"How do you do?"

"Hello," said Billie, looking. Martha nodded.

"*Dansez vous?*" said Wendell.

"*Pourquoi pas?*" said Martha.

They walked off and merged and continued where they had left off. Alan zigged as the *Gama* zagged and said "Would you care to dance, Billie?"

"All right."

They moved off to "Oh Mein Papa" and to his unconditional delight he found himself commanding the floor with smart toes and relaxed knees. He began to hum along.

"You have a nice voice," said Billie. "Did you study singing?"

"No. Music in general." Well, she had asked a direct question.

As always the music answer did something. She arched back and looked at him, then came close, "I like a quiet voice," she said.

He felt so good that he began to sing along with the band, quietly, with his best phrasing, suiting method emotion to the words. "You sound like someone," she said. He merely kept on singing. "At Last" and "Amapola" and "On a Little Street in Singapore." Billie, who was tight-bodied, although she didn't wear a girdle, relaxed and let him do all the work. By the time they were into "Elmer's Tune" she was asking him not to stop. He complied and at the end finished up with a neat little dip which left them close and hand-holding. She looked up at him and said, "Edward

236

G. Robinson. You sing like Edward G. Robinson, if he could sing."

"I guess so," he rasped.

She squeezed his hand. "Let's sit down, see," he snarled.

She punched him lightly on the arm. "That's cute." Hand in hand they walked back to the table. As they sat down, Wendell was saying, "Buffalo Bill."

"Nyeah," snarled Alan. "What about him?"

Billie punched him again. Wendell turned. "Buffalo Bill Motels. A string of them across France."

"Nyeah."

Again she punched; she had sharp little knuckles. "See?" said Wendell to Martha. "He understands."

"Nyeah."

"Jesus," Billie said.

"What?" said Wendell.

"Nothing. I just think Alan is cute."

Wendell glanced at Tab and fluttered an eye. "Hey," he said, "it's awfully warm down here. How about a stretch on deck?"

The girls looked at each other. Wendell looked at Alan.

"All right," said Martha.

"All right," said Billie.

"Nyeah," said Alan.

Wendell paid the check and they walked out and up and aft. Alan glanced up once as he climbed behind Billie; nice fat behind the knees. They walked back to the fantail and stopped at the semi-circle of rail that rounded off the ship. The *Gama* bounced a little, but he didn't mind. A few feet away Wendell was leaning against Martha who was leaning back. Billie stood beside him and they gazed off into the night. He sighed.

"It's pretty," said Billie.

"Nyeah," he snarled.

"That's enough, Alan," she said quietly.

"I'm sorry."

"No. It's all right. How come you talk and sing like Edward G. Robinson?"

"I don't always."

"Well why do you when you do?"

"I'm an actor."

"Really?"

"Really. Though not too successful yet."

"I met George Raft. At a Hadassah benefit. He was very short."

"He tosses coins."

"Uh huh. Who else do you do?"

"Cagney and John Garfield and Nick Conte."

"Richard Conte?"

"Nick. Before he went to Hollywood."

"Do him."

He sang "Old Black Magic" as Nick Conte.

"That's cute. Do you like to do them?"

"Sure."

She squeezed his hand and the suppository he was holding dropped into the ocean. Drat. He looked for Wendell and Martha, but they were gone. He turned back and as he did Billie turned too and before he could change direction she had her arms around him and was kissing. He felt the ship twitch and grabbed her and kissed back. He could taste cigarettes and whiskey. She tightened around him and started the breathing thing. She reached down and before he knew it, *almost* before he knew it, he was in. They rocked with the boat. "I like cute boys," she breathed.

"Uh huh."

They rocked some more.

"Especially when they don't get fresh."

"Uh huh."

"I can't understand fresh boys."

"Uh huh."

"Do Nick Conte."

"Do Nick Conte."

Rock.

"Singing?" Rock. "Or talking?" Rock.

"Ahhhhh. Sing-ging. But . . . don't . . . get . . . fresh."

"All . . . right."

She was digging into him now. Goddam sharp little claws. He sang "Elmer's Tune" as Nick Conte would sing it. At the last bar, she shuddered and sagged against his shoulder.

"Don't get fresh," she moaned.

"I won't."

WHEREIN TCHAIKOVSKY STEALS FROM FREDDY MARTIN

The next morning he doled himself out one of the friendly bullets in his friendly head and then meshing with confidence went topside to meet with that (third) world. For'd he walked, past the focs'le and the bridge, to the busy bow. The other half lived here in the morning sun, sprawled out on hatch covers and coiled ropes. Students—young, old and has-been—in levis and chinos and bras and sweatshirts and T shirts and Coppertone and beer and red wine. A genuine obstacle course, but with his new knee-sense he navigated easily through and up to the fat prow. He squinted out professionally at the slosh. No sweat. Not with his asshole buddies. He patted same and made his way through the clutter and sat down on a hatch cover. He leaned against a funnel, turned up to the sun and peeled up his T shirt. He closed his eyes and gave himself 15 minutes for the initial solar bite.

He was up to 12 when he heard Freddy Martin. Well not exactly Freddy Martin. Well Tchaikovsky as Freddy Martin. Or Freddy Martin as Tchaikovsky. Well, either way, "Tonight We Love." Or "Concerto for Two." By Claude Thornhill. You pays your money and takes your choice. Softly he popped his tongue against the roof of his mouth along with Freddy-Peter-Claude.

"Please stop making that noise."

He opened his eyes. She was sitting on a coil of rope, guarding a small portable phonograph. She was long and thin, with nice smooth legs encased in chopped-down levis. Loose T shirt with little to show topside except two buttons. Pageboy bob. Oh, and a small, wild nose that started out for the right ear, hesitated, then

239

plunged straight down. The voice, somewhat ball-breaking, was Wisconsin or northern Illinois, if three months in speech class meant anything.

"If you listen carefully," he said, "you will note that my pitch is absolutely correct."

"I don't care about your pitch, it interferes with my record."

"I certainly wouldn't want to interfere with Tchaikovsky's Piano Concerto."

"Oh," she said. Just Oh.

And she looked at him with that wild nose. Then she put her finger to her lips and pointed to the phonograph. He nodded and to himself pitted the world's sweetest sax against the world's lightest piano. Sax won. Naturally. He smiled and closed his eyes and went with Freddy, superimposing the Tony Martin vocal. When all was quiet, he opened his eyes. Wildnose was locked around her smooth legs, her own eyes bye bye. Just then she popped them open. They were big and brown and wet. She smiled and he smiled back. She reached down and clicked off the phono.

"Aren't you going to turn it over?" he said. He was going to say flip, but you flipped Freddy, not Tchaikovsky.

"No." Said with no trace of a broken ball. "That's all of the Concerto I can take at one time. Hello. I'm Mona Witkin." She held out her hand.

"Hello. I'm Alan Katz." He took the hand. It was long and cool and he had the sure feeling he was sliding along her leg. Then the hand slid away.

"Not everyone recognizes Tchaikovsky," she said.

"No? How could they not?"

She smiled again. It really changed the silly putty in the center of her face, therefore the face. It helped her resonance mask too. "You would wonder, wouldn't you?" she said. "But they really don't. I'm sorry I was nasty about your noise."

"That's all right."

"Do you really have perfect pitch?"

"Yes."

"And can you really play along?"

240

"Not quite play. Accompany. Although I *can* solo."

"Let's hear."

"Some other time."

"Let's hear." She said hir-r-r.

He inhaled deeply. She said she couldn't take too much of Peter I., so he riffled through his repertoire and came up with Puccini. He popped out *"Un Bel Dì."*

She clapped her hands and exclaimed, "You really can. That was 'Butterfly.' "

He shrugged. "It's just something I do."

"Well I never heard of anyone else who can do it. It's really quite creative. Couldn't you get on Ed Sullivan with something like that?"

"Nah, I'd never do it for money."

"That's nice."

He felt a little blip. "Well," he said, "that's my position."

"I just wish more people in this lousy world felt like that."

"Oh there's a few."

"Like hell. That's one reason why I like Tchaikovsky."

"What is?"

"If he were alive today don't you think he could make a million dollars in our wondrous land of opportunity? He'd say the hell with it and stay where he is."

"Well he was supported by patrons in Russia." Was also queer as a three-dollar bill. He didn't say that.

"I should hope so."

"Therefore he doesn't need America."

"Precisely my point."

"Oh."

Then she said something that sounded so corny, he could never think about it without blushing. She said: "I like to talk to you, Alan."

He blushed. Tab Katz *blushed*. "You're from Illinois or Wisconsin," he blurted out. Tab Katz *blurting out*.

"Wisconsin. Eau Claire. That's marvelous."

"You're easy."

241

"Well you're not. Ohio?"

"No," he said, terribly pleased.

"Pennsylvania? Oregon?"

"Come on. You're guessing wild. New York City."

"You don't sound at all like New York."

"Well I've cleaned it up a little."

"Are you a speech teacher?"

"No . . . I'm an actor."

She looked, no gazed. Yes she did. And he leaped in with "What school do you go to?"

"How do you know I go to school?"

"You sound like it." That was a little better.

"You win. Northwestern."

"Charleton Heston's school." Yeah.

"It is? I'm sorry you told me that. I detest Hollywood."

"Well it can be pretty bad." Fink.

"The hell with it. I'm leaving the wondrous country for a whole year."

"Junior year?"

"Yes. Geneva."

Shee-it, seven years ago, he had *saved* this "wondrous" country. He considered, then decided, yes, he must do it.

"You know Freddy Martin made a hit record out of the Piano Concerto."

"I don't believe it." Christ, she was strangely innocent.

"It's true. And another one out of the Grieg Concerto. Called it 'I Look at Heaven.' "

She looked him in the eye, then reached down, scooped up the record, got up and walked to the rail and scaled it far out into the ocean. It sank slowly. She came back and sat down.

"I'm sorry," he said.

"It's not your fault. I should have known." Her nose waggled as if the *Gama* were floating over Newtown Creek. "Don't *you* ever go popping at the Copacabana," she said, "or I'll throw you overboard."

"You asked me if I could get on Ed Sullivan," he said, smiling wickedly to himself.

242

She frowned and he was instantly sorry. "I did, didn't I?" she said. "But you said you'd never be a whore. Promise?" The smooth hand was out. He took it and blipped again.

"I promise, Mona," he said. Her hand remained. They looked at each other. Just then someone yelled, "Hey, the *United States*." He looked up and sure enough, there she was, thin and sleek and blue, whipping toward them. They stood and hand in hand walked to the rail. The *U.S.* caught up and soon was racing away to the horizon.

"Her maiden voyage," he said. "She's out for the record."

"Oh she'll get it," Mona said, withdrawing her hand. He glanced at her. "Its a hundred percent aluminum," she said disdainfully.

A MORAL DILEMMA

What a stable, gut-packing, pleasant supper!

She walked past during the soup and smiled and helloed. She was wearing a slender dress that dropped straight down from the two buttons and did fine things with the smooth legs. He helloed back. Wendell murmured into his hand, "Not bad from the neck down, but no tits." He ignored it and packed in some bread and Cagneyed with Mrs. Bruckel through the meal. He sneaked several casual looks across the dining room and saw Mona turn on the transforming smile as she focused on her table mates. The *Gama* tried to bug him with a sharp drop and a shudder; he looked at Mona. No sweat.

After supper he walked topside and aft with Wendell. They studied the sunset and Wendell said, "You're not letting me down tonight, are you buddy?"

He looked at the purple and black and orange. "How do you mean?" he said.

"I mean I think I can get in."

"I thought you got in last night."

"Hellno, that was just a finger. Tonight's the night. Zig zig."

"Good luck."

243

"Not if Billie's hanging around. I need help."

"Yeah?"

"Yes. How about it?"

"Forcrissakes, she's a consul's wife."

"Fifth consul."

"Same difference."

"Shit, I'm doing her a favor. It's patriotic. She'll be sweeter to her husband and our foreign policy will improve."

"It's not kosher."

"What are you, my conscience?"

"No."

"Listen, how did you make out with Billie?"

"That's different."

"Shit me easy. She's somebody's daughter, no? Daddy's little girl?"

"I get the point. It's still not the same."

"All right, let *me* agonize, OK?"

"I'm just posing the moral dilemma, that's all."

"Screw *that* moral dilemma. She's over 21. The real moral dilemma here is are you gonna help a friend or not?"

"Oh all right."

"Gee thanks. Come on I'll buy you a drink. And throw in some philosophy. Just remember this whenever you start to think too much: Quiff is quiff."

He stuck to white crème de menthe and at 8:30 Wendell said here they come. And in they sauntered, carefully, without looking around. They sat down at an iron table. "Come on," said Wendell, "we can finish the drinks at their table."

His duodenum blipped. "You go ahead. I have to go to the john."

"OK, I'll meet you at the table. Let's synchronize. I'll cut out at 11. From 11 to 12 I'll be on A deck forward behind the blue and white ventilator. I've set up two deck chairs there. By 12 she should be ready. Up to 12 the cabin's all yours."

244

"Thanks. See ya."

He walked out and aft until he found friend john. Inside he waited for his special seat, then fixed up with a magic bullet. Then pulled himself together and walked out to perform his moral duty.

As soon as he walked back to the casino he saw her.

She was sitting with two girls on the other side of the dance floor. He looked at the moral table. Wendell was all over Martha who was nothing loath. Billie was . . . Billie. He turned and hustled back to the throneroom and took another bullet. Then, gutfull of sizzling confidence he returned and walked across the room.

"Hi, Mona."

She shifted up to him, every slender bit of her. "Hello Alan," she said with sincere, complete delight. "Oh I like your jacket."

Simple, so simple; the duodenum blipped. "Thanks. I like *your* outfit."

She smiled and gave herself a face job. "Alan," she said, "these are my friends, Juliann and Fay."

N.Y.U., City, Hunter, Queens, take your pick. They had obviously been briefed on the actor. He smiled down at them and said, "Mind if I dance with your friend?"

"Of course not," said Juliann.

"Of course not," said Fay.

"Mind if I dance with you?" he said to Mona.

Out of the million things to say, she picked, "I'd love to." He blinked and followed her out on the floor. She turned and slipped in and they moved off to "Our Love." Peter Ilyitch. He said into her ear, "You hear that?"

"Yes, and I recognize it, darn you."

"Shall we go overboard together?"

"Not tonight. Maybe tomorrow."

She snuggled in and piddled with the back of his neck. Dorothy Foster at her sweet 16 party. He shivered. The combo switched into "Underneath the Arches," he dared a quick spin, she timed it perfectly and they nestled back together and stayed that way

245

through "Lili Marlene" which he sang with the clean lyrics. They never missed a beat.

"You dance New York style," she murmured.

"What's that?"

"Loose and smart-alecky and kicky."

"Thank you."

"It's nothing to thank me for. *You* do it."

"Depends. On who I'm dancing with."

She threw him a glance; no it was better in French, *un coup d'oeil,* an eye shot. *"Merci bien,"* she said.

He reached far back. *"De nada."*

Again the eye shot. Then the snuggle. "Smart-aleck," she whispered. Someone kicked him in the ankle. He lashed back and swung around to protect her. It was Jay. And Billie. He nodded at her; she threw him a thunder of the eye and folded into Jay who looked at the ceiling with a moth-eaten grin. Thanks, Vulch. He Katzed Mona in a reverse circle and dipped like mad on the final bup a dup. They stood there on the floor as the records came on and at "Let's Get Lost," moved together, the only couple on the floor. He sang with Eberly vibrato but Garfield intonation into her ear; it was thin and shiny and whorly, like a piece of fine lettuce. In no time at all he had her giggling. Suddenly she said, "Gosh, we're the only ones on the floor."

"So?"

"I feel so conspicuous, Alan."

"So?"

"Let's sit down. No. Let's go outside and get some air."

"OK."

Hand in hand they walked through the casino and out to the passageway. He led her aft until they reached the rail. Two couples already in position. Perhaps Billie and the Vulch; Wendell and his moral duty were up for'd by now. He hoped the Vulch could synchronize.

They leaned over the rail and studied the white wake, straight as a plumbline. Then she said, "Alan," and he was kissing her and trying to maintain some starlight between them. She was all per-

246

fume and soap and dampness and Gordon's Gin and he drank her in. She drank back and then he felt the thinness boring into him and he bent backwards until he figured oh hell and stiffened against her. She murmured into his mouth and reached up and firmly unlocked his arms and guided his hands to her chest. He pulled away. She pushed them back. This time holding him tight against the two buttons. Slowly, as if testing the glue, she dropped off; he stuck.

Then she began to writhe softly beneath his hand and he found himself massaging in the opposite direction. She was suddenly pointy hard. "Mmmm good," she murmured, "tha's good." He nodded, quite amazed at all the things they were doing at once: the belly-rock, the button-stroke, the reciprocal drinking, the murmuring, to which he contributed yes and uh huh. He was even more amazed by the elasticity of what had seemed a rather cute, small mouth. It just kept on stretching bigger and bigger and he kept on sinking in deeper and deeper. At one point he even said to himself Christ this must be Capistrano, here comes another swallow. At another point he had a (quickly erased) image of himself as the tamer disappearing into the lion's mouth.

Then he felt something new: he felt *her* hands. They had been neutral, except to glue him on, but now, sonofagun, they were moving around downtown. Yes, around the vital stress and strain area. This co-ed from Northwestern. He waited until he was absolutely sure, then reached down and gently pushed her away. She opened her mouth wider, lifted his hand to the uncovered button, then descended again. Again he pushed her away, not quite so gently. In tandem they went back topside. Pause, and so help him she was down around the crotch, which was now beginning to really bulge. He pushed. She said into his mouth, "Yes, dammit!"

So yes it was.

Then, whatthehell, if that was the story, Wendell, or for that matter, the pre-*Gama* Alan Tab, wouldn't have hesitated. Leaving one hand to cover a button, he lowered the other and rolled up until he felt the hem of her dress. He lifted and pushed in. Yowsah, the legs *were* smooth. He slid around there for awhile and then

247

pushed in between the smoothies. She opened slightly and he slipped his hand in neatly. He then started to move up until he felt the tight panty crotch and a smattering of hair. He took a deep breath, pulled the panty out and snaked in.

She clapped together and with a violent swipe pushed his hand away.

"Whatthehell do you think you're doing?" she snapped.

"I thought . . ."

"The hell with what you thought. Don't you dare touch that."

"I . . . was . . . only . . ."

"I know what you were only."

"I'm . . . sorry, Mona."

She looked at him. "The all-American syndrome," she said. No, sneered.

"I said I was sorry."

"Yes, I'll bet."

"Well you . . . Never mind."

Her hand was on his face, turning it. "All right, Alan. I accept that. And I believe you are sorry. I do. Also I take back what I said. You're *not* like the others."

"Don't be too sure."

"I'm sure. I can tell."

"How?"

"Never mind. If you were a girl you'd know."

"Christ, Mona, Mona. I think I'm falling love with you."

"Oh Alan, don't say that."

"I said it."

"You don't even know me."

"What's to know? You're not the first girl I ever knew."

"I'm sure of that."

"Well."

"Well. You're sweet."

"Uh huh."

"Oh Alan."

She was kissing again and the mouth was opening again and she had his hands on her again. He held on, then slowly unfolded

248

and stepped back. She was trembling all over. "Come on," he said. She nodded and he put his arm around her and they walked forward and down to B deck, not too far from last night's station. Billie and the Vulch, thank God, were nowhere in sight. She turned, put her arms around him, sagged and kissed wide open. He kissed back and they began to rock and massage and drink, though he kept his hands strictly uptown. Then he broke off and said, "Good night, Mona," and hurried away. He could hear her breathing all the way down the corridor.

He walked back to his room feeling big and pulsing and a little dizzy. Wendell was already in bed, arms behind his head, smoking and smiling.

"Hi."

"Hi," he said. "Say Wendell, I—"

"Forget it. Jay stepped in."

"I'm sorry. I just couldn't push it."

"I said it was all right. How'd you make out?"

He looked down. He'd been very close to rusty-zipper time. Well he sure wasn't diving into the sack to finish the job; she deserved more than the imploring face in the air, the moaning take me, take me and the whipping hand.

"Wendell," he said, "I'm no prude, but I'd rather not discuss it."

STARS IN THE SKY WERE DANCING

Mona. In a bathing suit. Mona. Bottoms. Two peanut shells and a rubber band. You had to admit it. You had to. Ah but the legs, attached like a newborn colt's to the small stuff upstairs, the legs they were smooth and soft and firm. So was the ass. No, *derrière*. And the transformer smile. Feed in 60 volts, get out 120. And you put up with buttons and tiny, flat belly. It was all sexy as hell somehow. And sad. That was the way the afternoon swept by in and alongside the swimming pool. Kicky and smart-alecky and sexy and sad. Rolling the Coppertone into the mournful, bony back and down the firm sexy legs. And when the *Gama* got frisky, you just floated in the postage stamp, dead center and stayed flat and confident.

Twas a glowing, suspended afternoon. Everything in place. Wendell and Martha having their matinee forward. Billie and the Vulch cooking beside the pool.

And at 5:30 he did his special dive.

The back flip with the half twist. The only one he could ever do. Could never push himself into a front dive, for then you could *see* all the danger. And a simple back dive landed him flat on his face. But a flip and half twist brought him feet first into the water and turned him, importantly, out to the world. So he did it. He stalked out on the board and with Mona gazing, turned smartly, balanced, counted two and flung. The world spun, so did he, he spied a smokestack and the horizon and a cloud and then his feet were digging into the surface tension and he knew he was home free. When he thrust up and stroked to poolside Mona was leaning down and kissing.

"I've always wanted to be able to do something like that," she said as they lay beneath the approving clouds. "Just *one* thing like that."

He patted her hand. "I'll show you."

"Never. I'm chicken."

God that was touching. He rolled over and looked up at her. She had the dive expression: Lila Levenson at Schroon Lake, Marge O'Grady, the mick modern dancer at the Concord.

"Gee willikers," she said, "it's six o'clock. I have to run and make myself beautiful and don't you dare say it's gilding the lily."

"Hellno, it's the Mona."

"Smartaleck." She kissed him on the shoulder. He shivered. "See you, sweetie," she said and gathered oil and towels and Kierkegaard and scudded away. He watched the colt legs disappear down A deck. He rolled over. The pool was deserted, while everyone gilded, helped no end by the copper sun. He looked out at the flying fish doing their stuff. Not really flying. Leaping. Like salmon. With terrific dorsal muscles. He must remember to tell that to Mona.

For each of the five remaining days he saw her every afternoon, for'd, or at the pool, and every night after supper, to dance and drink and gaze into one another's eyes. Then topside to do the fabulous things that brought him close, but never quite as he always stopped short at the brink. She had this thing of clamping his right leg with both of hers, bending back and sliding up and down as if she were a V-shaped buzzsaw and he a delicious hunk of pine. It did great things to his autonomic nervous system, not to mention his voluntary motor control. Especially on the night that he forgot himself and reached. She growled and dug her nails into him and made his thumb bleed. He could feel the wet stickiness with his index finger. He pulled away at once (of course), stifling the yell. At that moment, she grunted and reached for *his* crotch. He forgot himself and slapped down hard. She yelped.

"Oh I'm sorry," he said, shaking his thumb out behind her back. "Christ did I hurt you?"

". . . No," she breathed. "It's all . . . right. Oh Alan, I respect you more than anyone I've ever known."

"Respect."

"Yes."

"Not love."

"Alan, please. Don't push."

"Sorry."

"Oh baby, now I've hurt you."

"No, I deserved it. I was stupid."

"No, you're not. You're sweet."

He stuck his hand in a pocket and wiped off the blood. "Let's get you back," he said. She looked up and kissed him. He took her arm and walked to her cabin, concaving a bit so the big bulge wouldn't show. He didn't think at all about the *Gama*'s motion (had even given the extra suppositories back to the beefy nurse who'd smiled, the goddam nazi, and asked how they tasted). When he bent down to Mona, she clamped on his leg and they swung and swayed until he pulled away and he ran to his cabin.

SOUS LES TOITS DE PARIS

Le Quatorze Juillet. Bastille Day. Thank you, Louis and Marie. The going-ashore parties started after lunch, when they first saw Le Havre. Le Havre was brand new and shining. 1945 and the pontoon bridges and the conquerors. The war was very important to you, Mona said over a toast to France. Yes, it was a good war. *No* war is good. Let's not argue, OK? OK, I respect your opinion. Yeah, I'm great in the respect department. Kiss and make up. They drank and danced till three o'clock. Then the *Gama* berthed at one of the bright new piers (made possible by the conquerors) and they went ashore.

They took the boat train and he sat with Mona and her friends and the Vulch and Billie. Wendell insisted on entering Paris first class so he and Martha did it in their own private car. At four o'clock they saw the tower. Mona wiped her eyes; he felt the blip again and kissed her tenderly. They pulled in and she said, Oh Alan, I'm so glad I saw it first with you.

They had six hours to do Paris. They did. First, of course, the tower, and some more tears. Then the Arch and both gardens and Nôtre Dame. She insisted on Père Lachaise, so they went out to gaze down at poor Oscar Wilde. They can't hurt him any more, she said. The English, he reminded her, we treated him pretty well in America. I'll bet, she said. He kissed her and they walked out and joined the dancers at République. They danced to "Frou Frou" and "La Vie En Rose" and "C'est Si Bon" and a blousy-pantsed boy did a passable Georges Guétary on "Stairway to Paradise." They walked over the Pont Neuf and scurried through Montparnasse and then Sacre Coeur and Utrillo country where she dabbed her eyes some more. They drank to Paris at each place (she could really hold her booze, this one) and kept going with only a *jambon* sandwich right up to train time. At a quarter to ten he walked her through the Gare de Lyon and put her on the train to Geneva.

"Are you sure you'll be all right?" he said.

"I don't know. You won't be there."

He kissed her and she moaned.

"I'll come down as soon as I can," he said.

"No, I want you to see Paris. That's what you came for. Not an American girl."

"Not *an*. *This*."

"Sweet thing."

He kissed her and she moaned some more. Mona.

"I meant what I said," he whispered into her lettuce ear. "It goes double now."

She shivered. "Thank you," she whispered back.

"I don't want thanks."

"I know, sweetie, oh I know. Oh Alan, whatever it is I feel, I never felt anything like this before."

The conqueror blipped. He smiled down at her. "That'll do for now," he said.

He walked back to Boulevard Raspail and the Hotel du Nord. Wendell was waiting.

"I thought you'd never get here," he said.

"I was saying goodbye."

"Is she finally gone?"

"Yes."

"You ready?"

"For what?"

"This is Paris, buddy."

"I know."

"Come on, we're going to the Place dee Opera."

"Oh Christ. What happened to Martha?"

"Are you kidding? She's on her way to Brussels and mama. Are you coming or not?"

"No. Go on. Have fun."

Wendell left and he stared out the hotel window at the dancing below. Then he went to bed. But the room would not sit still; it swooped and dived and spun and did a regular *Gama*. He made it to the toilet and was sick as a dog. Oh was he sick. And not one goddam suppository.

He paid his call on Hannah's cousins in the *Quartier Juif,* the Rue des Rosiers. He cashed some traveler's checks on the black market, doing business with an old man in a skull cap and despising him for it. (Mona also despised this kind of thing, she had told him; well what she didn't know wouldn't hurt her.) Then he did the things he had come to do:

1. He went to *Le Tigre,* an existential club in St. Germain, where he drank to Jake Barnes and his poor lost cojones.

2. He took in a *Grand Guignol.* It was boring; he left early.

3. He went to *Le Vieux Colombier* to see Sidney Bechet and his soprano sax. He sat in with Sid and it was great.

4. He caught Django Reinhardt at the *Tabou.* Also great.

5. He walked into the Montana and asked in his best New York French *pour la table où* Jean Garfield *a bu.* They showed him and he drank to Julie. He picked up a girl named Beatrice, who said he looked like Ree-shard Cohntee. He said thanks, he knew Nick. They went dancing and he took her home, to one of those great Paris courtyards, but all she wanted to do inside the gate was dry hump, so he said yes he would call her and walked back to the Montana to Garfield's table.

6. He saw the uncut version of the *Wages of Fear. Les Salaires de la Peur.* Very anti-American. Mona would have loved it; he walked out. But surprisingly, a singer named Montand could really act.

7. He went to the Comédie and saw *Andromaque.* Gérard Phillippe. *Magnifique.*

8. He picked up a girl named Anne-Marie in the Luxembourg. He took her to see *An American in Paris.* Then back to the hotel. Wendell had discovered the high class stuff on the Champs and was paying for Michele Morgan's double (in mink) for the fourth night in a row (also thinking he was falling in love and could reform her), so the room was again all his. The hot, sexy, knowing French girl went obediently to bed and did it passively the same old way. He put her in a cab and sent her home.

9. He went to the *Deux Magots.* He saw someone who looked like Sartre and decided he was Sartre. He drank John-nee Walkaire Scutch and was picked up by a Swédoise who out of a clear blue

sky said she detested Jews. He left her panting against a wall.
10. He went to Pigalle. He walked down the line of shills. He left.
After ten days he got a letter from Mona. In French. It was
trembly and silvery and so sweet he almost couldn't stand it. He
told himself not to be so stupid over a pair of colt legs and two
buttons and a wildnose and that night when Wendell said how
about coming down the Champs with me, he said why not? They
walked out after ten and went directly to the charming sidewalk
cafe where Wendell's bimbo was waiting, all mink and class and
4,500 francs of her. At Wendell's insistence, she called up a friend
and a few minutes later in swayed a brunette, minked, gorgeous,
equally snooty. They drank Moët and at midnight walked back to
their hotel, just off the Champs. When he was alone with Edwige,
she insisted on carefully washing off his private parts, then just as
carefully asked him what he wanted, fuckee, suckee or *les deux.*

"*Combien?*"

"*Deux milles* fuckee, *trois milles* suckee, *six milles pour tout.*"

"*Pourquois pas cinq?*"

"*Oh là. Tout. Au tour de la monde. Tout.*"

"*C'est quatre milles cinq cent pour* Wendell."

"*Bien sur. Il est un grand ami.*"

"Uh huh. OK."

"*Le quel?*"

"*Tout.*"

"*L'argent s'il vous plaît?*"

"Oh shit."

He dropped her a thousand, got up and walked out, walked
back to the hotel and went to bed. He got up at six, checked out
before Wendell returned, took a cab to the station and caught the
train for Geneva.

THE JET D'EAU

That was the first thing he saw. The tower of water. The liquid
Eiffel of Geneva in Lac Leman. It was all so clean and fresh and
new, almost *American,* especially after the shmutzik of Paris. He

felt better already. He pulled in around one, checked his bag at the station and went straight to the dormitory on Avenue Henri Dunant. He walked through the lobby, past all the international girls, took the *ascenseur* to the *troisième étage,* got out and walked to 305. He knocked. A zaftik blonde girl answered.

"*Mademoiselle Mona Witkin,*" he said.

"*Elle n'est pas ici.*"

"*Où est-elle?*"

"*Je ne sais pas.*"

"Oh."

"You are . . . the actor?"

"*Oui.* Yes."

"I am Brunhilda Mueller."

"Oh yes, she told me about you in her letter."

"And she has told me of you."

"She has?"

"Yes."

"Well, I just arrived in Geneva."

"And you came directly here?"

"Yes."

"Mona will be very pleased."

"Well, I wanted to see her."

"*Bien sur.* Of course."

"Do you know a decent hotel *bon marché?*"

"The Hotel Alpe is good. It is very near the station."

"*Danke schoen.*"

"Ah, You are welcome."

"What time will Mona be back?"

"I really do not know."

"May I come back this evening?"

"If you wish."

"Thank you. *A tout à l'heure.*"

"Goodbye."

He returned to the station, picked up his bag and checked into the hotel across the street. From his bay window he could see Mont Blanc. Clean, it was all so clean. Then he walked out and rented a bicycle and pedaled around this clean town, this League of Nations

256

town. He had a quiet little *biftek* in a bistro beside the lake, close to the *Jet d'Eau* and at seven o'clock hurried back to Henri Dunant, who, his research informed him, had founded the Red Cross and not Florence Nightingale. His heart was pounding, no sprinting, when he knocked at 305. Brunhilda answered. Her hair was in braids.

"Mona?"

"*Non.* She has still not returned."

"Oh."

"I am sorry, Monsieur Katz."

"Alan."

"I am sorry, Alan."

"That's all right. I didn't tell her I was coming, so what the heck."

"I see."

He looked at the blonde braids, the pigeon-pouty chest. "Would you care to have a drink with me."

"Thank you, yes. Won't you come in?"

So he walked in. Into Mona's room. And he waited for the German girl, all the time feeling Mona. Then Brunhilda came out and he smiled at her in a ratty fur jacket and they left. Whew. They had a drink at the *Moulin Rouge.* And they danced. And he practiced his wartime German and she smiled very seriously and told him he was the second American she ever knew. The first, in Kassel, was a huge black soldier who had frightened her badly when she was 13 and had given her a chocolate bar and said don't cry, honey, and then soared away in a jeep. Yes, he nodded, night fighters. Night fighters? Yes, we used them to fight the Nazis at night, they did not need to blacken their faces. She hesitated, then laughed very seriously. He patted her cheek. Too bad he hadn't met her before Mona, heinie or no heinie. They danced some more, very correctly, but with chests touching, something Mona couldn't accomplish in a million years. He smiled tenderly at the thought. And he began to talk about Mona. Haltingly at first. Then in a great rush because she listened so well. And her chest was so soft and *sympathique.*

At midnight they walked back to the dorm by way of the lake. The tower of water was glistening in the moonlight. That's Geneva for me, he said. For me also, she said. And you're Geneva, too.

Vraiment? Of course, honey, he smiled, didn't I spend my first day with you? Yes you did, she said very gravely. Mona should be back by now, he said.

"Mona is not coming back, Alan."

"Whatayou mean, not coming back?"

"*Jamais,* Alan."

"Whatayou mean never?"

"She is not to you. *Pas à toi.*"

"Whatyou mean not mine?"

"*C'est vrai.*"

"Whathehell is true? Speak English, will you?"

"She is in Albania."

"Albania? That's a Communist country."

"*Oui. Ja.* Yes."

"What is she doing in Albania?"

"She is there with a *journaliste.*"

"What's she doing with a journalist?"

"She met him here. He was studying for the summer."

"You mean while I was in Paris thinking about her, she was here with this . . . journalist?"

"*Ja.* Yes."

"Why?"

"She is in love with him."

"Bullshit."

"It is so."

"How do you know?"

"She told me. Many times."

"How many?"

"Many."

"She told you that?"

"Yes."

"And you didn't say anything?"

"I told her to be careful. To . . . reflect with care."

"And what did she say?"

"She said she had . . . reflected. She would go anywhere with him. Back to Albania. For he would not come to America."

"She told you that? She would go off with a Communist?"

"Yes."

"The fucking little whore."

"Oh Alan, you are . . . *blessé*."

"Balls. Did he lay her? *Coucher?* Zig zig."

"Je crois."

"Yes or no?"

"Yes."

"Once?"

"Oh Alan—"

"Twice."

"Beaucoup fois."

"Bitch."

"I did not want to tell you."

"I'm glad you did. What are they gonna do in Albania?"

"I don't know. Be together."

"Get married?"

"I don't know."

"He got himself a nice American piece. I bet she's paying their way."

"Do not be so bitter, Alan."

"Who's bitter?"

"It is God's will."

"OhJesusChrist not that."

"Will you come to church with me, tomorrow, you will feel better?"

"Ich bin ein Jude. I'm a Jew."

"I know."

"I bet your father was a Nazi."

"Yes, he was."

"Nazis and Commies. Great."

"Will you try to seek peace with me?"

He looked at the blonde braids, the kirschwasser lips, the swelling chest. He put his hands on the chest. She let him.

"All right," he said. "I'll go to church with you."

He went to church in the morning and she taught him how to cross himself. Then on bicycles they rode far up behind Geneva and she showed him Madame de Stael's house. Very quietly he let her show him around and tell him about the madame in French and German and English. She had prepared a picnic lunch and they ate it far above the *Jet d'Eau*. Then silently they pedaled back to town and he left her at the dormitory. At nine he called her up and asked if she would like to go out for a walk. She would. They walked down to the lake and watched it and the shooting tower. He thought of Albania. He reached for Brunhilda and kissed her. She lay very still in his arms. Then he said oh shit and lay down on the grass and cried. He cried for a long time before he finally felt her roll him over. She was gazing down at him.

"Ah, *tu est beau*," she said.

"Say it in German. *Deutsch*."

"*Du bist schoen*."

"In English."

"You are beautiful."

"Fucking Nazi."

"*Nein*."

"*Ja*."

"*Si tu veux*."

She bent down and kissed him. He grabbed her and pulled her down on top of him. He ran all over her, inside her blouse, kneading the great pouty chest, the Nazi ass, the Nazi legs. He reached under the skirt and drew down her panties. She crossed herself and put her hand on his crotch.

"*Pas ici*," she said.

"Whythehell not?"

"*Nein*."

"Where?"

"In your room. I want you in your room."

They walked back to his room. She undressed, then she undressed him like a little boy. She crossed herself, then kissed it, lay back and pulled him down on top of her.

260

"Je suis encore fille," she whispered.

"Well then let's not do it."

"Ja. Alan, *tu est pure?"*

"No."

"Ja. Dans ton coeur."

He raised up and stared down at her. He started to cry again. She wiped away the tears and said, "Alan, *je veux en enfant de toi."*

"Pourquois?"

"Je t'aime."

He reached down and took off the rubber. "Fucking Nazi," he said, going in. She nodded and held his head and moved very slowly and surely, all the time whispering *je suis encore fille.* Then she moved faster and he began to move with her. Just as he came, he reared up and yelled NAZI!, then burst into tears and buried his head in the fantastic chest. She stroked his hair and crossed them both and whispered over and over, *"Je t'aime."*

They went to church again the next morning, then went back to his room. Afterwards they took the boat ride around the lake, got off near Vevey and walked into the woods where he laid her. They hitched a ride back to Geneva and did it in her dorm room. That night they went out dancing in the Moulin Rouge and then returned to his hotel, past all the (clean) ladies *du soir,* and he took her fiercely, this time yelling Ilsa Koch before the tears. They went to midnight mass that night.

For eight days they did this. On the ninth night he finally was able to sleep. The next morning after church he told her he was going home.

"Yes, I knew it."

"Well I couldn't stay here forever. I'm not in love with Europe."

"Non. Would you take me with you?"

"Ich bin ein Jude."

"Would you?"

"Why don't you say will you?"

"Because I know you will not."

"Well I guess I wouldn't."

"I knew."

"Katz and his Nazi."

"Yes, I know."

"Do you love me, Brunhilda?"

"*Ja.*"

"Say in German, I love the Jew."

"*Ich liebe der Jude.*"

He put his hands on the soft breast. The nipples were stone. Of course, she was a shiksa, a *heinie* shiksa. "*Auf wiederzehen,*" he said.

"*Au revoir,* Alan."

"That is not quite goodbye."

"*Ja. Je sais.*"

He went back to Paris that night. The next day he crossed an agent's palm with some black market silver and got a berth on the *United States*. It was a very rough trip, but he never got sick.

So.

So.

So.

So.

How do you feel?

Not too bad. Surprisingly.

That was quite brave.

Thank you. I believe it is exorcised.

I doubt it.

You do?

Reality has been transmuted.

Oh stop it.

Oh but yes. Now when you think of her, of *them,* you won't know which version to believe.

Nonsense. I told it like it was.

Did you? How many times did Alan make it with Brunhilda? Once, twice, twenty times, *never*?

Alan doesn't remember.

Aha.

Just leave Alan alone.

It's you who brought him up.

Well I'm leaving him in peace. In piece.

Oh that's nifty.

All right, all right.

Tell me, Major Bowes, before we leave Alan, who paid for the trip?

You know damn well.

I want to hear you say it.

Hannah. Well he went back to school for her.

For her?

I thought you were going to help me on this one.

I am. Oh I am.

With friends like you . . .

You're getting smartalecky again.

Please don't use that expression.

I'm sorry. *Vraiment.*

And don't use that fucking language.

Ah but it is exorcised.

Yes, yes. Anyway I got a story out of it.

Oh that you did.

And, Bligh, I know which version I prefer.

Oh? Which?

The next one.

XX

Little Sidney Birnbaum. He used to wait for Izzy's footsteps, his key in the door, the creak of the bed, the soft Hannah-Izzy voices. Then and only then would he smile into the covers, turn over and go to Lily White's party. He always worried that one day he wouldn't hear, and one day he didn't. Benson. He, too, waited. For the phone call. Sooner or later the phone call. Well, it came, later, but it came. Manny.

"Sid?"

"Yes?"

"Something's happened."

"I knew it. Mama?"

"Yeah."

"She died."

"No, Sid."

"What Manny, for crissake?"

"She had a accident."

"What kind of accident?"

"We had a holdup."

"Oh God."

"The guy had a gun."

"Yeah, Manny?"

"She made a grab for it."

"Oh God, Manny, why'd she do that?"

"You know your mother."

"Yes I know."

"So she made this grab for it."

"Yeah, Manny?"

"Well they grappled."

"JesusChrist. Why didn't you stop her. Grappled."

"You know your mother."

"He shot her."

"Yeah, the gun went off while they were grappling."

"Oh Christ, where?"

"In the region of the abdomen."

"Jesus. Is it bad, Manny?"

"Yeah, I think so, Sid."

"Where is she?"

"Jewish Memorial. They got her in intensive care."

"Oh Christ. Manny, are you in the store?"

"Yeah, Sid."

"Well you stay there, you hear me, stay there."

"I'm a little shaky, Sid."

"*You stay there.* I'll pay you double time."

"It ain't that, Sid, jeez I don't care about money at a time like this. But this was a helluva ordeal."

"I know, Manny, I know. *Please* stay. For Mama."

". . . Sure, Sid, OK, I'll stay, goddammit."

"I won't forget it, Manny."

I hung up and called Sue.

"I'll be right over," she said.

"I'll wait for you."

"No, you get over to the hospital."

"No, I'm not so sure I can. I'll wait for you."

"No, Sid, go to the hospital. You hear? I'll meet you there."

"Oh God, I just knew this would happen. Why didn't I take over the goddam place?"

"And drive you and her nuts? Not now, Sid. Get going, Sid."

"Promise you'll come?"

"Yes. Now *go*."

I put on a tie and jacket and took a cab uptown. They said I could go up. I didn't like that. I went up and stood outside the door. I looked up and down Broadway. There are blossoms on Broadway when I'm looking at you. There's a broken heart for every light on old Broadway. Not now, Sid. I couldn't go in. But I had to, I had to, I *had* to be a decent son, goddammit. Then I had a brainstorm. If I *acted* it out, I could do it. OK. I stared out at Broadway. I closed my eyes and did a method preparation. I was Cagney in *White Heat*. I was in stir and we were eating and the whispering chain reached me that Mom had died. I went nuts. I busted out and went to her. Only when I got to the hideout they told me she wasn't dead, just bad hurt. Oh God. I charged in. She was small and thin, except for her face which was puffed up. Her eyes were closed and she had a tube in her nose. She had another in her wrist attached to a bottle overhead.

"Mom," Cagney said, "it's me."

She didn't move or flutter her eyes. I pulled up a chair. She was breathing very heavily. A good sign. A bad sign. I would get the mob or the bulls or my boys for this. I stroked her wrist. I had never done that.

"You got to make it," Cagney said.

She didn't move.

"You been through too much not to make it," Cagney said with a crooked grin. "Jesus, this is nothin compared to the *tzuris* you've had." She still didn't move, but something, I don't know what, told me she had heard. "You can't leave me," Cagney begged. "I need you, Mom. I wouldn't know what to do without you." He leaned his head against the side of the bed; he could feel her breathing; he sat up. "What would Pop do without you?" Cagney said. "And Abe? And what about all the customers? What would *they* do? Mrs. Plotkin and all the *shvartzim*? They call you Mom. And what about

Manny? He got a family to support. Mouths to feed. Would Mrs. Roosevelt let them go without what to eat? You know the answer, I don't have to tell you. Listen, didn't *she* have trouble with her man? Did she give up the ghost? Heck, she opened up a *bigger* store. You got more upstairs than the rest of the family put together. Your cousin in Paris told me that. In French. She said you were the smartest girl and smarter than most of the boys. Would Izzy pick a dumbell? Listen, I wanna go to Paris this summer and I need a couple of dollars. Abe needs some more books. Izzy needs an overcoat. Carlie needs a slip, her old one is a *shmotta*. I swear I'll make her wear it, they won't see a goddam thing. Also a brassiere. I make a solemn promise she will not be *gontz* exposed. Basically she has a very good heart, she does. So has Garth. He's like me, not very demonstrative, but he cares. Who's gonna put him through college? Hell I'm a dreamer, I couldn't in a million years and you know Pop can't. You see? What about that tree you planted in Israel? It needs you. I'll tell you who else needs you. The Prince of Wales. The King. The true king, Mom, the only one you ever recognized. They cut his kishkas out, but you stuck by him then, well he's very sick now and he needs you also."

Cagney looked down. She was very still. Cagney sobbed into his hands.

I felt someone. I wiped my eyes quickly and looked up at Sue. She was very calm and collected. She nodded. "She's going to get another transfusion," she said.

"Another?"

"She's had two."

"Can I give? I'll give."

"I think they have enough. But you can ask."

"Did you tell the kids?"

"Yes. They'll be over later."

"She wouldn't want them to see her like this."

"They should. They'll be here."

"All right, Sue."

"She's very tough, Sid."

"You're telling *me?* She has a little color, don't you think she has a little color?"

"I'm no doctor, Sid."

"But she doesn't have that terrible gray color."

"No, she doesn't."

"What did they tell you? They didn't tell me a goddam thing."

"She's doing as well as can be expected."

"Straight out of *Medic*. She loved *Medic*."

"Why don't you get a cup of coffee. I'll stay."

"You will?"

"Of course."

I got up. She sat down and tucked in a loose end of the bedsheet. Cagney sighed and walked out. It was all right, Virginia Mayo was here.

I had coffee in a grubby little joint that was straight out of *Little Caesar*. OK, Sid, not now. OK. At the second cup I made up my mind. Just like that. The hell with not being a person. I must now not be bullshit, but boy. Me, myself and I. Benson Benson and Benson.

Is that wise?

Uh oh.

Is it?

Look, buzz off, I got no time for sergeants.

I merely don't want you going off half cocked.

You said it, I didn't. I will go off three-fifths cocked or nine-tenths cocked or fully cocked if I so choose. The fact is I always rise to the occasion.

What about Cagney?

Never mind Cagney, he hasn't had a job in a long time, I was just being nice to him.

Yes.

I'm warning you.

Yes.

Don't interfere with family matters.

Very well, Christian, but I'll be around.

I won't notice, amscray on the oubleday.

I ran back upstairs. I walked into that room. That room with no *rachmunes* in it. I filled that room with me. Benson cubed. I brushed her wrist. I willed her to hear, the ancient sleeping beauty. I leaned over.

"I'm gonna get Pop," I said.

I asked Sue if she would come with me. She said shouldn't she stay here. Don't worry, she'll hang on, she knows I'm going for Izzy, she knows and don't tell me I'm crazy, I'm crazy, but I'm not stupid. All right, Sid, I'll go.

I went straight home and packed.

I didn't sleep. I listened to WNEW all night. It was the Steel Pier and the Trianon and Glen Island and waiting for Izzy and the key. I even made myself some hot milk. Straight. I didn't have any Ovaltine or Cocomalt. I got up at five, ate some stick-to-the-ribs oatmeal and took a cab out to Kennedy. Where did I come off to ride cabs? I came off, I came off.

Sue was there. Calm and collected. Not Virginia Mayo, Myrna, Nora Charles. Stop it, Benson. Stopped. I called the hospital. No change. I called Manny and told him he must keep the place open. He understood. I read three Hercule Poirots and a Maigret and at noon we took off. Did you know, I asked her, as we swooshed up, this used to be Trans-*Western* Airlines? No, I didn't, thanks for telling me, now read your books. I read. I read two Nero Wolfes to Kansas City and three Travis McGees to New Mexico. Someday I will write the world's greatest detective story. Over Oklahoma I reinforced my decision. I would be Benson, the whole Benson, nothing but the Benson, so help me Hannah. Twas one of my greatest anti-sadsong decisions. To help, I reviewed every girl I'd ever had, from second base to home plate. Also my Benny Goodman or gold period, my Stanislavsky or blue period, my first stories or burnt sienna period, when the man at *Kenyon* told me that even though they weren't taking them, these were the most exciting things since Sherwood Anderson. Also two chapters of my autobiography, second person.

We landed in Albuquerque at four. As soon as we stepped onto the ladder, I took out the dirty, frayed 26-year-old piece of paper and looked at the address, which suddenly I knew by heart. I hailed a cab and said the number and the street and the cabbie said sure, Old Town. I sighed and settled back on my tenterhooks. I feel funny, I said to her. To my wife. I know, she said. Maybe he's deceased or something. Maybe, I don't think so. Neither do I, but maybe he's not there any more. Well it's a starting point. Yes, a starting point and he hated to move, you had to give six months' concession to get him to move. We'll see. Yes, we'll see, maybe he'll take me by the back of the neck and throw me down the stairs, he did that once to Abe when he came home late, I was scared shitless. Don't think about that. No, Pulitzer always looked to the future. Are you writing about Pulitzer? No, forget that, I never talk about my writing. All right, Sid. Suppose he says even a dog in the street got the A.S.P.C.A.? He won't. No he won't, but suppose he does. We'll cross that bridge when we come to it. He hated bridges.

We drove through Old Town. Spanish Town, Tourist Town. Hot peppers. Lupe Velez. Lili Damita. Steffi Duna. La Cucaracha. *Rio Rita. The Three Caballeros.* He took us to the Roxy to see that. I hear bout dis money, she no good. *The Cisco Kid. Robin Hood of Eldorado.* He always liked Warner Baxter. Said he looked like a man. But the only genius out there was Sam Goldfish. From gloves to gelt. His secret? He never mixed business with pleasure, remember that, Sidney. The cab stopped. In front of a bar with plastic swinging doors. Over the bar were two windows. A taxpayer. I paid the driver and we got out.

"Well," I said.

"Do you want me to go up?"

"Of course. He always liked shiksas."

"For laying or marrying?"

"He was very tolerant. He always said not all of them were whores."

271

"Oh, all right, then, let's go up."

"Sure, let's go."

The hallway beside the bar was dark but clean. He hated two things in hallways: catpiss and dryhumping. The inside door was open, so we walked through and up a flight of stairs that creaked like mad. *Kiss of Death.* No, kiddo. OK. There was one door. I hurt my knuckles on it.

The woman stood there.

She was darker than I had planned. A flat face and silver-gray hair, moist, drawn straight back. I swear she was a good 75, but the dress was barely down to her knees, her legs were bare, brown and solid. Leather sandals. Red toenails. Her hips were wide and pushed out against the dress. The breasts hung down, but at the top the beginning of the split showed. Izzy, the tit man. Over the years I had blocked on the name.

"Señora Maria Serrano?" I said.

"Jes."

"Yo me llamo Sidney Birnbaum."

"The son?"

"Si, el hijo. Mi padre, el es aqui?"

"Jes. Chew want to come in?"

"Si. Este es mi esposa."

She looked at Sue, turned and walked into the room. The antique ass switched. We followed. The room was small, but neat. Keep the goddam Sunday paper together. A white rug on the wall. A red and black one on the floor with an eagle in the center. A small table T.V. Much pottery, from cups to trays, all around the room. Of course, the stuff he had pushed all these years. The outside man for the reservation. The woman was standing aside, pointing gracefully. I walked into the kitchen. My head began to float. He was sitting beside the kitchen table in a straight-backed chair. He was wearing a shirt with a huge thunderbird on the chest. Around his neck a string tie. He was very thin. I couldn't tell if he had shrunk. The shirtsleeves were rolled up. The tattoo of the flag and Miss Liberty rested on the arms of the chair. The forearms were mahogany, veiny pencils and the hands curled around the chair like yellow-brown claws. The face was also mahogany. He still had the great head of hair. It was albino white, smoothly cut, not a single goddam step. He used to send me back when they gave me steps. I hadn't seen him for 29 years. I was in the army when he done what he done.

"Hello Pop," I said.

His head swung toward me. The eyes were empty. Then he swung back, looking for the woman.

"It's me, Pop," I said. I grabbed my head and put it on my neck. "Sidney. Your son. *Su hijo,* goddammit."

The woman brushed by me and bent over him and whispered sibillantly in English and Spanish and pointed at me. Once she shook him. He stiffened up and nodded and smiled. Then she walked to the other side of the table, sat down, folded her arms and stared at the four walls.

"Hey it's Prince Sidney," I said loudly. "Who's that coming down the street? Good old organ grinder Pete."

"Sid," said *mi esposa,* "I'll wait for you downstairs."

"You don't have to."

"I'd rather."

She walked out and closed the door softly. I looked at the woman. She was passive, impassive, blank. I turned back to Crazy Horse of Washington Heights. I walked right up to him. He smelled like Izzy. He raised his head. The empty eyes looked into mine. Who would blink first? I blinked. I touched his shoulder. He didn't do anything. I squatted down in front of him in my Gus Mancuso catching position.

"Believe it or not, it's me," I said. "The clinker artist." I made like a Chromonica. He looked. "Listen," I said. I shot a thunder of the eye at the woman. She was still sitting and staring. I wriggled my chops. Then I popped my tongue against the roof of my mouth in "My Country Tis of Thee." The eyes narrowed a little.

"How was that, Pop?"

His head wavered. I quickly snapped into "Must Be Jelly Cause Jam Don't Shake Like That." The head firmed up. Whatever you do, no daydreaming in school.

"Not one clinker, Pop."

273

He looked for the woman and lifted one of the brown claws
with a great effort. I stood up.
"OK, Pop, you win, Benny Goodman is no Al Goodman."
The hand flopped on the chair arm.
"Listen, Pop."

Tore ray a door ray
don't spit on the floor.
use the cuspidor,
that's what it is for.

His mouth moved. He smiled a little, not the smile of beauty,
but a smile. "Sure Pop, that's the ticket. Listen."

Trail the eagle
Trail the eagle
climbing all the time.
First the star and then the life
will on your bosom shine,
keep shi-ning.

He was very stiff. With the smile, the moth-eaten smile. I
crouched down again. Arndt Jorgens, the poor bastard, had to
play behind Bill Dickey.

"Pop, I want to talk to you very serious. Straight from the
shoulder. Mama is very sick. That's right. It's a whole lot worse
than her acute indigestion. She had a very bad accident. She wants
you to come home. She told me so herself. Whatayou say, Pop,
forgive and forget?"

He smiled down on me. The shrewd pupils were big.

"I promise not to call her 'she' if you come home. Is it a deal,
Pop? Listen, I don't go in for music anymore, I'm a writer now
like Abe Cahan and Mike Gold and Sholom Aleichem. If you
come home I'll write a novel about you. OK, Pop?"

The smile stopped.

"I'll put Feibleman in it. Just like he was in my bird study
merit badge: a yellow-bellied sapsucker. I'll have a scene where
you walk right up to the White House and tell the president since

274

he can't do it, you'll be happy to kick his kids in the ass for him. Is it a deal?" I stretched up and stepped to his other side and his head followed me. "Attaboy. What happened when they threw all the tea overboard at the Boston Tea Party? It floated down to Atlantic City and that's how they got salt water teaffy. Right, Pop?" I stepped to the other side, drawing his head with me. "I was also a terrific actor, Pop. Another Jacob Adler. Look." I did my Pat Rooney soft shoe from *Lefty*. "How was that, Pop?" He got the grin back again. I bent over him. I smelled Bay Rum. She must have shaved him. He always rubbed it into my face; he never did that for Abe. "I'm gonna tell you a secret, Pop," I whispered loudly into his ear. "The *shviga* always wanted her Hannah to marry Moe Tannenbaum, but she only wanted *you*. She told me that, no shit. I'll tell you something else and I'm breaking a cardinal rule in telling you this. I'm writing a terrific novel now. A real novel. Like *Oliver Twist* or *Jews Without Money*. It's got action and suspense and foreign intrigue and enough screwing to keep them all happy, but it's high class. It's all about the Boxer Rebellion in China, you know, where they kidnapped Chiang Kai-shek, or Chancre Jack as we called him, and this hot-shot reporter like Floyd Gibbons except he's got two eyes, who works for old man Pulitzer. Who are the two greatest Jews? Goldfish and Pulitzer. Listen, Pulitzer's *shviga* didn't care for him either. In this terrific novel my guy rides his horse all over China getting one scoop after another and also some zig zig. Hey Pop, why was Eva Braun jealous? Because Hitler was fucking the whole world instead of her."

I walked slowly back and forth and he stayed with me. I stopped and he stopped. I rubbed my hands.

"This reporter, he's talking about Peking now. Or Pekin. Or Bay-ping. One Long Pan, Pop. Fu Manchu. How about our laundry man, Wong Soo? That's right, Pop, everybody wants to get into the act. You always said you wouldn't trust him as far as you could throw him, with those eyes. You always said that. You said he probably belonged to a tong. Just like the Boxers. They were a sort of tong. And they burnt and pillaged and raped and set siege to

Peking in June, 1900, where all the Allies were holed up, except these Allies, believe it or not, included the Germans and the Japs. And then this reporter goes on to relate how the Japanese minister, Sugiyama, had his belly cut open by the tong with the red sashes and sores on their foreheads. Where did they get the sores from? OK, I'll break another rule and tell you. From striking their heads on the ground so they would be impervious to bullets. No shit.

"For the first two weeks of June these Boxers destroyed churches, hospitals, schools and houses while the Chinese Imperial troops looked on impassively. The same look Wong Soo had. You wished you had five dollars for every thought that passed behind that look. Well they desecrated cemeteries and massacred priests. Not that that was so terrible. The next day they started fires that consumed much of the Chinese City. Not a single engine responded to the conflagration and you know why? Because the Boxers conned the people into believing the Gods were angry at water. I kid you not. Three thousand shops and houses were destroyed. All communication with the outside world was cut, just like the Battle of the Bulge.

"I reached Peking on June 18.

"On the same day Baron Von Ketteler, the German minister, set off on a mission of peace to Prince Tuan, who was the inside man, and he was shot and killed in his sedan chair. That's a little bit back for Munich, not much, but a little. I liberated Leon Blum in Buchenwald, Pop.

"On June 20, *China* declared war!

"Well we were now effectively cut off from our respective countries, or any other countries for that matter. Yet this only served to stiffen backs and reinforce wills. Under the steadfast guidance of Secretary Prouty, proving that not all Civil Service were goniffs, the missionaries and their families were evacuated to the British Legation, where Claude MacDonald, the limey minister, was now fully awakened to the grave import of the situation. The Catholic and Protestant converts shifted as best they could for themselves, which served them right, the patsies. They finally found refuge in the courtyard of the palace of Prince Su, a decent guy and an opponent of the regime, although there were some who called him a Quisling. Za zeetz is own.

"I could not get my dispatches off to Mr. Pulitzer, or Andes, as he was known in our secret code book. By now my stories were being featured in the morning, evening and Sunday *Worlds,* or Senior, Junior and Seniority and I could just picture the boss, floating around on his yacht, gnashing teeth and breaking balls over the interruption. Hey Pop, what do you think we called the Republican Party? *Malaria.* So I contented myself with taking notes and helping out when and where I could."

He finally blinked. I slapped my fist into my palm. He blinked again.

"Yessir, you are absolutely correct, the Polacks were much worse than the Germans. You're right about something else, darn it, Melvyn Douglas *is* Jewish. OK, now hear this. The line of defense was a thousand yards long, that's all it was. Along Legation Street and a little north and south of it to the Tartar wall. A pitifully small rectangle that held the eyes of the world in focus for a good two months. It just goes to show what you can do if you want to. You always said where there's a will, there's a way. I always keep my promises, Pop. I promised you when they sent me overseas I would always keep a rubber in my wallet, well I kept that promise. I also promise never to whip my pony in front of the mirror.

"Very well. Our firepower was almost ridiculous. One Colt automatic machine gun, Captain Whitmore and his men in charge. The British had a Nordenfeld, the Austrians a Maxim gun, not that they knew what to do with it and the *Talyainas* a one-pounder. We also had an international gun, a British piece of 1860, that took Russian shells, ran on an Italian carriage and was fired by an American gunner, A splendid example of the League of Nations in operation until Henry Cabot Lodge, Hitler, Mussolini and the Japs killed it. A *shvartz* year to both sides in Spain after what they done to the Jews.

"Naturally the Americans got the shit end of the stick. They were moved up to the wall between the Tartar and Chinese Cities and with Captain Whitmore barking out commands, and with the putative aid of several Austrians, they set up the Colt automatic. I passed my thirty-thirty test in '43 with absolutely no strain. Night after damnable night the Boxer hordes charged in the Kamikaze attacks and night after night Whitmore and his gallant band repulsed them. Arnold Rothstein was terrible for the Jews, Pop.

"Now all during this time our rations were growing ever more short, even though the redoubtable Prouty did yeoman's service in laying by stores of rice and other comestibles. But by the final week of June the decision we all dreaded had to be made: we must eat the mules and horses. So in groups of twos and threes the poor dumb beasts were rounded up, led to the garden of the Jap Legation and there slaughtered and butchered. Then quite fancily did the cooks serve them up, including liver and other miserable parts I never could stand, even going so far as to make curry sauces and sausage. If not *traife* by definition, then by God by effect! Naturally the native converts had to make do with the entrails and hooves.

"On the night of June 27 a Jap captain named Mitsuyama appeared in my quarters in the American Legation, whence I was observing the action and taking notes for Andes. The midget soldier clicked his oversized heels as they had recently learned to do, the Japs being very quick studies, and said in English:

" 'It has come to our attention you got horse.'

" 'That is so.'

" 'I regret that you must part with horse to us.'

" 'To what purpose?'

" 'So we all got to eat.'

" 'Very well. He is in the garden in the rear.'

"He smiled one of their Tojo smiles. I walked out ahead of him into the garden, there to look on my peacefully grazing Herald. The *wojen's* face grew positively rapacious.

" 'He is yours,' I said, stepping to one side.

"He walked past me and reached up for Herald's bridle. As he did I fetched him a corkscrew clip alongside his ear. He hit the ground with stunning force and lay absolutely still. I must say that Herald regarded the scene with complete equanimity. I whistled and he trotted over. I swung aboard and turned him to the wall and tapped my heels. This fellow was dearer to me than Equipoise, War

Admiral, Twilight Tear or Tarzan and I was damned if he was going to end up as special and beans on Yamamoto's table.

"We galloped like crazy toward the sluice gate, the only remaining opening to the Chinese city. Once through, somehow I knew he would get himself safely lost in that maze of humanity and chaos. As we approached the cut in the wall I slid down to his left side even as Ken Maynard on Tarzan and I whispered in Mandarin, 'Keep on going, old fellow, no matter what obstacles intervene.' Just as he was about to bound into the depression, I dropped off, rolled over and came up lightly onto my feet. For a terrible moment he was out of sight, then, there he goes, the gallant fox of a head held high, the nostrils flaring with fierce exertion. But hold! Above him on the wall a shout! An Austrian soldier rises up and points his gun. Unarmed, I watch in extremes of agony and helplessness. Herald is on the other side now and the Boxers, no matter what else they are, are not animal killers. Austrians, as we all know, are a different story. The fellow takes dead aim. Oh it cannot, it *must* not be! It will not. In that instant a tall, slender figure stands up on the wall, some twenty yards from the Austrian. Tis Captain Whitmore! He points his revolver and shoots the man between the eyes. He turns to me and salutes.

"In that glorious moment a volley. It rings out from the Boxer side. It sounds like the patter of a snare drum. Alas a deadly patter. With his hand to his hat, Whitmore turns, smiles disdainfully and falls off the wall in a heroic parabola. All is silent. Shouts, alarums, volleys. His brave men, ignoring the danger, rush to him and drag the splendid corpus to safety. It is, I know, too late; I have seen too many good men crumple. The typewriter in my head pays a grateful farewell to the man: Jedediah Whitmore, a little bit on the chickenshit side, but taken all in all a most gallant officer and a credit to his nation.

"I look at the sinister darkness of the Chinese city. Mott Street at midnight could not be more foreboding. Somewhere in that tortured web of life and death a noble steed is sure to understand the sacrifice that has been made for him, a peculiarly *American* sacrifice."

Oh Jesus crax, Izzy was looking for the woman!

"Ford, Father Coughlin, Bilbo and Rankin," I said. "Take them by the back of the neck and kick their ass down the stairs."

He looked for the woman.

"Hey Pop, it's 1929. Well dressed man: 'I'd like a room please.' Hotel clerk: 'For sleeping or jumping?' "

I walked over and stood between his eyes and the woman.

"They should shoot the doctors, what they done to Gershwin. I personally guarantee Hannah will never throw it up to you the *shviga* bought the store."

Ah, he looked at me.

"Thus we entered the month of July," I said, "some 600 defenders which became 400 as time went by, against as many as 10,000. It wasn't as overwhelming as the Arabs against the Jews, but then the Chinese could fight. Independence Day passed unobserved, no cherry bombs, no sparklers, no getting my ass kicked for burning my thumb. In addition to 15 Boxers, we also blew up one of their crude mines. Bastille Day came and went, marked on our side by the death of a French marine and the wounding of Lieutenant D'Arcy. Indeed the French Legation had become a scene of strife that rivaled the British, but I am happy to report that the French held on with grim determination, which, knowing their history in the Prussian conflict, not to mention the Maginot Line, I found quite amazing. You always said they never got Dreyfus out of their system. Lepke was also rotten for the Jews. It wasn't only that Zelda Cushman had no tits, she spit when she talked. Additional accolades and huzzas must be accorded the ladies of the legations, who throughout comported themselves with utter dignity and fortitude. This certainly proved a surprise to Andes who believed that woman's place was in the home, barefoot and pregnant, but I for one shall ne'er forget that it was they and not the Boxers who proved impenetrable. I do not care if they were goys. Hannah can also make it, but only with your help, whatehell, stocks are falling again, how can you watch the board from here?

"We made every shot count, unlike the enemy who fired at any and all targets, real or imagined. Soc Zlotsky always did that. Yet Allied soldiers continued to drop and twas the sad duty of the burial detail to inter them even to the extent of burying American boys alongside Russian boys in the Russian Legation, proving that World War II really happened. Trotzky had more in his little finger than Lenin, Stalin and Kerensky put together. Cardozo had the highest I.Q. in the history of the Supreme Court. As August crept on apace, the Boxers attacked us with ever more desperation and wild ferocity and it became increasingly clear that the final challenge was being hurled at us. Hitler's last gasp at the Bulge. We or they must fall and we were damned if twould be us. 'Nuts,' said the defenders of Peking. From 5 A.M to 5 P.M. on the 13th of August we were subjected to a continuous fusillade. Night descended and still the very heavens were aglow with the awful beauty of attack and counter-attack. Ah what a night that was. I shall never forget its agony and ecstasy as American, Frenchman, German, Austrian, Russian, Briton, Italian, Japanese fell to the ground, only to wave their comrades on!

"I watched on that terrible night from an upstairs window in the British Legation, pacing back and forth, as nervous as Andes himself, wondering if the world, or the *World,* had indeed forgotten us. Dawn's early light arrived and still the human waves flooded toward us without interruption. Grimly we mowed them down. It was Verdun all over again.

"Then on the following afternoon, from the direction of the main gate, the Chien Men, I heard it. The high thin note of a bugle. Billy Bimstein in camp couldn't even play swim call, but this unknown fellow knew his 'charge!' Twas the most blessed noise these old ears had ever heard. Far better than Bix ever blew, or Harry or Ziggy and yes, I know, Ziggy played at your cousin's wedding. Despite the danger, I stuck my head out the window. Suddenly I was aware of a deafening sensation. What could it be? But of course: Silence! The firing had ceased. All I could hear were the echoes in my head. A puzzle. I strained this way and that. And then, oh glorious moment, I saw them: the fiercely bearded Sikhs, as noble as the Khyber Pass, tough as the House of David, marching through the Chien Men. I heard cheers. I saw hats being waved. I tossed my fifty-dollar pith helmet into the air. I ran downstairs and outside waving my precious pencil and pad. I picked up my pith helmet and put it on. A stolid British face rode toward me.

" 'Norris Blake, reporter from the *World*,' I shouted. 'Which outfit is this?'

"He observed me cooly.

" 'An element of the Seventh Rajputs,' he offered. I jotted the information down. 'Leftenant Colonel Vaughan in command,' he added.

"We were saved, Pop! Patton had broken through. We were saved!"

He sat stiffly. The brown claws with the yellow nicotine stains were digging into the arms of the chair.

"How about that, Pop? Saved. But was that the three-o mark? You better not believe it. Remember W.J. Boody Junior's mother, the one with the big tits? For beginning that very day mopping-up operations began, as well as the drive into the Forbidden City, carried out naturally by the Americans. Impelled by my professional curiosity, I accompanied them. Thus I was the first journalist to enter that sacred plot of ground. His mother was married to a Christian Scientist from Houston, which not only made her a whore but also stupid, how could a Christian be a scientist, right? I wandered in awe and pent-up excitement through the once exquisite grounds, now strewn with the rubble of war. To show the extent to which law and order had broken down, Chinese civilians also wandered hither and yon, something completely unheard of in pre-war, sacred days. But now, poor things, they were pushed along by the unsacred pangs of hunger-swollen bellies. Twas 1945 and Europe all over again. One of the poor creatures caught my eye, a woman of indeterminate age, dressed in faded pajamas, scrounging in a trash heap. I went up to her and as she raised her head in fear I offered her a tael. She shook her head. Her eyes were glazed over with suffering. I pressed the coin into her rough hand.

" 'Thank you, Norris Brake,' she said. 'This time I accept.'

"I drew the woman up to her full height. A graceful form confronted me. I gazed into a pair of sad, glistening eyes.

" 'By God!' I ejaculated. 'Are you, *can* you be Ah Soon?'

"She lowered her head in the exquisitely shy nod I had known so well in my dreaming. I folded my arms about the slender form and clasped it to my person. Oh this dear girl, sweeter to me than

282

Anna May Wong, Tillie Losch or Sybil Soo who played kneesie with me in Civics.

" 'Ah marvelous girl,' I murmured. 'I can see how you have suffered.'

" 'Yes, Norris, but tis my people who have suffered. We are lost.'

" 'No, say not. Not yet, dearest. For you shall remain with me. Now and evermore.'

" 'Oh how splendid those words! Would that I could. But I cannot. I have come here only to convey to you a piece of news, or as you call it, a scoop.'

" 'Touching, so infinitely touching. You are still watching out for me?'

" 'Should I not? Is it not my duty? Does not Joan watch over you?'

"Thinking she referred to Joan Walsingham of Newport, I maintained a silence on that point, but did respond that I wished her duty would become a lifetime affair.

" 'As would I. But it cannot be.'

" 'Then what news, dear one?'

" 'The Empress is on the point of fleeing.'

" 'Egad, that *is* news! When?'

" 'Within the hour. By way of the northwest gate.'

" 'Where will she go?'

" 'To Sian.'

" 'Once the capital of the three kingdoms?'

" 'The very same.'

" 'With whom does she flee?'

" 'The Emperor and his son.'

" 'The heir apparent?'

" 'Yes.'

" 'Well well.'

" 'You must make haste. There is no time to lose.'

" 'Yes. Of course. How can I ever repay you?'

" 'By writing beautiful memorials and by thinking of me when the trees blossom in your capital city as I understand they do each spring.'

" 'Ah dearest, but those are Japanese blossoms.'

283

" 'Oh? Well so they are from this side of the world.'

" 'Indeed they are. I shall make a solemn pilgrimage to the blossoms every spring.'

" 'Ah beloved.'

"She emitted a soft and lovely cooing sound. A horse clattered up. A familiar-looking animal.

" 'Herald, old boy, you are a sight for sore eyes!' I turned to my benefactress. 'You are truly magic.' I exclaimed with utter sincerity.

" 'There is no time for that,' she said. 'Now begone.'

"I swung aboard the familiar back and essayed one more glance. Twas too painful. Her eyes were cast down, the smooth shoulders slumping. I lifted up my head, clucked once and in a thrice was pounding for the northwest gate."

I began now to pace with alacrity. "Who," I said, "did all the shiksas get on line for? Give that man an Admiration, Max Baer. Who knows more about the market than Mellon? Sure, Winchell. I reached the northwest gate in fifteen minutes flat. Was I too late? I could not tell, I could only hope and wait there and pray for the scoop of the infant century.

"At precisely 3:22 P.M. on the 15th day of August, 1900, three plain-looking carts hove into view, rolling slowly toward me. I felt a flood of excitement, not unmixed with gratitude, then taking an educated guess, tapped Herald toward the middle cart. No one dared stop a westerner. Cantering up alongside, I leaned over and opened the door. The interior was dark, but not so dark that I could not see the shrouded form of a woman and that of a child.

" 'Good afternoon, your majesty,' I said in high Mandarin.

" 'Who is that?' said a voice that was a thousand years old and as young as a spring blossom.

" 'Norris Blake of the *World*.'

" 'And what is that?'

" 'You do not know? A writer, your majesty. A writer of memorials to the people of this earth. Of this good earth.'

" 'All the people?'

" 'At least one-half million. Plus all those who read the papers on a secondary basis and all those who are influenced by the one-half million.'

"There was a moment of assimilative silence. I knew that moment well. Then the shrouded woman spoke to the youngster at her side. I saw a proud little head nod and then he was stepping outside the door and climbing up to the cart driver. I offered a hand, but he waved me imperiously off. When he was seated beside his impassive companion, I heard the remarkable voice say:

" 'Enter, Mr. Brake.'

"I did as I was commanded. I sat down and found myself opposite an enigmatic and diffused presence. An odor of marvelous yet cloying sweetness filled the cart's interior.

" 'Do I understand,' said the voice in businesslike tones, 'that you wish to ask me questions and record my answers for the people of the earth?'

" 'Yes I do, Madame.'

" 'Do I understand that if I do this thing it will be an achievement on your part of the first magnitude?'

" 'You do.'

" 'What would you give for such a thing?'

" 'Ah, what would I *not* give?'

"Another moment of silence filled the cart. I could hear the rumble of the rough wheels. Then, to my astonishment, the presence opposite me was reaching daintily down to the hem of the gold brocaded gown. I saw the famous nails, two feet in length, blood red, delicately raise that hem. Before my wide eyes the skirt drew up above the imperial knees. Suddenly into my searching mind swept the rumours, the whispers, the sly tales.

" 'Halt!' I exclaimed.

"The ten daggers poised in their salacious flight.

" 'What do you say?' queried a surprised voice.

" 'I said halt. No interview is worth *that*.'

" 'Do not be impertinent.'

" 'I shall be whatever I please. I am an *American*.'

" 'Ah.' The voice all at once was soft and soothing. 'An American. I have never known an American.'

" 'And you never shall if *I* have anything to say about it.'

" 'Oh but you are wicked to speak so. Why do you treat me thus, Mister Brake? A poor, helpless, defeated Empress.'

" 'Defeated, yes. Poor and helpless, I categorically doubt that,' I said with a sneer.

" 'Brutal man.'

" 'Madame, I simply will not be coerced into a scoop, by you or anyone like you, come hell or high water.'

" 'Oh my. Would that someone in my court could speak like that on occasion. I would not be here now.'

" 'You mean there is no one on whom you can rely for utter frankness?'

" 'They are all eunuchs.'

" 'All?'

" 'Practically all. Those that are not are eunuchs in their head. Tell me, are there eunuchs in America?'

" 'God forbid!'

" 'Well they do have their uses.'

" 'Not in my country, they do not.'

" 'Well they do.'

" 'You shall never convince me of that.'

" 'Quite well and bravely said, Mr. Brake. Where are you going?'

" 'Out. I presume the interview is concluded, or is not to take place.'

" 'Did I say that? How cruelly you treat me. Stay!'

" 'Never on your terms.'

" 'Oh bother. Very well, on your terms then.'

" 'That is more like it. First raise your veil.'

" 'Pig!'

" 'Very well, I go.'

" 'No, no, please. I will do as you say.'

"She flipped the hem to the floor, then lifted back her veil, revealing a face of a thousand wrinkles, yet smooth as cream. We gazed at each other.

" 'All right then,' I said. 'We will now converse as equals.'

" 'Equals!'

" 'Yes.'

"The eyes, which had been two glittering snake pits, gradually grew quiet. She seemed to draw into herself. Then she said, as if thinking aloud:

" 'Equals. The Western Empress and a hairy devil. Equals.'

" 'Tis the only way I will consent to the interview,' I said.

" 'But I must have this interview!'

" 'Well then . . .'

" 'Equals eh? Actually the thought is rather delicious. What must I do?'

" 'Nothing in particular. Merely sit there and respond.'

" 'Well well. I learn something new every day. Please proceed to interview me, Mr. Brake.'

" 'Thank you. First of all, why did you turn the Boxers loose?'

" 'Dog!'

" 'Madame, I must insist.'

" 'Yes, yes, forgive me, repeat the question.'

" 'The Boxers. Why did you give them carte blanche? In other words, your official sanction to rampage, loot, burn, destroy and turn anti-Christ?'

" 'I? I did that? Nonsense. It was Tuan. He might as well be a eunuch for all the backbone he possesses. If only I had someone like you. You have no idea what it is like to be surrounded by such weak-kneed imbeciles.'

"I committed her words to memory, which is my unique technique and which makes these remarkable conversations even more remarkable.

" 'Do you,' I then asked, 'believe the Boxers to be immune to bullets?'

" 'Not the ones who were killed.'

" 'Why did you have your troops join the Boxers?'

" 'Did I do that?'

" 'Do not play coy with me, Madame.'

" 'Oh how nicely you say that.'

" 'Well Madame, the question.'

" 'Yes. Equals.'

" 'Precisely.'

" 'Precisely equals.'

" 'Yes. Now then, why did your troops join the Boxers?'

" 'To give my people some backbone.'

" 'I see. And has it been worth the candle?'

" 'We have paid with blood, not candles.'

" 'I mean, are you satisfied now?'

" 'I am never satisfied, Mr. Brake. It is my curse.'

" 'What I mean is, now that your country is a shambles and you are in flight, do you not regret your part in this affair?'

" 'I do now. If we had won, I would not.'

" 'What do you propose to do now?'

" 'Run away.'

" 'What then?'

" 'I will throw myself on the tender mercy of the victors. In particular, the Americans.'

" 'Would you not abdicate?'

" 'Never.'

" 'Why never?'

" 'What else could I do? A poor old concubine and an empress?'

" 'You wish to remain the vortex of evil, intrigue and licentiousness?'

" 'Ah, it is my character.'

" 'What will you do at Sian?'

" 'Wait. Things will calm down. They always do.'

" 'Why did you murder the Eastern Empress?'

" 'I have never murdered anyone.'

" 'Why did you have her murdered?'

" 'Let us say simply that she awoke one morning lacking a heartbeat.'

" 'Do you care for your people?'

" 'Only if they care for me.'

" 'Do you have any words of advice for the American people?'

" 'Do not trust the Japanese.'

" 'What of the Russians?'

" 'The Cossacks are most interesting-looking.'

" 'What do you regret the most as you look back upon your long and momentous life?'

" 'That I have not been interviewed before.'

" 'Do you believe that east is east and west is west and never the twain shall meet?'

" 'Yes and no.'

" 'Would you care to explain that?'

" 'No.'

" 'I thank you, Madame. Mr. Joseph Pulitzer thanks you.'

" 'Is the interview concluded?'

" 'Yes.'

" 'Would you care to join my court? I will behead Tuan and put you in his place.'

" 'I report political affairs. I do not become a part of them, except as a last resort.'

" 'Would that my generals behaved in like manner. Well then it is farewell, Mr. Blake. I will add one more parting to my long list. Tell me, would you care for anything as a remembrance of this occasion?'

" 'Yes I would.'

" 'Name it and it is yours.'

" 'May I have a fingernail?'

"She smiled with understanding and assent. Then she withdrew a small golden sword from the sleeve of her gown. It occurred to me that I had had rather a close shave. With a deft, lightning-like movement, she sliced through one of the glistening, red daggers. It stabbed into the floor of the cart and remained there upright and aquiver. I bent over and yanked it out. It was curiously warm to the touch, hard and smooth as glass. I thrust it carefully into my tunic.

" 'Thank you,' I said.

" 'May *I* have something from you, my equal?'

"I drew out pencil and pad, wrote my name down and tore off the leaf and handed it to her.

" 'That is my by-line. It is not without some importance and value.'

" 'I shall indeed treasure this. When next I see it, I shall think of my equal in the west and the delights of an interview. Farewell, Mr. Brake.'

" 'Farewell, Madame Empress.'

"With a quick and decisive movement, I opened the door and

propelled myself through it and onto the back of the waiting Herald. I yanked him back and he pawed at the sky. With the precious interview tucked safely into my head, I turned him on his hind legs, eased him down and made straight for Ah Soon.

"What do you think of that, Pop, a *worldwide exclusive?*"

His head was slumped down on his chest. You would think he had just run the cross-country at Van Cortlandt. I looked at the woman; Helen Wills Moody.

"Pop, Pop, listen to this. That ain't the end, I was just teasing. Hell, I raced straight back through the gate, I came to the head of the stretch, I picked off nags one after another. I was Charley Kurtsinger on War Admiral. I had so much horse under me it was almost funny. I just let him do all the work, a hand ride all the way. We ate up Roman Soldier and Seabiscuit, that's right, Seabiscuit, sure, that race was fixed, and we burst into the Imperial City by six lengths. You hear that, Pop? Don't go way now. I galloped into the courtyard looking this way and that, Pop, looking for a certain someone who shall remain nameless for the nonce. I saw only the conquistadores carrying on something terrible. That's right, I could tell you some stories about Bavaria. It has become known as the sack of Peking, or as I named it, the Shame of the West. It must be said. I was present. I saw it all. Twas a terrible spectacle, one that cannot be condoned by invoking the cry of the spoils of war. No, these soldiers were spoiling this noble war. The terrified populace was scurrying this way and that, seeking escape for themselves and their loved ones, for tis true the yellow man has his loved ones also, but there was no escape from the vengeful, besotted, swaggering troops. Frankly I was disgusted, it was worse than that gang bang on Audubon Avenue in the school yard with Hedda Obrinsky, I swear I didn't touch her, but Abe did.

"I kept on searching, keeping my mind on my business, yet recording everything for posterity. After I ran away from the school yard I kept going till I saw Sybil Soo coming out of her father's shop. From behind an exquisite marble fountain I heard a piercing cry, half human, half bird. I asked Sybil if she would like me to walk her home as it was getting dark and some nasty things were going on. She said sure. I dashed toward the source of that sound. What I saw made my very blood run cold. I took her by the arm and vowed to myself that the only way they'd get her was over my dead body. She cuddled right up to me. There on the ground was my beloved flower. Above her in a position too awful to describe was a soldier. He was clad only in his tunic and helmet. On 181st Street I saw W.J. coming toward us. A *spiked* helmet. W.J. said hi, but he wasn't fooling me; I belted him in the solar plexus. With a terrible oath, I hurled myself from my steed and onto the despicable back of the hun. W.J. went down for the count and we stepped over him. I sent the savage sprawling even as the pitiful moaning sounds filled up my ear canals. W.J. looked up at us and I said I wouldn't trust him as far as I could throw him. The brute stared at me with cold stupidity. Then with a cry, the like of which I have never heard, save in my nightmares, he launched himself at me. Sybil said she never did like the way he looked at her in Biology. I heard W.J. sucking air as we walked away and I just waited for the counter-attack. As the Uhlan came at me, I reached into my tunic and withdrew the warm, blood-red fingernail. He just lay there and Sybil hung onto my arm. With all the strength my pent-up emotions possessed I plunged the dagger into the dastardly heart. W.J. didn't talk to me for two weeks, tough shit. Fritz looked at me, his eyes clouding over with dumb surprise, then he gazed at the offending weapon. I went to the park a lot with Sybil after that, but I stayed strictly on top, never *once* went for bare tit. He clutched frantically at it, then as if clubbed from behind, he toppled, never more to rise. He lay there with that petrified epidermis protruding from his chest, drawing blood like a magenta magnet. Her old man caught us in August and said he'd kick my ass in if he ever caught me again.

"I looked to my pitiful precious. Even as I did her hand was inside her blouse, then reaching up toward her mouth. After that, she only went with Jimmy Kee from the Happy Carp. I bounded to her with all the strength in my athletic legs. Even in mid-air I saw her swallow with a great effort. I'm absolutely sure Jimmy was getting in, but that didn't matter to the old man. I gathered Ah Soon to my grieving body and asked over and over:

" 'Oh what have you done?'

"She smiled wanly up at me.

" 'Only what I had to, Norris Brake.'

" 'No, I forbid it. What you have done must not come to pass.'

" 'Yes, Norris Brake. it must.'

" 'But you are a goddess, therefore immortal."

" 'Alas, no more. I have been defiled. My power is lost forever.'

" 'I care not. My love for you is not one iota less strong. I swear it.'

" 'I thank you for that, beloved of the west. But I know how these things go. In time that powerful emotion would of needs change.'

" 'Never!'

" 'I would become a detriment to your career.'

" 'I will enter another career. I will write novels.'

" 'Beautiful dreamer. You must not grieve. I am not unhappy.'

"With that she gently closed the gentian violet eyes and sighed a heartbreaking sigh. I stared down at the magnificent, mud-stained, pure face. Ever since Sybil, I made it a cardinal rule to take it whenever it was there, but I swear I never dipped my wick just for the sake of dipping. I tried desperately to come to grips with what had just transpired.

" 'She is gone, scrivener.'

"I looked up. A fierce countenance, the color of jujube, with caterpillar eyebrows, gazed down into mine. Suddenly, my trained and questing mind understood all. With one exception.

" 'Why, Kuang Yu?' I entreated.

" 'Because it is written. Need I explain that to you?'

" 'No, you do not.'

" 'I will take her now. She belongs to us.'

" 'Yes. Although she will always be mine.'

" 'I understand.'

"I lifted the lovely body and handed it up to the God of War.

" 'Where will you take her?'

" 'Far to the west. To the most magnificent of tombs. Where the earth meets the sky. Where our people may make a pilgrimage and gain inspiration for all time to come.'

292

" 'Go in peace.'

" 'For the moment, yes. However, we shall surely meet again. Farewell, reporter to the world.'

" 'Yes, I fear we will meet again, God of War. Till then.'

"We measured each other across the quiet form. Across ten thousand miles and a thousand years. He turned and strode off. I watched as he entered a throng of natives. As though by pre-arranged signal, they closed about him. The last thing I saw was an exquisitely tiny, limp foot."

I kept very still. I looked very naturally at him, careful to avoid any sudden moves. I was positive he had come to himself a little. "Pop," I said softly, "what do you think? You have an opinion about everything. You said *Pins and Needles* would make it and everyone thought you were nuts. How about it? This'll make it, won't it, Pop? I'll clean up the clinkers and it'll make it. Right, Pop? Prince Sidney can't miss, can he? Tell the whole cockeyed world, Pop. Shit, I'll make you my agent. It'll make a million and you can skim a hundred thousand right off the top. I'll write a sequel. A series, just like your Moe Fagin stories. No more lousy rummage sales for Hannah that drove you wild, OK, Pop? We'll make a movie deal, if you want Warner Baxter, you got him. What's the verdict, Pop?"

Oh he was sitting straight up now. He had a look on his face, a *real* look.

"I'll buy the biggest co-op in Washington Heights. The entire top floor. You'll look out the window and practically see Bear Mountain." I winked at him. "Hey listen, Pop, you don't have to explain a thing. I was born in Brooklyn, but it wasn't yesterday. Mama loves papa, papa loves mambo."

The eyes, they got a little sense. The face worked.

"What's the big deal here? We got *real* Indians in New York. They're king of the hill, they got pride and they make damn good money. They work in high steel. Mohawks. They built the George Washington Bridge. *Your* bridge."

The lips trembled. A string of spit dropped to his chin. "Attaboy. Listen, I'll buy you a candy route. You can be on the outside all day. Or you can put a man on it and fuck off anytime you want. In Bryant Park, Radio City, or 42nd Street. You wanna hear something? The Yanks finally got a Jewish ball player. You wanna hear something else? Another depression is coming! Yeah, you can smell it. You know why? We got Malaria in the White House. But you'll be sitting pretty watching all the big butter-and-egg men swan dive out the Waldorf."

I got down on my knees in front of him. The mouth was going this way and that and the spit was hanging down. "Yeah, Pop, give your girl a gorgeous Gruen for Christmas. Come on, Pop, you can do it, whatayou say?"

The mouth opened very wide. I could see gold fillings.

"Curtains," he said very clearly.

I sat back on my haunches. I sat there looking at his slippered feet I don't know how long. When I finally looked up his face was covered with sweat and he was staring toward the woman. I got up and walked out. I walked slowly downstairs and out into the brilliant New Mexico sunlight. Suddenly I had to lean against a hitching post.

Are you all right?

Shit no.

I told you.

All right, please don't throw it up to me.

I just want to make sure you know.

I'll eat shit. I know, I know.

After all, I warned you.

I said I knew. Get off my back.

My my, all that jism.

All right already.

What will you do now, Mr. Christian?

I don't know.

Should I tell you?

Yes, tell me.

Are you sure?

294

Yes.
Say please.
Please.
Will you listen?
I will listen.
Will you behave?
I will behave.
You will remember who is in command?
On my honor I will do my best to do my duty. Tell me what to do, Captain . . .

I managed to look through the sunlight to the other side of the street. Sue was running toward me.

THE END